THE PALE HORSE AND THE UNICORN

KENNETH ARBOGAST

Dedicated to the medical professionals
who treat the patients and comfort the families
during these terrible times.

To Ed,
Thanks for your
help & encouragement.
Stay Safe & Sane.
Ken

TO JESS:
This political intrigue
(a la Covid) will help you stay
up to date with your
Michigan roots.
LOVE DAD

"I looked, and there was a pale-colored horse.
Its rider was named Death,
and Hades followed close behind.
They were given authority
over one fourth of the earth,
to kill by means
of war, famine, disease, and wild animals."
— Revelations, 6:8.

February 24

"The Coronavirus is very much under control in the USA. We are in contact with everyone and all relevant countries. CDC & World Health have been working hard and very smart. Stock Market starting to look very good to me."

— President of the United States of America, on Twitter.

February 27

"We have done an incredible job. We're going to continue.
It's going to disappear. One day — it's like a miracle — it
will disappear. And from our shores, we — you know, it
could get worse before it gets better. It could maybe go away.
We'll see what happens. Nobody really knows. The fact is,
the greatest experts — I've spoken to them all. Nobody
really knows."

— President of the United States of America,
at White House photo event.

February 28

"This is a reality check for every government on the planet:
Wake up. Get ready. This virus may be on its way and you
need to be ready. You have a duty to your citizens, you have
a duty to the world, to be ready, and I think that's what this
alert says. It says we can avoid the worst of this, but our level
of concern is at its highest."

— Executive Director,
Health Emergencies Program,
World Health Organization.

March 11

While the President has throughout the coronavirus outbreak sought to minimize it by comparing it to the seasonal flu, the Director of the National Institute of Allergy and Infectious Diseases noted the novel coronavirus is significantly more lethal.

"I mean, people always say, well, the flu does this, the flu does that," the Director said. "The flu has a mortality of 0.1 percent. This has a mortality rate of 10 times that. That's the reason I want to emphasize we have to stay ahead of the game in preventing this."

– The Washington Post.

March 15

"This is a very contagious virus, it's incredible, but it's something that we have tremendous control over. I think very important the young people, people of good health and groups of people just are not strongly affected."

— President of the United States of America,
at White House coronavirus daily briefing.

March 15

"The worst is yet ahead for us. It is how we respond to that challenge that is going to determine what the ultimate end point is going to be. We have a very, very critical point now."

— Director of the National Institute of Allergy and Infectious Diseases, at the same White House coronavirus daily briefing.

March 16

"To mitigate the spread of COVID-19, protect the public health, and provide essential protections to vulnerable Michiganders, it is reasonable and necessary to impose limited and temporary restrictions on the use of places of public accommodation."

— Governor of the State of Michigan,
Executive Order 2020-9.

March 17

"I felt it was a pandemic long before it was called a pandemic."

— President of the United States of America,
at White House coronavirus daily briefing.

March 19

The city of Southgate said a resident of the city was the first person in the state to die from coronavirus on Wednesday.

According to the city administrator, the city was contacted around 5:30 Wednesday afternoon by the Wayne County Health Department and informed the death was a Southgate resident.

The health department said the health department informed them that they would dig in to find out more possible exposure locations.

According to a press release from Beaumont Health, a man in his 50s died at Beaumont in Wayne County. As of right now, over 100 other cases have been confirmed in the state. The conditions of these patients have not been released.

– Fox 2, Detroit.

March 19

Frank clicked off the television power and hurled the remote at the couch. He lowered the foot rest on the big leather recliner, pulled himself out and stalked into the kitchen. He was a regular big and tall customer, so he ducked as he went through the doorway. Frank was not a fat man, just built like the guy who had spent his college years at Michigan State University as a center on the basketball team. Until he tore something called an anterior cruciate ligament in his knee early in his senior year.

Regina was dicing carrots for a venison stew. She was trying to stretch the meat in the freezer to avoid going into a supermarket. And to avoid spending. Her cotton apron draped from her neckline to her knees.

"I swear, none of these people seem to have a clue what's really going on," he groused. "They can't all be morons. Hell, that's why I voted for him, to drain the swamp. Now it looks like a bunch of swamp people standing behind him when he talks."

"Please, Francis, keep your voice down. Mary just laid down."

"I'm sorry. I worry most about her, but you, too. How do we keep you both safe?" He leaned into the refrigerator and removed a can of Miller Lite from the carton. "Jesus, what do we do?"

Regina looked at him. "Early?"

He looked at the open can of beer in his hand. "What does it matter? I feel like nothing we do is going to change the situation. She's sick, and you're not healthy. The plant is going to be closing, and we'll be on unemployment. I think we'll keep health insurance. But I don't know how to keep you and her from catching this thing. Rush says it's like the flu, but then why put the Vice President in charge of dealing with it? Flu comes every year, and we get our shots. So what's the big deal now? The president says it's a pandemic. Maybe as bad as the Spanish flu."

She put her knife aside and sat back in her chair so she could look up at her husband. She pushed her eyeglasses up her nose with one finger to the bridge. "I'll tell you what I think if you won't be mad about it."

Frank stepped back, shocked. Was he so difficult to talk with? He took a sip of beer. Nodded. "I'm sorry. Go on."

"I read online that it's something brand new. Not like anything before. It's not the flu, not even the Spanish flu. It's something that destroys your whole insides." She paused, tearing up. "I don't want it, Frank. What I've read is that when you go to a hospital, you can't ever see your family again. They put you on a machine and that's that. I don't want that, and I don't want that for Mary."

Frank stepped around the kitchen table and hugged his wife's shoulders. He kissed the dark curls on the top of her head. She removed her eyeglasses when she began to cry, and soon he was fighting back tears as well. "I won't let that happen to you, or to Mary. I promise."

They remained embraced for several minutes. Frank thought about how to keep his oath. When Regina took up her knife again, he went out to the small garage. Three years back he had converted the space to something of a den after she stopped driving and sold her car. She called it his "man cave," but with the high ceiling and exposed joists, it was more like a man cavern. On the walls hung photos from the trips they had enjoyed before Mary took sick. From a young age, she had loved fishing and never squirmed at putting a worm on a hook. Mary loved to reel in trout, salmon and even once a northern pike in the Upper Peninsula of Michigan. Her smile as she held her catch was luminescent.

Her favorite campground was Sand Lake on the Huron-Manistee National Forests. Because it was so close, the family could drive there easily in just a few hours. Mary could fish and swim in the lake, and there were hiking trails nearby. They made all these trips in a 38-foot Damon Challenger RV. Frank inherited it from his father, who had spent a few years as a roving campground host after retiring from General Motors. That was a life Frank hoped to pursue if he ever retired. Meanwhile, the RV sat in the driveway of Frank and Regina's home.

Frank went back into the kitchen where Regina was dicing potatoes for the stew. Already, the stock on the stove smelled delicious.

"How long do you think we could live in the camper before I drive you crazy?" he asked.

"You mean us running away? Like that Seger song, but in an RV instead of a 'big two wheeler'? I don't know. Where could we get the care Mary needs?"

Frank picked up the can of beer he'd left on the table. "I don't know. We'd have to do some research. Maybe a hospital in Marquette or Escanaba? Wouldn't someone there be able to treat her?"

"I suppose, but I don't know what you're suggesting." She settled back in her chair to study his face.

He leaned closer and lowered his voice. "Let's get away from people, from this virus. We find a spot to live out of the camper until it's safer. When Mary needs treatment, I'll drive her into town. And pick up any groceries we need at the same time. We'll keep you away and safe."

"There's a magical place to keep us all safe?" Regina asked. "Even in the camper, we'll have neighbors."

"Don't worry, we'll work it out. I think we'll be better off than here."

March 20

"The healthy and optimistic among us will doom the vulnerable. A successful shelter-in-place means you're going to feel like it was all for nothing, and you'd be right: Because nothing means that nothing happened to your family."

— The Chief Infectious Disease Epidemiologist at University of Chicago Medicine.

March 20

The curbside pickup at the Meijer in Grandville moved quickly. But loading his massive order into the back of his Ford Explorer took nearly ten minutes. Ordering more than $700 of food made Regina anxious; he thought stuffing their RV to the gills was more sensible than frequent runs into a store during the pandemic. They agreed to invest a few hundred dollars in books and Wii games to keep Mary occupied during their isolation.

"Going to the Yukon?" the young woman in charge of the loading asked.

"Someplace like that," Frank said, wondering about the tattoo of a rose that stretched from her chin to her collarbone. "You a lot busier these days?"

"Like crazy. Hardly nobody shops inside now. Of course, that makes my job easier if I have to go into the aisles for something."

"OK, but you stay safe." He gave her a folded $20 bill, even knowing that Regina wouldn't approve if she knew.

"You sure? It's not store policy. And hardly anybody does."

"Yeah, I'm sure. Stay well."

Frank drove home, thinking about everything else he would need to load into the Damon today if they were going to get away early Monday morning: bedding, clothing for the three of them, fishing gear, his deer guns, a shotgun, tools to deal with whatever they encounter. If he forgot something, there was an Ace Hardware and a general store in Dublin near the campground.

Mary became excited hearing the family was going camping, especially at Sand Lake. In past summers, the family had taken their Grumman canoe out for cool mornings of fishing. For lunch they would have the fresh panfish caught that morning, fried in the cast iron skillet over the open fire. In the afternoons, she liked to read on a canvas camp chair in the sunlight. There were times on those trips when she was so happy that Regina and Frank almost thought their daughter's leukemia had relented. Clinical tests relentlessly proved them wrong.

March 21

Once you break your back, mornings suck. Whatever drip-drip-drip of sleep came in the night burned off any benefit of whatever your ingested, inhaled, or injected the night before. And anything taken at dawn won't kick for at least an hour.

Rick found the fastest morning relief was to wash down a couple each of store-brand naproxen and ibuprofen with a slug of Irish cream. A doctor over at the VA clinic warned him that mixing alcohol with pills could hurt his liver or kidneys. Rick figured either would be a slower death than relieving the pain with a .357.

He rolled onto his right side and pulled an old quilt up to his shoulders. Shouldn't March start getting warmer? With so much on his mind, Rick debated whether to get out of bed. He could load the wood stove and stoke the fire until he felt the warmth. He hoped to hold off ordering more propane until his disability check reached his bank account. As a result, he kept the thermostat set at a balmy 55 degrees. His joints were cold and stiff, especially his fingers. Maybe movement would help. In the waiting room at the clinic, they play a video of some guy performing a slow tai chi dance to ease his pain. Rick believed in better living through chemistry. Morphine's best, but Demerol is a nice chaser.

After about 45 minutes twisting and flopping from side to side, he surrendered to the day. He sat up and pulled on a thick flannel shirt. He discovered his jeans were not on the bedpost. Instead they lay on the floor waiting for a wash. Rick rummaged in the closet until he found a pair of tan cargo pants from the army surplus store in Grand Rapids. Good until Monday. On a weekend, the laundromat was just a daycare, full of crying kids in that decade before they reached an age to be turned loose on the town.

In the pantry were boxes of cereal. Rick opted for a bottle of Founder's Breakfast Stout from the fridge. He turned on the radio to a hard rock station then settled on a kitchen chair. He also flipped on the television to see the morning outrage. On Fox News, a guest was explaining how a disease becomes a disaster. On CNN, the pundit panel discussed the governors in California and New York putting their entire states on lockdown. Frank decided to wait for Major McKittrick to explain the whole issue. On a Saturday, the major would come knocking around 1500 for a ride down to the Legion. Major Mac was an army combat surgeon in the first Gulf War who later worked at the VA hospital where Rick met him.

Saturday afternoons, American Legion Post #58 became an informal clinic. Major Mac brought along a leather doctor's bag. A gift from his officer's mess when he retired. He carried a stethoscope, blood pressure cuff, a forehead thermometer, a penlight otoscope, a pulse oximeter, a rubber reflex hammer and a stack of tongue depressors. The Post executive committee voted to fund Major Mac with a steady supply of exam gloves. Any vet was welcome in the post when the doctor was in the house, member or not. The doc also wrote up his opinions in support of their medical claims for VA disability evaluations.

Rick fetched another stout and looked out the kitchen window. His next-door neighbor, Frank, was pulling the cover off his big Damon camper. The Class A looked enormous beside Rick's 27-foot Coleman Lantern. Seemed early in the season to Rick for a family camping trip. Maybe Frank was planning to get some maintenance done before the weather warmed.

If he was going with Major Mac to the Legion Post, Rick decided he should shave and shower. Maybe even eat.

March 22

"Getting away for an early vacation?" Rick asked as he came up the driveway while Frank was busy packing groceries from the Explorer into the RV. Rick moved slowly, with something of a limp, but he carried surprising heft.

Frank turned in surprise. "Jesus, you scared the hell out of me."

"Sorry, buddy. I just saw you clearing off the Damon yesterday. Now you're packing enough supplies for a trip up the AlCan. You need me to watch the house while you're gone?"

Frank knew Rick as a neighbor for nearly 15 years. They took turns watching each other's property while the other was out traveling with their campers. Once, over a few bottles of Founder's Porter in his backyard, Rick described the accident on a Navy frigate that left him crippled for life. Short of his 20-year retirement, Rick now relied on the VA. He often said the agency's goal was to deny veterans care until they died. For years the administrators had tried to blame Rick's injuries on his high school football rather than his fall into an open hold on a ship's main deck during resupply operations. After years in the auto industry, Frank figured that was the same plan for private industry as well.

"I don't mind keeping an eye on things," Rick said. "Not like I'm doing much else now."

"I'm taking Mary and Regina away," Frank said. "If this disease is what they say, like the Spanish flu, they won't survive. But maybe we can get away from people far enough so they'll be safe."

"Where you thinking?" Rick asked in surprise. "Canada?"

Frank turned to sit on the step of the RV. "No, we need to make sure Mary has care available. Canada has their government health care, so she wouldn't qualify up there."

"Jesus, that makes it tough," Rick said, leaning against the side of the Damon. "So where you thinking? Going to the UP?"

"No. Regina didn't want to take Mary too far from her own doctors. You know Sand Lake? It's near Wellston. We've camped there before. The wife did her research. She says we'll be within an hour of hospitals in Traverse City, Ludington, Manistee and Cadillac. Two hours to get back here, if we need to."

"The campground's already open?" Rick asked in surprise. "I

never got into a Forest Service campground before May. I would have used them for turkey season."

Frank looked at Rick and lowered his voice. "They're closed for six more weeks, so we'd be all alone. When they open, we'll pay for three sites each night, so we'll have space on either side between our closest neighbor."

"How long do you think you'll have to stay up there?"

"Till they figure out what they're doing with this thing, or when the ranger throws us." Frank stood and climbed into the RV to continue stowing the groceries.

"Say goodbye before you go," Rick called.

March 22

Regina was loading the dishwasher with dinner plates. Frank sat at the kitchen table, comparing her list of needed staples with the Meijer register tape to confirm they had everything they needed. The rapping at the front door surprised them both. Not knowing who was outside, he closed the kitchen door so she would be safe from a sneezing or coughing stranger. Then he went to answer the knock.

"Hey, Frank, sorry to disturb you," Rick said. He nodded toward the gray-haired man standing beside him. "You know Major McKittrick from over on Birch Street, right?"

"Sure. How are you, doc?" Frank waved rather than extend his hand in greeting. "What's up, guys?" The Major reminded Frank of no one more than Jimmy Stewart when he played the doctor in John Wayne's last movie — tall, gaunt and weathered.

"Listen, we've been talking this afternoon about your plans," Rick said. "Major Mac thought it might be good for us to come along with you. Between us we have a very particular sets of skills. Skills we have acquired over very long careers."

"OK, stop that. We're not assassins," Doc said, pushing at Rick's shoulder gently. "But I've been a doctor for 40 years. I've handled a lot of situations."

Frank looked at Rick, "And you?"

"Well, if you must know, I have an acetylene torch. And I know how to use it." Rick laughed. "Skills that make me a blessing for people like you."

"You guys spend the day watching Liam movies, or what?" Frank asked. "So what have you been discussing?" He leaned against the door frame.

The door opened behind him just a little. Regina's face appeared. "Everything OK?" she asked. "Oh, hi, Rick. Major. How are you?"

"It's all good. I'll tell you in a couple of minutes," Frank said.

"Ignore Rick," the Major said after the door closed behind her. "He's had a few this afternoon. Brings out his inner Irish. Sad that he's all Czech and Polish."

"Now, wait. This was my idea," Rick said.

"Yes, it was. Be quiet, and I'll explain it to him. Frank, we can help you. Might be good to have a doctor closer than an hour away. And if you need something fixed, he's pretty handy to have around."

"A fool with tools," Rick observed.

"And when you don't need us, we'll be in his camper or enjoying the outdoors," Doc said. "He said there's good fishing, especially on the rivers."

"They don't need you at the hospital?" Frank asked, shifting so that his back was flat against the door.

"No, the good folk at your friendly VA decided to stop seeing patients in person because of this crisis. It's all telemedicine now, just that 'take two aspirins and call me in six months' crap. Not about seeing patients. Besides, I've got more than a year of leave on the books. I could sail around the world while collecting paychecks."

Laid-off from GM because of the economic slowdown, Frank couldn't help but feel jealous of Major McKittrick's good fortune. Regina worried every night over the checkbook, calculating how to cover the bills. They'd heard there might be federal money coming if a law got passed in Washington, but he was no more inclined to believe in it than unicorns. So he couldn't ignore the doctor's generous offer to assist in keeping Mary healthy through the pandemic. Of course, Frank also realized that he hadn't gone to medical school like the major had, so he should expect different outcomes in their incomes.

"I appreciate the offer. I do," Frank said. "But I only bought enough supplies for the three of us."

Rick leaned forward and smiled, tipsily. "Oh, we've thought of that, too. You know, it might look strange to have a couple of RVs traveling together this time of year, before campgrounds open up. So we thought if you go up 131 through Cadillac, then we could take the scenic route on 31 and stock up at the new Meijer in Manistee. We'll leave before you so we'll get there about the same time."

Frank took a deep breath. "Well, it's a free country, so I can't tell you not to go up to Sand Lake Campground tomorrow morning. I was thinking we might get there before noon. Might be nice to run into someone we know there. And if you aren't happy, you could always come home."

Rick poked an elbow into Major Mac's ribs. "See, sir, I told you he was a reasonable man." They turned and stepped off the concrete stoop. Rick turned and said, "Perhaps we'll see each other again someday."

As Rick headed down the sidewalk, Doc McKittrick took a step back toward Frank. "It'll be good for him, too. To steal from another movie, he's in more dire need of a detox than any white man in history." McKittrick started to walk away but then turned and came back to Frank's stoop. He removed his cap and brushed back his thinning hair. "I'll tell you this in confidence, though. I've been reading enough that I'm worried about Rick, too, if he were to catch this thing. He's a diabetic now, and he hasn't exercised since the accident. With the drinking, his liver's probably shot all to hell. I chalk about half of it up to my colleagues. But this thing will kill him in weeks."

"Are you coming with me or proposing to Frank?" Rick called from the sidewalk.

"Sorry, if I don't walk him home, he could end up in Grand Haven."

"Oh, dear. No telling what they'd do to a squid in Coast Guard City," Frank said. "Maybe I'll see you in the next few days."

March 23

"The goal here is simple; stay home, stay safe, save lives. This is not a recommendation. This is an order. Even with today's action, the number of cases will go up today, tomorrow and the days ahead."

— Governor of the State of Michigan, at a press conference.

March 24

"Look, you're going to lose a number of people to the flu. But you're going to lose more people by putting a country into a massive recession or depression. You're going to lose people. You're going to have suicides by the thousands. You're going to have all sorts of thing happen. You're going to have instability. You can't just come in and say, 'Let's close up the United States of America.'"

— President of the United States of America,
in an interview with Fox News

March 25

A Phoenix-area man is dead and his wife is under critical care after the two took chloroquine phosphate in an apparent attempt to self-medicate for the novel coronavirus, according to the hospital system.

"It does not appear they took the pharmaceutical version of the drug, but rather 'an additive commonly used at aquariums to clean fish tanks," the hospital said in a statement.

NBC News spoke to the wife, who said they learned of chloroquine's connection to coronavirus during [the President's] news conference, which "was on a lot actually." They took it because they "were afraid of getting sick," she said.

— CNN News

March 27

"Ferguson, Dispatch. LE wants to talk to you. Do you have any bars where you are?"

Jack eased his lime green pick-up onto the shoulder of the dirt road. He retrieved his cell phone from the leather holster on his belt and checked for coverage. He picked up the mic on the two-way radio and pressed the talk button. "Uh, oh. Somebody park in Rory's spot again?"

"Ferguson, Dispatch. It's Monday. New week; new whine," the dispatcher said. "Can he call you? Are you someplace safe?"

"Dispatch, Ferguson. Better here than in my office. You know how dropped calls happen."

"Ferguson, Dispatch. OK. Good luck. Out."

In 20 years as a district ranger, Jack Ferguson had worked with several law enforcement officers on his district. He had good relations with most, until Rory Winchester arrived. The man caused endless conflicts with the public, by issuing a citation to practically every visitor to the National Forest. Once, an 87-year-old man had come into Jack's office asking forgiveness for 27 tickets he received. Rory accused the man of mowing the grass along a Forest Service road that passed in front of elderly gentleman's home. One ticket for each mowing. Jack prayed for Rory's promotion into a job where he would never again deal with the public.

The cell phone thumped with a heavy hip-hop beat. Jack's wife liked to change the ringer to annoy him. Barking dogs one week to screaming Italian polizia siren the next. "Yeah?"

"Hey, Jack, it's Rory. You got a few minutes?"

"Sure, out here looking at a couple of timber sales that just wrapped up. What you got?"

"You been out to Sand Lake lately?"

Jack thought about the last time he'd been out to the campground, which remained over the past winter. "No, not since last fall. What's up?"

"I had a call that maybe the gate was open. I asked some neighbors to keep an eye on things. I didn't know if you had told the campground host they could go in early."

This required a little mental calculation on Jack's part. Early at this point would mean six weeks before the official start of the camping season. Maybe someone was in the campground to test the well water. Michigan waters can hold lots of nasty surprises. "Listen, I'm out near Caberfae now. Let me drive past and see what's going on."

"Fritz and I can meet you out there," Rory said.

The district ranger hesitated a moment before responding, not wanting to reject the offer too eagerly. "Nah. Long way to come if it turns out to be nothing." Jack did not care for Rory's canine unit, Fritz, any more than his handler. The dog had a habit of cruising the office, on the prowl for unattended food. Jack questioned whether Fritz was any better trained than Rory.

Jack drove west on the gravel and dirt roads, meandering through the forest toward Yuma. There was still a decent snowpack on the ground in the woods. When Jack brought his pick-up to a stop on Michigan 37, he watched two logging trucks pass before he followed them south. More loads of trees destined for the cardboard plant in Manistee or the electricity furnace east of Cadillac. As the years went on, he found his timber sales included a lot more pulp than hard wood. The best species, like oak and cherry, were most vulnerable to poachers. With so many roads and so much private property inside the National Forest, it was easy and profitable to steal trees off public land. Jack wished he could interest Rory in timber theft more than parking permits. He turned on the radio on the dashboard, but found it tuned to a Christian music station rather than his usual sports talk channel. He couldn't recall who had last borrowed his rig. He turned off the music and picked up the mic on his two-way radio.

"Dispatch, Ferguson. I'm going to stop by Sand Lake before I head back to the district. Following up on the LE complaint."

"Ferguson, Dispatch. Copy that. ETA back to the office?"

"I'm going to say when I get there. Just a guess."

"Affirmative. I won't hold you to that. Dispatch out."

When Jack stopped at the intersection with M-37 at Garlett's Corner, he ended up again behind yet another fully loaded logging truck, likely headed for the container board plant in Manistee. He considered passing, but once over the crest of the first hill the truck accelerated sharply. The driver was probably concerned when he saw the Forest Service truck following him. Jack slowed to avoid the shower of limbs and bark blowing off the logs on the back of the truck.

In a few miles, he crossed a bridge over the Pine River. MDOT rebuilt the bridge because it had a similar construction design as a bridge over the Mississippi River in Minneapolis that collapsed in 2007. The detour annoyed Jack, although he used the bypass as an excuse to stop at the general store in Dublin.

From M-55, Jack followed South Seaman's Road to the right-hand turn into the Sand Lake Recreation Area. The campground was small; much of the nearby land was privately owned. Still, the area was popular because of the beach, boating, campground, fishing and picnicking. Half the year the site a private company operated the site to make a profit and relieve the Forest Service of the costs and workload. The other six months, the beach and campground remained closed because of Michigan's unpredictable weather.

Even before he reached the entrance, Jack could see there was an issue. The big iron gate at the entrance was still closed, but over in the group camp area to the North sat a large RV next to a camper. A big F-250 pick-up truck and an Explorer sat nearby. He stopped to unlock the barrier but found that someone had welded closed the swinging gate to the latch post. Somebody intended to stay. He now faced one of those decision that everyone in the Forest Service does at some time; whether to proceed to encounter the problem or retreat and wait for back-up. Weighing his options, Jack decided he would rather not have Rory and Fritz as his back-up. He honked the truck's horn twice, then climbed out, walked around the barrier, and headed toward the group camping area.

"Hallo," the ranger called as he headed toward the campers. "Anyone home?"

Soon three men emerged; two from the trailer and one from the camper. They didn't look armed. They seemed to saunter casually toward him, so Jack wasn't expecting trouble. Certainly not the outcome he would expect if Rory were there. Jack held his hands out to show he wasn't armed. In response, the three men did as well. They stopped a respectful distance apart; none were wearing face masks. The three appeared mostly harmless: a middle-aged guy in jeans and a flannel shirt; a bulky man in outdoor clothes who walked with a limp and an older gentleman with spectacles and a sparse beard on his chin.

"Hello, I'm Jack Ferguson," he called. "I'm the district ranger here. I manage this whole area, including the campground. I had a call because we don't open the campgrounds for a few more weeks." He stopped, hoping they would respond that it was all a big mistake, even though the welded gate suggested otherwise.

"I'm Francis DuLong. That's my big RV." He stepped forward but didn't invade Jack's social distance. "These are my friends. Doctor McKittrick. He's a retired Army major. Works for the Veterans Administration."

Major Mac stayed where he was but waved casually.

Frank continued. "This is Rick Bocek. Former Navy Chief Boatswain's Mate. I asked them to come help me. Thought I might need their technical skills in getting settled in here."

Rick laid his palms together and bowed rather formally.

"OK. How long you planning to stay?" Jack asked, relaxing some. He assumed two veterans weren't suddenly going to go rogue and attack.

"As long as you let us," Rick said. "At least until the handcuffs come out."

"Well, I'm not law enforcement. You may be trespassing. Our campgrounds are closed to the public as long as the gates are locked. It looks like the gate was, uh, modified,"

The three men exchanged looks between them. Frank spoke for them. "I need to tell you why we're here. You know about coronavirus. My wife and daughter are in the camper. My wife is a diabetic. Type 1. My daughter Mary has leukemia. I can't pronounce the kind. She's waiting on a bone marrow transplant at St. Jude's. If either of them are exposed, it could be fatal. So we're here."

As Jack looked between the three men, they all nodded together.

He thought about this for several minutes. "I get why here. But don't they need medical care?"

Major Mac raised his hand. "I'll do the day-to-day stuff. I've made contact with doctors in Traverse City and Ludington in the case they need more than I can handle."

"Don't you open up the campground in mid-May? Couldn't we stay here until then?" Frank asked. "We'll clean up after ourselves so you'd hardly know what's here."

Jack looked at his watch. "Let's do this. You're here tonight. I'm going to give you my business card in case anyone else comes along. I have to talk to my boss and the law enforcement people about this situation. No guarantees beyond tonight, at least for now." He set the card on the top of the sign post and stepped back.

"Thank you," Frank said, stepping forward to retrieve it. "We won't cause any trouble."

"Ranger Ferguson, here, take this," Doc McKettrick said, laying down his own business card from the Veterans Affairs hospital in Grand Rapids. "In case you need to check us out."

After retrieving the Major's card, Jack turned and went back to his truck. When he got into the pick-up, he saw the three men wave before heading back to their campers. He didn't need this on top of everything else. Most employees on his ranger district were working at home because of the pandemic. They were planning to move out to a new office at a rehabilitated tree nursery in Wellston, not far from Sand Lake. In addition, he had to deal with all the usual budget and personnel issues. He backed the truck around and headed out of the campground. When he got to the intersection at the county road, he pulled to the side of the road and dialed his phone.

"Hey, Bill. You got a few minutes or more to chat?" he asked when the response came.

At the forest headquarters in Cadillac, Bill Reinhardt sat in the cramped public affairs office. "Just a casual chat, then? Cause I'm sitting in my office."

"Can you close the door?"

"The walls have ears. Eyes. Cameras. Recording devices." Bill looked up and scanned the ceiling.

"Good time for a walk?"

"OK, but you do know there are three other districts on the forest, right? You aren't the only ranger who needs help. You just need the most."

"Maybe you'll want to know about this one before anyone else."

"All right, give me a couple of minutes. I've got to sneak out the back door. Otherwise, I'm tracked."

"Five, then."

"I'll call you."

Bill picked up his jacket and planted his hat firmly on his head. He glanced both ways in the hallway before he headed for an exit. The forest supervisor had recently begun monitoring the activities of those employees who came into the office despite the pandemic. The boss acted as though there was a resistance movement against him. His poor performance reviews were no secret amongst the office staff, whom he frequently accused of spying on him for the Regional Forester.

"What's up, Jack?" Bill asked the ranger when he reached the parking lot. A slight wind garbled his cell phone reception, so he decided to take the call in his personal vehicle.

"Out in your POV?" Jack asked. "Can we talk now?"

"Depends. I've got a meeting with the boss in 20 minutes. Can you give me the gist in that time."

"I'll try." Jack launched into a description of his afternoon at Sand Lake. When he finished, he heard Bill groan.

"How do you manage this? You're a crisis magnet."

"Just another trespass, right?" Jack asked. "Can I turn this over to Rory now?"

"If you want your face on CNN and Fox News. Sick wife and child in the midst of a pandemic? At the next public meeting, why don't you just break out singing 'I'm a lumberjack and I'm OK.' That'll get you some attention."

"Only if you tell me what the hell a buttered scone is."

"Should I worry that you know all the lyrics?" Bill asked. "I think I need to sleep on this overnight."

"Sleep on which? The scones?"

"On whether to bring Rory and Fritz into this. Although at least the dog behaves for treats."

Jack laughed. "Listen, I'll handle Rory and Fritz, if you think you can get the boss to heel."

"You really owe me. And I don't mean another gas station hot dog."

March 29

DETROIT – The number of confirmed cases of the coronavirus (COVID-19) in Michigan has risen to 4,658 as of Saturday, including 111 deaths, state officials report.

As of 6:30 p.m., the total number of confirmed cases has reached 4,658 according to the state, an increase of 1,001 cases since Friday. The death toll increased by 19.

– ClickonDetroit.com

March 30

Jack sat in Bill's office waiting for the public affairs officer to finish another meeting. He had bought a coffee and Danish on the way over from Manistee to Cadillac. Decorated with a gray steel file cabinet, gray steel book case and a gray steel desk, the office looked like a set from a World War II movie. Bill liked to joke that all expense was spared when it came to furnishing his office. The only proof that Bill had a life outside work was a framed set of miniature medals and ribbons hung on the wall. Jack wasn't a military man himself, but he assumed that the number of awards and the gold stars attached to them meant something. The remaining space was wall-papered with maps of the ranger districts and the boundaries of the tribal treaties.

"Sorry. Hope I didn't keep you long," Bill said, when he came in. He navigated around Jack's long legs in the small office and settled behind his desk. "Is it me, or does coronavirus cause mass stupidity?"

"Isn't the usual mass stupidity enough for you?" Jack asked. He passed a bag over. "I know you don't drink coffee, but I thought a jelly donut might help you today."

Bill took the bag and peered inside. "Ah, infinity and jelly donuts. You think you can bribe me?"

Jack tipped his head slightly and made his best Tom Selleck smile. "Will it work?"

"You're lucky I like jelly donuts," Bill said. "But next time, go big or stay home."

"That bad, huh?"

Bill pulled out the lower drawer on his desk to rest his foot on it. Then he leaned back in his desk chair. "So here's the thing. Just last month the boss signed the latest updates of the Occupancy and Use orders for the entire forest. It's pretty clear that people can only occupy campgrounds during the open season. Even then it's for a limited time. We don't welcome homesteaders or squatters."

"Yeah, I initialed off all those updates that law enforcement requested before the boss signed. You've got to be a lawyer to visit the forest now."

"So, let's say you're willing to ignore that the campground is closed. Then technically, they can only stay in one spot for a couple of weeks before they have to move. That gets them to the middle of April. But the campgrounds won't open for at least three more weeks after that. Where they going to go in the meantime?"

Jack leaned back and rested his head against the wall. He pondered this dilemma for a few minutes. "Could we move them out of a developed camping area? Dispersed camping in the general forest?"

Bill shook his head. "That was my solution at 3 a.m. An hour later, I remembered that even then they're required to move every 16 days. But, we'd still be in April. We get hit with another blizzard with two feet of snow like we did a few years ago, they wouldn't be able to get out. What if the little girl needed medical attention?"

"Do you sleep?" Jack asked.

"No. You do?"

"But you've got an idea?"

"More like suggestions. First, we need to keep Rory as far away from Sand Lake as we can. Has he mentioned any temporary assignment opportunities? Training? Extended vacation to Tierra Del Fuego?"

"No, but I'll call the Special Agent in Charge over in Milwaukee to see what we might arrange for him. What else you got?"

"You talk to the concessionaire who runs the campground to inform them of the situation yet?"

"Left a message this morning. Nobody in the office regularly this early in the year."

"We should ask about their plans for opening next month." The phone on Bill's desk rang. He sat forward on his chair to answer it. "OK. This my five-minute warning? Thanks. We're ready." Bill sat back and smiled at Jack. "We're going to need more information about the girl. If we're going to take a humanitarian approach, we need to know what we're working with. Hopefully it's more than claustrophobia due to the lockdown. But the family has to give us that. You know the whole HIPPA thing with medical records, right? So maybe a letter from the parents?"

Jack nodded, putting the soiled napkin in the waxed bag. He stood and brushed the crumbs from his trousers. "Time to go?"

"Yeah, let me get my sack cloth and ashes. I don't know what I regret, but I soon will." Bill picked up his binder and water bottle. As he led the way through the maze of hallways toward the forest supervisor's office, Jack asked about the flavor of the cheese at the end. Just a few years ago, Bill's office was next door to the supervisor's office. New boss; new priorities. After the move, he sometimes joked that he was not let out to pasture, just given a different view on life. His current office window faced the adjacent cemetery.

They halted outside the office of the executive assistant to the boss. She was on the phone, but when Bill tapped on the glass, she looked up and nodded. So they walked a little way farther toward the end of the hallway. Bill knocked and leaned through the open doorway. "Still a good time?"

"OK, but we need to keep it short. I have to call back the Regional Forester in 15 minutes."

Jack went in while Bill lifted the stopper so he could close the office door. Perhaps intending to keep the meeting brief, the boss didn't invite them to sit either in front of the desk or at the conference table. Instead, they stood together near the boss's desk like a pair of truants sent to the principal's office.

Robert Fulbright checked his watch, a fancy gold band with a black face that might well have been a Rolex. "OK, thirteen minutes." He sat back in his chair and crossed a foot over the other leg, revealing a well-polished Italian shoe. Most employees on the forest wore a variation on common hiking boots. "Go."

Jack launched into his description of the prior day's events. While the ranger talked, Bill's eye's roamed over the impressive grid of framed photographs on the wall: Fulbright with the past six Chief of the Forest Service; Fulbright with the past four Secretaries of the Department of Agriculture; Fulbright with three vice presidents; Fulbright with the past two presidents. The frames created a pyramid; Bill assumed the top spot remained for a photo of Fulbright golfing with God. When Jack finished, the boss glanced at his watch and stood up to usher them out of the office. "Thanks, Jack, keep me informed. Bill, write up a briefing paper and give me some options." From the doorway, he called to his assistant, "Liz, get me the Regional Forester's office." The office door closed behind them.

"He calls her Liz?" Jack whispered, as they walked back down the hallway. "I thought she liked Elizabeth,"

"She does. How much do you suppose those leather suspenders cost?"

"Wouldn't know. The only suspenders I have came with my waders."

Bill chuckled, "I've heard you should dress for the job you want next. I guess the boss wants to run for Congress." When Jack stopped to go toward out to his vehicle, Bill tugged his sleeve and motioned with his head toward his office. Once inside, Bill turned on a loud fan to muffle their voices. "You sense the same level of support I do?"

"Yeah, it's on us."

"So I'm not the only one feeling a target on my back."

"Your back? It's on my forehead."

"OK. Let's stay in touch. You have my number." Bill extended his hand.

Jack accepted the handshake. "No elbow bump?"

"No. Now I have to go deal with the public from home."

March 30

On his drive back to Manistee, Jack stopped into the Sand Lake Campground to see if anything had changed with his guests. The gate was still welded closed. The same two RVs remained parked in the campground. Little suggested anything amiss. He parked his rig and hiked toward the campers. When he hollered, only Rick emerged from the trailer.

"Hey, Jack, right? How are you?"

"Oh, yeah. I'm good. Everyone around?"

"Sure, sure. They're just in the Damon," Rick said, nodding his head in the direction of the big camper. "I'm the only one who doesn't need to interact with Mary, so I'm going to be your contact for now. You know, to make sure she doesn't get infected."

"Makes sense to me. Limit outside contact." Jack glanced about, wishing there was a picnic table nearby where they could sit for this conversation. Because the campground was officially closed for another six weeks, the picnic table were stacked together against a tree and tethered with a chain. "Listen, I was wondering if Frank could give us something like a letter outlining the girl's medical condition. Nothing too detailed. Just explaining the dangers to her."

"I'll ask. At the same time, Regina and Mary found this online." He handed Jack a thick manila folder.

When Jack opened the folder, he found more than a dozen printouts copied out of newspaper from several years earlier when the Rainbow Family of Living Light had a gathering on his district of the Huron-Manistee National Forests.

"They said you let these people stay on the forest because of their First Amendment right to free assembly. Regina said that we would like to invoke our right to free assembly."

"OK, I'll look over this if you ask Frank and Regina for that letter. Sound good?"

Jack turned and headed back toward his truck. He remembered the Rainbow Gathering all too well. From the time one of his forestry techs identified a Family scout's vehicle on the National Forest until the group left almost a month later, Jack had little rest. Nearly 2,000 people gathered on the forest in a display of unity and love that defied nearly every Forest Service regulation. They drew water from a spring without proper testing; they dug pit latrines as needed. They drove vehicles farther into Forest Service lands than legally permitted. In fact, nothing they did was legally permitted because no one accepted the authority and responsibility of signing a permit for the gathering. All those things made the forest law enforcement crazy, which Jack now thought would do Rory some good. In retrospect, Jack thought there wasn't much about the Rainbow visit that he couldn't have managed better without visits from the offices of the Forest Supervisor or the Regional Forester. In fact, one representative of the Regional Forester seemed ready to strip naked and join the Rainbow festivities.

Before he reached the main road, he pulled to the side of the road and took out his cell phone once again. After a few rings, a voice answered. "Houston, we have a problem," Jack said.

"A donut doesn't cover do-overs. G&D's in 20 minutes? On you," Bill said.

"Do you charge the other rangers this much?"

"No, but they aren't on a frequent whiner plan. You gotta pay to play."

"Crap."

March 30

When Jack arrived at G&D's, the popular party store/pizzeria in downtown Cadillac, Bill was already standing outside the door. Both ordered the full-size pizza pockets, basically a Stromboli with any filling you requested from the pizza menu, topped with marinara sauce and cheese. The clerk was the son of the forest biologist. He was home from Michigan State because the university closed due to the coronavirus. Jack paid and led Bill outside. They left Bill's Jeep in the parking lot and rode in Jack's pickup down to a park overlooking the Lake Cadillac waterfront.

"You know you haven't done anything for that yet," Jack said, looking at the pizza pocket Bill had just unwrapped from the aluminum foil.

"I'm just taking advantage of you while I can."

"OK. But no surprise retirements in the middle of all this." He removed the manila folder from his canvas briefcase. "They're claiming the right of free assembly, just like the Rainbows."

Bill flipped through the printed news clippings. He stopped to read aloud one quote in particular. "'We believe in the First Amendment right of assembly of the Rainbow Family,' Reinhardt said.'" He closed the folder. "I hate having my own words thrown back at me." He opened his mouth wide and bit into the pizza pocket.

"Well, it sure takes away one tool. I was thinking we could ticket them for damage to the gate. The Rainbows put in a water system and slit latrines. And the gathering covered almost 20 acres. Now I've got five people sitting on two campsites, and they're socially distancing on top of it." Jack unwrapped his lunch. "And they're in a designated camping area. Hard to object."

"Unless you're Robert Fulbright," Bill said after his first bite. He looked at the lake as he chewed. "You know, I'm thinking about getting a Coast Guard license so I can run a charter fishing boat when I retire. Be nice to be my own boss."

"You own a boat?"

"Not yet. I'm looking to see what's available. What kind do you have?"

Jack swallowed a bit of the doughy crust. "A 28-foot money vacuum. I should have waited until I retire to buy. Work gets so busy in the summer that I haven't even put it in the water the past two years."

"Sucks. Actually my main goal is to retire before the administration figures out how to screw us out of our pensions. They do it in the private sector all the time. Like those Kentucky miners who discovered that the owners looted the retirement fund before selling the company."

"I've got three years before I can go out. What about you?"

Bill looked at his watch, then tapped the folder with a forefinger. "I may punch the button when I get back to the office."

"You got any ideas on how to handle this one?" Jack finished with pizza pocket and opened a bag of potato chips. "Just fix this last one before you retire, and I won't ask you for anything else."

"First, I have to go look up the legal definition of assembly. Are five people an assembly? The Rainbows claimed a kind of quasi-religious assembly, with the big drum ceremony on the Fourth of July and all. I see a call to the Office of General Counsel in our future."

"You think we may be making too big a deal out of this? We should issue citations and send them on their way?"

Bill wiped his mouth with the paper napkins. "Yesterday, you said this was a trespass. Then you told me about a sick little girl. Today, it's about the First Amendment. What's next? You come back and tell me they're tribal members exercising treaty rights, and I'll walk straight out the door to buy a boat."

"OK, OK. I wasn't going to spring that on you during lunch." Jack turned to look at his colleague and laughed. "You should see your face. I'm just fooling. I don't know they're tribal members. I'll ask next time I see them." He laughed again.

"You, sir, are an evil bastard."

March 31

"I want every American to be prepared for the hard days that lie ahead. We're going to go through a very tough two weeks."

— President of the United States of America,
in a White House press conference.

March 31

Rick sat at a wooden picnic table in the early morning. He had liberated several from a stack that chained to a tree. He had placed two tables about six feet apart between the campers. He named them: one for the washed and one for the unwashed. He usually sat alone at the unwashed table and never entered the big Damon. Frank and Regina sat at the washed table. Mary sat with them on the rare occasions she came outside. Doc sat at the washed table because the VA hospital monitored his temperature every day at the hospital and twice tested him for coronavirus, an intrusion he found more uncomfortable than painful. Rick had to remain separated from the others until he had completed a 14-day quarantine. With a map and a calculator, he was plotting the work day to come.

"Early start today," Major Mac said, as he came down the steps of the Damon. He had moved over from the camper to reduce any risk of infection to Mary. He carried a cup of coffee to the opposite picnic table. They sat nearly 10 feet apart.

"I've got to do a little work today. We've been here since March 23, right?"

"Geez, I think so. Hard to keep track without looking at the internet or the television." He held the mug tightly in his hands to capture the radiating heat. "If it weren't for Regina and Mary parking by the Wellston library and snagging a little wifi, we wouldn't know much of what's happening out there." He nodded toward the world beyond the campground gate.

"So maybe the three of you can decide how you want to pump our tanks. The closest dumping station I recall is the state campground in Cadillac, but the parks are still closed. The next closest would be Traverse City, but seems like it defeats the purpose to drive the Damon up there."

Doc Mac nodded, equally perplexed. "Well, we can't pump into the lake. That ranger will come back with Smokey Bear in SWAT gear." He drained the mug as he pondered the problem. "Other options?"

"Just a quick fix," Rick said as he surveyed the campground. "We could tap into the campground system. Looks like a vault toilet over there, your basic latrine. We could pump into that easily enough, depending upon the capacity. But I thought Frank mentioned showers. They probably wouldn't run showers into a pit, so maybe there's a septic system we could tap into. Even then we couldn't use it forever."

Doc stood to go back into the Damon. "I'll ask Frank how his tanks look and when that ranger might be back out here." As he walked back toward the big camper, he stopped and looked down at Rick. "Regina made a whole lot of food. How about I bring you a plate of whatever's left? Maybe scrambled eggs and toast?"

Rick waved him off. "No, I'm good. I drank." He chuckled.

Doctor McKettrick turned and came almost close enough to violate Rick's social distance. "OK, but you remember our agreement. Only until your birthday. That's still just three days? No changed birth certificate, right?" He paused for Rick to nod in the affirmative. "Then you start Doc McKettrick's program to detox and live pain-free, unapproved by any VA voodoo practitioner. You agreed." He waited again.

Rick raised his right hand. "Yes, Doc. I do solemnly swear that I will submit and endure the constitutional rehabilitation imposed by Doctor Charles McKettrick against all alcohol, foreign or domestic; that I will bear true night sweats and terrors from the same; that I will obey the orders of Doc Mac and order only non-alcoholic beverages."

"You've been thinking about this," Doc observed.

"Like a lobotomy."

March 31

"Hey, I just want to confirm with you that our current plan is that we don't have a plan, current or future. Is that right?"

"I've got to do a better job screening my calls," Bill said.

"I'm on my way out to Sand Lake, and I'm hoping for a little guidance," Jack said.

"Ready? Wash your hands frequently for 20 seconds. Don't lick doorknobs. And don't eat from a buffet. Thanks for calling."

"Any suggestion?"

"I keep coming back to that old Kristofferson song, 'Tell me, Lord.'" Bill began to croon. "What have I ever done, to deserve even one, of the calls that, I've taken from Jack?"

"If I ever hear you sing again, you will die with my hands around your throat."

"Yeah, I get that a lot. So I gave the boss my write-up on the situation and alternatives. And I'm going to guess since I haven't heard anything back that he would like us to move forward and not involve him directly."

"We're strictly on our own?" Jack asked. "Again."

Bill laughed into the phone receiver. "You had a different impression the other day? Something like law, regulation, or policy? It sounded to me a lot like 'good luck.'"

Jack chuckled. "Yeah, I heard something like luck, but it started with an F."

"Same message, different vernacular. Bottom line is we're screwed."

"Message received. I'm almost there. I'm doing a standard safety check this morning. I'll let you know if it has gone tribal or Congressional."

"Or if you see a media van with a big antenna in the air; call me; have me paged; call my cell; send a St. Bernard with brandy." When Bill put down the phone receiver, he saw Elizabeth waiting at the window in his office door. He waved her in. "The morning shopping list?"

"Just in case you have nothing to do this morning. Ready?" she asked.

Picking up a pen, Bill glanced back at the list from the prior day. "OK, go."

Elizabeth took a deep breath. "There hasn't been a press release about the boss participating on the governor's forestry council. Or the boss speaking to the Chamber of Commerce over in Oscoda. Where's the employee newsletter for this month? Can you arrange television interviews for the boss regarding Covid-19 and Department of Agriculture food initiatives?"

Bill leaned back in his chair. Given his military background, he chose not to mock the boss in front of a junior staffer. Instead, he took a deep breath. "Nothing about Sand Lake?"

"Not on my list."

"Thanks. I'll get on it."

The red light on Bill's phone flashed, indicating waiting messages. He picked up the receiver and listened to a pair of voicemails, first from a Congressional staffer and then a district ranger warning him that a Congressional staffer might call. At issue was a constituent's recurring request for grazing rights on National Forest System lands in lower Michigan. This was the fifth request from the same farmer since Bill arrived on forest; apparently the herd owner submitted the same inquiry each time the Congressman for the district hired a new staffer. Bill would call the ranger and explain the recurring letters before copying the same response going back over the past 20 years. But not now.

He took his hat and went out the northside entrance. He walked up the slope into the Maple Hill Cemetery. He knew his fellow employees walked here each day for exercise. When he came, it was for another reason. Beneath an bare-limbed white oak, a massive *quercus alba*, he knelt between two grave stones, removed his hat and bowed his head.

April 2

"I think they're going to be coming out with regulations on that [masks]. And if people want to abide by them, frankly, I don't think they'll be mandatory. Because some people don't want to do that. But if people want to — as an example on the masks — if people wanted to wear them, they can."

> — President of the United States of America,
> in a White House press conference.

April 3

"What a lot of the voters are seeing now is that when you elect somebody to be a mayor or governor or president, you're trying to think about who will be a competent manager during the time of crisis. This is a time of crisis and you're seeing certain people are better managers than others."

— Senior Advisor to the President
of the United States of America,
in a White House press conference.

April 3

With the district ranger's permission, Rick had pumped the brown and black water from the two campers into the vault below the campground toilet. This task finished, the trespassers were well-off as long as the groceries held out. With Regina's cooking skills, the Damon passengers — even with the addition of Doc Mac – were in fine shape with the supplies Frank had loaded in Grand Haven. Not as well-prepared for the challenge, Rick hadn't stored quite the same variety of staples in his camper. He had focused on frozen and other easy prep meals, even over the objections of Doc Mac who had recommended more economical grains and legumes.

"So, I was thinking about a quick run into the Meijer in Manistee," Rick told the doctor in the afternoon. "I'm planning to go in tonight before they close."

Doc McKettrick shook his head slowly. "No, we can't risk that. You going into town increases the danger."

"Wait, so I'm stuck here until we know what happens with Mary?"

Doc sat down on the "washed" picnic table opposite where Rick relaxed at the "unwashed" table. "No, you can leave. But you have to promise to not come back. And I can't help you detox."

"So you tricked me."

Doc Mac laughed. "No. Remember, you brought me into this. Before you told me, I didn't know how sick Mary is or that Regina is vulnerable. If you'd left me out, it wouldn't matter now. But if you go now, you'll bring back beer and whatever else. You knew my terms. Are you squelching on our agreement?"

"No, no, no," Rick said. "I'm running out of food. And I'm perfectly able to walk down an aisle and not pick up a six-pack. I just don't want to use up all the supplies I have." He sat back on the bench defiantly.

Doc Mac looked at Rick for several minutes. "OK, give me a list of what you think will tide you over for a few more weeks. I'll ask Regina to do the same. We'll put in a pick-up order to the Meijer store in Manistee. Maybe we can convince the ranger to bring the groceries out to us."

"All right. I'll see if I can hold out for a day or two. But I'm running low on aspirin and naproxen, too."

McKettrick shrugged with a lack of concern. "I can manage that for you. Just let me know when it gets bad." He stopped and looked at the Damon. "You'll never guess what Mary asked me a few days ago."

"Career advice?"

"Almost. She asked whether an epidural would help your back pain." He chuckled in astonishment.

"Now where does a nine-year-old child get an idea like that?" Rick looked at Doc for a long moment. "Is she going to med school online?"

"I think she could. At least she knows more about what's happening to her than 90 percent of the adults I treat."

"Is an epidural even possible for me? If it can help a woman in labor, why not me?"

"You haven't had an epidural in your thoracic?" Doc asked in surprise. "Has anyone suggested that?"

"No, just steroids and those, what are they, radio-frequency needles? I guess they burn off the nerve roots."

Doc groaned as he stood. "Well, one thing at a time, I guess. When we get back to Grand Rapids, I'll see if I can get your doctors to consider it. Assuming I still have a job there." He headed toward the big camper. "I'll come back in a little while for your nightcap."

"Hey, thank Doctor Mary for me," Rick called.

April 4

"This is a very important — the next two weeks
are extraordinarily important, and that's why I think you've
heard from [the] Doctor, from myself, from the President
and the Vice President that this is the moment to do
everything that you can on the presidential guidelines. This
is the moment to not be going to the grocery store, not going
to the pharmacy, but doing everything you can to keep
your family and your friends safe, and that means everybody
doing the six-feet distancing, washing your hands."

— Ambassador
and Coronavirus Response Coordinator for
the Vice President of the United States,
in a White House coronavirus daily briefing

April 5

"Late night?" Doc asked when Rick emerged from his camper blinking in the late morning sun. "You want something to eat or do you need something for the pain first?" McKettrick sat on the far side of the washed table with a piece of toast in one hand, a coffee mug in the other.

As if emerging from a cave, Rick slowly pulled himself up to full height. "I am not an animal," he growled. "I think I'm good for now. Just had a few naproxen and ibuprofen, with a handful of aspirin. They should make a cereal with that recipe."

"With just water, right? No stout this morning? Because we can't be mixing what I give you with your home remedies. And nothing that I don't give you after noon, remember?" Major Mac's tone did not sound comforting in any way. "Check with me before you take even an aspirin."

"Were you also a drill sergeant?" Rick settled at the unwashed table and removed a pack of cigarettes from his shirt pocket.

"For you, for the next month, yes. And then we start work on getting you off those damn things." He took a sip of coffee.

Rick flung his arms out in a display of mock rage. "What the hell is it with you VA people? No painkillers. No alcohol. No cigarettes. No hitting on the pretty nurses. I didn't think getting hurt meant I had to become a monk."

"I never said anything about the nurses. Why do you think I still go to work? I could have retired six years ago."

"Must be good to have a job to go to," Rick muttered.

Not certain he was meant to hear that comment, Doc Mac decided not to respond. "Regina took the truck over to Wellston. She's hoping to find wifi at the library or somewhere so she can download this morning's Mass from St. Andrew's. She promised not to get out of the truck. When I came out, Mary had beaten Frank in Chutes and Ladders twenty-seven straight games."

"Wow. Twenty-seven? So which one do you suppose is cheating?"

"Oh, the first twenty or so I thought it was him. But after that I was wondering how he found so many ways to throw the game without her catching on. So I think there's three options: she cheats, he cheats, or he doesn't understand the game at all."

Rick jerked upright. "Uh-oh. Looks like we have a visitor."

Doc turned on the bench to see a big Ford pick-up truck coming toward the campground gate. "It doesn't look like a Forest Service truck. They seem to be white or that minty green."

"Should we call Jack?"

"Give it a minute. Let's see what we've got."

The Ford came up to the gate but then made a three-point turn so it's back end was just a few feet from the campground's steel gate. The driver got out and came aft. He dropped the tailgate and lifted the back window on the bed topper. Inside were dozens of white plastic bags with red and blue print.

Jack came to the gate with a few shopping bags in each hand. "You guys had exactly the right idea. I'm going to tell my wife to start scheduling her grocery pick-up for Sunday mornings." He set the bags at the gate and went back for more. "Nobody around, and the young woman who brought it out seemed happy for the distraction."

"Tall girl with pink hair?" Rick asked as he came toward the gate. He and Doc had picked up an order there on the way over to Sand Lake.

"I wouldn't say tall, but definitely pink." There weren't many people Jack considered tall. As early as junior high, he was already taller than most of his teachers and coaches. "I'm just going to drop the stuff here for you to sort out. I won't get no closer than this."

"You sure you don't want to come in? We've got an epic Chutes and Ladders grudge match going." Rick laughed.

Jack chuckled as well as he laid a few shopping bags on the gate. "Chutes and Ladders, huh? That takes me back. I just sent my oldest daughter off to college. It's hard to throw that game when the kid gets to be about eight. They know all your tricks."

Rick doubled over in laughter. "Too bad you can't come in. Frank's lost 27 games, and he's probably about done out. Maybe you could share a few of your cheating ways with him."

"That's one clever dad," Jack said, nodding in agreement. "But

I'll bet she figured him out at least ten games ago. Now she's just being nice to him."

"If I'd tried that, my daughter would have gotten up in my face about it." Doc also laughed. "From about five on, you couldn't get anything past her. But she used it to the good. Went to law school, worked for a district attorney down in Lansing, and now she's a federal prosecutor in Bay City. I pity the defendant or any lawyer who tries to play her. I hope I live long enough to see her on the Supreme Court."

"Doc, I don't think I've ever heard you mention you have a daughter," Rick said.

"No, we don't talk much after her mother died. Blames my smoking back in the day for her mom's cancer." All jesting came to a full stop. "She could be right. Who can know?"

In silence, Jack emptied the pick-up bed, then closed the tail gate and the topper. Rick gathered up the shopping bags, even running down a plastic bag that escaped from the table. Doc McKettrick silently turned and walked down to stare at Sand Lake. He did not look back as Jack's Ford rumbled down the campground entrance.

April 6

Now that Rick had completed his quarantine, Doc McKettrick moved back from the Damon camper to the Coleman trailer. At first, he griped about the smaller accommodations. After a few hours, he realized he could now curse freely without being sternly corrected by Regina, both a devoted mother and a devout Catholic. He couldn't decide which of the two RVs offered the better mattress. He was drinking his second coffee when Rick emerged. He didn't seem nearly as bound up in pain.

"So what did you give me last night?" Rick asked. "That pill kicked my ass. I haven't slept like that in maybe twenty years." He eased his bulk into the bench seat across the table from Doc. "Man, that's some good shit. They should sell instead of all the other crap out there."

"I'm sure they do sell it. It's just harder to come by than oxy."

"So what was it?"

"Morphine."

"Morphine?" Rick's eyes opened wider. "You have a stash of morphine pills? Do you have any idea how much that stuff would be worth in we took it up to Traverse City?"

Doc Mac eyed his patient with suspicion. "First, I believe we discussed total secrecy. Second, any idea what the prison time would be if we sold just one pill? Third, these pills are time-release, so nobody is going to get a big high, unless they mix it with something else. That could be fatal. So, we're not selling it, and we're not talking about it — to anyone. Especially the ranger. Understand?"

"OK. Who am I going to tell out here?"

"I'm serious about this. You tell a squirrel, and detox done. Do you agree?"

"Yes, of course." He returned to the trailer and emerged again five minutes later with a bottle of diet soda. "So how is this going to work? I'm switching over from alcohol to morphine? Seems like a serious upgrade to me. In combat first aid, the instructor said to write the time we administered morphine on the patient's forehead so they weren't given a second dose too soon."

Doc McKettrick took a black marker from his shirt pocket. "OK, lean down here. Or, I can just keep you on a regular schedule.

We're going to teach your body to sleep without alcohol, then we'll find something to actually treat your pain."

Rick straddled the bench on the picnic table near where the doctor sat nursing his coffee. "You know what the pain clinic does for pain? The therapist showed me these stretching exercises. Of course she can bend her back like that." He created an arch with his hands. "But she's less than half my age. I let her go on, because I'm polite and she's nice to watch. But when she finished, she asked me to try while she guided me."

"Tell me you didn't do anything to her."

"Hell, Doc, I couldn't get into those positions. If I lost my balance and landed on her, I'd have crushed her. I didn't want to hurt the little thing. But she just wasn't understanding me. So I told her about getting knocked into that open hold and landing on my back some twenty feet below, half on a hatch cover. Shattered eight vertebrae, sheared off five ribs and two of those punctured my left lung. Put a crack in my pelvis. I needed her to understand it's too late for me to start yoga, so I pulled up my shirt in the back. When she saw that scar, she stopped being so chipper."

As Rick described his experiences with the VA, Doc Mac sat with his eyes closed, shaking his head in sympathy.

"Heck, you've seen my x-rays. Do you think I'm a good subject for tai chi or Cirque du Soleil? But the Navy put me out at eighteen years, and I hear the little bastard who knocked me into the hold is a lieutenant now." He tried to calm himself because usually when he got angry about how his career ended, he would think about opening a beer.

"What did the VA give you for pain?"

Rick smiled, as if remembering a promotion ceremony or a welcome home party. "Man, back in the day, they made it livable. Percocet for pain and valium for sleep. That was good for three or so years. Then a couple of years with oxycodone, no valium. Next just hydrocodone, which is like doubling down on Tylenol. Then we hit a wall about, what, seven years ago. Nothing that works." He began speaking in a cheerful falsetto. "Sorry, but you might sell a pill to a junkie. So here's some gabapentin for the burning in your hands and feet; won't do anything for your back, ah, discomfort.

Have some flexeril, it's not a pain reliever, but a nice muscle relaxant so you sleep all day. Try holding down a job like that. Would you like some amitriptyline? It's an anti-depressant so you feel better about being in constant pain. See if you can rub this lidocaine creme everywhere that hurts. To spread it up between your shoulder blades, you'll need to dislocate your shoulder like Houdini. And here's an electrical device to give you little shocks that distract you from the pain. And try watching *Joanie Loves Chachi* reruns, because laughter is the best medicine."

"Done?" Doc asked.

"Don't want to know what they did for me when one of my other ribs slipped?"

"Only if it worked out."

"Not yet. Think you could consult with Mary on that one?" He sounded surprisingly sincere.

April 7

There are now 845 deaths from COVID-19 and 18,970 confirmed cases in the state of Michigan, according to new numbers released by the state on Tuesday.

That's up 118 deaths and 1,749 cases from the day before, and is the largest single-day increase in deaths, beating the previous high of 110 set the day before on Monday.

The state still ranks third in the country for cases and deaths, behind New York and New Jersey respectively.

– WXYZ, Detroit.

April 7

"He did what?!" The boss stood, leaning forward with his hands planted firmly on his desk, in order to glare directly into Bill's face.

"He used his own vehicle on his own time." Bill wondered if he should worry about the cloud of saliva and spittle emanating from the boss when he was so angry. Not a particularly rare occurrence in Bill's experience. But in a pandemic?

"Are you at all familiar with the term 'aiding and abetting'?" Fulbright demanded. "Damn it, are the two of you intentionally trying to destroy my career? I can't wait until the Regional Forester hears about this."

"If I may, sir, last week you gave me and Jack the impression that we should resolve this as quietly as possible. He's been talking to the concessionaire and keeping that zealous LEO out of it. With the governor's shelter-in-place order, how would it look to throw a nine-year-old girl with leukemia onto the streets? With respect, I think that would be a career-ender." Bill wondered whether the boss's diamond cufflinks were real.

"I want you and Jack in here tomorrow morning at 9 a.m. And this time, I want real options. Understand? We can't just let people trespass on National Forest System lands with no end in sight. Am I clear?"

Bill smiled and nodded. That was always the best response to the boss. When he reached the hallway, he thought to himself, *Is today the day to push the button?* As he passed the office where Elizabeth sat, she waved furiously for him to enter and close the door.

"Good meeting with the boss?" she asked.

"You couldn't hear it? I figured everyone on this side of the building will be sharing it at break with everyone from the other side of the forest. In another 15 minutes, all the district offices will receive a complete transcript."

She shook her head. "No. I'm still typing it up." She looked at the small bits of paper pasted to the wall of her small office. "Are you flummoxed or flabbergasted?"

"Not sure. Maybe floundering? You're suddenly quite erudite. I'm impressed."

"It's this word-a-day calendar you gave me. I tack up the words I like. I'm thinking about moving over to public affairs. 'Course, I'd consider marking timber or cleaning toilets if I could get out of here."

Bill left her office and started the northerly migration to his office. He considered the desperation in her career choices, not certain which would be a worse fate. Timber marking means spraying the trunks of trees in a proposed sale area to differentiate trees to be harvested from those not for harvest. He had seen markers finish a day in the forest covered from boot to hat in paint. On the other hand, he had gone into toilets in the recreation areas on the forest where visitors had smeared the walls with human feces. His office phone was ringing when he arrived. He closed the door and punched the speaker button.

Jack started talking immediately. "How bad was it?"

"How did you know?"

"I heard a little bird calling my name."

"So how did Elizabeth describe it?"

"First she said blistering. Then she added suppurating. I had to look that up."

Bill laughed as he settled into his chair. "I admire her restraint. Did she tell you we have an encore performance before the king tomorrow morning? I think we'll have a choice between gallows and guillotine."

"That bad?" Jack asked earnestly.

"Did you have to take their groceries out to them? Please tell me you didn't pay for it."

"I was heading out that way," Jack said, defensively. "On my way to church. So I did my good turn for the day."

"Sure. You drive thirty minutes each way to church. Did you wade into The Church of the Sacred Salmon?

"That's my story, and I'm sticking to it."

Bill laughed again. "Good luck with that."

"But listen, I had an idea that might fix all this. I'm meeting with the concessionaire this afternoon. Here's my thought. Right now, Covid-19 closed all campgrounds. Suppose we ask the concessionaire to hire our visitors to be campground hosts. He's not making any money on closed campgrounds, but suppose we could reimburse him for completing any deferred maintenance projects on the camp-ground. I'll bet this Rick fellow could do quite a lot of repairs on a variety of things. I think he did this stuff in the Navy. Maybe Frank, the dad, can help him. The concessionaire gets paid for mainte-nance, and our visitors can stay on the site for free as hosts. What do you think?"

"This may be the most creative use of Granger-Thye authority in the history of the Forest Service." Bill paused. "And it's legal, right?"

"So here's the thing. My recreation people tell me we can afford it because they haven't spent any money yet this year. So if we can economize, especially if the state stays shutdown, we can probably give the company a little incentive to cooperate."

"OK, so maybe you can pay for it. Now listen carefully to my question, Jack. Is. This. Scheme. Legal? As in not violating law, regulation, or policy?" Bill paused to wait for a response. "Don't think too long. It's a simple yes or no."

The ranger laughed. "Nothing is ever a simple yes or no. Why do you think there are so many lawyers?"

"Keep golf courses in business?" Bill guessed. "The Mustang Ranch wasn't hiring?"

"You know the first lesson in district ranger school is 'it's easier to get forgiveness than permission.' And the second is, 'never ask the lawyer.'"

Bill chuckled. "Cute, but there's no such thing as district ranger school."

The phone line went dead.

April 8

"You will always have conspiracy theories when you have very challenging public health crises. They are nothing but distractions."

— Director of the National Institute
of Allergy and Infectious Diseases,
at the White House coronavirus daily briefing.

April 8

"OK, that could have been worse," Bill said as they walked away from the Forest Supervisor's office and headed down the hallway. The few people still working in the building scattered as they approached.

"I hope you're impressed." Jack seemed rather impressed with himself. "Did you like that I had the Concession Desk Guide with me? Complete with yellow sticky bookmarks."

"I'm betting you stuck those in at random, didn't you?"

"I can neither confirm or deny. But the boss was OK with the plan. Isn't that all that matters?"

Back in his office, Bill closed the door and turned on the same loud fan, now aimed at the wall. "You gave him plausible deniability, and that's all he wants. If this goes well, he's putting it on his accomplishments report. If it doesn't end well, it'll show up in our performance evaluations."

When Jack settled into the wooden visitor's chair, his legs stretched nearly across the small office. "What do they say, 'all's well that ends well'?"

"Yes. They also say 'don't do the crime if you can't do the time.'"

"Really? People still say that?"

Bill glanced at the flashing red light on his desk phone. He decided to ignore it. "Have you heard back from the concessionaire? Are they going to go along with this plan?"

"Not yet, but they'll probably get my message today. I'm offering a chance to have some income. They'll call. Meanwhile, I think that you owe me lunch for thinking of this. Anywhere nearby we can get takeout?"

"Take your pick of the best cuisine Cadillac has to offer in a pandemic. I think we can do burgers, subs or tacos."

"Oooh, tough choice. But no burgers, please. They're all starting to taste the same at this point." Jack opened the door and headed into the hallway.

"That's how I feel about subs now. How about tacos?" Bill asked, tugging on his hat. He followed Jack out to the parking lot.

"You want me to sit in the back seat or drive myself? According to Canada, we have to stay a caribou length apart."

Jack laughed. "Or four ravens. Are Canadian ravens trained to queue up like that?" They climbed into Jack's big pick-up truck. "Hey, have you tried this Zoom thing?" Jack asked. "I've got a planning board meeting tonight. I've got to figure out how to plug into the software."

"No, I haven't needed it because we have the region's teleconference system. Isn't it like Facetime, but with lots of small screenshots, like a kaleidoscope?"

Jack groaned as he ground the truck's ignition. "Great. Sounds like a headache coming on." He shifted into gear and drove out from behind the office building toward the highway. "The thing about this lockdown is there are no more excuses. What are you going to say, 'Sorry, I can't make the meeting. I'm going to be in the next room playing Call of Duty."

"Not Asteroids?"

At the stop sign, Jack looked at Bill and shook his head slowly. "You still have your Atari?"

April 8

Rick watched Regina and Mary down at the water's edge, dressed in their winter coats. They were fishing with matching pink rods. The mother seemed to prefer long casts that dropped a bobber about 30 feet from shore. Mary appeared to target an area maybe 15 feet closer. He didn't hear Doc Mac approaching, so the voice from a nearby table for the washed surprised Rick.

"My money is on Mary," McKettrick said. "Couple of bucks on it?"

"That how VA doctors supplement your pay?" Rick asked. "Dope somebody up on morphine and bet on fishing tournaments?"

"Not much else out there right now. Maybe ping-pong games?"

"OK. Betting on the number caught or by the pound?" Rick asked. "What kind of odds?"

"Were you a bookie in a former life?"

"I spent most of my life underway. What else could we do? There's only so much *Dungeons and Dragons* you can watch before you start to think about all that line coiled down in the forward hold."

"You haven't mentioned suicidal thoughts before," Doc Means observed warily. He sounded suddenly worried about his approach to treating Rick's alcoholism.

"Oh, I never gave it as much thought as all that. Especially after I did a funeral escort home for a seaman who went through with it. Hardest thing I ever did to present the flag to those parents." He stopped speaking for a long while. "Besides, I've got a new mission. We have to keep Mary safe. That's something to live for."

Doc Mac nodded, thinking *oh, and my mission is to keep you alive.*

April 8

After lunch, Jack drove back toward Manistee on M-55. There was almost no other traffic on the highway. Just after he left Cadillac, two Michigan State Trooper cruisers passed him heading west at high speeds. With timber hauling done for the year, and the campers were still grounded by the governor's stay-at-home order, he wasn't certain the gas station and convenience store at Garlett's Corner would be open. He did not see any vehicles in the parking lot. After stopping at the intersection, he headed up the hill. When he passed the blue sign for Manistee County, a cruiser pulled out behind him and flipped on its blue lights.

Great. Traffic ticket in a government vehicle, Jack thought. The boss is not going to be happy about this. He rolled down the window and turned toward the approaching officer. "Officer, I thought I came to a full stop. But you probably hear that a lot don't you?"

The officer laughed, a guttural sound from deep in his chest. "Jack, when we're done, you're going to wish it was just a speeding ticket." Pete Simmons stepped past the truck door and leaned against the outside mirror. "This is going to be way more trouble than that."

"Sheriff, you know I'm good for that fifty bucks. But you know the governor won't let me stop by your house. Not even for a chance to win my money back." Seeing that Simmons wasn't wearing a mask, Jack extended his hand.

After shaking hands, the sheriff removed his gray cowboy hat and dark aviator glasses. He hung the sunglasses on his uniform pocket next to the badge. "Your office says you've been in Cadillac all morning. So you haven't spoken with Rory today?"

"Oh, God. How bad is it?"

Simmons reached for the pickup's door handle. "Let's take the cruiser. We should run lights and siren."

"Oh, God. How bad is it?" As Jack stepped out of the truck, Simmons was already halfway back to his cruiser. Not stopping to roll up the window or lock his truck, Jack jogged to the passenger side of the sheriff's car. Jack's car door slammed shut when Simmons accelerated into the traffic lane. He fumbled for his seatbelt as the lights and siren came on.

"So we had a request from your boy a short while ago, needing backup at Sand Lake Campground. We might meet state police there, too. And the narcotics team."

"Oh, God. How bad …?"

"Come on, Jack. We survived the Rainbows. It'll be fine."

"The Rainbows were in Wexford County," Jack said grimly.

"Oh, right. We just got your spillover."

"What's Rory's problem?"

"I heard trespass, destruction of government property, narcotics, assault on an officer, kidnapping. Maybe treason by the time we get there."

Jack took out his cell phone and called the office. "Hi, Gwen, can you have somebody go get my truck out on 55, Manistee side of Garlett's?"

"You bet, Jack. Hey, the sheriff was trying to reach you earlier. Did he find you?" Jack turned the phone toward the partially open window. The siren wailed loudly. "OK, I guess we're good. Jack, be careful. Rory's a little amped up. Too many energy drinks, I think."

Simmons took the turn off the state highway onto the county road, fast, and the cruiser fishtailed in response. "This what you told me about at the gas station the other day? It's all about keeping a sick girl safe from this coronavirus?"

"It was when I left the office this morning. Sounds like Rory turned it into the greatest conspiracy since the 9/11 truthers."

As they turned into the campground, they saw a dazzling collection of red and blue flashing lights through the trees.

"We're too late," Simmons said. He drove his cruiser in a wide arc across the brown lawn to where they could see the campground host site: two RVs and private trucks on one side, and on the other a Forest Service LEO vehicle, three blue Michigan State Police sedans and two unmarked, black Fords with flashing lights in their grills and arrays of antenna on their trunks.

"Suggestions?" Jack asked.

"We go straight to the middle of it. I'll get the LE people together. See if you can isolate Rory. Maybe get him in his truck and have him call his supervisor. Then check in with your guests. You encounter a problem, give a shout."

They got out and walked toward the picnic tables that seemed to have become a sort of command post. Doc McKettrick and Rick Bocek sat together at one table in handcuffs and leg restraints. Not until they passed the front of the Damon did Jack and Pete see the worst of it. Two state troopers had AR-15s aimed at the side of the RV, while another officer stood nearby holding a megaphone in one hand and a cell phone in the other. The sheriff pushed Jack in that direction.

"Hey, Tom, can you bring me up to date?" Pete asked.

The officer with the megaphone glanced quickly toward him. "Jesus, Pete, I'm a little busy here. Guy in there admits me he's got a deer rifle and a shotgun that he won't throw out. Holding his wife and daughter. Won't let them come out either. Maybe a custody issue. Those two guys are holding a bunch of narcotics. TNT is looking around to see if this is a meth operation." He turned his attention back toward the big RV.

Simmons chuckled and said, "Tom, when you have just a moment, can I tell you about a little boy who cried 'wolf'?"

The trooper turned to face Pete and Jack full-on. "What do you mean?" he asked angrily.

"Who called for assistance?"

"Forest Service dispatch asked that we meet LEO Winchester out here."

"Now you've met Rory. Is his dog in the truck?"

"He said his canine was assaulted."

Pete laughed and patted the trooper's shoulder. "Welcome to the Rory and Fritz show. I hope we made it in time for intermission."

"No, wait. What's the story with this guy in the RV? He's holding two people and not coming out. Rory's not making that up."

Simmons turned to Jack. "Tell him. Short version."

With as little flourish as he could manage, the ranger explained why there were five people camped in a closed campground, starting with the concession agreement. Finally, he reached for the bullhorn. "May I?" Tom handed it over. After a moment of painful squelch, Jack spoke into the mic. "Mary, could you let the trooper know how you and your mother are doing?" The echo rang through the trees.

In a flash, Mary held a sheet of paper plastered against the glass window. "WE ARE FINE, JACK." A moment later, a second sheet appeared. "PLEASE ASK THEM NOT TO SHOOT."

As Pete walked toward where the Traverse Narcotics Team was strip-searching the Coleman trailer, he spotted LEO Winchester searching the far side of the parking area near the beach, perhaps looking for shallow graves. Pete was grateful for the time alone with the other agencies.

Back in front of the Damon, Tom called over the other two state troopers. The introductions were quick. Jack explained again in as few words as possible why there might be a family holed up in a big recreation vehicle in a closed campground, refusing even to open the door to answer the troopers' questions. The child's doctor had come along because the VA hospital where he worked no longer accepted patients in person. The two men were the new camp-ground hosts, there early to get the site ready for the coming camping season, that Jack expected to be extremely busy after people emerged a few weeks under the stay-at-home order. As Jack finished, he saw troopers Rex and Melinda set the safety on their weapons before they walked back to their vehicles.

"Your officer's going to get someone killed someday," Tom said to Jack before he walked away.

Not my officer, Jack thought, just my problem.

When the ranger looked up, he saw Frank and Regina standing together in the big window of the Damon. He gave them a thumb's up, then walked back to where TNT were questioning Doc Mac and Rick. Simmons was already attempting to intercede on their part as well. Jack had missed introductions, but didn't want to inter-rupt the discussions between the law enforcement agents.

"Can you go through what you've got for me?" Simmons asked.

"When we got here, we found these two cuffed and waiting. The new forest cop showed us this old bag with morphine, oxy, insulin, and a bunch of other stuff I can't even pronounce." The TNT officer wiped a rivulet of sweat from her forehead with the sleeve of her uniform. "We've been searching the camper to see if there's anything else. When the troopers clear the RV, we'll go through that as well."

Jack leaned into the conversation. "May I say something?" He waited for the TNT people to look in his direction. "I can explain the drugs. He's an actual doctor."

She laughed at him. "Sorry. Who are you?"

"Jack Ferguson. District Ranger for the Cadillac/Manistee Ranger District. Part of the Huron-Manistee National Forests. I authorized these people to stay on this campground." Pointing at Rick, he said, "He's a seasonal host for this campground, coming on to help us get ready to open." Jack pointed next at McKettrick. "And he's a doctor. He's here to treat the little girl in the camper until they're ready to leave. You can check his credentials here." He held Doc's business card toward the TNT officer. "A phone call?"

She accepted the card but looked at Doc closely. "So these other drug bottles and vials with the handwritten labels, what are they? They're not on a DEA schedule."

"I hope not," Doc said. "Those are for treating leukemia. I keep in touch with the girl's doctors. They'll instruct me what she needs, if she needs it."

The officer straightened and looked from Doc Mac to Jack. "If she has leukemia, why is she in a camper in the forest. Why isn't she in a hospital?"

"The hospital isn't ready for her," Doc explained. "They don't have a ready bed or a good bone marrow match yet. I trust St. Jude's more than I trust anywhere in the VA."

"And who's going to expose her to coronavirus out here?" Jack asked.

The officer shook her head. "You mean other than us?" She flipped closed her notebook, then stopped short. "Wait. Why do you have all these narcotics? They'd better not be for the girl."

Doc held up his cuffed hands. "May I?"

Doc Mac stood and leaned toward Rick, careful of their tethered ankles. "I'll be careful, Rick." He gently tugged Rick's shirttails out of his jeans and hoisted the material up past the massive scar. "Mr. Bocek is one of my patients at the VA. While we're here, I'm trying to identify a medication regimen to help with this injury, incurred on active duty. Would you like me to explain what they had to do to rebuild his spine?"

Jack sensed a tone in McKettrick's voice that he worried might offend the TNT crew. He leaned toward Doc Mac and whispered, "Easy now. You're winning already."

Three of the officers, including Simmons, looked at Rick's back. One whistled. Jack wasn't sure which one.

"And none of these drugs are for sale?" the lead TNT agent asked.

"No, ma'am," Doc said. "I'd lose my license."

"Are we done then?" she asked.

"OK, one question," the sheriff said. He swiveled his head to see where Rory was. "What's this about assaulting a law officer?"

Rick raised his hands. "That one's on me? That big truck pulls up, and next thing I know there's a dog trying to steal my burger off my plate. So I smacked his snout. After that, the officer searched and bound us up like a chain gang. And the dog ate both our lunches."

Simmons looked at Jack. "I'd have smacked the dog myself, unless he had a search warrant for my lunch."

"So you'll arrest Rory for a false police report?" Jack asked.

"Sounds like a Forest Service problem. And you know how I am about jurisdiction."

The Ranger looked down and then around him. "Don't we have some kind of cooperative enforcement agreement? Don't I pay you to patrol Forest Service lands?"

"You invited me. Now I'm disinviting myself. But thanks for an interesting afternoon." Sheriff Simmons walked away and caught up with the TNT officers. Jack couldn't hear exactly what they were saying, but he assumed there was nothing flattering about Forest Service law enforcement. Jack wondered if there was a way he could hire back a recent retiree who never thought that the number of citations was a performance measure. Henry was more inclined to welcome visitors like a lumbering Smokey Bear and intimidate miscreants with his sheer bulk. Bill remembered Henry as one of the biggest men he had ever met. A former tackle at West Virginia University, he had a neck thicker than most balsam fir.

When Rory returned from whatever quest he was on, Jack asked him to remove the shackles from Major Charles McKettrick and Navy Chief Boatswain's Mate Rick Bocek. As a former Army MP, Rory seemed willing to give the fellow veterans the benefit of some doubt. So Jack quickly explained the situation that brought the five people to Sand Lake at this time. When Jack mentioned that Rick was one of the new campground host, Rory seemed very surprised.

"That's kind of weird that the Forest Supervisor didn't tell me anything about that this morning," Rory said.

"You talked to the boss this morning?" Jack asked.

"Oh, yeah, when I couldn't reach you, I called the office in Cadillac. From what he said, I assumed you had just left his office."

Jack looked down at Rory, trying to determine whether to believe him. "And nothing about the agreement with the concessionaire?"

"No. Told me I should exercise my discretion."

"OK. Then are we good here?"

Rory stepped back, instinctively resting his hand on his pistol butt. "No. Fritz was assaulted. I take that serious."

Jack smiled. "Rory, your victim was stealing the perp's lunch. You want to take that to federal court in Grand Rapids? I'll testify for the defense that Fritz is a habitual lunch offender. Do you seriously want to put a disabled vet in jail for that?"

Rory seemed to debate this with himself for a long while, perhaps for the first time understanding the horns of a dilemma. "Fritz seems OK, but I have to talk with Monica. The Special Agent in Charge gets to make those kinds of calls on assaulting a federal officer."

As Rory walked back to his truck, Jack heard Fritz barking in excitement. Probably the dog looked forward to free food back at the district office, Jack assumed. He realized he would need a very honest chat with the Special Agent in Charge down in the Regional Office in Milwaukee about the assault on a federal officer, canine unit. But first, he needed to talk with someone much closer to home.

"Rick, do you think I could borrow your truck for a couple of hours? My staff picked my government rig up from the highway."

"Can we trust you?" Rick asked sarcastically. "I'm not sure about your relationships with law enforcement."

"If you'd rather do time for swatting the dog, that can still happen."

Jack caught the truck keys in mid-air.

In the cab of the big pick-up, Jack dialed his cell phone. "Caberfae Trailhead in twenty minutes?"

"I do go home sometimes," Bill said.

"Why?" Jack regretted that as soon as he said it. "Sorry. I didn't mean that."

"No, fair question. I go home to work so I'm not here at work. That would be pathetic. No one at home anyhow. OK. Twenty minutes."

April 8

After a brief stop at Garlett's Corner, Jack pulled Rick's Ford pick-up next to Bill's Jeep in the far back corner of the Caberfae Snowmobile Trailhead. After a moment, Bill climbed into the passenger side of the Ford. "You get a different rig again?"

"No, I had to borrow a ride. Long story." He made a kind of sweeping motion with his hand to indicate that was past history. Then he reached into the back seat and pulled up a plastic shopping bag. "Sorry. Limited selection back at the store. Better drink quick before it gets warm."

Bill pulled a Two-Hearted Ale out of the bag. "Ah, a man after my own heart. Best brew in Michigan. You got an opener?"

"In my truck, yes. Check the glovebox."

"It's OK. I've got my all-purpose service knife. Carried it for almost forty years now." After he opened his bottle, he handed the utility knife to Jack.

After opening his beer, Jack saw the initials "U.S." stamped into the side of the silver knife. "You'll want to hold onto this." He passed it back. "How many years in the Marines?"

"Twenty. We're here to talk about me? Cause if we're dating now, I expect better than this." Bill took a long swig. "Although great beer in a scenic place." He looked out the window at the towering red pines all around the parking area.

"We've got a problem."

"You brought me all the way out here to tell me that? I could be home, drinking the same beer, trying to understand the latest Bob Dylan. But you called me just to say we've got a problem?"

"OK, a new problem." Jack outlined the events of his afternoon, including the Great Sand Lake Campgate fiasco. "So, Rory said he talked to the boss this morning after we did. No mention of our discussion about the campground host thing, or anything else we're trying to do. So Rory goes in, guns drawn, and says they are, if I remember, trespassing, destroying government property, dealing drugs, kidnapping, assaulting a police dog, maybe trafficking endangered species."

"The boss talked to Rory? Didn't tell him what you're doing? Didn't tell us about Rory?"

"Correct."

"That …" Bill stopped himself.

"Agreed."

"What do you think we should do?"

"Move forward and watch our backs."

Bill took a long drink of ale. "I'm just thinking about Ringo's solo on the Sergeant Pepper album."

"Don't sing," Jack warned.

"You're safe. I was thinking, 'I get by with a little help from my friends.'"

"Do I want to drag my friends into this?"

Bill turned to stare at Jack a moment. "You dragged *me* into this, didn't you? Besides, I thought you played poker with Sheriff Simmons."

"I bought you lunches. I brought the beer. Enough criticism, already." He passed over another bottle of Two Hearted Ale.

"You have to bribe all your friends like this?"

"No. But I also lose money in poker." The ranger drank beer and stared at the twilight flickering through the pines reflectively. "Speaking of losing, when I dropped the groceries Sunday, Rick was telling me that Frank had lost more than two dozen games of Chutes and Ladders to Mary that morning. I think there's a Father of the Year Award somewhere with his name on it."

Bill leaned back in his seat, laughing. "That man's a genius." He took a long swig of ale. "You should never play poker with him."

"What am I missing here?"

"Always let them think they're winning." Bill chuckled in that sinister Hollywood villain manner. "Look I've got to get home and build a strategy. You're sure you want to bet the farm on little Mary? From here on, we're all in."

"Funny that you and I haven't met her. But we're fathers, so, yeah, I'm all in. But leave my dad's farm out of it. I may be driving the tractor if this blows up." He pushed the remaining beer across the seat at Bill. "Take this with you. I can't leave it in Rick's truck. And I shouldn't be drinking through a school board meeting."

Bill climbed down out of the pick-up and turned back for the plastic bag. "How else do you get through a school board meeting without drinking?" He closed the door and headed for his Jeep. He climbed in and started the big engine. Then waited while Jack drove away in a cloud of dust. At that point, he opened another beer and sat for several minutes before driving out, blasting a Warren Zevon CD.

April 9

"Michigan has the third highest number of COVID-19 cases in the country, and we're still on the upswing. We must continue to do everything we can to slow the spread and protect our families."

— Governor of the State of Michigan, extending the "Stay Home, Stay Safe" Executive Order.

April 9

When Rory and Fritz came in the back door of the ranger station on the next morning, they heard a repetitive choir.

"Hey, Rory, Jack was looking for you this morning," Gwen called from the break room where she was pouring water into the coffee maker.

"Good morning," Jane greeted him as she headed out the door to take her rig down to the shop for a set of new shocks. Forest roads are hard on trucks, especially when they develop a washboard surface from weather and grading. "You seen Jack? He was asking for you this morning."

A few feet farther along, another voice from the stockroom. "Yo, Rory, the ranger seemed pissed you ain't been here."

Stopping briefly to put down his jacket and lunch bag, Rory went on down the hall to the district ranger's office. He knocked and poked his head in the doorway. Jack was on the phone but motioned it would only be a minute. Fritz sat, his long tongue lolling off the side of his mouth. Jack's call took almost five more minutes. Fritz sprawled on the carpet. Each time Rory indicated mutely that he could come back, Jack held up a single finger as if asking for another minute. So Rory looked at the big district map on the wall, the well-mounted hide of a black bear and the Pendleton blanket weave of Smokey Bear. The bookcases against the opposite wall held volumes of the Code of Federal Regulations, binders of guidance from the Department of Agriculture and Forest Service, as well as scholarly textbooks, legal tomes, and guidebooks to identifying the trees, mammals, birds, plants, reptiles, fish, and amphibians of Michigan.

"Sorry, that took longer than I expected," Jack said as he placed the handset back on the base. "And longer than I needed. Grab a seat. Did you get coffee on your way in?" Jack knew Rory wasn't a coffee drinker; he preferred those caffeinated energy drinks. "So listen, I was thinking last night about the situation yesterday out at Sand Lake. I've changed my mind. I think you need to call Monica and get her OK to contact the U.S. Attorney. If we expect the public to treat K-9s like law enforcement, we can't let someone correct it like a dog."

Rory was nodding the whole time. "That guy's lucky Fritz didn't rip his arm off. If we let the public mistreat K-9 units, we're losing a critical part of the animal's effectiveness."

Surely this came directly from a training manual somewhere, Jack thought. Rory was not — what had Bill called Elizabeth? – erudite. "Exactly. I wasn't there to see what happened, but you can tell Monica you have my support." Jack looked at the Belgian Malinois lounging on his office floor and thought, that dog couldn't rip Rick's arm off because his mouth was already full of Rick's burger.

"What about destruction of federal property?" Rory moved forward to perch on the edge of his chair. "That's ten years or two hundred fifty thousand dollars or both."

Jack leaned his recliner back and took a paper clip off his desk that he proceeded to mangle in his fingers. "I'd like to hold off on that one. He's the new campground host, so let's see how well he can fix it. Are you OK with that?"

"Shouldn't we put them together? Give the USA something more to negotiate in a plea? This new gal likes to hit the defense hard."

Jack worried that he had done too good a job at winding Rory up. "Let's not start a charge that might have to go away. Could make us look weak." He sat forward in his seat and reached for the phone and began dialing, not because he had a call to make, but to bring the meeting to a quick end. "Have Monica call me if she needs to." As Rory and Fritz headed out, Jack added, "Hey, can you close my door?"

"Wouldn't it be easier for you to stand up and walk ten feet than for me to drive fifty minutes to close your damned door?" Bill asked.

"Sorry. I was trying to wrap up my meeting with Rory."

"And Fritz."

"And Fritz, the star of our show."

"Let's not give them too much credit. They're performing in just one ring of our little circus. Did you see the information I sent you about the new USA?"

"Anything in particular I should be looking at?"

"Know her bio, especially law school. And some of her family history. Just in case you get a chance to drop something into the conversation. Casually."

"And this is all legal, right?"

"I thought you were more of a forgiveness later, kind of guy." There was a knock on the glass of Bill's door. "Hey, I gotta go. Probably Elizabeth has my daily to-do list. Let me know how it goes with the tribe." After hanging up, Bill reached over and opened his office door to find Ruth waiting for him. She wore a bright blue face mask. Motioning her in, he settled back behind his desk. He put on his own cotton face mask.

"I'm not disturbing you, am I?" She entered and closed the door behind her. She seemed even smaller than the last time he saw her. Her sweater hung loosely from her shoulders, and a thin belt held her matching slacks in a tight bunch at her waist. Just a few weeks ago, he would have hugged her, but this pandemic made that too dangerous. She was battling her third bout with cancer that always seemed to find a new site to launch its cruel attack.

"Why are you here?" he asked. "Didn't the boss OK a telework agreement for you? We're in the midst of a pandemic, for Pete's sake. I've told you if you need something, you call and I'll take care of it. I'll even bring your groceries to your back porch if you want."

"I hope you can tell me what's going on around here. It's like a little conspiracy to keep information from me so I don't worry." She took a deep breath. "I'm still the Operations Staff Officer. So if there's a problem with a campground host, somebody should tell me. Why do we even have a host on site six weeks early? Especially someone selling narcotics and involved in a child sex ring."

Try or no, Bill could not stop before he laughed, prompting a surprisingly angry look from Ruth. "I'm sorry. You are the victim of one of the worst games of Telephone in the history of mankind." So he explained how the events at Sand Lake had progressed over the past three weeks, including the Great Campground Raid that Rory had orchestrated just the day before. Bill was certain she would sympathize with Mary's plight and the heroic efforts to keep her safe.

She shook her head in astonishment. "He's going to get someone killed one of these days."

"I hope not, but something tells me what you have heard is a collection of gossip added to radio chatter yesterday. I guess I need to go have a chat with dispatch about what they share with whom."

"Maybe not," Ruth said. She shifted on the chair and uncrossed her legs in order to bring her knees together. She opened a thick folder across her lap. Deep in a pile of papers, she pulled out a stapled sheath. "I read this a few weeks ago." She handed over a photocopy of an article entitled, *Information, Disinformation and Misinformation in the Post-Truth Era*. "I've been meaning to give it to you. I gave it to Ted, also. When he finished, I asked him what he thought. I suppose a guy who spent thirty years battling forest fires is going to think of things in that context. He said, 'Back burn.'"

Bill marveled at the after-dinner conversations Ruth and Ted must have now that their children were out of the house. She had a very academic approach; he was the ultimate tactician. "I'll have to read it. Thanks."

She closed the binder and put it on the corner of her chair. She sat with her feet flat and her hands in her lap. "I wanted to ask you another thing. You always seem to monitor everything happening in the media, even social media and so-called fake news. So what do you think about this coronavirus? Are we going to be able to stop it, or hold it back until the hospitals are ready for it? They say flattening the curve, but now it seems more like an incline than a curve."

He wanted to make a dismissive off-hand joke, but he sensed she wanted a very serious response — deathly serious given her condition. He searched for a way to emphasize the positive, but he couldn't see that. That was why he was so determined to help Jack resolve the brewing crisis at Sand Lake. Finally, he settled back in his chair, shoulders drooped.

"Ruth, do you remember when they found the first emerald ash borer killing trees around the metro Detroit airport? Fifteen years ago now? Probably came in a wooden pallet from China. Took the forest research labs a little while to figure out why the trees around the airport were dying off. You know what we needed then?"

"Time," Ruth said, simply.

"Exactly. We needed time to learn how the bug grew, spread,

and then how to kill it. Almost immediately researchers found it was laying its egg under the bark. So if someone hauled logs, they might also be carrying EAB. We asked people not to move firewood. Department of Natural Resources quarantined the lower peninsula and put dumpsters on the South end of the Mackinaw Bridge so people could dump their firewood before they took the bug into the Upper Peninsula. There were billboards on the highways asking people not to move firewood. We had brochures and bumper stickers. I spent weekends with DNR people at outdoor events. We went to home shows, hunting expos, events at Cabelas, Gander Mountain and Jay's. Simple message: Don't move firewood." He heard himself getting more vehement and took a deep breath to calm down. "And what was the most common question I heard from all these great outdoorsmen and hunters? 'So how much is the fine?' Yep, they were willing to risk killing off a big part of the forest they claimed to love if saving it would be an inconvenience."

"Oh, God," Ruth gasped.

"I'm sorry. But I think about that every time I fish the Manistee River. You can see whole sections of the valley where the ash trees are dead, just waiting for a good fire to burn it out. Because we had people who loved the outdoors too much to make any little sacrifice to save the woods. They say people can't see the forest for the trees; those clowns couldn't leave the firewood to save the woods. Will we see the better angels of our nature with this invasive new species? I don't think better angels hoard toilet paper and hand sanitizer."

When he looked, he saw tears in Ruth's eyes that she quickly blotted away with her embroidered handkerchief. "I'm sorry," she whispered.

"No, I should be sorry. You should really listen to that guy who's been in charge of infectious disease at NIH for 40 years. I probably know less than that scrawny frat boy playing éminence grise at the White House."

Ruth smiled at him. "Wow, éminence grise. You've become a student of French history lately?"

"Oh, no. I gave Elizabeth one of those word-a-day calendars on her birthday, and she left that on my desk last week. Besides, what would you call an idiot who think he's fixing the planet because a moronic president happens to be his father-in-law?"

"A few years ago, I would have argued with you. I'm a good conservative Catholic, but lately I've been thinking about the plagues visited upon us, starting in 2018. And this is the year the cicadas return."

"That year was the start of my troubles, in so many more ways than one." He could see she was visibly tiring. "Ruth, would you like me to drive you home?" He hesitated to hold out his hand to help her up, but decided it was safe because she was wearing a type of medical glove.

"No, Ted is waiting in the car out front. He won't come inside as long as Robert Fulbright works here. I just wanted to hear from you the truth about what's going on. You were too honest, as always. Thank you."

When she left, he worried about these iterations of her cancer, and how they became progressively worse. He looked out the window toward the cemetery, wondering if a sudden death is better than a lingering demise.

April 10

At mid-morning, the unhappy campers sat segregated at separate tables. Doc Mac and Rick sat together at the picnic table for the unwashed; Regina and Frank sat opposite them. They were once again segregated. Because of the risk that the police had exposed Doc and Rick to coronavirus the prior day, they went into quarantine for an additional ten days. Only her parents would be able to be with Mary, either inside the RV or outside. Although the Centers for Disease Control recommended six feet as a safe buffer, Regina preferred 12 feet distance for herself from Doc and Rick. And no contact with Mary at all.

"We start the clock back at day one," the major said. "We'll take our temperatures every 12 hours. If either of us starts to spike, the other moves into the tent."

"Doc, I've got the forehead reader in the camper," Regina said. "I've been tracking Mary's temperature every six hours since we've been here. Should I bring it out to you?"

"No, that's fine. I brought a few oral types. Rick and I won't even share the same one, just to be safe."

Frank looked at his camper to make certain he closed the door and windows so Mary could not hear the conversation that needed to come next. "Doc, what if Mary has a problem. Can you come in to see her? Do we go straight up to Munson hospital?"

After sleeping back on the cheaper mattress in the Lantern, Doc leaned back from the table in a stretch that seemed to move every joint from his waist upward. "For the next ten days, I agree with Regina. No contact. If you need to get help, just go. If I see your taillights, I'll call ahead. Wait outside until they come out for her fully garbed up: masks, face shields, gloves, and gowns. All three of you have to suit up as well."

Frank looked toward the closed gate and back toward Rick. "How do we get out? Didn't you weld it closed?"

Rick shrugged. "I guess now that I'm an official campground host, we don't need to have it sealed up. I'll rig something so the gate opens if you push on it with your bumper, but it won't be flapping in the wind."

"You're going to be living in the bubble for ten days," Doc told the parents. "Let us know if you need anything. Check your food and meds. We'll have to get the ranger to bring us anything you need again."

"I'd say he owes us after yesterday," Frank said.

"I don't think it was him that called the troopers," Regina said. "I think it was the little guy with the dog."

"You mean the lunch thief," Rick said.

The doctor studied his patient a moment. "You could stand to miss a couple of meals."

Ignoring this unsolicited medical advice, Rick said to Frank, "Let us know if we have to flush the tanks again."

"Anything else?" Doc asked.

"So we monitor supplies; we watch our tanks; we take our temperatures; and I get working on this little maintenance to-do list," Rick said. "I guess then all we have to do is hunker down and wait for the call."

Regina raised her hand, though it was entirely unnecessary. "I'm a little worried about Mary. Without regular internet access, she's not able to follow her classes every day. We download lessons at the library, but that puts her behind her class. Anyone have a suggestion?" she asked.

A long silence followed. Both Rick and Doc Mac were too old to be members of Gen Tech. Finally Rick spoke up, "Have you asked Mary? She probably knows more about it than any of us."

April 10

On most days, a receptionist answered the phones at the government offices of the Little River Band of Ottawa Indians promptly. Oddly, not today. No receptionist. No directory. No option to dial an extension. No voicemail. Jack tried three times before he gave up and decided to drive over. Perhaps their phone system was simply off-line that morning.

Not wanting to give anyone a wrong impression that a Forest Service truck was going up U.S. 31 in the direction of the Little River Casino, he took his own truck. He couldn't share with anyone his observation that the shutdown made driving through Manistee easier, although there was still the usual jerk trying to pass on the wrong side in order to get in front of him before the two lanes merged together up before the Coast Guard mooring. Jack assumed he could drive along Manistee Lake at 4 a.m. and still have somebody cut him off.

Just past the BP station, Jack made the right-hand into the Government Center of the Little River Band of Ottawa Indians. The newer building was a vast improvement over their former walk-up office in a building down on River Street. The parking lot was surprisingly crowded when he arrived. As soon as he turned off his engine, he heard the distinctive rhythmic drumming of a ceremonial drum circle. Despite the cool wind he felt coming off Lake Michigan, he saw people standing at the rear of the building. They clearly kept a safe social distance, and most wore face masks. He put on his own and headed back. He was tall enough that he rarely needed to scan the crowd to see whom he sought. Most often, people saw him coming. Within a moment, he saw Gertie Sam walking briskly toward him. He hoped he would be as spry when he approached his 70th birthday. When she neared, she put a forefinger to her mask to hush him, then took his elbow and turned him back toward the parked cars.

"Let's go speak in private," Gertie whispered. "We should not disturb anyone's grieving. I believe you knew Jimmie Cogswell from our meetings. He passed away last night. His daughter Delia called to ask if we could say goodbye this way. Jimmie has been living with her and her husband out in Brethren since his wife passed three years ago."

Despite his long legs, Jack still had trouble keeping up with her. She walked with her hands buried deep in the pockets of her wool coat. The wind blew her long, gray ponytail almost horizontal.

"The sun feels nice, but that wind is too cold for these old bones. Let's go into my office," she said, as she turned toward the building's front door.

He stopped walking. "Gertie, it might be better if we spoke in private. Would it be OK to sit in my truck?"

Her laugh shook her tiny body. "Oh, Jack. It's been years since a white boy asked me to sit in his truck."

Seated in his Ford, Jack experienced one of those eerie moments that had occurred a few times since he had begun working closely with the tribes of Northern Michigan. A man's voice was chanting over the rhythm of the ceremonial drum circle while the wind from the West gently shook the flat-sided pick-up truck. He sensed that if he closed his eyes he would feel in the middle of the circle of throbbing drums. He had no tribal blood that he knew about, and he never pretended like some whites do. But these feelings came over him at odd times. He decided to ask Bill if it ever happened to him.

Over the next 10 minutes, he explained to Gertie the situation with the people at Sand Lake. He did this in part because of his obligation under an agreement the Forest Service signed to protect the tribes' treaty rights. As he told her when he finished, he might also need to ask for help. "In a few weeks, the forest will be over-run with turkey hunters and then mushroom hunters. If the hospital isn't ready for the little girl when it's time to open the campgrounds, do you think the tribe could permit them to stay on tribal lands until they are ready to leave?"

"I must go back now. If the need comes, I will ask. For now, I will say nothing about your little secret. It may be best if it stays a secret. But it is nice to know that the big federal government has grown a heart for little girls. In 1956, a little Ottawa girl was sent off to the Holy Childhood boarding school in Harbor Springs. The nuns beat her every single day. So she decided she would prove them wrong and worked her way into law school at the University of Michigan." Gertie held her left hand toward Jack. Ancient scars furrowed the flesh on her knuckles. "Turns out nuns don't like lefties. Our cursive isn't up to divine standards." She opened the door and lowered herself onto the pavement. "Stay in touch, Jack."

He watched her walk back to the ceremony, the wind whipping her ponytail in the opposite direction around her neck. She was one of the smartest women he had ever met. He included Ruth, the forest operations officer in that group, along with a past Chief of the Forest Service. He hoped that the new U.S. Attorney for the Western District of Michigan could match their intelligence. The success of the circus depended upon it.

April 10

Bill was in the office early. After spending the early morning hours looking over his work e-mail and various online media, he returned the Congressional call at 7:20 a.m. He knew the best staffers were in the office early and stayed very late. This would help him judge Fred Anderson. Bill needed to know what kind of a challenge Fred would be in bringing Congressman Anton Van Den Berg into another ring of the circus.

Not until 10:15 a.m. did Anderson call Bill's cell phone. "Hey, sorry, had a breakfast thing with the Congressman this morning. Got a meeting with the Lake County commissioners at 11," he said. "Can you hang on a second?"

Pre-pandemic, there would have been no way for Fred to have breakfast with Van Den Berg in Washington and then meet with the county commissioners in Baldwin a few hours later. He had watched Van Den Berg live on C-Span earlier that morning on the floor of the House attacking expanded unemployment benefits during the pandemic for making workers too entitled and weak. The social welfare of FDR's New Deal weakened America for generations and made way for the Green New Deal, Van Den Berg raved. His voice quavered in rage. In his own anger, Bill hit the mute on his computer. Now that all breakfasts, lunches, and meetings were virtual, Fred could be chatting with the Congressman and commissioners while naked from the waist down. Bill put that vision out of his head. Somehow coronavirus had flipped the world's switch from virtual reality to all reality being strictly virtual.

Fred came back on the line. "Sorry, it's been a hectic morning."

"Big announcement coming soon?" Bill asked.

"Sorry? What big announcement?" Fred sounded confused.

"Oh, my mistake." Bill tried to sound a little befuddled. He was a fly fisherman himself and knew that the secret to good angling is false casting — just putting a little line out there before delivering the dry fly in front of the prey. "I was calling you on that Visser letter about running cattle on the forest over in Oceana County. The Baldwin District Ranger sent the request on to me."

"So, here's the thing. Mr. Visser came up to the Congressman after a town hall meeting in Hart back in February. He lives near the forest and wants to run some cows on an old farm that the Forest Service bought. I guess he's been asking for years and never gets a straight answer."

Bill came within a hare's whisker of obscenity. Obviously Visser was not a man who could take an answer for an answer. "First, let's set the record straight on that. I have written at least five responses to him myself, and I understand there were three or four others before I arrived. I will send you copies. Visser has approached every new ranger down in Baldwin with the same sob-sister act. He has gone to all of your predecessors, as well as the past three Congressman in your District."

"Sorry, he didn't mention any of that." A pause. "Obviously."

"I'm perfectly willing to write another letter, and attach the copies of all the prior letters. The Baldwin ranger and I can meet with him. You could join us if you'd like. It's a minor annoyance to keep going back over this and over this, so I'll do whatever you think will bury this issue."

"I'm glad to work with you if you have any ideas," Fred said.

"You know, it occurs to me that all of the agencies letters have come from the district ranger or the forest supervisor. Maybe we could get a letter signed by the Regional Forester. Or even the Chief of the Forest Service." Smooth false cast. Don't rush.

"How about sending me the past responses and let me do my homework. And you can look into a higher signature?"

"Sounds good. I'll get these scanned and e-mailed to you." Cast and retrieve. "I know you can't talk about the big announcement, but have you thought about what you're going to do next? I'll be retiring in a year. And our jobs are very similar. But you wouldn't have to deal with Social Security issues." Then lay the fly on the water and let it drift.

"OK, I appreciate the heads up." Again Fred sounded confused, but also unwilling to come right out and ask. "I'll be in touch."

Bill sat back, rather pleased with himself. In politics, knowledge is power. But admitting what you do not know is a potential weakness. What was it that a former Secretary of Defense said? Bill googled it for a good reminder. "There are known knowns; there are things we know we know. We also know there are known unknowns;

that is to say we know there are some things we do not know. But there are also unknown unknowns—the ones we don't know we don't know. And if one looks throughout the history of our country and other free countries, it is the latter category that tend to be the difficult ones." Donald Rumsfeld was mocked when he said it. Bill rather agreed with him; it's the unknown unknowns that always come around and bite you in the ass.

Bill's desk phone rang, and he assumed Fred was calling back about another topic. "Reinhardt, public affairs. May I help you?"

"Oh, good, I caught you. I wasn't sure when you were heading out today."

"I've got a little more work yet." He paused a moment. "Ruth, you have my cell phone number. It's on the call list. You know you may call me any time. How are you feeling?"

"It's a good day. No chemo until Tuesday. Listen, Ted and I were thinking about driving down to Grand Rapids to see my sister Sunday, so he looked at the Weather Channel. We're not going now. But then I realized it's another Easter snowstorm. Would you like to come spend Easter with us so you don't have to be alone? Ted is making lamb. I'll probably do a hot dish if I have everything. And the strength."

Bill looked at the calendar in confusion. Easter already? "Ruth, that is such a sweet offer. You know I'm not good company. And that's on most days. Maybe invite me over for the Flag Day festivities. I hope you and Ted can get to Mass and back home safely. Planning to Zoom meet with the kids and their families?"

"Ted's trying to set something up so we can get as much of the family together virtually as we can." Ruth paused and took a deep raspy breath. "Such strange times."

"Is the church offering the Stations of the Cross online this afternoon?" he asked.

"Yes, Ted has it on screen now. They should be starting soon."

"Don't let me keep you. Have a Happy Easter, Ruth. Same to Ted. Call me next week."

The calendar claims that Winter should end in March. In Michigan, Winter can claw its way straight through April into May. When it does, Winter is unforgiving. Two years ago, his wife and son disappeared into an Easter blizzard along U.S. 131 between Boyne Falls and Alba. They were driving south, coming back from her parents' house in the Upper Peninsula. Long stretches of highway there traverse open farmland, where the wind spins the snow into dense, white williwas. Her Jeep was no match for the oncoming county plow truck.

Two years already?

Bill settled at his computer and, using his daily calendar as a guide, wrote an e-mail summarizing the events of the week, high-lighting the details of every humiliating interaction with the boss. When done, he would e-mail a copy to his personal e-mail account, then print a copy and send it to himself in the U.S. mail. That way he had a sealed and postmarked account of Robert Fulbright, week by week. Bill started this tradition exactly two years ago, when his then-new boss had demanded "administratively acceptable evidence" to support Bill's request for three days of bereavement leave in the wake of the 2018 Easter blizzard.

April 12

There was almost no traffic on the highway at mid-morning. Bill saw a group of three people riding down the shoulder of the road on their off-road vehicles, which he didn't think was strictly legal. But he had given up years ago trying to educate people about this issue. Two of the three were young boys, who should have been wearing helmets. But it was the same as people who refused to wear seatbelts. Or don face masks in the midst of a pandemic.

As he passed the gas station at Garlett's Corner, he checked the Jeep's gas gauge. The snow was just starting, but he didn't want to get stranded knowing that worse was coming. When the front arrived, the winds were expected to kick up. He had planned to be back home before the brunt of the storm crossed Lake Michigan. Just one quick chore.

As he pulled up to the gate at the Sand Lake Campground, he saw no one outside the campers. He parked and gave the horn a quick tap. Then he climbed out and went to the Jeep's tail gate. The hostess at the Bob Evans back in Cadillac had helped him carry the bags of food out to load his truck. When he said he was delivering the feast to a family in need, she had suggested with a kind smile that he return later for his own Easter dinner. Next he drove over to the Meijer on Boon Road, donned his face mask and went inside. In the main aisle between women's clothes and pharmacy was a display of Easter merchandise, from plastic eggs to enormous baskets stuffed with candy and toys. He was a little startled to see that some of those over-sized wrapped baskets included toy guns, which seemed a little incongruous with the message of the day. In the end, he chose a boxed chocolate bunny and a small basket with jelly beans and a floppy stuffed rabbit with outsized ears enclosed in a plastic wrapper. Bill assumed these sealed items would be safe for Mary.

As he brought the bags of food back to the gate, a stocky man emerged from the smaller camper. He came toward the gate with a bit of a limp.

"Chief Bocek, I presume," Bill said. "I'm Bill Reinhardt, the forest public affairs officer. I work with Jack Ferguson, the district ranger."

Rick stayed a safe distance away. "Good morning. What brings you out on a Sunday morning in the middle of a snow squall?"

"Well, I know you can't go anywhere, so I wasn't certain whether you were able to make arrangements for Easter dinner." He hung the bags on the gate, then went back to the rear end of the Jeep. "And I assumed that no one had a chance to get anything cute for the little girl." He went back to the gate carrying the plastic bag from his Meijer visit. "We can assume the food is virus-free. And I put alcohol wipes in the other bag, so you can wipe the packages with the bunny and the chick. If you need anything, just call Jack." Bill walked back to his rig.

Rick hung back from the gate. "It is very nice of you to think of us. And Mary. Thank you."

Bill stopped before he climbed into his Jeep. "How is she? How is Mary doing?"

"Doc McKettrick says she's holding her own for now. Best we can hope for."

Bill went back toward the gate but stopped six feet away. "I'm curious. Is it weird being out here? It seems strange to me that the split is between people who can get sick and those who don't care who gets sick. It's like that old Charlton Heston movie, where he's the only guy in a city who isn't infected with some mutant disease."

"I love that movie. *Omega Man*, right? 'It's Sunday. I always dress for dinner.' But remember, in the end they use his blood to create a vaccine."

"No such thing as a Hollywood ending." Bill went to the driver's door. "There's instructions on how to warm the food in one of the bags." He waved and climbed inside the Jeep. In a few minutes, he was back on the highway heading east, windshield wipers brushing aside the gently falling hail and blowing snowfall.

April 12

Before Bill opened his eyes, he heard a hub-bub of furious
activity around him. Strange. Who are these people? The last thing
he recalled was driving back from Garlett's Corner with the snow
swirling about. Please, not the Jeep. He became upset to think he
may have run his beautiful rig into a tree. He could hardly go find
another of its vintage.

"BP is coming up quickly; 110 over 75. Pulse now 65. Blood ox
at 80. Now 125 over 80." a female voice narrated.

"His eyes are open," a male said.

A woman's shimmering face appeared above him. Gleaming
light created a halo around her white skin. Above her was a flat
white surface, with small, fixed lights. He could see only her blue
eyes; she wore a blue cloth from chin to cheekbones. A gold crucifix
hung closely around her neck. As his eyes became more focused, he
realized that the overhead lights above her created the glimmering
luminosities on a protective plastic shield over her face. A doctor
meant the absolute worst outcome.

"Wagoneer?" He asked.

"No, sorry. I'm Doctor Pelletier. Can you tell me where you
are?"

"Jeep?" He realized abruptly that he was wearing a paper mask.

"No, Cadillac. Do you know what day it is?"

"End days."

"Can you tell me your name?" Doctor Pelletier began to worry.
This man did not present with obvious head injuries or other
wounds. Perhaps a stroke?

"Wagoneer?" the patient sounded more insistent this time.

"Anybody check his wallet? What's his name?"

The young nurse held up a baggie. "State police left his personal
effects. Give me a minute. Name's William Reinhardt. Lives in
Harrietta. Here's a picture." Steve passed to the physician a photo
of a small family standing beside a classic Jeep. "She's a beauty."

"Steve, that's so offensive," Pelletier whispered harshly. "I never
want to hear you talk about a patient's family that way."

"Oh, no, ma'am. That's not what I meant. That's a classic Jeep, like a 1987. Probably has the big eight. Rims alone are probably worth close to a thousand."

She smiled to show her forgiveness, forgetting a mask covered her face. She leaned over the patient. "William? Or do you prefer Bill?"

"Bill, please. Ask him about my Wagoneer. Please."

Finally, he was communicating, even if it was about his truck. "OK, let me see what I can find out. Steve, do you know what happened to his truck?"

"Nothing. It was sitting on the side of 55 near Caberfae. He just passed out in the front seat. They couldn't rouse him. He didn't smell like he's been drinking."

"Good to know. Bill, it sounds like your truck is fine." She held the photo where he could see it. "Is that your wife?"

Bill nodded.

"Would you like to call her?"

Bill nodded. "Very much."

Pelletier handed the photo back to Steve, then spoke to Bill again. "OK, as soon as we know a little more about what happened to you, we'll try to reach her."

Bill nodded. "Promise?"

"Of course. Are you in acute pain?"

He shook his head. "No. Chronic anguish."

She looked at him quizzically, then stepped back to address the nurse and the technician. "Ask the labs to run CBC; comprehensive metabolic; lipid and liver, tox screen. OK, let's get him up to radiology. Quick head x-ray to see if we need to do an MRI. Remind everyone that he's not cleared for coronavirus. So everyone who comes near him in full dress; gown, gloves, mask, goggles, hair net, and face shield. No exceptions."

The doctor went out to the nurses' station. There were five people waiting there, anticipating the need to mobilize the Covid-19 team because they could not immediately determine this new patient's status. Every incoming patient was assumed to be positive until tested negative. Guilty until proven innocent. This protocol meant a full quarantine treatment. For the unlucky patient, it also meant no visitors, not even family, until the test results came back. Not that it mattered to Bill. A coronavirus test, that involved Steve shoving a long, white swab up Bill's nostril and into the back of his sinuses. Done right, Bill thought, the CIA could add this to the torture cookbook.

The staff hooked Bill to more monitors than a NASCAR Cup Series car getting a tune-up. He had wires connected to an array of metal nipples on stickers attached to his chest. To his annoyance, that required some shaving with an electric trimmer. A blood pressure cuff clung to his left bicep. Three separate times a tech had returned to clip an oximeter to his finger before switching to a style that held the sensors in place with glue strips. Unable to get a good vein in either arm, the nurse had put an IV into the back of his right hand. Laid out on his back with no way to move, he was at least relieved that there was no catheter involved. Yet. A nurse came into the ER bay where Bill lay to wheel him upstairs for the x-ray.

Doctor Pelletier stood waiting when his stretcher returned to the small ER room prepared for a suspected coronavirus patient. There were plastic sheets taped in place around the door frame, and a large, loud fan forced air into the duct.

"You prefer Bill, correct?"

"If Exalted Grand Poobah is taken, Bill is fine."

She laughed behind her mask and face shield. "Good. Humor intact. We can rule out injury or illness to the lower frontal lobes."

"Even after that Covid swab?"

Another chuckle. "I'm told your classic Jeep Wagoneer is very nice. The state police called to say that rather than get a tow truck out on Easter, they drove it into their office on South Mitchell. Not too far from your office, right?"

"Thanks for letting me know."

"So could you now answer some questions for me?" She raised a clipboard. "Full name and date of birth?" Her interrogation echoed the questions the recruiter asked when he went to enlist: Height? Weight? Medications? Illegal drug use? Any underlying medical or mental conditions? Criminal record?

"I'd say you are invading my privacy," he said, raising both arms so she could see the medical hardware there, "but I guess you've been doing that since I arrived. You didn't cut my shirt off, did you? It's an Orvis, one of my favorites."

"No, Steve refused to cut it. He managed to get it off you. Look, Bill, you asked me to contact your wife. We couldn't find any emergency contact information in your wallet. You don't have an ICE identified on your phone. The only women in your contacts list appear work-related."

"I'm sorry. I shouldn't have asked you to do the impossible. She passed away."

"No, I'm sorry. I didn't understand what you were asking. When did she die?"

"Two years ago. Today. It's still Easter, right?"

Doctor Pelletier laid the clipboard aside. "Was she ill?"

Bill nodded. "Toxic hubris. Tried to drive through a blizzard."

Her eyes widened, realizing that he may have identified the cause of his hypotension, the dangerously low blood pressure he was experiencing when he arrived at the ER door. The shock of remembering her death may have caused a sudden, unusual level of stress. "Bill, I'd like to admit you because I want to run a few more tests that I won't be able to do until tomorrow. I'd like a sonogram and an echocardiogram. Are you OK with that."

He shook his head and began to struggle to sit up. "Not today, please. I can't be in a hospital today. If you schedule the tests this week, I will try to get time off from work. But no promises there." She stepped back as he stood and began removing the stickers on his chest.

"OK, then I'll need you to sign that you are leaving against medical advice. Wait while I go write this up." She started through the door and plastic curtain, then stopped and poked her head back inside. "Please leave the IV alone. I'll have someone come take it out." If she had seen the long scar across his shoulder earlier, she would have asked about that during his medical history.

As she left, Bill thought to himself, *If I can put one in, I can take it out, too.* Of course, he hadn't done that in almost thirty years.

Steve came in to remove the IV needle from Bill's hand and

taped a piece of gauze over the wound. "You can take that off in 20 minutes or so. It won't bleed much. But I need you to wear this until you leave." He handed Bill a paper mask. "Here's your phone if you need to call someone." He gave Bill a white plastic bag that contained all of his possessions, including his Orvis herringbone shirt. He found his coat folded into a separate bag. "Is the Wagoneer in the picture the one you still have? That's a nice ride." He ripped off the disposable yellow gown he wore and dumped his hairnet in the garbage.

Bill thought it odd that a man who shaved his head was still required to wear a hairnet in the emergency department. "Yeah, same one. I bought it 20 years ago, while it was still in great shape."

"Can I call someone to give you a ride?"

"I'll probably just walk. It's just through the cemetery, past my office, the furniture store and the car dealer. Half hour tops."

"You know Winter just came back from the dead, right? I think it's gotten much colder since you came in." Steve asked. "A lot of us have a shift change in 15 minutes. Maybe someone is heading in that direction. Can you wait?"

"Yeah, the doctor has some paperwork for me to sign."

At that moment, Pelletier came in through the shrouded door. She was no longer wearing a sterile gown, but she retained the mask and gloves. Without her hairnet, her blonde hair fell to her shoulders. "Thanks, Steve. Let them know up at the desk that they can get in to sterilize here in a few minutes. OK, I've got a few things you need to sign that you are requesting a discharge AMA."

"AMA?"

"Against medical advice. You could have a serious underlying condition. Maybe a heart problem."

"No. Got to have one first. OK, I promise to hold you harmless. If anyone ever asks, I was never here. I only came for the lunch menu. I had a great doctor, but I forgot her name. All good?"

"I'm giving you my card. Office number and e-mail. Any problem, you call me."

"Normally, I take my problems to my bartender."

"What's your drink? I'll learn how to mix it," she chuckled, but her voice became more serious. "You can't just ignore this. And your bartender could make it much worse."

"Is that your medical advice?"

She groaned. "Yes, you are signing a statement that you're ignoring my medical advice. Please no more. I'm tired. I'm ready to go home. Just sign so I can leave."

"Any chance you're heading south? Past the state police post?"

As he finished dressing, she looked him over. At least he wasn't wearing a Detroit Lions jersey and sweat pants. He was right to worry about the Orvis shirt. Nice fit. Bill pulled on his coat.

"OK. In a blizzard on Easter Sunday, I guess I can manage this. But don't get any ideas."

"You already said you want to see me again."

"In a strictly professional capacity. You may make an interesting specimen." She left and returned in a few moments, pulling on the winter coat that she had to bring back out of storage for this wintry weekend.

Bill tugged his Stetson fedora into place, grateful it was not crushed along the afternoon's travels while he was unconscious. He wore a hat whenever he was outside, a habit ingrained in the service. "I don't think I've been called a specimen before."

They walked down the short hallway and out into the early evening twilight. Steve was right — it was much colder than Bill remembered. Both wore their face masks. She wore latex exam gloves.

"Get used to it. Around here, you're either a patient, a specimen, or a patient giving a specimen."

"Doesn't sound very merciful for a hospital called Mercy Cadillac," Bill observed as he followed her into the parking lot. She led the way to a Volvo XC-90. He couldn't recall ever riding in a car with another person while both were wearing face masks. During the short trip down South Mitchell Street, Doctor Pelletier didn't begin any discussion, and neither did he. At the state police post opposite the Holiday Inn Express, she dropped him off.

"Be sure to call for an appointment," she said. "We really need to figure out why you blacked out."

He thanked her and climbed out. "It's been very nice to be your specimen today."

After a brief wait inside the trooper post, the deputy on duty returned Bill's car keys. He drove home to a special Easter dinner. Between cooking and stirring, the turkey with stuffing meal finished in eight minutes. Calories without nutrition.

April 12

Early in the evening, Frank came out of the Damon carrying three plates covered with aluminum foil that he placed on the picnic table. After he had gone back inside, Rick went out and brought the plates inside the Coleman. He placed one in front of McKettrick and the other at his own seat. The third plate he set aside. He brought the plasticware he had stored in the kitchen. When they peeled off the foil, they marveled how much Bob Evans food that Regina had managed to squeeze onto each plate.

"If this is our share, Bill must have bought the 12-person feast," Rick said.

"Who is he again?"

"I guess he's the public affairs officer. I know Jack is trying to keep our contacts with outsiders to a minimum. But this was a nice gesture."

Doc pulled back the foil on the third plate and discovered dinner rolls, banana bread and two types of pie. "And a good celebration, too. Today is your first week of sobriety in, how long?"

"Wish I could remember."

"And you're still feeling OK?"

Rick swallowed a forkful of turkey. "I guess. I was a little edgy Wednesday after the police left. If there had been a beer in the fridge, I'd have opened it up. Or a six-pack."

Doc studied Rick as he ate. "That could be habit. You've trained yourself to grab a beer whenever you're stressed or in pain. You know the whole 'fight or flight' thing, right? You don't flee; you drink."

Rick took a drink of diet soda. "You know, I like the drug part of this. I'm not as keen on the talk therapy."

"All part of the process," Doc Mac said. "Which I'm making up as I go along. If it works, I'm going to open a clinic and make millions."

"So I'm your guinea pig? But I get a percentage of the millions, right?"

April 13

Ohio has 17% more residents than Michigan.

Its first confirmed case of coronavirus COVID-19 was Feb. 15, more than three weeks before coronavirus came to Michigan.

Yet as of April 13, Michigan had 24,638 confirmed cases of coronavirus compared to 6,518 in Ohio.

Why?

– Mlive.

April 13

"When somebody is President of the United States,
your authority is total."

— President of the United States of America,
answering a media question
on opening state economies.
As reported by CNN.

April 14

"The governors are instituting their own opening. Numerous states are doing well, and we're gonna let them open sooner than the date, at the end of the month, maybe sooner than the end of the month. Many states are out there reviewing it and say 'we shouldn't be included in this.' If we disagree with it we're not gonna let them open. We're there to watch, we're there to help. And we're also there to be critics."

— President of the United States of America, clarifying his authority to re-open state economies, as reported by CNN.

April 14

A protest called "Operation Gridlock" is planned tomorrow
at noon in Lansing to protest [the governor's] stay home,
stay safe order by a group that says they've "had enough of
Lansing's erratic, unilateral orders that threaten
Michiganders' economic existence."

As debate rages about the intersecting priorities of public
health and economic vitality, the Michigan Conservative
Coalition is calling for people to head out in their cars and
display signs, make noise and be disruptive.

"But stay in your vehicle so that the 'Governor's
police' cannot say you are ignoring the 'social
distancing' order,'" the group says in a press release

.

— WWJ, AM 950.

April 14

Bill came into the office early to prepare for a couple of conference calls set for the morning. The Regional Office wanted to discuss how individual National Forests were addressing public needs during the pandemic. There was a national emphasis on consistency. He figured this was another initiative from some political appointee up in the Department of Agriculture with a little too much time on their hands, like a prior suggestion that henceforth all agencies within the U.S. Department of Agriculture would all be considered OneUSDA. Bill anticipated the day he would go inspect an Iowa meatpacking plant. Maybe a specialist in Asian soy bean markets could come over from the Foreign Agricultural Service to help rebuild eroded trails on the National Forest. Surely the staff of the National Agricultural Library was ready to head west to fight forest fires. Ah, that old, all-for-one; one-for-all *espirit de corps*.

The hammering on his office door came at 7:05 a.m. He stood and reached for the knob, but the door swung open, neatly clipping his fingertips. "OK, come on in."

"Did you see this stuff in the news?" Elizabeth asked as she came in, still wearing her coat. She was surprisingly breathless. "I heard it on the radio coming in." She placed her iPad on his desk. "I found a few stories like this online, so I think it's real."

Bill looked at the headlines as she swiped through screens with her fingertip.

Michigan Conservatives Plan To Protest April 15th;

Protesters Plan To Swarm Capitol In Cars Over Michigan's Stay Home, Stay Safe Order;

Why Michigan Residents Are Preparing To Protest The Governor's Stay-At-Home Order.

"Let me guess why," Bill said when the screen landed on that last headline. "They missed school the years science was taught."

"Hold on, this article says they want everyone to stay in their cars with only family members," she said. "So they don't want people getting sick while creating a traffic jam at the Capitol, but singing in church is just fine? Don't they know about that choir practice where most of the members tested positive for Covid and two died?"

"As Reagan said, facts are stupid things."

"He did? Wow. So this stupid craze started before I was born."

He looked at her face as he did a little math about the end of the Reagan era. He suddenly felt very old. "He wasn't actually attacking facts," Bill explained. "He was trying to quote John Adams, who said, 'Facts are stubborn things; and whatever may be our wishes, our inclinations, or the dictates of our passion, they cannot alter the state of facts and evidence.'"

Elizabeth gazed at him in bewilderment. "Is this what you do at night? Memorize dead presidents?" There was a worried tone in her voice.

He laughed. "So you think I should be following the current president on Twitter?" He picked up his cell phone and swiped. "This morning it was 'Tell the Democrat Governors that *Mutiny on the Bounty* was one of my all-time favorite movies.' So now he thinks he's Captain Bligh."

"Hey, I liked that movie, too," she said defensively. "Mostly the second half, when Mel Gibson didn't wear a shirt."

He settled back in his seat and motioned her toward the visitor chair. "So what does this mean?" he wondered.

She removed her coat and sat down, pushing the chair against the wall. "I like watching buff guys. A lot of women do, you know."

"Stop. Don't make me report you for sexual harassment."

"OK, Boomer. You wish." Elizabeth shook with laughter. She stopped abruptly. "I'm sorry. I didn't mean — oh."

"Seriously. Stop now," he said. "Please."

She sat quietly for a minute, then asked, "So you're wondering about the Michigan Conservative Party, and how they're connected to the Republican Party? And why they're targeting a Democratic governor?"

Bill chuckled at how quickly she had analyzed the politics of the situation. "Very good. You want my job when I go?" He fiddled with his smart phone a few minutes before showing her a major polling site. "538 has the Democrat up by three points in Michigan."

"OK, but 538 had the Democrat up by a thousand in 2016."

"Yes, and she won the popular vote by two points. That's why these state-by-state polls are so important. To paraphrase a famous strategist, 'It's the Electoral College, stupid.'"

Elizabeth checked the time on her phone, stood, and slung her coat over her arm. "I'd better go be in the office when the boss arrives." She reached to open the door then stopped to face him again. "If you ever call me 'Liz,' I will deck you."

Given her stature, he chuckled at the thought. "Understood. Just remember my standing offer to write a solid reference for you. Like Pogo said, 'We're surrounded by insurmountable opportunity.'"

"Pogo? Is that some caveman mythology?"

"OK. And offer withdrawn. Thanks for coming by."

April 14

Regina and Frank sat at the Damon's dining area. Mary was in the big bedroom at the stern of the RV. She had written in her notebook a little list of her concerns that had come into her mind over the past several days.

1. *Weather?*
2. *Doc's quarantine*
3. *Police come back*
4. *MONEY*
5. *WORK????*
6. *Gate (out)*
7. *Campground opening?*

"Where do you want to start?" Frank asked with a deep sigh.

Regina heard his sigh and responded by bringing both hands palms-down on the table top. "Where do you want to start? First, maybe you can tell me how you sit in this camper with me day after day and never say a word to me."

He began to slide across the vinyl bench as if to get up.

"Stop!" Regina said in a harsh tone. Her face reddened. "Is it really that bad? You can't sit and talk for five minutes?"

"Could be. Maybe worse. I could double that list."

Regina leaned forward and looked up to see his downcast face. There were tears on his cheeks. "What is it?" She grew concerned. "What haven't you told me?"

Frank twisted on the bench seat to face her. "I haven't said anything because I know you're worried about Mary. You saw Rick crawling under the camper Friday? He thinks our black water tank has a seam splitting open. It's not much now, but we have to deal with it before it lets go. That would be a hell of a mess." He sensed she was ready to say something. "I'm sorry for swearing. I'll confess it next time we can. I guess I'm kind of banking my sins for now."

Regina felt relieved if that was the extent of his troubles. She added concern "8. Damon tank" to her list. "Is that all there is?"

He shook his head so sharply that his shoulders swayed as well. "No, just the start. Rick thinks we should replace all the belts."

"How much will that cost?"

Frank shrugged. "It may not be that easy. He doesn't think we can get belts for an old rig without going to an RV service garage. Which we can't do without breaking quarantine. As soon as it gets warmer, he wants to get underneath to look at an area of rust. When we were looking at the tanks, he noticed some scale on the ground in that left rear corner."

"Can you guys weld a plate over it? Just to get us through the next two months?"

"That's what Rick's thinking, but there has to be something solid enough to weld onto. Rick says we'll have to go under first and remove the loose scale to see what's still solid. He mentioned arc welding a little support shelf onto the aluminum shell, but he doesn't have what he'd need to do that right. And we don't want the floor to drop out of the bedroom as we're bouncing into Traverse City."

Regina reached across the table and placed her hand on his wrist. "It's not your fault. Since your father died, you've been telling me that we needed to put money into this."

"When he was sick, he just couldn't take care of it."

"With Mary sick, we can't take care of it either. Now we're stuck with it. Doc thinks that now the state's been locked down longer than three weeks, people are going to want to get out of their houses soon. We go home now, we're not any better off than we were a month ago."

They sat together at the table in silence for several minutes, watching sunset reflected in the placid waters of Sand Lake.

"Any ideas?" he asked.

"We push through like we've always done. Maybe ask Rick to put together an estimate of what he needs for each project. You two figure out what's most important. You may decide it's all equal. If so, we'll have to figure that out, too."

"We should go through your list, too. Read it to me again?"
She did.

"Want the good news first?" he asked. When she nodded, he began: "Rick said he fixed the gate so we can get out if we need to. There's no point talking about the police or the campground opening soon. We have no control over either, so we have to wait and see. What about the weather?"

She looked from the reddish lake surface to his face. "I feel like we were lucky yesterday's snow wasn't worse, because we had no idea what to expect. I liked it much better when I got those weather alerts on our cell phones."

"You mean back when we could afford to have cell phones?" Frank smiled at her to hide the shame he felt in not being able to provide for his family. "I can ask Rick if he could look at the radio on the console once he's out of quarantine, but I don't get the sense he does electrical repairs. Meanwhile, I'll sit in the Ford twice a day and listen to news and weather on that talk radio station out of Traverse City. Besides, you know they can't know in advance how far north it'll be rain and how far south snow."

"You're right. I just worry about being stranded in ten inches of snow when she needs help. So I'll try to download the Weather Service forecast when I go wifi hopping in Wellston. You listen to the radio, and I'll go online. Best we can do for now."

Folding her hands on the table in front of her, she said, "And if there's another storm coming, we need to take the camper as far as the main road, just in case."

Frank nodded in agreement. "You also have work and money on your list. What were you thinking with those two big subjects?" Frank felt his stress rising again. Why didn't she just come right out and say what she thought of him? *Lots of other people kept their jobs with GM, what's wrong with you?* he imagined her thinking.

"I believe we need a plan for that. If we start running out of money, maybe one of us needs to go home and get a job. With the repairs and her medications, I'm not certain how long we can hold out."

"If it comes to that, I can take the Explorer and go home. I can get a job without worrying about bringing the virus home to you and her," Bill said. He hoped this offer would quell any concerns that she had that he wouldn't do his part for Mary.

"I think that should be me, instead. I can get a job, probably easier than you now. The jobs are in fast food. They would think you would expect enough money to support a family. They'll look at me like a housewife just looking to earn pin money."

"No, you need to stay here to take care of Mary. You know her meds and routines. Imagine me trying to give her an injection. What would I do if she has a nightmare?"

"You'll be with her, just like you did when she was little."

Mary emerged from the bedroom at the back of the camper where she stayed. She held two folded pieces of vanilla construction paper. "I made these for Jack and that man who came tonight." Both had pictures of bunnies drawn in crayon. "I wanted to thank them. My bunny is very cute."

"We'll make sure they get them the next time they come here." Regina hugged Mary. "Did you tell your Dad the solution you figured out for getting internet access out here?"

"Oh, no, I'm sorry. Daddy, I think we could get a hotspot that will give us access. There are a bunch online. I think we could even rent one."

"Did she show you this?" Frank asked Regina.

"When we went over to the library tonight. If it works, we wouldn't need to drive over there every day."

"Maybe we could look into renting one," he said.

"You know, I have two hundred twelve dollars and sixty-three cents in my savings," Mary offered.

"I hope it will never come to that. Your mother and I can figure this out. But thank you. You're very sweet." He leaned forward and kissed the child's forehead. Once Mary had returned to her bedroom at the back of the camper, he leaned forward and whispered to Regina, "Do you think she feels warm tonight?"

"Yes, I'm checking her every hour. Just to be sure."

Frank went to the small refrigerator in the Damon and took out a beer. There weren't many left, but he felt he needed one so he didn't cry in front of Regina.

April 15

LANSING — Demonstrators drove thousands of vehicles — many draped with protest signs — to Michigan's State Capitol on Wednesday, loudly protesting the Governor's stay-at-home order intended to fight the coronavirus pandemic.

Police watched as horns honked and commercial and private vehicles from around the state jammed Capitol Avenue and other streets surrounding Michigan's seat of government.

"Liberty once lost is lost forever," read a sign draped across a commercial van. "Security without liberty is called prison," read another, stretched across the Capitol's front lawn.

– The Detroit Free Press.

April 15

With most of the staff working at home, the district office was unusually quiet for mid-April. During this time most years, they would be bringing on the seasonal employees, getting the recreation sites ready to open and preparing fire crews for the upcoming fire-prone months, both on-forest and across the country. So Jack sat behind closed doors in the conference room, listening to the noon hour news on WOOD-TV out of Grand Rapids. Almost half the show focused on the anti-lockdown protests in Lansing. He found himself agreeing with a few of the protesters, like the man upset because he couldn't take his Bass Tracker down the road to the state boat launch for a few hours of fishing. Another guy asked why you could go to Dairy Queen, but not buy paint. What was the danger in buying seeds to get the garden started? That issue affected Jack personally.

On the other hand, he could tell when someone was reciting a talking point provided by the protest organizers. The word tyranny came up often, as did the phrase "she overstepped her bounds." Jack couldn't remember ever saying either one. Not once in his lifetime. And he thought about the lockdown from the perspective of the DuLong family.

Just as the meteorologist came on screen, his phone rang. Assuming it was Gwen calling from the front desk, he answered with a casual "Hey." Suddenly Gwen appeared in his doorway, mouthing the words, "Regional Forester."

"Well, hey, right back at you. Is this casual Wednesday in Manistee?" the regional forester asked. "Or is it casual all week there?"

Just from the tone of her voice, Jack could hear Judith Oden's displeasure. "To tell the truth, it's been pretty casual around here since everyone is working from home. It's challenging to have a staff meeting with *Sesame Street* in the background."

"Really? From what Law Enforcement tells me, your district operates like *The Secret Garden*." Now her tone sounded more ominous. "Or would you call it *The Secret Campground*? You don't offer asylum to undocumented workers, do you?"

He wondered exactly what Rory had told Monica about the campers at Sand Lake. "Judith, this has all been a misunderstanding. I arranged with the concessionaire to let the campground hosts get an early start on some Granger-Thye projects."

"And the new hosts happened to bring along a family with a very sick child and, just by coincidence, a doctor with a large stash of narcotics. I want you to think carefully before you say anything more. I don't like to be misled. Clear?"

"Very."

"Good. Monica and I had a chat with Robert this morning. He said he wasn't aware of the situation until Rory Winchester called him."

Jack tried to recall if his phone cord could reach as far down the hallway as the closest fire alarm pull station. Unlikely the desk speaker would hear theft alarm on his truck if he triggered it on his key fob. He was good and snared, like a bobcat in a foothold trap. It would do his career no good to accuse his immediate supervisor of misleading – OK, actually lying to — the regional forester.

"Robert said that you have overstepped your bounds," she added. "I understand you came to us from Alaska. Would you like to go to Yakutat?"

"Oh, I didn't know it was open. Is Griff leaving?"

"No. You wouldn't be district ranger. Maybe something in timber."

Having worked his way up through the timber side of the Forest Service, Jack was not eager to go back. He had visited Yakutat once and was not eager to go back. He had been a bachelor once and was not eager to go back, which was a likely outcome of being shipped back to Alaska. He wondered if there was a way to get back inside his bounds.

"So, do you have an explanation for what you've done?"

Jack thought carefully for a long moment, just as Judith suggested earlier.

"Did you not hear my question?" she asked in an insistent tone.

He wasn't certain quite how to respond, so he decided to tread carefully. "I hope you won't think I'm dodging your question, but I don't think a phone call is the best way to defend my career, which I feel like you're asking me to do. I know everyone's in a lockdown, but I want to come talk to you in person."

"OK, Jack, but you'd better have a damn good explanation for all this, especially what looks like insubordination. I'll have Tara call you to arrange a date and time. Be sure you're available." The line went dead.

Jack took a deep breath. *Further proof that no good deed ever goes unpunished.* With that, he picked up his handset and dialed his phone.

April 16

As the death toll from the novel coronavirus pandemic continues to spiral, most Americans do not foresee a quick end to the crisis. In fact, 73% of U.S. adults say that in thinking about the problems the country is facing from the coronavirus outbreak, the worst is still to come.

With the Administration and many state governors actively considering ways to revive the stalled U.S. economy, the public strikes a decidedly cautious note on easing strict limits on public activity. About twice as many Americans say their greater concern is that state governments will lift restrictions on public activity too quickly (66%) as say it will not happen quickly enough (32%).

– Pew Research Center.

April 16

They ate lunch in the old Wagoneer at the state rest stop over-looking the Pine River on M-55. Jack was experimenting with the chicken combo with French fries from the Corner Express, back at Garlett's Corner. Bill stayed safe with the grilled cheese, along with a bottle of Vernor's diet ginger soda and a small bag from the Great Lakes Potato Chip Company. Over the years, Bill had augmented the Jeep's original sound system with a remote Pioneer CD deck and upgraded speakers, which were now playing an R. Carlos Nakai CD of Native American flute music.

"I was so surprised, I didn't know what to say to her," Jack said.

Bill swallowed the gooey bit of cheese sandwich he'd been masticating — today's word, according to Elizabeth. "Good strategy for no time to plan. How far forward do you think you can push this out?"

"I don't want to keep the regional forester waiting, so I was thinking of next week."

Bill choked on a potato chip. He took a drink of Vernor's to clear his throat. "You think I have a magic wand, or something? I was a Watersmeet Nimrod, not a Hogwarts' Gryffindor. I need a little bit more time."

"Look, I've got to be very, very careful. I can guarantee that Melissa is not going to follow me to Alaska. She didn't like Happy Camp on the Klamath, so she's not going to Yakutat. Christ, I have a kid in braces. There are no orthodontists in Klamath. Do they even sell *Orthodontics for Dummies?*"

"So give me your best defense. What were you thinking about before you called me the first time? Did your inner Eagle Scout take over, and you needed to move your Good Turn Daily coin into your right pocket?"

"So I shouldn't mention making Eagle Scout?"

"Not right off. You're a poker man, right? Think of that as your kicker."

"OK, it's going to sound too simple, but I was thinking about going with the Forest Service motto: Caring for the land and serving people." He sprinkled a packet of salt over the French fries before he began to eat.

"Anything else?"

With his mouth full, Jack asked, "What's the Hippocratic Oath say? First do no harm?"

"A, you're not a doctor. B, that isn't technically from Hippocrates. C. We gotta do better than that."

"I was thinking donuts. Would bear claws be better?"

"Too bad you can't find *paczki* after Lent."

The two men sat quietly for a few minutes, thinking about how to meet this next challenge. A car with a young couple in the front and two children in the back seat rolled through the parking area, stared at Bill and Jack and drove off.

"Too bad. The kids would have liked the view of the bridge," Bill said.

Jack shrugged. "It's kind of an insult. If I were looking, I could do a lot better than you."

Bill snorted out a laugh. "You're so vain. They were looking at the Wagoneer."

"And you're a time-warp jukebox. *You're so vain, you probably think this song is about you.*" The ranger offered a share of the fries, but Bill waved him off.

"No thanks. My bad cholesterol is already maxed out." He wrapped his hands around the steering wheel and stretched his fingers to relieve the early start of arthritis. Too many bouts of frost-bite. "Have you scheduled your talk with the new U.S. Attorney in Grand Rapids yet?" He started the Jeep's engine, and they drove back toward Garlett's Corner where Jack's pick-up sat.

"I asked Rory to set it up. Do I need to nudge him along?"

"Maybe ask the dog. He's trained to respond to commands." Bill finished his Vernor's and reached back to place the empty bottle on the back seat. "And you said you talked to Gertie, right?"

"Oh, yeah. Last week. Did you know she was went to law school at Michigan?"

Bill nodded. "She told me during lunch at the annual meeting. Two years ago. After the funerals. Camille's family invited the Little River Band, because they didn't think many members of the Lac Vieux Desert tribe would travel here to attend. I think she was trying to tell me that it is possible to recover from tragedy. She helped the tribe to get federal recognition thirty years after they lost it."

"One remarkable woman."

"Maybe convince her to write a letter of support for you. Completely unsolicited, of course. Great partner, responsive to tribal needs, respectful of treaty rights. You know, the usual pablum."

"So you mean trustworthy, loyal, helpful, friendly, courteous, kind, obedient, cheerful, thrifty, brave, clean, and reverent." Jack rattled off the list without any hesitation.

"So Eagle Scouts are kind of like St. Bernards without the drool."

"OK, wise guy, what were you doing when you were a teenager?"

"Getting the shit beat out of me for dating a Chippewa girl. One day the Native boys; next day the whites. They had a schedule. Benefit of a racially mixed high school."

"Really? What did you do?"

"Started talking to the Marine recruiter in Marquette when I was sixteen. Day after I turned seventeen, we went into the Immaculate Conception Church with my Dad and her parents, then Camille and I drove down to Parris Island."

"You know, I was looking at that case of little medals on your wall. Did you ever see Greg's shadow box? He had silver and bronze stars. What did he do to win those?"

"In the military, you earn rather than win." Although he knew exactly what Greg had done as a military policeman, Bill did not feel comfortable talking about someone else's service.

"So, what would he have to do to earn a gold star?"

"Die." Bill said dryly. "That would be the Medal of Honor."

The Wagoneer came to a stop next to the Ford. Jack gave Bill a quick salute and climbed out. After he closed the door, he knocked on the window. Bill put the power window down with a switch next to his armrest.

"Hey, did you know the boss is a Republican?" Jack asked.

For a man who rarely smiled, Bill had a wicked grin. "Oh, I'm banking on it."

April 15

"I'm just here to support my people. I have a lot of constituents down here right now. They want go back to work. If they can't access the website to get (unemployment) benefits, then they want to go back to work. Nobody is suggesting we just go back to work willy-nilly, we are recommending we adopt the federal guidelines and do it safely."

– Republican State Legislator watching the Operation Gridlock protests in Lansing.

April 16

Bill had a busy morning of phone calls planned, but Elizabeth came into his office before he could get started. Without any invitation or ceremony, she sat and pulled out her tablet. "OK, maybe you can explain this to me. Yesterday a state representative said that all the protesters want is for the state to re-open following federal guidelines." She tugged off her face mask.

"Right, I heard that. I think she's from Manton."

"OK, so how is a state supposed to follow federal workplace guidelines if they don't exist yet?"

"Have you ever considered the philosophical challenge that reality and politics don't exist on the same astronomical plane?"

"Stop screwing with me, Yoda."

Bill smiled at the comparison to a Jedi master. "You know that we are in the midst of a presidency in which the nation's chief executive has now officially lied to the American people more than 18,000 times, right?"

"Oh, yeah, I have the ticker running on my Fitbit."

Bill stopped, wondering if that was even possible. He'd always assumed those fitness devices were just spyware, whether foreign or domestic. "My point is that a state legislator is just reciting the talking points. Doesn't it sound reasonable to say, 'Oh, let's follow the federal guidelines.' But the media didn't immediately say, 'And what federal guidelines would that be?' So, these protesters look more legitimate, and the governor looks more like a dictator for not following federal guidelines."

Elizabeth's head drooped on her shoulders. Then she shook her head before asking, "How do you deal with all this? I read the Congressional letters that you write for the boss to sign. I see there's another one about cows on the National Forest. Don't you get tired of saying the same thing over and over?"

"Yes, I do. And so will you when you're sitting here."

She raised her hands in a gesture of surrender. "I'm sorry. I don't see any way that is going to happen in this lifetime. Not with this boss."

Bill changed the subject abruptly. "And how are you doing at Baker College?"

"Done next month. What's the song, 'If the Good Lord's willing, and the creek don't rise'?"

"Jerry Reed or Johnny Cash?"

"Does it really matter?"

"Well, Cash added the 'Good.'"

She touched her fingers to her forehead then splayed her hands out in front of herself in a quaking motion. "How do you know this stuff? No. Why do you know this stuff?"

"I grew up in the Upper Peninsula. When I was little, all we had was AM radio."

"No library? Sports? Girls? Selling GRIT magazine subscriptions door-to-door? Let me know when I can stop."

"I don't want to play this game anymore." He stood and turned on the big fan on top of the steel file cabinet. The fan faced the wall, but it still provided a loud noise to befog any conversations coming from his minuscule office.

"Oh dear, is it that time?" she asked.

"I'm afraid so. Listen, Jack is in trouble with the Regional Forester."

"Oh, yeah, I read the e-mails that the boss sent to Judith. I guess he forgot that I have access to his e-mail, and I forward his phone calls."

Bill leaned back. This might be easier than he thought if he was cautious. "So here's what I'd like to ask you. You've been his executive assistant the past two years, and I know there have been some issues."

"If you knew the half of it." Her voice sounded grim.

"Would you be willing to write up the rest for me? I'm going with Jack when he meets with Judith in Milwaukee. I'd like to have your statement in case I need to use it. But I promise that I will only use your letter if I have to. I have a lot of other documents to give Judith before I would get to your letter."

"Gee, thanks for not throwing me under the bus. Let me just lie down in front of it." Her eyes studied Bill's face closely. "And what are you submitting with your name on it?"

Bill stood and fumbled in his trouser pocket for his key ring. He unlocked the battleship gray file cabinet, then motioned for her to look into a drawer. Inside were two dozen file folders, each labeled with month and year, going back to April 2018. He pulled a file at random and handed it to her. In addition to a set of letters to file, the folder contained print-outs of e-mail messages from the boss with particularly snarky comments highlighted. In another message sent to the entire Forest Leadership Team, the boss directed that all calls from forest employees to the Regional Office required prior approval from the boss personally.

"You keep records?" she asked, handing back the file folder.

"Oh, yes. Very carefully." He thumbed through the files back to August 2019. He flipped over a few pages and turned the folder to where she could read it. "Remember this?"

She read his handwritten note aloud quietly. "Boss scolded Elizabeth in front of entire Forest Leadership Team when she came late to an FLT meeting because her husband had a flat tire coming from work. She couldn't leave two-year-old alone. Boss failed to check either phone and text messages." When she looked up, a tear rolled down her cheek. "Father Roberts tells me, 'Anyone who hates is really a murderer at heart.'"

"Yes, and Ecclesiastes says, 'there is a time to love and a time to hate.' But I'm not asking you to hate or love, just write out the things that I may not know."

"Like fetching his dry cleaning or wearing a skirt three days a week?"

Bill chuckled a little. "Sorry, I thought you just liked skirts." He mused to himself about what the local cleaners thought when they encountered the boss's French cuffs.

"When do you need my letter?" she asked.

"I'm not certain. Jack doesn't have an appointment yet. I've asked him to try to push it into May. But could be as early as middle of next week."

She nodded, gathering up her coat. "I have to talk with Randy first. He won't be thrilled that I could 'accidentally' lose my job. But he's not at all happy with what the boss puts me through." She opened the door and headed out. "I'll let you know. Door open?"

"Pull it closed behind you? Thanks." Bill locked the file cabinet then settled back at his desk. He flipped through the contacts on his tablet then dialed the number for 9&10 News. "Hi, Renee? Hey, it's Bill Reinhardt over at the Forest Service."

A woman laughed. "I think you already owe me a favor or two."

"And I am calling to pay up. This one could pay off in three ways. Maybe more."

"Always with the promises."

"I never promised you a rose garden," he said, careful not to sing a single note.

"That k.d. lang is so great."

"No, Lynn Anderson. 1970."

"Takes an oldie to know the oldies."

"I've been getting that a lot lately. Would you like to know what I have for you?"

"Sure, now that we've gone this far."

"I got a heads up that the Department of Agriculture is announcing a food assistance program specifically to address the coronavirus. Some of it will go for farmers and some to help consumers. Details coming in the next few days. But I was thinking you could interview my boss for your morning program, and then edit out a news story for the noon and evening programs. Sound good?"

"You said three chances."

"I am working on that, but there could be a big announcement coming. To be determined."

Renee laughed again. "After fifteen years, you're too late to play the man of mystery."

"I'll send you the press release as soon as I get it. Can we talk Monday?"

"We can always talk. But I'm not promising your boss an interview until I see what we have to work with."

"I'm sure it will be scintillating."

"Like the tree fungus with a name I couldn't pronounce on air?" she asked.

"Come on. *Heterobasidion* root disease just rolls of the tongue."

"Yes. I couldn't even sell that story for the early, early morning show. So call me skeptical."

"OK, Skeptical. I'll call you."

Bill put on his jacket and placed his fedora on his head. He went up the hill to the cemetery. There he removed his personal cell phone from his pants pocket and dialed a Cadillac number. When a male voice answered, Bill asked, "Hey, Ted, do you think it would be OK for me to come stand on your porch this afternoon? Great. See you then."

April 16

(HealthDay News) – As the number of U.S. coronavirus cases neared 637,000 on Thursday, the President announced that new federal guidelines will soon be issued to help state officials re-open parts of the country.

Meanwhile, 5.2 million more Americans joined the unemployment rolls, as new jobless claims numbers were released Thursday morning, *The New York Times* reported.

A team of officials from the U.S. Centers for Disease Control and Prevention and the Federal Emergency Management Administration is crafting a national plan to get Americans back to work, the *Post* reported.

The plan lays out three phases: a national communication campaign and community readiness assessment until May 1. After that, there would be a ramping up of manufacturing testing kits and personal protective equipment, and increasing emergency funding. Then, staged re-openings would begin, the *Post* reported.

– U.S. News & World Reports.

April 17

Michigan has now suffered 2,093 deaths in the state as a result of COVID-19. State officials released updated case counts and deaths related to the virus Thursday. The state reported 172 new coronavirus-related deaths, but also said 65 of those are coming from previous days that weren't initially confirmed to be caused by the virus.

The state also added 1,204 new confirmed coronavirus cases, bringing the total to 29,263. Michigan continues to have the fourth most confirmed cases in the country and trail only New York and New Jersey in total deaths.

– Mlive.

April 17

LIBERATE MICHIGAN!

> – President of the United States of America,
> on Twitter.

April 17

Just hours after saying it's up to the governors to implement
re-openings in their states, with the federal government
providing three-phase guidelines, the President on Friday
encouraged protests against stay-at-home orders in 2020
election battleground states with Democratic governors,
appearing to try to take advantage of public restlessness
amid the coronavirus pandemic.

The president did not mince words on Twitter this
morning in support of Michiganders, Minnesotans and
Virginians protesting against restrictions, saying in separate
all-caps tweets: "LIBERATE MICHIGAN!; LIBERATE
MINNESOTA!; LIBERATE VIRGINIA, and save your
great 2nd Amendment. It is under siege!"

– ABC News

April 17

The district ranger office in Manistee remained dark when Jack arrived. He wanted to catch Rory before he and Fritz headed out to patrol the National Forest. He did not have a line-of-sight view of the law enforcement office, so he pasted a yellow sticky to the door, requesting Rory come visit. Then he went into his own office. While his computer was warming up, he read again the guidance for fire-fighting in a Covid-19 world. He shook his head, thinking about the challenge of managing fire crews in an already dangerous environment with addition of a pandemic laid over top.

While waiting for Rory, he put in a call to the U.S. Attorney's office in Grand Rapids. The USA prosecuted crimes on or against federal property in the lower peninsula of Michigan, including the Manistee National Forest. The Huron side of the National Forest fell under the jurisdiction of the U.S. Attorney in Bay City. Typically the USAs prosecuted crimes like timber theft, trespass, illegal use of an off-road vehicle on National Forest System lands, and violations of the different permit systems. Between the Code of Federal Regulations and the Forest Closure Orders, Jack figured that just about anyone could get a citation for something.

The receptionist at the USA office sounded far away, like she was standing twenty feet from her speaker phone. Jack made a brief introduction of the cases he had worked with the prior federal prosecutors, including a dead body dumped on the National Forest by a serial killer. Joyce said she remembered that case very well, because the murderer had become a death row celebrity, attracting lots of feminine attention for his winsome looks and lame prison poetry. Jack explained that his LEO was trying to arrange a meeting on a case, and Jack would like to bring a little treat to welcome the newcomer to west Michigan.

"That is so sweet of you," she said. "Every morning on her way in, she stops by Starbucks for coffee. She's always talking about their lemon loaf. I think she'd like that."

He thanked her for the information and said goodbye.

When his screen finally came up, he immediately opened his e-mail. Of the nearly hundred messages that had arrived overnight, about 20 were retirement announcements. Jack scanned the names carefully to be certain Bill Reinhardt wasn't among them.

When the hallway lights came on, he knew he was no longer alone in the building. Gwen did that upon her arrival each morning, followed shortly by starting the coffee in the breakroom. Even though most district employees worked at home during the pandemic, she still prepared a full pot each morning.

Shortly after 8 a.m., his desk phone rang. Fearful it was Judith again, he answered cautiously. "Jack Ferguson, District Ranger, speaking. May I help you?"

"Hi, Mister Ferguson. This is Allison from Interlochen Public Radio."

"Oh, hello Allison. Didn't you float the Big Manistee with me a couple years ago when we were looking at an alcohol ban on the Wild and Scenic Rivers?" Jack remembered her as a slight young woman mostly worried about getting her recording device wet in the canoe.

"Oh, yeah, thanks for that story. I was nominated for a regional Edward Murrow Award for that."

"Really? Congratulations. Very cool. Anytime you want to visit, just give me a call." He suddenly remembered he was hijacking the PAO's job. "Or call Bill Reinhardt over in the Cadillac office."

"I wasn't sure if you can tell me about this or if I need to call Bill. I understand your campgrounds are still closed, but you have a family camping out at Sand Creek or Sand Lake, because their little girl is very ill, and they are in like deep quarantine. What a great human-interest story."

Jack slumped into his chair, his head lolling back on his shoulders. He hadn't discussed this possibility with Bill. What would it mean to the DuLong camp if they were suddenly exposed? "Hey, Allison, as it happens, I'm about to head out the door to go to Sand Lake. Do you think you could call Bill? He should be in the office in about 20 minutes."

"Oh, sure. I'll call Bill. Can I call you this afternoon after you have a chance to check on the family?"

"You bet. Talk with you then."

Jack stared at the black bear pelt displayed across the wall of his office. From his time living and hunting in Alaska, he knew how protective mother bears are of their cubs. He had heard stories of sows taking on much larger male bruins to protect their broods. He wondered what Regina would do to protect Mary. Or how far he and Bill would go for the family. What had Bill said last week? How they were 'all in.'

When Bill answered his personal cell phone, Jack asked about his location.

"Am I heading outside?" Bill asked.

"Oh, good. How convenient." After a quiet pause, during which Jack heard Bill trade pleasantries with several people, he heard a truck door slam. "Safely in the Jeep of Silence?" he asked.

"It's a Friday. You know, Thank God and all that. Why does it feel like you're calling with bad news? Maybe because you only call me with bad news?"

Jack chuckled into the handset. "Good news is that I arranged for a lovely young woman to call you this morning. Her name is Allison."

"And now?"

"She's a reporter with the public radio station in Interlochen."

"Thanks. After all I've done for you. Thanks."

"You're welcome. For all the lunches I've bought for you. You're welcome."

"Any news from Gertie or Judith? What about Rory on meeting with the USA?"

"Yes, no and no."

"Uh-oh. My work cell is vibrating. I'd better go. It's probably Allison."

Climbing out of the Wagoneer, Bill removed the other cell phone from his pocket. "Forest Service. Reinhardt."

"Hey, Bill. It's Fred Anderson."

"Hi, Fred. Did you get that set of letters that I e-mailed you about cows?"

"Yep, but I just finished reading this morning. Sounds like this farmer isn't capable of taking no for an answer. And why won't the Forest Service say yes? He says the prior owner ran cows out there."

"Long story. Did you see my 2012 letter? The Huron-Manistee

is not funded to manage rangeland, because we're pretty much a woodland forest. So if we misspent appropriated dollars to make him happy, our budget people and the Inspector General wouldn't be happy with us. Congressman Van Den Berg's not on the agriculture committee, so we wouldn't have any friends to help us in a hearing."

Fred laughed heartily. "You're probably right. You sure know the politics of it all."

"So you think you want to elevate this to the Regional Forester or the Chief's office? I can try to schedule a call if you can find time on the Congressman's calendar."

"So Bill, how long you been doing this work?"

"Almost nineteen years now."

"And you were military before that, right?"

"Not military. Marine Corps. Twenty years." Sensing this might be a longer conversation starting, Bill headed toward the office building.

"You said you were getting ready to retire soon?"

"Unless you can assure me there are absolutely no discussions about cutting federal retirements during this Administration." He paused for a moment, trying to remember the combination to the door lock. The four-digit code was based on the month and date of employee birthdates, rotating every month or whenever an employee left. With 59 people working in the building, that meant Bill could recall the code about one month out of five years. Finally, he recalled the new combination. As he walked down the narrow hallway toward his office, other staffers scurried away from him. Maybe he was the target du jour of the boss' ire, and they wanted to avoid guilt by association. Then he recalled that he had not donned a face mask before coming inside.

"Hey, Bill, what's the big announcement you were expecting? This USDA release on Covid-19?"

Bill paused, again letting the fly drift on the surface a bit. "Oh, nothing, I guess. I thought you guys might have something big coming up. But I do think that my boss may be on 9&10 next week to talk about the Covid-19 thing. I guess the Department really wants to play this big. I'll let you know date/time when we get to it.

Could you share with your boss? My boss likes to know your boss is in the loop."

"So, you've no inkling about this announcement?"

Bill went into his office, closed the door and turned on the big fan. "Hey, I could be wrong about it all. Just a hunch. After the Governor's breakfast here in February, I saw my boss chatting up Jerry Barr, the car guy." Bill was a little worried he was leaving too much line on the water that might tangle. Everyone in Northern Michigan knew of the Barr Cars franchises in five cities Up North. Only some people knew that Barr was Van Den Berg's top donor. "I thought it might mean something. I guess not."

"Well, I'm not aware of anything." Fred sounded painfully uncertain. "Let me know if you see anything else."

"Same by you, right? Thanks, Fred."

Bill scrolled through his morning e-mail haul. Retirement. Retirement. Retirement. Social distancing reminder. Retirement. Retirement. USDA Announcement. Retirement. Retirement. He opened the On The Move notice of recent promotions within the Forest Service. He let a call to his desk phone go to voicemail. His work cell phone vibrated in his pocket, but it stopped before he could get it out of his pocket. The front desk receptionist paged him on the office intercom. His personal cell phone began to vibrate in the other pocket. He fished for it and flipped it open.

"Jeez, can you just give me a minute?"

"No. We've got a crisis."

"Crap. Rory and a SWAT team?"

"Worse. Mary's sick. Her temperature spiked."

"What's Doc Mac say?"

"Nothing. Thanks to Rory's raid, Doc is under quarantine until Monday. But when he called the hospital, the doctor there said it might be more dangerous to bring her into the hospital."

A long silence followed.

"You all right? Any ideas?" Jack asked.

"Can you please give me a minute?"

Another long silence.

"What does Regina say?" Bill asked.

"She's freaking out. She really wants somebody medical to look at Mary."

"Think an ER doctor would do?"

This time the pause was on Jack's side. "You know an ER doctor?"

"Oh, yeah, going way back to Easter. A little thing that happened."

"I don't guess I have a need to know. OK, can your doctor come out to Sand Lake today?"

Bill fished out his wallet to look for a business card. "I have to make a phone call. Where are you?"

"Call my cell. I'm at the campground. Can you make this today?"

"Let me make a call."

Bill immediately dialed Dr. Pelletier's office. He decided to lie. "I may be having another episode."

"I can put you on at the end of her schedule today, or you can go to the ER," the receptionist said.

"Doctor Pelletier already knows my case, so if I could just see her that would save a lot of retesting."

"OK. How's 3 p.m.? But if you feel worse, just go to the hospital."

"Will do. Thanks."

When he hung up from the doctor's office, his office phone rang. He looked at the ceiling and muttered a soft curse. "Hello, Huron-Manistee National Forests. Bill Reinhardt. May I help you?"

"Hi, Bill, it's Allison Kiefer from Interlochen Public Radio. I was wondering if you had a minute to talk about the people staying out at Sand Lake."

"OK. Are you recording now?"

"No, just doing my homework first. So I'm taking notes. When I'm ready for tape, I'll call back on another line. That OK?"

Bill dropped into his seat. "Sure, I'll tell you what I can."

"So I understand they arrived the week that the Governor imposed this 'stay-home; stay-safe' order, is that correct?"

"I'm not certain if it was that same day or the day before. But about then, which presented a problem with them traveling back home."

"And do you know why they are there?"

"The concessionaire has hired two new campground hosts this year. We've got some maintenance work that they're going to get done before the site opens for visitors. Have we talked about our campground hosts before?"

"Not that I recall."

Bill signed in relief. Explaining how the National Forests have private companies operate some developed campgrounds through special use permits would take some time and possibly bog Allison down in the detail of how the campers got there. There were times when the tedious regulations that run federal agencies can confound people to the point they just surrender to the madness. By his office clock, it appeared Bill had spent seven minutes explaining the Granger-Thye Act of 1950 that authorized concessionaires to operate a Forest Service-owned recreation site.

"So why did they bring a little sick girl?" Allison asked.

Seven wasted minutes. "You know, I have to look into what I can release on that topic. She's a minor, so we've got a Privacy Act question. And then there's HIPAA. When do you need answers?" He needed to deal with Mary's health first.

"I'll probably roll it together Monday."

"OK, give me your questions, and I'll pull together everything I need."

They talked for another ten minutes, as she detailed a long list of inquiries. Her requests indicated a fairly detailed knowledge of the situation at Sand Lake. He wondered who had shared all this information. And why? Who gained from making trouble over all this? Unless somebody thought it was happy human interest story. Reporters were struggling to find those in the midst of the pandemic. He assured her he would be in touch as soon as practical. Immediately he dialed a number from his personal cell phone.

"Jack, we got trouble."

"Just noticed?"

"Allison knows everything about our guests. She was really just calling us for confirmation."

"How does she know?" Jack asked. "Rory?"

"Better not be. LEOs aren't authorized to talk to the press without permission. Rules out Fritz, too."

"Wouldn't be Pete Simmons. I doubt it was the state troopers or TNT. I think the whole thing embarrassed them."

Bill groaned. "The boss."

The conversation paused as they each considered the implications.

"I hope to be there about fifteen thirty. Can you wait?"

"You bring a doctor, I'll arrange a sheriff's escort from the county line in."

"Think your friends over at the trooper post would help, too? I plan to leave the hospital as close to fifteen hundred as possible. I'm sure they will recognize my Jeep."

When Bill arrived in the hospital parking lot at 2:45, he spotted a dark blue Dodge Charger parked near the street. He smiled seeing at the old gumball style roof light, but it always reminded him of the opening scenes of those police comedies. He settled his Stetson on his head and strolled over. The young woman at the driver's wheel put down the window. "You Bill?"

"Yes, Bill Reinhardt." He reached for his wallet. "You want to see ID?"

She waved him off. "You're good. My lieutenant says we owe you a favor."

He looked at his watch. "I'm going to go get one of the doctors. And then can you lead me out to the Sand Lake campground, near Wellston?" He pointed back at the Wagoneer. "Don't worry. She'll keep up with you."

The trooper laughed. "Oh, I know. I drove it in from Garlett's Sunday night."

Doctor Pelletier was not as easily persuaded as the trooper. She was reluctant to commit to treating a patient she did not know; Bill reminded her that they had not met before she had him poked, tested, and shaved, and his chest with monitors like Christmas lights. When she raised the question of medical equipment, he assured her that they were already onsite, courtesy of the Veteran's Administration. Finally, he invited her to look out her window office. "I want to assure you that is an actual trooper, who is going to escort us to our destination. You may ride with her if you'd prefer. Just bring your phone, so I can brief you on the way. But I beg you to come with me now."

Bill felt surprise when they reached the parking lot that she climbed into the passenger side of his Wagoneer. He gave her a sideways glance.

"How could I pass up the chance to ride in a classic 1987 Jeep Wagoneer, with something called a 'big eight?'"

"How could you indeed?"

The gumdrop light atop the cruiser was already turning, and Bill fell in line behind the trooper's car.

(Washington, D.C., April 17) – The U.S. Secretary of Agriculture today announced the Coronavirus Food Assistance Program. This new U.S. Department of Agriculture (USDA) program will take several actions to assist farmers, ranchers, and consumers in response to the COVID-19 national emergency.

– USDA

April 17

"This is the craziest thing I've ever heard," Pelletier said, as the Jeep rolled to a stop at the intersection at Garlett's Corner. "Why isn't this child already in an ICU bed somewhere?"

"Money?" Bill asked. "Does a GM worker keep his health insurance if he's furloughed? I think her parents are hoping to just go straight from here to St. Jude's."

"And the VA doctor who came with the family is now in quarantine? How did that happen?"

"To the great dismay of four law enforcement agencies and one dog. Beyond that, I shouldn't say. We needed a doctor on short notice, and I suppose you get swabbed and screened almost every day."

"So this is something you and your district ranger friend cooked up?"

"First, I wouldn't say 'cooked up.' Second, at this moment, you may still have some plausible deniability. After we arrive, I'm not so sure. I can't predict how this is going to play out over the next few days."

"You are just so much fun." She laughed. "By the way, nice ride. You have anything in the jukebox beside Native flute music?"

As they rolled up the hill beyond the intersection, a sheriff's cruiser pulled out from behind big 'Welcome to Manistee County' sign, lights flashing. With the Jeep wedged between the trooper and the deputy, Bill smiled at Pelletier. "Now this is the kind of treatment that a classic Jeep deserves."

"Not really very discrete, are we?" she asked.

"Did I invite you on this outing?"

"Practically at gunpoint."

With her face covered by a medical mask, he could not tell whether she was smiling. As they rolled into the campground entrance, both cruisers disappeared. Bill barely had time to honk a thanks. He drove around the gate and headed for the group campground. There, he found both campers, the Explorer, and two Ford pick-ups. Rick and the doctor sat at one picnic table. Jack sat at a separate table a few feet away. As they rolled up, Frank stepped out of the Damon with a stash of sanitary medical wear.

"Hello, doctor," Frank said. "We're very grateful that you were able to come see our daughter. Jack says you get tested and screened at the hospital every day, but my wife would still like you to suit up." He handed Pelletier a sterile gown, gloves, new surgical mask, hairnet, face shield, and surgical booties.

"Your wife is a very careful woman," Pelletier said. "Very prepared. Very smart."

"Yes, she may also be a little grouchy," Frank explained as the doctor dressed. "She's been sitting up with Mary since the 4 a.m. temp check. I've offered to spell her, but she's not able to rest now."

When Pelletier followed Frank inside, Rick motioned for Bill to come over. "So we now offer three levels of seating," Rick said. "You are welcome to join your friend at the unwashed table. We have added a nearly washed table where Doc and I hang out. Over there is the washed table for Regina and Frank."

"I don't have a reservation," Bill said.

"We do our best to seat our guests," Rick said.

"Hey, fancy meeting you here," Bill said, as he settled next to Jack.

"Thanks for arranging this house call," Doc Mac said. "I can't go see Mary until Monday. Slight fever but no other symptoms; we have to make certain we're in the clear."

Jack raised his hand. "No, this one is on us. I had no idea my LEO was going to go all Wyatt Earp."

"When was the last time Regina went over to the library to download the news?" Bill asked as he set his fedora crown down on the table. "You been following the crazy down in Lansing?"

McKettrick held up his smart phone. "Crazy in Lansing? How about this one? 'Liberate Michigan.' We've been locked in here a couple of weeks, so did I miss the pogroms and the gulags?"

The ranger put his hands back up in the air. "We just work for him. We're not actually responsible for what he says."

Doc nodded in sympathy. "I work for him, too. At least until I sort out how to retire from a smart phone."

Rick suddenly laughed sharply. "I don't work for anyone now. So maybe I got the best deal of all of you."

"So, chief, what was your specialty in the Navy?" Bill asked.

Rick seemed to sit a little more erect. "Boatswain's mate. Spent most of my time as a cargomaster. Until some jerk knocked me down an open hatch cover."

McKettrick jumped into the conversation. "Please don't get him wound up now. Otherwise I have to listen to it all night. If you didn't know better, you'd think the Navy and the VA exist to screw Chief Bocek personally."

"Now you're taking their side?" Rick asked, awkwardly turning his body toward Doc Mac.

McKettrick seemed to have reached a physical limit of his patience. "I did not say that."

"I kind of agree with the chief," Bill said. "I saw a lot of guys who deserved better than they received."

Rick looked at Bill closely. "Corps?"

Bill nodded. "Twenty years. Private to captain."

Rick let out a low whistle. "You kicked butt."

"Got my butt kicked plenty of times, too."

Jack leaned toward Bill. "When you've got a minute, we've got to talk about the boss."

"Whatever happened to TGIF?" Bill asked.

"You can still keep weekdays and weekends separate?" the ranger asked. "With lockdown, seems like every day slides into one another now."

"I have an easy way to remember which day it is. Weekdays are when I wake early and work late. Weekends are when I sleep 30 minutes later and then work late."

"And they say, all work and no play makes Jack a dull boy," Jack said.

"Maybe you're just dull."

"Or maybe Bill needs a hobby. You could work up to stamp collecting."

All four men turned to look when the door of the big camper opened. Frank stepped outside. "Doctor Pelletier says she isn't worried about Mary's immediate condition, but she plans to stay with us overnight to monitor her symptoms. That will also give Regina a little rest. So I'll be buttoning up the Damon for the night." He pulled the door closed behind him.

"Thank God the child's all right," Rick said.

McKettrick agreed. "Got to keep her healthy until Regina gets the all clear from St. Jude's. Just wish we knew when that would be."

"Caberfae." Bill said.

"You buying?" Jack asked.

"I brought the doctor."

Jack stood and stretched to full height. Sitting at a picnic table is a unique challenge after a certain age. "I'd say that's high card. Two Hearted again?"

"I could be persuaded." Bill also stood, but he came only to about Jack's shoulder. "See you in fifteen." He approached the nearly washed table at a socially tolerant distance and raised his right hand to his forehead. "Major, have a good evening. You, too, Chief."

Doc Mac returned Bill's salute. "Captain, I hope Jack has told you how grateful we are. You've both been very generous with a bunch of trespassers. And something tells me that generosity is not something the Forest Service," he paused, as if searching for the right word, "encourages."

Captain Reinhardt fished a business card from his wallet and set it on the unwashed table. "Call me when the doctor needs a ride back into Cadillac. You can't break quarantine now, being so close."

As he left, Bill waved at the Damon where Pelletier was watching from a big window. She didn't wave, instead kind of shrugged. He thought briefly that her expression suggested that she was being abandoned to live among cannibals. Then he realized that was the first time he had seen her full lovely face without a mask.

April 17

LANSING – Two days after a massive protest tied up traffic for hours in Lansing, the city's mayor said he's prepared to call in help from other agencies to enforce local ordinances and emergency health orders if another protest happens.

"We're hearing there are going to be future protests," the mayor said during an online briefing with reporters on Friday. "We're not excited to hear of people coming in and spreading COVID-19 even further."

Thousands of people converged on downtown Lansing on Wednesday to protest the governor's stay-at-home orders intended to fight the coronavirus pandemic, jamming streets around the state Capitol and tying up traffic on some roads for miles.

If it happens again, the city can't send its entire police force to cover it, the mayor said.

"If we're going to see this many thousands of cars, and we need assistance, then we will request assistance," he said.

– Lansing State Journal.

April 17

The tall red pines around the Caberfae trailhead parking lot swayed gently in an easterly wind. Bill thought he had better check the weather forecast for the coming weekend. He wasn't certain if the airstream foretold more wintry air. He turned off the engine and put down the window to inhale the forest air, until a dust cloud enveloped the Jeep as a big Ford pick-up rolled up next to him. Jack transferred from the truck to the Wagoneer like engaging in a drug drop.

"Got your church key?" Jack asked, as he fished two dark brown bottles from the plastic bag.

Bill leaned to the side so he could fish his knife out of his pocket. "Isn't an Eagle Scout supposed to be prepared?"

Jack chose not to take the Scout bait again. "Somebody told Allison about this, and maybe other reporters, too. So who do you think our prime suspects among those who know what's going on?"

"How many people actually know what's going on? The boss. Elizabeth. Rory. Fritz."

Jack interrupted. "I've never trusted that dog. He's foreign."

"I don't think it's anyone in law enforcement. Not Rory. Not Pete Simmons. Not the troopers; at the moment, we seem to be on their good side. Anyone in your shop?"

"People know. I mean people talk among themselves, so probably the entire district staff knows what's going on. But I don't know why any one of them would be calling the media." Jack waved his bottle and looked around the interior of the Jeep. "Was this thing built before they invented cupholders?"

"Just put it back in the six-pack. So you tick off anyone lately? Any letters of caution or discipline? Suspension? Removal? Executions? Ride-along with Rory?"

"You think I'm as cruel as that?" He paused to open another ale. "I did have to let a new firefighter go. Sent a dick pic to one of the botany seasonals. To make matters worse, her mother found it on the phone. Talking to the mom was something I won't forget anytime soon."

Bill also exchanged an empty for a full bottle. "So right there you have three unhappy people: the guy, the girl, and the mom.

Any one of them know enough about Sand Lake to call the media?"

"Doubt it. I had a lid on the situation until we started looking at using Granger-Thye. I think he was gone by then."

"Well, maybe it doesn't matter. I've got Allison's questions. Yes, the new campground hosts are there. Rick has a personal physician helping him to adapt to the new work arrangement because of his service-connected disabilities. And Doc Mac can't be working at the VA hospital right now, because they're not seeing patients in person. Frank brought his wife and daughter because hosts can have their families, and the schools are closed. I'll talk to Allison Monday morning. But I'm worried about some other reporter just coming out to Sand Lake tomorrow or Sunday.

"Meanwhile, I have to arrange meets with the US Attorney and the Regional Forester. And you think I should invite the boss, too? Why do I have to do the heavy lifting in this relationship?" Jack stepped out of the Jeep.

"Speaking of heavy lifting, next time get the twelve pack." Bill started the Jeep, and the sound of Seger's *Ship of Fools* filled the interior. *I alone survived the sinking. I alone possessed the tools. On that ship of fools.*

There was a knock at the passenger glass of the Wagoneer. Bill lowered the window.

"That was the first cassette tape I ever bought," Jack said. "Junior high, I think. Remember *Night Moves*? *I was a little too tall, could have used a few pounds.* That song was about me with my first girl-friend. *Out past the cornfields where the woods got heavy.* I played that cassette until it was so worn it screeched."

"Still timeless," Bill agreed. "Now go put together our circus acts."

After Jack's pickup was rumbling out of the parking lot, Bill opened another Two Hearted Ale and punched up *Night Moves* on the CD player. He put his window down, then stepped out the door into the cool air. *Out in the backseat of my sixty Chevy. Workin' on the mysteries without any clues. Workin' on our night moves.* Back when the song hit the charts, Bill cared about just two things, a 1964 Chevy Nova SS and Camille.

Now it seemed the most important thing in his life was a nine-year-old girl he had never met.

April 18

When the Wagoneer rolled up to Sand Lake Saturday morning, the two women were sitting at the washed table. Rick and Doc Mac sat nearby at the nearly washed table. Just one more day remained of their quarantine. Bill donned a face mask before climbing out of the Jeep. He was in the lowest caste there — the utterly unwashed and recently arrived from the virus-infected outer world.

"Back so soon?" Rick asked. "It is a nice little corner of the planet. You're welcome to haul your camper over."

"You're going to make a great host," Bill said. "Just remember that nothing is open until the governor gives the all clear. If you start Camp City now, Jack will be a farmer again."

Pelletier stood and walked around the table to bend over Regina. "You're doing great. Mary's holding up well. Come Monday, I will poke a friend I have at St. Jude's just to see what she knows. Meanwhile you have my personal cellphone number. Any change, call me. And in another day, Mary gets her personal physician back on duty. And I want you to think about nursing school, like I said."

As Doctor Pelletier walked to the Jeep, Doctor McKettrick stood and gave a slight bow. "Thank you for this professional courtesy. I hope to repay you some day."

"Entirely unnecessary. This was my pleasure and privilege." Pelletier said.

Bill saluted. Both the Major and the Chief returned his salute. He climbed in and started the big V-8.

"No flute music today," she said. "This is nice."

"*Hope in the Night*. William Dawson." Bill turned left toward the state highway.

"I don't think I've ever heard of him."

"He was an African-American composer. He wrote this in 1934."

"It's beautiful. So you listen to Native American flute and African-American symphonies. Rather eclectic."

"Have you listened to FM radio lately?" Bill asked. "They still play that pina colada song."

She laughed. "I can beat that. Last week I heard *Muskrat Love* and *Afternoon Delight* back to back. No, really. On a Traverse City station."

"I hope you filed a complaint with the FCC." Back on M-55, they headed east toward Cadillac. "That's why I don't listen to the radio. I don't need anyone talking total gibberish on AM or playing colossally bad music on FM."

"My, aren't you a little judgmental?"

"Yep. We get a little bit of time on this big blue planet. Why waste our limited minutes sifting through dreck?"

"And a philosopher, too?"

"For the record, full-on judgmental; only amateur philosopher."

"Speaking of, when was the first time that you thought you might die?"

Bill didn't hesitate. "April 1983. Beirut. Well, maybe it was Somalia in '92."

She gave him a questioning look. "Ten years ago, I had a cancer scare. I was 37 at the time. Knocked me for a loop."

"Sorry to hear that," Bill said. "It's easy to forget we're not immortal."

"I just spent 24 hours with a nine-year-old who has a better attitude than I did. She knows what will happen if there's no match for a bone marrow transplant, and she understands how hard finding a match can be. But she is as happy and cheerful as any child I've ever treated. I've had them cower at the sight of a needle. But Mary just accepts what comes."

"Her parents are certainly devoted to her."

She twisted in her seat to face him. "I'm sorry I didn't understand what you were saying in the ER the other night. Your wife and son died in an accident?"

"Yes, a few years back. A whiteout on the highway. They hit a plow."

She gasped. "I'm so sorry. What a terrible thing."

Bill nodded, not really wanting to talk about those events. "What about you? Family in Cadillac?"

Her laugh sounded brittle, like crumpling paper. "No. I failed three times. A few things about being married to a doctor on call:

My lack of time, our lack of communication, our lack of intimacy, his lack of fidelity."

"I'm sorry."

"I wish I could be as philosophical about things as Mary."

As they came into town, Bill made the right-hand turn onto M-115. Beyond Lake Cadillac, he made a left onto Sunnyside Drive.

"Can you drop me back at the hospital?" she asked. "My car is there."

"You bet. Thanks for helping Mary. Jack and I are betting a lot to make certain she survives."

"Oh, I heard all about Jack. Regina would like to nominate him for sainthood."

"Don't you have to be dead for that?" Bill asked.

April 19

The number of new COVID-19 cases reported by the state of Michigan have come in at less than 800 for the fourth day in row.

Figures released Sunday, April 19, by the state's Department of Health and Human Services show 633 new cases reported, more than 100 less than the 768 cases on Saturday and 760 on Friday.

Sunday's numbers raise the total COVID-19 cases in Michigan to 31,424, with 2,391 deaths.

– Mlive.

April 19

A trio of far-right, pro-gun provocateurs is behind some of the largest Facebook groups calling for anti-quarantine protests around the country, offering the latest illustration that some seemingly organic demonstrations are being engineered by a network of conservative activists.

The Facebook groups target Wisconsin, Ohio, Pennsylvania and New York. By Sunday, the groups had roughly 200,000 members combined, and they continued to expand quickly, days after the President endorsed such protests by suggesting citizens should "liberate" their states.

— The Washington Post.

April 19

"How you feeling today?" Doc Mac asked as Rick came outside.

The chief made a kind of Tarzan pose. "I haven't felt this good in years." He raised himself to full height and stretched his back muscles. "Probably since before the accident."

"Good. Time for Phase 2," the doctor said emphatically. "Hopefully you won't notice any difference in the level of your physical pain."

Rick settled at the picnic table facing Doc. "But if I do have more pain, we can go back, right?"

The old doctor sat erect, studying Rick's face closely. "I need you to be clear about this. I can't keep you on morphine forever. I needed to break your nightly binges. Now we have to find the right mix of pain relief to make your life livable. But if you backslide, it will kill you. Understand?"

Rick tipped his head to one side, studying McKittrick's face closely. "OK. Thanks, Mister Happy Ball. Any other words of encouragement?"

"Rick, you've gone two weeks without any beer. And you've been sleeping through the night, from what I can tell."

"And, wham, I'm on my own again."

"No, that's not what I'm saying. Look, I spent years in combat hospitals and VA hospitals. I know pain. I'll work you through this. And on the other side, you won't be drinking yourself to death, a six-pack at a time. You're already two weeks sober."

April 20

About 22 million Americans filed for unemployment over the past four weeks, a number expected to grow as the coronavirus and subsequent lockdowns ravage the economy. The unemployment rate is nearing 18 percent, according to Fortune, the highest rate of real unemployment since the Great Depression.

JP Morgan Chase has estimated it will hit 20 percent before the end of June.

Poverty, hunger, crime, and social upheaval are a real threat in the US, according to a professor of sociology at Albertus Magnus College. Especially if the government doesn't step in to soften the blow.

"There's no doubt this is going to have huge economic and social impacts, and the worse it is, the more likely that people are going to get to the point where social action is the only move forward," the professor said.

Anti-government demonstrations could become more widespread: In Lansing, Michigan, "Operation Gridlock" has seen armed protesters holding Confederate flags and signs calling the governor a Nazi. Similar demonstrations took place last week in Indianapolis, Salt Lake City and Columbus, Ohio.

Hoarding is already an issue in the United States: As people stockpile canned goods, cleaning supplies, and toilet paper, it could put more pressure on supply chains and keep supermarket shelves empty.

On Wednesday, the International Monetary Fund warned that the coronavirus could spark turmoil in countries around the world if people were left without jobs or money for food during and after the pandemic.

"If the crisis is badly managed and [the response] is viewed as having been insufficient to help people, you could end up with social unrest," the IMF chief economist told Reuters.

April 20

AN ANTI-LOCKDOWN protester was spotted carrying a
vile "sacrifice the weak" to coronavirus sign at a ReOpen
Tennessee rally. The woman, who wore a scarf and
sunglasses, was seen holding the placard in Nashville as calls
grow across the United States to lift lockdown restrictions.

– Newsbreak.

April 20

Frank was not aware that Regina had returned from her daily run into Wellston. She would park next to the library for 30 minutes and use the wifi there to check their e-mail accounts and look over a couple of news sites like the *Detroit Free Press* or the statewide online news wire, Mlive. If she saw something Frank needed to see, she would download a screen capture.

While Mary was napping, he stepped out of the RV for a breath of fresh air. Then he noticed their Explorer parked in a remote part of the campground. Regina sat in the driver's seat. As he walked over, he could tell that the Ford's engine was not running. When she saw him coming, she put down the window. He could see that she had been crying.

"What's wrong?" he asked. "What's happened?"

"People!" she wailed. "These people are just the worst."

"Which people? I don't understand what's happened."

She lifted the laptop and turned the screen toward him. She played a video of a young blond reporter describing an anti-lock-down protest in Tennessee. Directly behind her was a woman holding a sign that read "Sacrifice the Weak: ReOpen TN."

"They want to kill Mary. They really want to kill my baby."

He closed the laptop and set it on the hood of the truck. "No, honey, no. That's just one nasty person in Tennessee." He put his hand on her shoulder to soothe her.

"You didn't see the comments. All these people agreed with her and support her. Somebody wrote that she should run for governor and use that as a campaign slogan: that comment has 200 likes. People are just awful."

"Not everyone. Rick and Doc Mac dropped everything to come help us. Look how much Jack has done. And Bill brought Easter dinner. Mary loves that bunny he gave her. Doctor Pelletier stayed overnight so you could get some rest. And that young woman from the radio station who came out Saturday was nice. She was very concerned about Mary. It's not that everyone is evil."

April 20

Sitting in his Jeep, Bill reflected on what he considered a very productive day. There was a full week of events ahead.

He had arranged with Renee at 9&10 News an interview for the boss on the Tuesday morning show to discuss the Department's Covid-19 relief program. Bill was not clear on why that was so important to the boss, but at this point he did as told. As promised, Bill had given Fred Anderson a heads up on the interview and also arranged for Congressman Van Den Berg to speak with the Regional Forester about the cattle matter on Tuesday afternoon.

Also on Tuesday, Jack was set to go with Rory and Fritz to meet the USA for Western Michigan in Grand Rapids.

Come Thursday afternoon, Jack would detour through Cadillac so Bill could ride along on the drive to Milwaukee. Their appeal for Jack's career was planned for Friday morning.

Now he was waiting for the local news on Interlochen Public Radio. He was curious to hear Allison's coverage on Sand Lake.

Overall, her reporting pleased Bill was. Allison didn't use anything from Bill; instead, she focused on the DuLong family. Regina did a great job in her interview. Bill went inside and gathered up his laptop and some papers from the printer. On his way out of town, he stopped at the party store on the west side of Lake Cadillac to see if he could get a few cans of Manistee's IPA from Manistee's North Channel Brewing. He was developing a taste for the local craft brews.

April 21

Technology is marvelous, Bill often said; he preferred to marvel than engage. He readily admitted that his smartphone was smarter than him. The phone was capable of texting and tweeting; Bill was not. Nearly everyone in his circle of acquaintances knew this. So he was surprised when the phone vibrated to indicate a new text.

The phone number began with a 616 area code, indicating southwest Michigan. The preview window read: "OMG! At a protest in Grand Rapids today."

Bill opened the message and found a photo of one particular sign in a sea of campaign and Confederate flags. In blood red, the poster read: "Sacrifice the Sick: Liberate Michigan!"

April 21

The boss agreed to appear on the Morning Show at 6:40 a.m. He intended to join live from his home by Skype. At 6:25, Bill texted Renee that he was grateful for the time and asked her to keep her phone handy.

At 6:30, Elizabeth came into Bill's office, carrying her tablet. "Sand Lake made the news overnight. You're on AP, 7&4 News, Detroit Free Press, WOOD-TV in Grand Rapids, Mlive, I could go on. You want to see any of it?"

"Not at this moment. The boss is coming up after the next commercial break." He was busy typing a text on his phone. "I imagine Renee will bring that up after he talks Covid-19 for a minute. And then the April surprise."

"What are you planning now?" She looked at him closely. "I don't like the little twitchy thing you're doing in the corner of your mouth. You look like the Joker."

The boss appeared on the television screen, and Bill turned up the volume so he could monitor the conversation carefully. "Is he wearing bronzer?"

"Or spent the night in a tanning bed. Cause when he left yesterday, he was as pasty white as the rest of us after a Michigan winter."

The boss ran through the Departmental talking points in under less than two minutes. So Renee moved onto the report in the news overnight of campers at the Sand Lake campground. Robert expressed some discomfort with the new line of questioning but adhered to Bill's talking point. Bill, meanwhile, hit send on his latest text.

Renee was back on screen. "Mister Fulbright, one final question before we let you go. Would you address rumors that you plan to run in the August primary to unseat Congressman Van Den Berg?"

The boss froze like a possum in the headlights. He picked up the new thread after another moment. "Yes, I am aware of the rumors, which they are at this point. I have received some encouragement and will be making a decision soon."

"Thank you. We hope you will come back when you're ready to make the big announcement." Screen went back to Renee in the studio. "That was Robert Fulbright, Forest Supervisor on the

Huron-Manistee National Forests, hinting that he may be making a surprise move into national politics. And now, Jackie, how's the out-the-door weather looking this morning?"

Bill sat back in his chair laughing rather hysterically. Soon a small crowd of employees gathered at the window of his office door. He raised a forefinger to request a moment before opening the door.

"He can't do that, can he?" Elizabeth asked. "Isn't there a rule? You always send out reminders before the election."

"The Hatch Act." He was grinning at her. "And the incumbent's reaction will be?"

"Uh, shock? Anger?" She paused to think about it for a moment. "But how will Van Den Berg know? Who watches the 9&10 early, early morning show?"

Bill shrugged nonchalantly. "This morning? Fred Anderson, the Congressman's district chief of staff. Unless all these years have been wasted, I expect him to call me very soon." He looked at his watch. "Any minute now."

Bill waved at those standing in the doorway to come in. He faced a barrage of questions, mostly having to do with Bill's prior knowledge of the boss' possible run for Congress. Elizabeth watched his Oscar-caliber performance as a man flabbergasted or bewildered by this sudden news. She smiled thinking at first that she could do this public affairs work and then realizing that she really, really wanted Bill's job when he retired.

April 21

From Manistee to Grand Rapids, Rory and Jack made only one stop, at the Starbucks in Walker along I-96. Jack ordered a coffee for himself with the lemon loaf for the new USA. Rory was already halfway through his second caffeinated energy drink. They proceeded into the city and finally on to Michigan Street, traveling east. Rory knew the directions because he had been to the U.S. Attorney's office and the District Court. The two buildings sat on opposite sides of Ottawa Avenue. When they stopped on the upper parking deck, Fritz joined them from the back of the rig. The dog did a good job of staying at Rory's side. Jack and Rory wore face masks; the dog did not.

When they went into the suite for the Office of the U.S. Attorney, a receptionist stood to greet them, donning a blue face mask as she did. She was tall and elegantly dressed, perhaps having also learned to dress for the job you want rather than the job you have. "Good morning, Mister Ferguson. Officer Winchester. I'm afraid Miss Crum is running a little late in court this morning. I just spoke with her by phone. I expect her in the next fifteen minutes or so. My name is Joyce. Would you like to have a seat? May I get you coffee or tea?"

Rory wandered off, perhaps looking for a restroom, leaving Fritz with the ranger. Jack smiled, "No, thank you. However, do you have a plate or something for the lemon loaf? I wouldn't feel comfortable just giving Miss Crum a bag of pastries."

Joyce chuckled a little. "I'm sure we can do better."

He walked over to the floor-to-ceiling window that looked out over Grand Rapids. They did not encounter much traffic on the highway, and there did not appear to be many cars on the streets downtown. Perhaps it was best to drive into the city in the midst of a pandemic.

Rory came back into the suite just as Joyce stood and came toward them. The dog also stood. "Miss Crum is on her way. Let me show you into her office."

For a federal office, Miss Crum's furnishings and decorations were extremely nice. Comparing her mahogany furniture to Bill's suite of recycled battleship metal would be like comparing the

White House to Jack's little cabin on Hamlin Lake near Ludington. Hanging alone on one wall was an enormous painting of a beautiful house overlooking a wide misty river. The gilded frame looked to be nearly four feet by five feet. A brass tag affixed to the frame read, "Crum Hall on the Hudson River."

"Do you appreciate the Hudson River School?" a woman asked as she came into the office. "A Thomas Cole original."

"Oh, it's just amazing," Jack said, straightening. "I think his eye for architectural detail is as exceptional as his landscapes. Have you seen his painting of Fort Ticonderoga?" He could see a look of surprise on her unmasked face. "Oh, I apologize. Jack Ferguson. This is Rory Winchester. And Fritz, the victim." They all maintained a respectful distance, except Fritz walked directly up to Miss Crum.

"I'm Victoria Crum." She leaned down to lift the dog's snout. "And I will be representing you, if I choose to take your case."

Joyce came in, still wearing her face mask, carrying the lemon loaf on an oval silver tray. She placed it on the corner of Miss Crum's desk. "Mister Ferguson brought this for you, as a welcoming present."

"Call me Jack, please. Yes, welcome to Michigan. I don't think we'll give you the most cases, but they'll probably be among the most interesting." Miss Crum did not wear a mask, and Jack thought she looked a little young to be a U.S. Attorney. But she had a clear business-like efficiency. Given her taste in fashion, he didn't think that having the same name as the estate in a 160-year-old painting was a coincidence. He left his canvas bag on the chair in front of her desk, then walked over to the conference table where Rory was already sitting, uninvited, fiddling with his smart phone. The LEO did not look comfortable trying to squeeze into the office furniture while wearing his bulky belt loaded down with a holstered pistol and other tactical gear.

When Miss Crum joined them, Rory gave his account of events at Sand Lake leading up to April 9th. He had a flip notebook open in his hand that he referred to back to document the dates and times. "On March 26, I received a phone message from Martha Previn who lives in Dublin in Norman Township. She reported seeing two recreational vehicles in the Sand Lake Campground, located on National Forest System Lands within the Huron-Manistee National Forests. The campground was not open to the public at that time of year because of the seasonal closure. After retrieving this message on the morning of March 27, I contacted District Ranger Jack Ferguson by phone at approximately 1230 hours and informed him of this potential trespass."

Miss Crum raised a hand, the forefinger elegantly extended. "Officer Winchester, I'm sorry, but I am due back in court later. Could we jump ahead to the day of the complaint? I believe that was April 9, correct?"

The attorney gave Jack a questioning look as Rory flipped through numerous pages in his notebook. His features hidden by a mask, Jack responded with his most non-committal nod. Finally Rory began again. "On April 8, I received a further call from Missus Previn that the same two recreational vehicles, along with the two passenger vehicles, remained in trespass at the Sand Lake Campground. I retrieved that voicemail on the morning of April 9. The district ranger was unavailable at that time, so I established contact with the Forest Supervisor, Robert Fulbright. I informed Mister Fulbright of the information in my possession. He recommended that I proceed with the normal enforcement activities I am authorized to pursue in such cases of trespass."

Jack watched the U.S. Attorney's eyes appear to glaze over from the boredom of this presentation. Although she had the complaint on the table in front of her, she paid no attention to it. Instead she seemed to be glancing, discretely, at the screen of her smart phone resting next to the charging documents.

Rory plowed on, apparently oblivious to the response his presentation was receiving. "Upon entering Sand Lake Campground, I found that the standard Forest Service gate mechanism had been illegally modified, which supports a charge of destruction of federal property. I then observed two suspects sitting at a picnic table in immediate proximity to the two recreational vehicles. Because the campground is closed, those picnic tables are not available for public use. During the off-season, those tables are, in fact, secured with a heavy steel chain and padlock. Removing that chain constituted a second occurrence of destruction of federal property."

By now, Jack was starting to wonder whether he wouldn't rather just confess himself than continue to listen to this endless account of Rory's relentless pursuit of what came down to two old guys having lunch and a family staying in a camper. Miss Crum looked as equally bored as Jack.

"At that time, myself and Canine Unit Fritz made contact with the two suspects, one Charles McKettrick and one Richard Bocek, both of Grand Rapids. Mister Bocek appeared to be preparing lunch, supporting my suspicion that they were staying on the campground, which was trespass at that time of year and also a violation of the Governor's shelter-in-place order. When Canine Unit Fritz approached the picnic table, suspect Bocek struck the Canine Officer across the snout. That assault constitutes a violation of 18 U.S. Code, subpart 1368. At that time, I immediately apprehended both suspects and placed them in restraints before calling for back-up from other law enforcement agencies."

Miss Crum interrupted Rory's recitation at that point. "Mr. Ferguson, Jack, were you a witness to these events?"

"No, I arrived only after the other law enforcement agencies."

"I see. But the notes I received indicated that you spoke with those other agencies that led to a resolution of the events, including, if I understand correctly, the possession of narcotics by Charles McKettrick."

"Yes, ma'am. Doctor McKettrick is on leave from the Veteran Administration in Grand Rapids. He cares for Mister Bocek, who was injured in service to the U.S. Navy. The doctor also treats the daughter of the DuLong family."

"And this other family is at the campground. Why?"

Rory jumped in again. "Well, ma'am, I did not know that Rick Bocek and Frank DuLong were hired as campground hosts for the upcoming season."

"Do either of you know why Mister Bocek struck the canine unit?"

Jack spoke first. "He told me that the dog …; sorry, canine unit was trying to steal the hamburgers he had just grilled for their lunch."

Miss Crum sat back in her chair. "So it sounds like we have some confusion as to whether they were trespassing or just early arrivals for their seasonal camp host jobs. These other statements in the complaint about kidnapping and illegal distribution of narcotics are inaccurate. Is that correct?"

Again, Jack spoke before Rory was ready. "You know, I think it might be helpful for you to have some idea of the geography. So I brought you a map of the forest and the campground. Give me just a moment." Jack stood and walked back to where his bag sat on a chair in front of Miss Crum's massive oak desk. After removing the folded forest-wide map and diagram of Sand Lake, he reached over and gently nudged the silver tray closer to the edge of the desk. Then he walked back to the table where Rory sat across from Miss Crum.

He stood at the table and unfolded the big map that showed his ranger district. He laid this across the table and then put the Sand Lake brochure on it. "So Sand Lake is located about halfway between Cadillac and Manistee. As Rory said, the campground closes from September to May, especially now with the governor's lockdown. So I approved a request from the concession operator to get his campground hosts in there."

A sudden racket erupted behind Jack as the silver tray tumbled to the floor. He turned, as did Miss Crum and Rory, to see Fritz wolfing down the lemon loaf. He licked crumbs from the carpet and looked up, like he was expecting a chai tea to wash it down.

"I think we're done here, gentlemen. I don't see a case I could prosecute in good faith." Miss Crum rose and strode to her desk, leaving the two men and dog to find their own way out.

April 21

The home phone rarely rang at Bill's house, especially after 10:30 p.m. The last person he had spoken to was Jack, reporting that the animal act in Ring One had gone flawlessly. In the future, the new USA was likely to carefully consider prosecuting the voluminous citations that Rory issued like raffle tickets. In return, Bill reported that similar success in Ring Two because, according to Fred Anderson, Congressman Van Den Berg was rather chagrined after watching the boss on 9&10 News.

"Hey, that thing about the Hudson Valley School was a nice touch. Glad I did a little research. Did you know she has the original Crum Hall painting in her office?"

"I read a profile about her in *The Washington Post*. Most DOJ attorneys don't have half-million-dollar paintings hanging in their offices."

Jack whistled. "Shouldn't she be in private practice? Isn't that where the real money is?"

"She's got the money. Her family has had money for two centuries. I expect she'll be transitioning to a political career at some point soon. We live long enough, we'll watch her run for president."

"I should have gotten an autograph. You have a good night."

When the house phone rang late, Bill had just finished working and settled onto his sofa with a can of the Manistee IPA to watch the latest episode in the Picard spinoff to the Star Trek franchise. Who called on a land line these days? He picked up the receiver. "Hello?"

"You are so fucking trending right now," a woman's voice said. "You're trending above the Governor of Michigan."

"Does that convert to frequent flier miles?" he asked.

"This is so bad." Elizabeth's voice turned into sobs. "How can people be so evil?"

"Wait, I thought trending was a good thing."

She let out a deep, long sigh. "There's all these people on Facebook and Twitter claiming they are the Liberation Army of Michigan."

"You mean like the Liberation Army of China?"

"No, like the protesters with signs saying 'Sacrifice The Weak.'

The people who don't wear masks and block streets into a hospital. They wear guns to a protest. Bill, they want to liberate Sand Lake."

"What?"

"They're saying it's not fair that with the lockdown that campgrounds are closed, but we're giving a sick child special rights. Here's a tweet, 'Lockdown the dying; free the living.' They're talking about coming in force. Maybe bring heavy equipment."

"Elizabeth, send me the links. Then, please go to bed. I will need your help in the morning. OK?"

Bill paced around the house from room to room, debating whether to call Jack again so late in the evening. He worried that the Liberation Army of Michigan could spin the situation out of all control. From the refrigerator's bottom shelf, he took out another IPA. Back in his study, he opened the laptop and searched for an e-mail from Elizabeth. In the faraway past, Camille would have been standing next to him at this time of night, encouraging him to put away work and go to bed. Her father served in the Navy in the Pacific Theater, and she often recited something he had told her: "Think of your life like a ship, and work is water. If you float above it, you are fine. If it gets inside, it fills all voids and you sink."

He scrolled through the appalling online screeds that Elizabeth had sent. He had been thinking about one of his first deployments as an officer, when his unit deployed to Zakho in northern Iraq to help protect the Kurdish people fleeing their homes and villages away from Saddam's retribution, an operation named Provide Comfort. Now, almost 30 years later, he was once again providing comfort to people fleeing their home in fear, and he had to hold off another hostile "army."

His personal cell phone rang a few minutes after midnight.

"You're seeing all this, right?" a woman asked.

"Yes. Having a little trouble grasping the insanity. But, yes, I'm seeing it."

"You have a plan?"

"Walk the dog. Another beer. Watch a *Hogan's Heroes* on DVD."

"You don't have a dog."

"Good. Skip straight to the cold beer. You know why I like Hogan? He's the patient running the asylum."

"You need help?"

"Like therapy, no, I gave it up. And I know where the beer is."

"You want to know who's in the Liberation Army of Michigan?"

"As a start. But I also need to know who is funding them. Funny thing about these astroturfing outfits; they always have an invisible support network. Like all these people driving down to Lansing last week, crying poverty because of the lockdown. How many clunkers were pushed down the street because they broke down or ran out of gas? They didn't look homeless or hungry to me. So the lockdown has been a terrible burden to them?"

The woman laughed. "Think how much money they're saving because they aren't getting the weekly mani/pedi."

"Annette, I would like your help, yes, but it can't be on government time or equipment."

"Other than a massive data dump, are there particulars you would be looking for. If I'm going to venture into the dark web, I want to make sure I have something to show for it." Annette was a master webmaster in the Regional Office.

"Mostly I would love to know when this is going to happen."

"You don't know? You've got all the way until Friday, the 24th."

April 22

LANSING, MI -- The ongoing COVID-19 pandemic continues to impact more and more people as Michigan hospitals facing economic struggles announce layoffs and furloughs at a time when they are treating thousands of patients.

Testing numbers continue to fluctuate as a backlog of cases led to a record high of daily deaths being reported in the state on Tuesday, April 21.

Meanwhile doctors across the state say finding proper ways to treat COVID-19, which stands for coronavirus disease 2019, change almost daily as experts work to better understand the virus that causes the illness.

– Mlive.

April 22

The roads surrounding Michigan's Capitol were supposed to be full of cars Wednesday as residents planned to protest against the extension of the Governor's "Stay Home, Stay Safe Order" Instead, only a handful of people showed up.

"Operation Gridlock 2.0" was planned for 10 a.m. to 2 p.m. Wednesday, according to the event page on Facebook, which was taken down within a few hours. Even after being deleted, the event gained attention and was shared widely on other social media platforms.

"It's becoming very disturbing, the way our government thinks they can just shut everything down," a protester said. "They're becoming a tyranny and I think it says in the Declaration of Independence that we have the right and the responsibility to stand up, that we can't just stay in our houses and let people lose their jobs and their dreams and their lives. They're shutting this all down based on inaccurate information and that can't keep happening."

She was one of the few protestors who showed up at the state Capitol.

– The State News, MSU.

April 22

There are 999 new cases and 113 new deaths as of Wednesday morning, according to data from the Michigan Department of Health and Human Services. The total number of cases is now at 33,966 and the death toll is 2,813.

There was a spike in the death toll on Tuesday, after a several-day decline, however, that was due in part to the addition of death certificates from the week prior. The state will review death certificates weekly. If a patient who dies is matched to a confirmed COVID-19 case, this will count towards the state's death toll, which applies to 95 deaths reported Tuesday. This accounts for spikes in the death toll on April 10 and April 16.

– WZZM13, Grand Rapids.

April 22

When Jack climbed into the Wagoneer, Bill handed him a sausage, egg, and cheese sandwich on a croissant. "It's from the deli at Garlett's Corner. Only place open this early between home and here." They met back at the state rest stop on M-55 just east of the Pine River bridge. At 6:30 a.m., they were the only visitors. Bill thought they needed a very private place to talk.

"What's so hush hush this early in the morning? The Congressman still on the Regional Forester's schedule for this afternoon?"

"Yeah, that's happening. But we've got a bigger problem than the boss. You've been following all these people protesting down in Lansing, right?"

"Oh, yeah. People angry they can't go to the gym or the hair salon."

"Yep, those are the ones. They're coming here."

"What?" Jack sounded panicked. "Why?" He twisted in his seat to look at the driver.

"They want to liberate Sand Lake. Apparently it's not fair to them that a sick 9-year-old child is in a closed campground if they can't go camping."

"But we took care of that. Frank and Rick are campground hosts."

"Must you try to be logical?" Bill asked angrily. "They want old people to die if it helps the economy. Suddenly the right-to-life crowd that doesn't believe in evolution are in favor of survival of the fittest."

Jack tried to sound reasonable again. "It's OK, Bill. People are just stupid."

"Sorry." Bill took a deep breath to calm himself. "You know who they mean when they talk about letting the old die? My dad. He was with Patton in Africa. Camille's dad was in the Navy at Guadalcanal. They want to kill the Greatest Generation."

"And now they're coming for Mary," Jack observed. "How we going to stop that?"

They sat quietly in the Jeep for a few minutes. Touching the automatic window control, Jack let in the songs of birds rousing for the day, along with a mild breeze.

"We don't have much information yet, except that they plan to be here Friday. Annette is peering into the dark web to see if she can learn more. Maybe you can talk with your friend Pete to see if anything has come through law enforcement channels."

"Speaking of LE, should we tell Rory?" Jack asked.

Bill finished the last of his breakfast bagel. "Seriously? He's the kid I'd give to the other team in pick-up hoops."

"OK, then how do we keep him out of it?"

"We have him guard the doghouse."

"I heard about your hospital visit. Did you have a stroke? Because that didn't make any sense."

"Is that any way to talk to a possible stroke victim?" Bill opened his Vernor's soda. "Back when, my grandfather had a dog called Rex, short for Tyrannosaurus Rex, because he was the meanest dog ever. He bit just about everyone he met, except my grandmother." He tugged up the sleeve on his jacket to show a crescent of small scars on his wrist. "Well, my grandpa was having trouble with a coyote killing his hens in the coop. When he got down to only a few hens, he moved them into the doghouse one night and closed up that pen. Then he put Rex into the henhouse. A couple of nights later, problem solved. Grandpa had that coyote pelt long after he got rid of Rex."

"So we put Rory in the RV?"

"No, we need to find a doghouse to put Mary and Regina for a few days, maybe the major, too. We have Rory watch over them, because this mob will be looking for them. Then we create another reception for the Liberation Army at Sand Lake. But first we need a doghouse. I ruled out my place, because it isn't sterile. So we need a place away from people, that preferably no one has visited in at least a week to ten days."

"Maybe a place vacant since November?" Jack asked. "I've got that little cabin over by Ludington, on Hamlin Lake. Most of the neighbors are snowbirds, so there won't be anyone poking around. I can give the Mason County sheriff a heads up that somebody'll be staying there a few days to get away."

Bill looked over at Jack. "In all these years, you did not tell us that you are a genius."

"I don't like to advertise," Jack said, modestly. "But what are we going to do at Sand Lake, so that we're not overrun by idiots?"

"Call Rex."

"Seriously, about that stroke thing."

Bill was back in the Cadillac office by 7:30 a.m., eager to get a start on what he needed to do in about 48 hours. He left voicemail messages for three retired Forest Service law enforcement officers. He boxed up the files from his locked file cabinet drawer. Finally, he left a voicemail for Ted, assuming that he was busy taking Ruth for chemo or radiation therapy.

Just after 8, a knock came at his office door. "Come in," he called.

The door swung open to reveal Robert Fulbright in a royal blue Italian-cut suit that looked bespoke. Bill considered whether he should get out of his desk chair to genuflect. "So how did you think we did yesterday morning?" the boss asked.

Bill pondered for a moment whether the boss was including him in his perceived success of the 9&10 interview or was merely using the royal "we." "Well, you were good on the Covid thing, handled the Sand Lake question well, and I guess you got to where you wanted with the question about running for Congress. I wish you had given me a heads up on that. I could have given Renee a little background to give you time to talk about your interests."

The boss laughed as he closed the office door behind him. "She completely surprised me there. But it will be informative to see what interest it generates now. You know, just throwing bait in the water to see who bites." He started to turn to leave.

Bill's inner angler wanted to scream, *No, chumming is what you do if you're after shark.* "Quick reminder. Congressman Van Den Berg has that call with the Regional Forester this afternoon about the cattle letter."

The boss reacted like a man stepping on a live electrical wire. He twisted awkwardly back to face Bill. "What?! Why didn't you tell me about this?"

"I sent you a text and an e-mail last week. Fred Anderson set it up because we discussed elevating our response on the cow grazing to the RF because it keeps coming up year after year. If you win the election, you'll probably have to deal with the cow shit yourself."

The boss turned angrily and left, muttering "Damn cows," as he went.

When the door closed, Bill picked up his personal cell phone and placed a call to Traverse City. He kept his voice low when the other party answered. "Hey, you have any time this afternoon? I need some strategic advice."

"You know that Veteran's Park on 115 west of Mesick?"

"Yeah. Time?" Bill asked.

"18:00?"

"Sounds good."

"You'll provide the libations?"

"Of course."

April 22

Jack's meeting with Pete Simmons went about as well as you could expect when you tell a sheriff that his county will be overrun by a horde of angry vigilantes within a few days. And they might be heavily armed.

"Seriously, Jack, what do you want me to do? I've got a sheriff next door who won't enforce the governor's lockdown orders because he'd afraid to piss anyone off. You know what happens to a sheriff who makes voters unhappy?" He leaned against the fender of his cruiser.

"More time for fishing?" Jack asked with a smile.

"Only if the governor opens the boat launches. Seriously, what can I do?" He threw his hands out in a display of frustration.

Jack rested against his truck. "How about doing exactly what you are comfortable with. You don't want your folks anywhere near, that's OK; it's on federal land. Maybe you could have a cruiser looking for expired license plate or registrations, that's OK, too. The only thing off the table is dropping me from your poker games."

"OK, let me think about it. But why go up against them at all?" Pete asked. "If the little girl's not there, why not let them have the run of the campground for a night? Give them a little victory so they go away happy."

Jack reflected on this idea for a few minutes. "I'm not sure I can claw back from the end of the limb I'm on. First, I've got the Governor's shut down order. Next, the Regional Forester wants to send me back to Alaska; my wife is not happy with that idea. The boss in Cadillac thinks that I should have never let them stay to begin with. And I've got an ex-Marine planning tactical maneuvers to respond to this Liberation Army."

Pete laughed. "Jack, I'm sure I've told you this before; there is no such thing as an ex-Marine." He unbuttoned a sleeve to reveal a globe and anchor tattoo on his wrist. "Once a Marine, always a Marine."

April 22

The President on Wednesday criticized the decision of a political ally, the Governor of Georgia, to allow many businesses to reopen this week, saying the move was premature given the number of coronavirus cases in the state.

"I want him to do what he thinks is right, but I disagree with him on what he is doing," the President said at a White House briefing. "I think it's too soon."

"I love those people that use all of those things — the spas, the beauty parlors, barbershops, tattoo parlors," the President said. "I love them. But they can wait a little bit longer, just a little bit — not much, because safety has to predominate."

— President of the United States of America,
as reported by *The New York Times*.

April 22

When Bill's cell phone rang, he checked the screen. A 414 area code meant Milwaukee. He wasn't at all sure he wanted to answer. Milwaukee is home to the Regional Office for the Eastern Region of the Forest Service.

"Reinhardt."

"Bill, how are you? I hear you've got a lot of things going on over there." Rachel sounded a little too perky for this to be good news. She was the director of Congressional Relations at the Regional Office. She had worked her way up through the ranks from frontline receptionist, then writer/editor to forest public affairs officer. Bill thought she would next move into a district ranger job and then onto a senior leadership role in the future, like Regional Forester. So he tried not to get on her bad side.

"Oh, the usual. For the midst of a pandemic."

"So, hey, I sat in on a call with Congressman Van Den Berg and the Regional Forester."

He closed his office door and turned on the loud fan. "Oh, sure, the cow thing. We keep giving the farmer the same answer over and over, so I thought it might be time to elevate it for signature."

"Yeah, the Congressman mentioned that. But he mostly wanted to know if your boss is serious about running for Congress this year. Know anything about that?"

"Did you ask him?"

"So he hasn't discussed it with you?"

"Robert?" Bill chuckled. "Not a man to ask for advice."

"I feel like you're avoiding my question. Did you see any indication that he plans to run for Congress?"

"Rachel, he hasn't said anything to me. I saw him talking with a big donor after the Governor's Breakfast in Cadillac a few months ago. That's all. When he confirmed some rumors on the local show yesterday, that was the first I'd heard him talk about it. You want me to send a notarized statement?"

She seemed to pause for a long few minutes. "The Congressman may take this to the Chief, maybe even the Secretary. He's worried that one of his major donors hasn't been very responsive the past few months."

"I'd worry, too, if I were him. But the boss has plenty of time to retire before the primary. Michigan's primary isn't until August."

"True. But if Robert's fundraising now, that would also violate the Hatch Act. Not sure anyone in the Department or the White House would be happy about that."

"So you think the current administration cares about the Hatch Act? They sure didn't listen to the Office of Special Counsel when they recommended firing the creator of 'alternative facts.'"

He heard Rachel's laughter faintly, like she was 10 feet from a speaker phone. He wondered if there were others listening in to the conversation.

"Well, Judith would like us to keep him out of trouble. Can you do that?"

"I'm sure Robert knows what he's doing. Quite sure. But let me know if you need to talk more about the cows." As he hung up the phone, Bill stifled a triumphant laugh and a celebratory jig. Instead he took his rabbit-felt fedora and headed up the hillside into the cemetery.

April 22

Jack met Gertie at the Rainbow Bend boat launch on the Big Manistee River just after noon. She pulled up alongside his personal pick-up truck in an ancient AMC Eagle that looked like it was mostly rebuilt with Play-doh. The car let go a series of five or six belches of black smoke when she turned off the engine. There appeared to be about a year of magazines thrown into the back seat.

She groaned as she climbed into his truck. "Is it possible you jacked this thing up on springs before we met, or am I just getting older?"

"Maybe I just overinflated the tires."

"Nicely said, Jack. Don't insult the old woman, especially if you want something from her."

"I didn't even have to go to law school to learn that rule." He opened the small cooler on the seat between them, offering her a choice of beverages containing alcohol, caffeine or mere water.

She selected a Leinenkugel Northwoods Lager. "The usual white man trick to weaken us with alcohol?"

"Not on purpose. Just a drink?"

"Jack, after 500 years, nothing is just anything."

He sat watching the river flow a few minutes. He opened a Leinie Original. "I've been trying since I've been here to do what I can," he said haltingly. "What's within my little square of National Forest. I'm sorry it's not more."

"Jack, it's all so much more. Do you know the story of the Burt Lake Band?"

He shook his head.

She turned toward him and leaned back against the door of his truck. "Burt Lake is up near Cheboygan. The Burt Lake Band are Anishinaabe, just like the other Ottawa and Chippewa. They were assured a reservation by the Treaty of 1855 with the federal government. But the county assessed property taxes on the tribal properties, forcing the tribe to sell off good timber land to pay the taxes. Finally a white man bought the rights to their taxed lands. He convinced the county sheriff to clear the Anishinaabe people off their homes, then burned out the whole community. That was in

1900, not hundreds of years ago. But because of the bu⌐
Burt Lake Band lost their federal recognition. They have⌐
back yet. Think about that, Jack, the Cheboiganing people
been there so long, that their name is on the river, the coun⌐
the town — have no place to call home."

Jack sat silent, still watching the Manistee. He took a sip of beer.

"Thank you," she said. "You may be the first white man I ever
met who understood that an apology is so pointless."

He chuckled. "I don't know if I ever told you about this. A while
back now, I was at a tribal meeting over at the Lac Du Flambeau
Reservation. A scientist from the Wisconsin DNR was talking about
emerald ash borer and the threat of invasive species. When he
finished, I think it was the chairman of the Red Cliff Band who
said, 'We sympathize. The tribes have been dealing with an invasive
species for 500 years.'"

Her small body shook with laughter so that she nearly spilled her
beer. "So true. So true."

"Sure made for an interesting afternoon," Jack said. "Listen,
thanks for the letter of support. But I have another favor to ask.
Don't know if you know Beth Coubmosay in our Baldwin office, but
she was thinking we could offer your drummers an outdoor practice
area at Sand Lake."

"This would be a favor for me? Or for you? Or for your little
sick girl?"

"How about all three? I was hoping the drummers might stay
over both Thursday and Friday nights, just to keep our campground
full."

She took a long swig of Leinenkugel. "I should laugh at all this,
but it is too hard now. Years ago, your government gave my people
blankets infected with the smallpox virus. Here you are now, asking
my help to save a child from another virus. It's a big ask. A very big
ask."

April 22

At the intersection where M-115 meets M-37, Bill pulled into the BP gas station at Ellens Corners. He had three relatively urgent needs: gasoline for the Wagoneer; a restroom for himself and libations for his next meeting. Standing in the beer cave, he found the range of choices daunting. Finally, he concluded you can never go wrong with Leinenkugel. He took a six-pack of Original and another of Northwoods Lager. When he put the beer up on the counter, the clerk nodded out the window toward the gas pumps.

"You have the fuel in the old Jeep?" she asked. "What year is that?"

"She's an '87. Mostly original."

"Really? Me, too. But I'm all original parts."

Another clerk turned from stocking bottles of liquor on the shelves behind the counter. "Jeez, Carol, you've been 33 for the ten years now I've known you."

Carol smiled at Bill as she rang up his beer. "If you're having a party, I'm your best party girl."

He thanked her and hauled the beer out to the back seat of the Wagoneer. Although only five blocks long, Mesick can be a little harrowing to traverse as slower local vehicles mix with the through traffic determined to maintain highway speeds.

Veterans Memorial Park sits just beyond the intersection where M-37 turns south toward Baldwin and M-115 continues northwest on toward Copemish, but just shy of the bridge over the Manistee River backwaters of the Hodenpyl Pond. When Bill arrived, there was only one other vehicle in the lot, an older Ford conversion van with a pop-up roof. One man sat alone at a picnic table directly in front of it. Bill pulled to the opposite side, closest to where the Manistee River flowed into the impoundment. Bill was halfway through a Northwoods Lager when Greg's big pick-up truck drove up next to the Wagoneer. Like Bill, Greg had also enlisted at 17, going Army, then retired at 37 years old; he then came to the Forest Service and retired at the 57, the mandatory retirement age. In the eight years since, he had operated a rock and crystal store in a Traverse City shopping mall. There's a surprisingly good market for Petoskey stones among the tourist crowd. The pick-up truck spent a moment sputtering before the engine finally stopped. Greg stepped out of his truck and climbed into Bill's Jeep.

"I'm impressed you still keep this thing running," Gary said as he looked around the interior. When he spotted the Leinie's, he reached for an Original. "Thanks. Been a while." He raised his bottle in a toast. "To Camille and Brandon." They clinked their long-neck bottles.

"Amen," Bill said.

"Is this about your problem at Sand Lake?" He spoke with a deep voice in a slow cadence that some people mistook for indecision.

Bill shook his head, then took a long swig of beer. "I've got a new problem. You ever hear of a group called the Liberation Army of Michigan?"

"Are they connected to the Earth Liberation Front? Or the Animal Liberation Front? A friend who retired in Washington State told me about a Youth Liberation Front. Any connections?"

"Not so far as I know. From what I understand, these guys are an astro-turf group, like the old Tea Party. Rebels with a cost. From what I've read online, they mostly want to liberate barbershops." Bill exchanged an empty for a fresh bottle and popped the top.

"Do they pay?" Greg asked.

"Why? The rock shop not doing well?"

Greg lightly punched Bill's shoulder lightly. "Not why I asked. We closed the shop down until the Governor opens up tourism again. I'm asking because you can get people to protest for or against anything if you pay them."

"Were you this cynical before you retired?" Bill asked. "Did I just miss it?"

"I think it started back then, but I've gotten much worse now. My brother-in-law is a clinically diagnosed moron. My sister had to throw out every bleach product in the house, because he wanted to try it, like the President suggested. I swear if there was an African witch doctor who claimed to cure Covid, he'd buy in."

Bill chuckled at that thought, then stopped abruptly. "Wouldn't surprise me. Probably only a matter of time till it happens. Isn't there already a New Age church in Florida selling hydrochloric acid as a sacrament to cure it?"

"It's all a mess." A long pause in the conversation followed. "So you called me. What do you need?"

"Well, you know we've got a sick little girl camping out at Sand Lake, right? We can't risk having her come in contact with anyone, so Jack is going to put her up at his cabin on Hamlin Lake for a few days."

Greg looked over in surprise. "I didn't know he had a cabin out there. Nice area. Especially up on the north end, near Nordhouse."

"Right. She'll be safe over there, but I'll still have to deal with any Liberators at the campground."

"You? Why not Jack? Did he get fired over this?"

Bill reached for a third bottle. "Not yet. I'd like to prevent it if I can."

"All right. I'm game. What do you need from me?"

"A ground game. Jack's talking to the tribe. I've got a couple of people lined up for a 'hearts and minds' approach in Grand Rapids. I need some thoughts on how to subdue a group of people who will likely be armed. I figure that's an MP function."

Greg held up his bottle and turned it in his hand. "And you think this is enough? You'll have to do a lot better than this if you want to get me into a shooting war."

Bill shook his head strenuously and held up both hands in a gesture to stop the direction of their discussion. "Absolutely not. I don't want this fight to go hot. I want it to go away. No shots."

Greg grunted in an expression of doubt. "If they come with weapons, you may not control that."

"Right. And that's why I am asking a very experienced MP and Forest Service special agent for tips on crowd control." Bill reached into the back seat to get a new Original that he passed to Greg. "My goal is to stop them from breaching the campground, preferably stop them before the gate. Just tell me what you need. I don't even need to know the plan."

"Right off, I'd like to ask for some help. Any objection to inviting Jerry and Henry to come along? And maybe some people who know how to take orders."

"Give me your wish list." Bill raised his bottle in a toast.

"What are you going to be doing during this 'police' action?"

Bill chuckled. "I thought I'd make initial contact out on the county road. If I can't use all my powers of persuasion to divert them, I'd fall back to you at the gate."

"And non-lethal only unless they breach the peace?"

"Exactly. You have something in mind already?"

"Were you in Panama in '89?" Greg asked.

"No. Wasn't that mostly Airborne, Special Forces, and MPs?"

"Don't forget the PsyOps Group. I'm thinking about playing *Spinal Tap* at about 11?"

"Is that going to be loud enough?" Bill asked. "With Koresh in Waco, didn't they play Nancy Sinatra?"

"*These Boots are Made for Walking.* That's torture at any volume."

"OK. Call me with your shopping list. Surprise me with your game plan."

April 22

As dusk settled over Wellston, Jack used a small flashlight to search for the light switch. Contractors had recently gutted and rebuilt most of the former building of the Chittenden Nursery, just a few miles from Sand Lake Campground. Soon the district staff would be moving from their cramped quarters in Manistee out to the newly renovated building. Jack had spent years trying to convince the powers that be that putting the district staff in the center of the district they managed made a lot of sense. Common sense, as Melissa often reminded her husband, was as common as a good salmon mousse at a county fair.

He came to meet Bill. They had decided to use Chittenden as a command center for the coming days. First, they needed privacy from the prying eyes, eager ears and loose lips at the district office. Because they had invited a few retirees to assist, they needed a little secrecy in their coming and goings. Most worrisome for Jack, Bill had asked for a little outdoors practice area for a small tactical unit. He was not certain exactly what that meant. Hopefully Bill wasn't planning to take the Forest Service to war.

Bill came in the door with an armful of rolled maps tucked under one arm, carrying a six-pack of Bell's in his other hand. "Have a fridge yet?" he asked, raising the ale.

"Not sure we should be drinking alcohol in a federal facility." Jack said.

"Well, it's hasn't really been dedicated yet, has it? So it's only a potential facility, and this is just a potential drink, until we drink it."

"Just give me the church key. We only have to get all this rolling in about twelve hours."

Bill handed over his silver US knife and proceeded to layout a forest visitor map, a topographical map, aerial photography of the surrounding areas and a diagram of the campground. With duct tape, he draped a state road map across an old chalk board. With a bright red marker, Bill had drawn circles around a few cities in Michigan's Lower Peninsula: Lansing, Bay City, Ludington and Grand Rapids.

"I feel like we're planning for a big game of Risk," Jack observed.

"This may be more like Global Thermonuclear Warfare."

"Isn't that the one where nobody wins?"

Bill answered in his best presidential voice. "We're going to win so much, you're going to be so sick and tired of winning."

"I'm onboard with the sick and tired portion. But I recall that we started with a three-ring circus. By my count, we're now up to at least five."

Bill shrugged and took a sip of IPA. "Sounds about right. Want to go through how everything plays out tomorrow? Then we'll talk Friday."

"I feel like right now I have plausible deniability or qualified immunity or something. If you tell me too much, I'll be joining you in whatever conspiracy you have in mind." Early Wednesday morning, when this new danger emerged, Jack had called Jane in the RF's office to postpone his personal trip to Milwaukee to make his mea culpa. Since that call, he'd been thinking about what this challenge would mean. On the other hand, going back to Alaska did mean another drive up the beautiful AlCan.

"I'm not suggesting anything illegal, especially for you. Even better, you'll have video to show the RF." Bill paused as he sipped his ale. He felt safe knowing that he was within the retirement window, and he tried to recall how much longer Jack had until he was safe, too. "Maybe we just go through your to-do list. What you don't know, the bosses can't hurt you with."

"If you insist on saving my bacon, how can I complain?" Jack turned his head and smiled in that way that made him look like Magnum, minus the Hawaiian shirt. Those had been co-opted by an anti-government group. Jack didn't follow those kinds of fashion trend, but Melissa did. She insisted he stop wearing a wallet with a chain and that he change from A-shirts to plain T-shirts without any half-witted inscriptions.

"Were you able to contact Gertie today?"

"Yes, she thought she could round up a least a half dozen campers and tents. I like that idea."

"Beth down in Baldwin suggested it. She's a tribal member and heard that they were looking for a place to practice. And Melissa is OK with Regina and Mary staying at your cabin?"

"Oh, yeah. She was ready to go stock the kitchen, but I explained that it's sterile now because no one has been there since last year except seagulls."

"And you talked with Sheriff Pete about having his deputies on Seaman Road and 12 Mile Road?"

"Yup. I said between 10 and 2 would work best."

"And you got me a couple of sawyers for Friday morning, too?"

Jack looked up from the maps spread across the table. "Again, why do I feel like I am doing all the heavy lifting?"

"Because you don't know what I'm doing. So what about Rory?"

Jack laughed. "Is being *gung ho* still an OK thing? If so, he's the poster boy. I asked him to get to the cabin at 6 a.m. Friday. Instead he's going to camp in the Nordhouse parking lot overnight so he can monitor traffic on Nurnberg Road going into our little neighborhood throughout the night."

"What is it the Army says? Hoo-ah?" Bill shrugged.

"So what do Marines say?"

Bill chuckled. "Mostly, 'Sir, yes, sir.'" He finished his beer and reached for another.

"Where were you assigned?"

Bill shrugged. "Lebanon under Reagan; with Bush it was Somalia and Iraq; under Clinton it was Haiti and the Balkans."

Jack stood and went to the state map on the chalkboard. "What's with the circles?"

"Potential targets." Bill followed Jack to the map. "Annette is doing some research." Then he paused. "Maybe this is a gray area you don't need to know about." He began peeling the map down.

"Hold on. If it's legal, you can probably tell me about it. Is it legal?"

"Yes, legal and moral." Bill folded the map, then picked up a piece of chalk. He drew a square in which he wrote "SL." Next to it, he drew an arrow aimed at the initials, then another box at the tail end of the arrow. In that box, he wrote "Home." He pointed at the first box. "On Friday, we will be here at Sand Lake. We can expect the main action to be here. But suppose we make a separate offensive action?" He drew another arrow from Sand Lake toward Home. "This is called pacification, where we try to change hearts and minds back home. During World War II, the Allies dropped billions of leaflets to convince the Germans at home and the occupied countries that we were winning."

Jack waved his hands. "You're going to dump leaflets?" He stopped and looked at Bill. "Wait, wait, you've got a plane?" He sounded incredulous.

"No, we've got something better. Social media. And the advantage is that it can be very personal and targeted. Look, let's get back to you and the heavy lift. So at 5:30 Friday morning, you're going on Skype with Katie Jaeger on UpNorthLive, then 6 a.m. with Renee at 9&10 and 6:30 with Theresa at WOOD in Grand Rapids."

"And where will you be while I'm playing public affairs officer?"

Bill pointed to the SL scrawled in the chalk box. "Thought I'd hang out to see who showed up."

April 23

The Michigan governor said Thursday that she's assessing reopening parts of the state's economy, as the Democratic governor faced angry protests last week over her stringent "stay-at-home" order intended to fight the spread of coronavirus.

"I have one of the most aggressive orders in the country, and so to start to release maybe a few things that are, you know, pose very little risk. I think it's appropriate to keep doing that assessment and we may have announcements in the coming days," she told CNN's "Newsroom."

The governor held off from going into further detail because she said the changes have not yet been finalized.

The governor last month signed a "Stay Home, Stay Safe" executive order, closing down nonessential businesses, and she recently extended it through April 30. Fed up with the restrictions, protesters defied the stay-at-home order and social distancing guidelines last week and gridlocked the streets of Michigan's capital. Protests have also popped up in other states as Americans grow concerned about the economic fallout of the coronavirus pandemic.

– CNN.

April 23

LANSING, Mich. — A group of protesters gathered outside the Governor's home in Lansing, urging her to re-open the state's economy sooner rather than later.

The demonstration comes after 'Operation Gridlock' brought Lansing to a stop Wednesday, April 15 when thousands of people blocked the streets surrounding the Capitol. That protest, one of the first of its kind in the country, sparked other similar events in states with stay-at-home orders in place. Michigan's current stay-at-home order is set to expire at the end of the month. Wednesday, the Governor said it's likely that some version of the order will be extended, but it's unclear when that will happen and for how long.

"The Governor is tyranny, this is like a third world country. It's like *V for Vendetta* and *Idiocracy* hooked up and they produced this baby that is 2020," said the organizer of the event. "We also want to ask her why she does not follow her own order and 'Stay Home, Stay Safe?'"

Despite several people at the event claiming Michigan's first-term governor was not inside her residence, she in fact was. Earlier in the day Thursday, the Governor appeared live on CNN talking about the state's next move and after the protest, a political reporter spoke with the Governor from her home.

– WWMT-TV.

April 23

Bill arrived in the dark at the Cadillac office. Only a few green government vehicles lined the back of the lot in the rear of the building. Was it already time for another vehicle auction of the high-mileage used trucks? It was common to see a Forest Service vehicle in town with the agency markings painted over in black. After three attempts, he finally remembered the correct door code. As he walked down the hallway, the motion-sensitive lights came up in each sector. He felt oddly like a prisoner escaping from Stalag 17.

He turned on his office computer, then plugged in his personal computer. He scrolled through his phone, looking at all the news of the Michigan protesters. Some reasonable, some blatantly political, some just vile. The Liberation Army was gathering plenty of Likes and more than a few 'Thumbs Up' or 'Angry' emojis. Depressing that so many Americans wanted to take up guns to see if they could make a sick 9-year-old child even sicker. One meme read: Send Mary Home, next to a child-like drawing of a tombstone.

Suppressing a desire to hurl his phone against a wall, he took out simple pencil and paper to compose a shopping list based on a lengthy voice mail from Greg on his personal cell phone. *No electronic record.* In column A and B, he wrote the quantity of the supplies he needed and when; in column C, he listed sources. Skull masks – Halloween store. Reagan face masks — Halloween store. Personal security — Cadillac Armory. Bodycams — Fire Staff or Troopers. Hearing protection — Home Depot or Meijer. Googles — Meijer. Posterboard — Meijer. Markers — Meijer. Ponchos — Meijer. Leaf trash bags —Meijer.

When the lights of surrounding offices began to come on, he checked his Timex. 5:30 a.m. Already? Time to send a few e-mails, on the government system and his personal computer, as well as make a few phone calls, also on the office phone and his personal cell. First up, he completed an Office of Personnel Management Form 71, the government's official Request for Leave or Approved Absence for both Thursday, April 23 and the following day. He marked Purpose as: Other. Under Remarks, he typed: "Urgent situation requiring close personal attention." If the boss asked for "administratively acceptable evidence," Bill's first inclination was to strangle him. His second choice was to promise plausible deniability. But no, there would never be qualified immunity for Robert Fulbright.

His first call was to the forest fisheries biologist. "Hey Roger, it's Bill. Can you give me a call when you get in? Call my personal cell. I'm wondering if your brother still owns that Halloween store in Traverse City? Was it in the Cherry Pit Plaza? I have an urgent need for some masks. Like today. But Roger, please don't say anything to anyone else. Need to know only."

A few years back, the forest fire staff had purchased a few body cams, mostly so they could create training videos of prescribed burns and actual fire incident responses. These were popular for a while, until the recordings captured inappropriate comments. This was particularly unfortunate as the Forest Service was trying to tamp down on sexual harassment, especially among fire crews. Bill assumed he could have free use of any body cams not already *accidentally* destroyed in the field.

Next he sent an e-mail to the wildlife biologists in the Baldwin, Cadillac and Manistee offices, asking who had cans of bear repellant on hand or, if they didn't, did they know somewhere Bill could purchase a half dozen cans on short notice.

He settled back and reviewed his scribbled list. When had his handwriting become so illegible? He shook his head in frustration. He had forgotten to write a timeline of events that he needed to follow for the next 36 hours to ensure that people were in the right place, doing the right thing, and at the right time. He would need to go shopping for the remaining supplies, then reach out to Pete Simmons in the Manistee County Sheriff's Department, as well as call back to three retired Forest Service LEOs who still lived nearby. He also hoped to recruit a handful of volunteers from American Legion Post 93. He checked his wrist watch again and wondered if 24 hours was enough time. He sent an e-mail to check-in with Annette to see how her research was progressing.

Before he unplugged his personal laptop, he posted an ad on the Grand Rapids Craigslist page, seeking help for an Event in the Gigs section:

NEED 5 PEOPLE TO BE PART OF A CREW OF

SIGN WAVERS OR STREET THEATER!
You get paid $50 PER HOUR, up to three hours.
Must be available 10 a.m. to 1 p.m. Friday.
Must have a phone and reliable transportation.
Must have a professional attitude.
Fun and good paying job!
Sign-on bonus if you respond now!
TEXT THE PHRASE "THEATER" now!

That should get some response. If they didn't have enough replies by the end of the day, Rick would need to reach out to the members of Legion Post 58 in Grand Rapids.

Next he called Elizabeth and invited her to join him for a walk up the hill into the cemetery. She arrived at his office door in 10 minutes. As they went out the back door, she extended an open cigarette pack toward him. "I've quit three times since the boss got here."

Bill accepted a smoke. He told himself that no one should smoke alone. "I quit after Bosnia. But this seems like the same thankless work."

"Thankless, hell. Try Sisyphean." She held out a Zippo. "Am I saying that correctly?"

"Oh, yes. Nicely played." He stopped and cupped his hand to light the cigarette. "Did you know that in England they call a cigarette a 'fag'?"

She fired up her own smoke. "Really? I'd expect something more like 'Prince Albert in a stick.'"

He chuckled. "Listen. Do you have any time you could take off? I need someone to hold a smartphone in Grand Rapids about 10 a.m. tomorrow. I'm paying fifty dollars an hour."

She stopped abruptly and turned toward him. "Yes, I've got plenty of credit and comp hours. And yes, I could go down to Grand Rapids as soon as Randy gets home from work. Is this about that little girl?"

Bill nodded as he inhaled on the cigarette.

"And you think I need to be paid to help her?"

"I know what your salary is; it's in the forest budget."

She took a few steps toward the cemetery and looked up the hillside as she pulled her coat closed with one hand. Her other hand held the cigarette away from her body. When she turned back, she took a long drag on her smoke. "So only you and Jack can worry about a sick child? What do you call it 'noblesse oblige'? Well, I've spent the past two years of my life worried about a child, day after day and night after night. Fevers, pink eye, ear infections. Up endless nights. I can't imagine what that mother is going through, but I think I know a lot better than you."

Bill stood there a few minutes, finishing the cigarette. People tended to forget that he recently had a family of his own, so he could relate to the many tribulations of childhood and adolescence: the constant colds; learning to read; the embarrassment of spelling bees; sports tryouts; and the first discovery of an opposite sex.

"I'm sorry," Elizabeth said. "Brandon was an amazing kid. Of course I want to help."

"Thank you. I never intended to insult you. But I need your help." He dropped the butt on the ground and stamped it out. "I'll text you an address. Tonight I'll call with details once I have everything in place. Please check your mailbox before you leave work. There'll be an envelope for you. Don't open it until you hear from me."

April 23

"I see the disinfectant that knocks it out in a minute, one minute. And is there a way we can do something like that by injection inside, or almost a cleaning? Because you see it gets inside the lungs and it does a tremendous number on the lungs, so it would be interesting to check that."

— President of the United States of America,
at White House coronavirus daily briefing.

April 23

Regina worried about moving Mary to a temporary home. The ranger's cabin had been unoccupied for at least six months, well before the arrival of coronavirus on American shores. Still, she was anxious about leaving Frank alone if the protesters did come to Sand Lake. Also, she would lose her access to the internet at the Wellston library. What if St. Jude contacted her with a potential opening?

Her forehead rested on the shank of her hand, her elbow propped firmly on the table. Yet the ranger himself insisted how necessary this move was. Frank would remain behind, along with some type of protection. The idea was to have Mary safely far away for at least a day. Now their quarantine was threatened, just as she worried as when she first saw the protest signs that read "sacrifice the weak."

"Frank, is this going to be OK?" she asked when he returned to the Damon. "If we go to Hamlin Lake? The doc is coming with us, and Rick is going down to Grand Rapids for some reason. That means he'll have to quarantine when he gets back. But you'll be here alone. What if these protest people break through the gate? Will you be safe?"

Frank motioned with both hands that she could calm down. "I think Bill has a plan. The sheriff's department will be out here, and there will be some retired law enforcement officers, too. Bill's talked about getting some other help as well." He settled into the booth seat opposite her. "Are you ok going to Jack's cabin? Would you rather try to find a motel that's open?"

Regina sat up and put on the game face she wore back at Sacred Heart Academy when her basketball team was down by ten or more. "I think the cabin's a good choice. Jack says no one has been there since November. And I'll pack us some food and what things we need. I'm glad to have the major with us, just in case."

"I'm more worried than you, stuck out there with that crazy Rory and his dog. Who knows what trouble he can cause."

Regina reassured her husband a smile. "I think our friend Jack has handled Rory for us. Notice he hasn't been around lately?"

"That's why I worry. Why has Jack felt he needed to keep him and the dog away? Now Rory's going to watch over you?" He stood and went to the coffee maker for another cup.

"I wouldn't wonder but that Rory learned a lesson after that terrible day. We'll be fine. And the good doctor is bringing one of Rick's shotguns."

April 23

When Bill delivered his request for leave to the boss's inbox, he felt relief that Robert was busy on the telephone. So he walked back down the hallway and told Elizabeth his plans, just so he would have a witness. He also told the front desk, and sent an e-mail to ALL EMPLOYEES to notify everyone that he would not be available for two days, except by cell phone. And he filed a copy of his signed request in the week's folder in his file cabinet.

On his personal e-mail, he sent a request for assistance to the membership roster of American Legion Post 93 in Cadillac. He asked interested individuals to call him or arrive at the Sand Lake in Wellston Friday morning at 0900 hours; he offered fifty dollars per hour. Then he headed out to enjoy his day.

First stop was an ATM machine at which he withdrew a few hundred dollars on a credit card. Next stop, same routine with a different credit card. Third stop, more cash, new card. Then a stop to withdraw cash from his credit union. And one last stop to make a withdrawal from his bank account. If he shuffled the cash wearing gloves, he would end up with about $5,000 cash that would be difficult to trace back to him.

Next stop at Meijer on the North end of Cadillac. Bill selected one of the big shopping carts and headed down the main aisle. He spent some time in the home improvement section before moving onto sporting goods, next office supplies and finally housewares. He found enough that a trip to the hardware store was unnecessary. Bill headed out to the Wagoneer. Time to move on.

He drove west on M-55 and arrived at Cadillac Archery and Armory just as the owner turned on the light and opened the door. Bill had been buying reloading supplies there for years, so Mark didn't question his purchases: a dozen cans of bear repellant and two dozen personal defense sirens. He also added fifteen sets of ear plugs and fifteen pairs of hearing protection ear muffs. Mark totaled it all up, looking at Bill like he'd suddenly gone all prepper.

"Hey, do you have a box of FMJ for a 1911 Colt?" Bill asked.

"Just for plinking around?" Mark sounded surprised.

"No, I was thinking a box of hollow points. I know nobody shoots them for fun."

"I think I may have a box in the back. Let me go look." In ten minutes, Mark returned with a box of Federal Personal Defense 45 ACP 30 Grain Jacketed Hollow Points. "I've got better rounds if you're taking down the Dogman."

Bill nodded, hoping not to give away too much of why he needed these things. "I wouldn't want to hurt the Dogman. He's a better story than Paul Bunyan."

Mark totaled up the damage, and Bill was on his way. As he loaded the items into the back of the Wagoneer alongside the Meijer haul, his personal cell phone rang.

"Hi, Annette. How's your day going?"

"Lots of fun stuff," she said. "Yes, looks like Grand Rapids will be a good place to visit tomorrow morning. Do you want an address?"

"Send me a text? Any chance you can you create a couple of shell Facebook accounts for me? I want to record what's happening there and also broadcast it."

"OK. Sure. Let me think through the logistics. How long do you need to have it online?"

"Might be less than 15 minutes."

"What platform are you thinking?"

"Just nothing agency related. Create an account with my name on Facebook or Instagram. Whatever is easy for just a little private video, with an option to take it broad."

"Viral. It's called viral," she said.

"OK, that too."

"Let me see what I can do."

Bill closed the tailgate and climbed into the Jeep. Other than a few masks from the Halloween store, he thought he was in pretty good shape for supplies. He'd received three responses to his Craigslist ad seeking a theater troupe in Grand Rapids. A good response before noon. Now several hours of logistics work and then a Sand Lake Surprise.

April 23

Another protest aimed at the Governor's stay-at-home order took place Thursday. This one took place outside the governor's mansion in Lansing. A handful of people were in attendance to express their displeasure with her. However, prior to the protest, the Michigan Senate Majority Leader spoke out against protesters who go to the homes of people involved. The Republican said he supports free speech and the right to protest, but the demonstrations should take place at government buildings.

"I strongly exhort those organizing the protests to limit the venue to public spaces and around government buildings. Don't protest at homes. Even the public Governor's residence. It is indeed public property. But the adjacent properties and neighborhood are not," he wrote.

– Mlive.

April 23

After Major McKettrick left for Hamlin Lake with Regina and Mary in the DuLong's Explorer and Rick headed to Grand Rapids in his own pick-up truck, Frank was alone in the campground. He ate a cold ham sandwich at the washed picnic table. He worried whether all these plans Jack and Bill had designed would keep everyone safe. And he regretted doubting Regina's fears when she first encountered the online hate.

Toward dusk, he heard a rumble of vehicles on the road into the campground. This was much earlier than the ranger predicted. He reached into the door of the Damon where he kept a Remington Model 870. As he walked toward the gate, already seven campers were in line, awaiting entry.

He carried his shotgun with the barrel skyward and a finger on the trigger guard as he approached the entry point. "Hello. I'm the campground host here," he called. "I'm sorry, but we're not open for camping yet."

The driver of the lead rig got out. "Hello. I'm Joe McClellan. Jack Ferguson said we could camp here the next couple nights. We'll be practicing our traditional drumming. We needed an outdoor space because of this damned virus."

Frank moved his gun to his opposite hand and aimed it downward. "Sure, Jack told me you'd be here. Sorry about the shotgun. I wasn't expecting you for a few hours yet. You heard we may have some trouble tomorrow?"

"Yeah, Gertie told us. We're to be, what you call them, Silent Observers, except for the drumming? But I think we all brought along a deer rifle, or something, in case we get an opportunity for target practice." He loosed a somewhat sinister laugh.

"I think Bill's hoping to avoid that," Frank said. "Jack said he's in charge tomorrow morning."

"I know Bill Reinhardt. He lives near me over in Harrietta. Shame about his family that way."

Frank didn't know what Joe meant, but he nodded in sympathy. "I guess Jack's going to be on television all morning."

"Good place for Jack. Reminds me of some actor. My wife

thinks he looks like a guy on her soaps. I think he was in westerns, like John Wayne stuff."

"Yeah, they were sure good, not like the new ones with robots and aliens." Frank stopped when he realized he was talking about cowboy movies with an actual Native American. "So Jack said you guys are going to camp on every other site so that you had a safe distance."

"Yep. Jack and Gertie worked this whole thing out. It's not a usual drum circle practice where we sit around one big drum. We borrowed drums from other tribes and asked some of our young members to bring the drums they created. We'll do our best to maintain social distance." Joe headed back toward his big RV.

"So you'll take care of spacing everyone out in the campsites?"

"Sure." Joe laughed. "We've got a long history of camping outdoors."

April 24

In the wake of the President's comments during the White House coronavirus news briefing on Thursday, the CDC reminded Americans on Friday not to consume disinfectants.

The CDC tweeted a link and added, "Household cleaners and disinfectants can cause health problems when not used properly. Follow the instructions on the product label to ensure safe and effective use. Learn more about cleaning and disinfecting your home."

Meanwhile, the Surgeon General encouraged the public to heed the advice of doctors.

"A reminder to all Americans – PLEASE always talk to your health provider first before administering any treatment/medication to yourself or a loved one," the Surgeon General tweeted. "Your safety is paramount, and doctors and nurses have years of training to recommend what's safe and effective."

– 7 ABC, Denver.

April 24

Early morning television is an interesting mix of news, pre-recorded health reports and upbeat anchor banter. Bill sat through all this patiently, waiting for Jack's appearance. At least no one on air was touting the president's Covid-19 cure of gargling disinfectants. There were already plenty of other groups, including some churches, promoting a bleach cure for coronavirus.

Jack's remote interview was conducted from his office in the district ranger station. He handled the question about the arrangements for campground hosts well. The reporters' summaries sounded too much like the suggestion that Jack was accepting comments on whether or not little Mary should live.

The ranger's most effective pitch accompanied a photo on screen of Mary snuggling her Easter bunny. As the photo played, Jack asked, "I hope people see that a little girl and her family who work at the campground should be safe is what the Forest Service means when we say, 'Caring for the land and serving people.' Of course, we'll open the campgrounds when the Governor's orders permit it." Jack done good, Bill thought. That should go well with the Regional Forester.

Bill watched only two of Jack's interviews that morning, hoping that during the third he didn't suddenly burst into a rousing version of, "I'm a lumberjack and I'm OK." Checking his field watch, Bill saw he had just enough time to meet a few retired law enforcement officers at Chittenden. If he hurried. These meetings used to be easier when he could drive just two blocks up the street to the Hillside Restaurant or over to the Frosty Cup on M-115. Then one closed, and the other burned. But maybe a remote location like the old tree nursery was better; they needed to devise a strategy for dealing with any trouble on the National Forest.

Bill wore the battle dress uniform he last wore in the Balkans. If he'd stayed on active duty another year or two, he would have received the newer combat utility uniform. But Camille was ready to come home. Wherever they had been stationed, there was never a warm reception for tribal women among the military wives. On one base, the wives' club hosted a showing of the Disney movie *Pocahontas* at their monthly meeting; there were no other movie offerings during his assignment there. In the bottom drawer of his dresser, he found a wooden box that contained his rank insignia and other badges. He secured the twin silver bars on the front of his green utility cap. Finally, he strapped his khaki web belt with the holster affixed at his back. His boxed Colt 1911 sat on the kitchen table, next to the box of FMJ.

In addition to the retired Forest Service LEOs, Bill expected help from other agencies. The sheriff had agreed that a few cruisers from the Manistee Sheriff's Department would be available along county roads. Jack had also alerted the State Police post in Cadillac that trouble might be arriving in Wellston on one of several possible state highways. In Bill's mind, the purpose of the operation was two-fold: Disrupt enemy action, then deceive and divert the enemy. Classic rifle squad tactics. Not having a rifle squad available, he had a third purpose in mind: Repel.

Instead of the Wagoneer, he went into the pole barn and pulled the canvas tarp off a 1952 M38 Jeep, a postwar model with no comfort features. The shorter wheelbase had a tighter turning radius than the Wagoneer and better maneuverability over land. He pulled up next to the bigger Jeep and loaded the contents from the back end into the smaller rig. He placed the Colt on the passenger seat and headed for the rendezvous at Chittenden.

April 24

A handful of GM employees and management will return to work next week to prepare for a restart in production soon. A few skilled trades and management employees will return to the Flint plant next week as planning continues on how to safely reopen the plant.

"That includes notifying some team members (primarily salaried and a small number of skilled trades) that we may need them to report to work soon. But we have not announced a restart date," a GM spokesperson said in an email to MLive-The Flint Journal.

However, the UAW president says the idea to reopen in early May is risky and wants to see more data before UAW members go back to work.

– Mlive.

April 24

A reunion of retired law enforcement officers has a unique ambiance. They stood together in the cool morning, leaning on the front fenders of a pair of pickup trucks. Their three trucks had rifle racks in the rear window. Bill noticed that the racks were full that morning. He assumed all three men also carried side arms, as he did. For them, it was a force of habit acquired over twenty plus years in the field. For Bill, the need had been strictly situational.

"Good morning, Captain," Greg said, touching his hand to his forehead in a friendly salute. "You're looking dapper this morning. I don't think I could fit into my old uniform."

Bill extended his hand, also a force of habit. Greg accepted the handshake, as did the other two men. Habit dies hard. None of the three wore a mask; not from any political stance, but simply because they were among friends. All three were clean-shaven, perhaps from habit as well. Henry had been a conservation officer in West Virginia until ginseng poachers began harassing him and his family. He went to a federal job on the Monongahela National Forest, moving more than a hundred miles away, but the threats didn't stop. So he transferred up to the Oscoda office on the Huron side of the Huron-Manistee. At 68, Jerry was the oldest of the four men, but still trim and agile. He had worked in the Baldwin office for thirty years after starting as a fire fighter in the summers during college. He had the unenviable job of dealing with the drunken anglers and boaters on the Pere Marquette River.

"So where's Rory?" Henry asked. "Isn't this his territory?"

"Hopefully at a safe distance," Jerry observed.

Greg chimed in last, speaking with a serious tone, "And working with Legos."

When the three finished laughing, Bill explained the strategy. "Jack asked Rory to sit over in the Nordhouse Wilderness to keep a watch on traffic along Nurnberg Road. That's the access to Jack's cabin on Hamlin Lake. We've got the girl and her mother staying there while we deal with this."

"OK, wilderness is a good place for Rory. Next time send him to the Bob Marshall, will you?" Jerry said, as he reached for the thermos of coffee on his truck hood.

"So, Bill, you still plan to make initial contact?" Greg asked. "Jack said he was going to be waiting in his office for media calls."

"Wait, isn't that your job?" Henry asked with a laugh. "You been demoted again?"

"It was one time. I refused to shoot a civilian and was demoted. Now kill a civilian and you get a Presidential pardon."

"So Greg, tell us your plan for today so we can rip it all to hell," Jerry said.

"Thanks for the vote of confidence. Let's go inside so I can draw it out on the chalk board," Greg said. Using Jack's key, Bill unlocked the restored tree nursery and led the way to the conference room.

When the lights came up inside, the three lawmen expressed their surprise at the renovations.

"Wow, this sure turned out nice," Jerry said.

"Heck, I might unretire to work here for a while. I never had an office like this." Greg wandered away from the others, studying the renovations. "Yeah, but I'll bet they're just going to move the same crappy furniture they have now in here. It'll look just as ugly as the old office," Greg said.

"Who pissed in your coffee this morning?" Henry asked Greg.

"Forty years in the government and never once had a comfortable office chair," Greg said. "Finally just bought one with my own money."

"You had your own money?" Jerry asked. "I thought Sue controlled it all."

At this point, Bill wished he had moved the reunion an hour earlier. There was still plenty to do before the anticipated start time of the protests. "If I may, gentlemen, I'd like to discuss an urgent matter."

The three laughed together. "Then why'd you call us?" Henry asked. "We're retired. The only thing urgent now is getting to the restroom at four in the morning."

"You, too?" Jerry asked. "I'm trying these saw palmetto pills from the radio commercials, but I don't know if they help."

"Please!" Bill said sharply. "There's a lot going on this morning. Unfortunately, our guests did not RSVP, so I don't know how many we may be dealing with." He quickly drew a sketch of the Sand

Lake Campground, showing the primary entry points, along with the key points to protect. The first objective was to keep the protesters from breaching the gate. However, the second objective was to keep the protesters from entering the Damon camper and potentially contaminating it with the novel coronavirus. Lastly, Bill did not want the protesters to know Mary was already somewhere else because he did not want them looking for her elsewhere. He hoped to resolve the matter here and now. "So far, none of these protests in Lansing has gotten violent, although some bring a variety of weapons. So we need to be ready for anything."

"I want to stress that. Annette thinks the Liberation Army may get some help from a couple of militia. Keep an eye out," Greg said, as he leaned toward the crude map of the campground. "I'd like to keep them together and force them back together before they get entrenched. Remember our back-up from the Legion Post aren't any younger than we are. Jerry, can you take a position at the camper? Try to keep Frank calm. If you hear gunfire, you'll also need to reassure the tribal drummers. I'm sure at least a few brought weapons, but we can't have them engage. Unless they're threatened directly."

Greg turned to Henry. "I'd like you with me. Depending upon how many vehicles they bring, that will put some of them out on the county road. The sheriff's folks will deal with any obstruction of traffic out there.

"If they try to push past Bill, we fortify the gate. The folks from the Legion will be positioned at the gate. Henry, you take charge of them. Their job is to make breaching the gate uncomfortable. All I ask is don't shoot Reagan. Jack sent a sawyer ready to drop a few trees behind the gate."

"That all sounds great, but what about if it goes south?" Henry asked.

"Yeah, these boys like to bring out their big guns. What if they figure out how to use them?" Jerry asked.

Bill smiled at the three men. "When we go over to Sand Lake, the sheriff has agreed to deputize us. In the case that we need to protect life or limb, I've brought along two paintball guns for each

of you. I expect they'll be wearing body armor, so aim at the vulnerable spots, other than eyes."

Henry put a hand over his groin. "That's a big 'ouch.'"

"A few last items to cover." Bill held aloft a small pocket radio.
"Here are some cheap walkie-talkies. Not much range so it's unlikely
anyone can monitor us. If you see intruders, click five taps. Second,
if it goes bad and we have to step up to superior firepower, try to
minimize loss of life. Finally, I'd like each of you to wear one of
these." He handed out the body cams. "Just in case we do need to
resort to firepower, this will give us evidence of what caused it."

The three LEOs exchanged worried looks.

Scratching his chin, Jerry said, "Always good to know where we
stand, I suppose."

April 24

"We ask every American to maintain vigilance and hygiene, social distancing and voluntary use of face coverings. We're opening our country. It's very exciting to see. We have a lot of talent involved, from governors down to people that just stand there and help you with the doors. There's been tremendous talent involved and tremendous spirit from our country. The country is a great place, and it's going to be greater than ever before. I really believe that."

> – President of the United States of America,
> at White House coronavirus daily briefing.

April 24

So Operation Safe Rabbit began. In his M38 Jeep, Bill led the three big pickup trucks to the campground entrance. Henry and Greg parked their rigs nose-to-nose parallel to the campground gate. Bill promised to return shortly, then led Jerry over to the campground, where they met Frank.

"They came looking for you," Frank said to Bill. "I didn't know what you wanted them to do, so I asked them to wait. I let that Forest Service guy over there come in because you said to check out the trees."

"That's fine. I'll deal with them all. Would you take Jerry over and show him around the campsite. He's going to stay with you until we get this resolved."

Bill turned back toward the line of cars waiting on the other side of the gate. He waved with his arm for everyone to come meet with him. The men who emerged from the cars wore in a mix of military garb and hunter camouflage. Based on appearances, his volunteer corps ranged in age from 40 to maybe 70. To ensure he had someone turn out, he had not specified either age or ability.

"Good morning, my name is Bill Reinhardt. I sent the message to the Legion membership asking for help. Some of you may have heard that protesters are coming here this morning because they think it's unfair that a little girl with leukemia is here with her father, one of our campground hosts. As you all know, the Governor has closed campgrounds and boat launches. They want to liberate this campground. But if they contaminate the camper or the campground with coronavirus, that little girl could die. I will be out on the county road. If I can't stop them, I'll come back to the gate. This morning you'll be working directly for Warrant Officer Greg LeMay. He was an Army MP and later a law enforcement officer on the forest."

Greg stepped forward. "Gentlemen, good morning. Thank you for coming out this morning. My goal is to keep the Liberation Army from entering the campground. We have what I think is a very good strategy for that. I also want to assure you that my plan is to resolve this without gunfire. If you hear any shots, I want you all to leave on 12 Mile Road west or if you can't drive out, head over to the beach. Any questions?"

A younger vet with a thick beard that reached his chest raised his hand. "Sir, so this is about that little girl who was in the news?"

"Yes."

"Wish things had been this clear in Fallujah. Hell, if a child is your enemy, you've got some serious mental problems."

One of the older men spoke to Bill. "Excuse me, Captain, I was an Air Force tech sergeant, mostly in Germany. Crewman. Never had combat training. So put me next to someone who's been through it. I'll manage. But I don't want your money."

The other men nodded. Another man raised his hand. "Have you thought about placing our vehicles on either side of the gate so they can't just drive around us? I could wrap my tow cable around the gate post or a tree to anchor either side."

"Were you a Seabee?" Greg asked.

The man nodded. "Can Do, sir."

"Then would you take charge of moving the vehicles into barriers? Any other suggestions?" Greg asked.

"You know these trees could really slow the enemy down if we drop them strategically. A dozen trees could be impenetrable," another said.

"I've got that covered," Bill said. "Now a couple of details. I'd like you all to wear medical masks, because most of these people will be coming from the South, where they have higher Covid rates. I also expect everyone to wear one of these." He hoisted a Ronald Reagan Halloween mask. "It's important that these people cannot identify you. If they do, they may harass you, steal your identity, whatever. And because we don't know what you'll encounter, I have bought heavy-duty rain suits for you. Questions so far?"

The same bearded young man raised his hand. "I brought my Glock 19 in the car. Can I bring it along?"

Greg stepped in front of Bill to reply. "Please don't. I've got two non-lethal weapons for each of you. I absolutely do not want any of you to engage in a gunfight today. Is that clear, gentlemen?"

April 24

More than a thousand people cheering "USA" and "open up" gathered on the steps of the Wisconsin State Capitol on Friday to protest the Governor's restrictions on their daily lives, rallying in close quarters on a day the state saw its highest daily increase in positive cases of coronavirus.

The crowd stood shoulder to shoulder — physically and in solidarity — in defiance of the Democratic governor's order to keep businesses and schools closed, and people apart, in an effort to limit the spread of highly contagious virus for which there is no vaccine.

Circulating among the crowd were petitions to recall the Governor and signs that said "All Workers Are Essential" and "Death ... is preferable to communism."

Dozens, perhaps hundreds, of American flags accompanied the protesters and some openly carried assault-style rifles. A guillotine also was on the Capitol steps among protesters.

The same day as the protest, Wisconsin saw its highest daily increase in confirmed positive cases of the virus — 304. Thursday night, nurses lined the state Capitol steps with 1,300 electronic candles in tribute to those currently hospitalized with Covid-19 in Wisconsin. The candles were meant to be a silent counter-protest.

– Milwaukee Journal Sentinel.

April 24

Elizabeth phoned just after 9:30 a.m. She kept the conversation brief and guarded.

"On location now."

"And Rick is there?" Bill asked.

"Yes."

"And our actors?"

"Three so far."

He checked his wristwatch. "Well, it's still early. And Rick brought the masks and signs?"

"Yes. Nice touch."

"And I now have a Facebook account?" This step worried him a little.

"Two. One to broadcast and one to view. Annette says it's not as hard to fake them as the Great Zucker thinks."

"And Instagram?"

"Of course," she said.

"OK, far and wide, but on my command."

"You know me. The very model of discretion."

April 24

Michigan's Governor lengthened her stay-at-home order through May 15.

The new order will require people to wear homemade face coverings when they enter enclosed public spaces. It will also lift some restrictions on outdoor activities and allow some workers to go back to work.

Per the governor's order, people won't have to wear face coverings when they're taking a walk in the neighborhood, but when they go to the grocery store, they should be wearing one. No one will be subject to criminal penalty for going without a mask.

Additionally, landscapers, lawn-service companies, and nurseries can return to work, subject to strict social distancing. Retailers that do not sell necessary supplies may reopen for curbside pick-up and for delivery. Big box stores can reopen "closed areas," like garden centers. And bike repair and maintenance can come back online.

The order will also allow motorized boating and golf, but no golf carts, consistent with sound social distancing. It will also permit individuals to travel between their residences, though traveling during the epidemic is still strongly discouraged.

The new executive order takes effect immediately.

– WXYZ, Detroit.

April 24

Henry did not seem comfortable sitting in Bill's M38. He still carried the heft from his days on the Mountaineers' frontline. He fidgeted and finally draped one leg over the open door jamb. "So, we sent a bunch of children to fight the Germans? No wonder it took years to knock them out."

"Imagine how you'd do in a submarine," Bill said. They sat 200 yards away from intersection of the county road and the entrance to Sand Lake campground.

"That's why you're stuck with me. I love the great outdoors." He flashed a big grin. "So what's the plan?"

"I'll try to talk them down. Won't work, but have to offer terms. Then we retreat to the gate." He glanced at his phone. When he called up Facebook, a half dozen protesters appeared, milling about on a residential street. They wore disturbing Halloween masks that covered their entire heads. They looked like serpentine ghouls.

Henry elbowed him. "You need five clicks?" He pointed toward the East, where several pick-up trucks appeared. "You think they're here for tea?"

"Why don't you get in your truck? If I click three, you head for the gate. But, listen, if something happens to me, feel free to shoot every last one of the bastards."

"That's legal?" Henry laughed. "If it matters to you, I'm fully locked and loaded."

Bill left the M38 running. As they stepped out of the Jeep, Bill dialed his personal cell phone. The other end picked up, but no voice spoke. "Go live," he said. He clicked off. Henry opened the driver's door of his truck, and Bill saw the two paint guns. There were also several long guns propped for easy access. He felt he may have come under-gunned in comparison.

A line of seven pick-up trucks came to a stop in front of Henry's big truck that straddled the gravel road to the campground. As he walked toward the new visitors, Bill tugged the strings of a surgical mask over his ears and casually reached to feel his Colt 1911 holstered at his back. Reassurance. The trucks began to rev their engines in frustration. Bill wondered why they didn't simply drive around Henry's rig.

When he was directly in front of the line of trucks, Bill raised his hands. Then he called out, "Hey, is Gary here yet? He's in charge, right? Is he here?"

The driver's window of the first truck opened. "Yeah. What do you want?"

"I think we need to talk for a minute? I want to clear up some confusion." To Bill's surprise, the truck door opened and a small man wearing tactical gear dropped to the ground.

"We're not confused," the man said. "Open the outdoors for everyone." The man wore a tactical vest and camouflage cargo pants. A semi-automatic weapon hung over his chest. Bill wondered how he managed to drive with that array. Was there an online course in pretend soldiering?

Bill checked the time on his watch. Four minutes to go. "So listen, you know all campgrounds in the state are closed, including federal sites, right?"

"That's why we're here, moron. It's time to liberate Michigan."

Bill smiled to see that a leader in a "Liberation Army" didn't recognize or acknowledge his rank. He glanced at his watch and parsed his words for time. "See, at the moment, the campground is full. Sovereign tribes may use the forest facilities while exercising their treaty rights. You may not violate a site closure, and you may not interfere with the exercise of tribal treaty rights." As if on cue, the sound of rhythmic drumming filled the woods.

"Screw you," the head of the Liberation Army of Michigan said. "We have rights. First and Second Amendment. Get the fuck out of our way."

"You know the First Amendment?" Bill didn't like how this was playing out, but as he and Jack agreed weeks earlier, *All in.*

"Sure, free speech, free religion, free gathering."

"Peaceably to assemble, you mean, right? Like this?" Bill took out his phone and showed Gary a screen of Facebook Live. Several masked protesters walked in a circle, carrying posters that read: *Liberate = Exterminate.* "Nice to see people exercising their freedoms, don't you think? This is live from Joliet Street down in Grand Rapids. Right now. Jeez, what's that street number?"

"What the hell is this?"

Bill chuckled intentionally. "This, Gary Reynolds, is that stage in military engagement in which the superior force offers terms. Usually unconditional surrender. But I'm willing to let you retreat. No harm, no foul. If you need me to explain these terms, you just ask."

Gary looked past Bill to where Henry stood behind his truck with a pair of long guns laid across the hood. "How do you know my name?"

"Look, Gary, you can go where you want. Dark web. 4chan. 8chan. 8kun. You're not invisible." Bill held up his cell phone again. "Would you like one of my friends to go ring your mother's doorbell now? What is it she has? Parkinson's?"

The leader of the Liberation Army of Michigan took two steps back. "Two of you? You're threatening me with just two? Look at us? And you're going after my parents?" He thrust out his chest.

Bill took another cell phone from a pocket and pressed a number. "OK, go viral." Bill smiled, even as he wanted to break the finger Gary kept across his trigger guard. "I tried to warn you. Right now, Facebook Live is watching the protesters at your folks' house. A colleague will be posting it to other sites for all your little friends to enjoy. Sure you want to push this? It only gets worse from here."

"My family!" Gary growled. His trigger finger tensed.

Bill stepped so close that Gary couldn't raise his weapon if he tried. "Your family? How about any family with a sick child? Or a grandparent? Didn't your bosses tell you that the sick will die if you win? Or are you too stupid to understand that? How do Parkinson's patients do with coronavirus?"

"Fuck you, moron," Gary hissed.

"Captain, to you. Don't come any farther."

"Fuck you!" Gary screamed.

"I warned you," Bill said. "Do not come any farther." As Bill climbed into his Jeep, he clicked the little hand-held radio three times in rapid sequence, then five more. Henry was already in the cab of his truck. They sped down the road to the gate, and Henry parked his truck directly in front of the gate. Bill drove his M38 around the array of vehicles to the left of the gate. When he pulled up behind the gate, he stepped out to watch the approach of the

Liberation Army. Henry was already behind his vehicle with an array of paintball weapons and long guns resting against the front fender. Greg came sauntering over with his own weapons, a paint-ball rifle and a 30.06.

The drumming that echoed through the forest stopped abruptly. The sudden silence sounded eerie.

Gary and his militia screeched to a halt in front of the gate and climbed out of their monster trucks. They also wore varying types of tactical gear. Not a one of them wore any face covering. All sported some kind of menacing weapon. If Bill hadn't watched several hours of video from their prior protests, he would be more concerned. But tactics matter.

On either side of the gate, the vets stood along an arc in front of their vehicles. Head to toe, they wore camouflage rain gear. Their faces were hidden behind full Ronald Reagan masks. Beneath the Halloween masks, most wore both medical masks and ear plugs. They were, as Bill thought briefly, ready to rumble.

The Liberation Army gathered in a huddle in front of Gary's Chevy crew cab pick-up. They seemed to be waiting for direction. Greg took advantage of their confusion.

"Ears," Greg called. At his order, the Reagans, as well as Henry and Bill, put protective earmuffs in place. He then blew a sharp whistle to penetrate their double protection. "Noise," he shouted. From their pockets, the Reagans each took personal security devices, removed the lanyards to activate the noise and tossed them at the feet of the protesters. At 130 decibels apiece, the racket of two dozen alarms interrupted any attempt to issue commands that Gary may have planned.

"Take out any itchy fingers," Greg said quietly to Henry. He gave two short blasts on the whistle. The Reagans advanced a few feet and then began to spray the cans of bear repellant over the heads of the Liberation Army. At 25 feet, the cloud had the desired effect when the mist began to settle, and the mask-less Liberators began to choke and cough violently. Some dropped to their knees. Bill saw Gary retching along the side of the roadway.

Greg blew his whistle again to halt the spraying and conserve the repellant for a second blast if it became necessary. A few members of the Liberation Army retreated to the protection of their trucks. They backed out and sped off in a flurry of gravel.

"You think I should go take their weapons?" Henry asked, pointing to the few attackers still crouched on the ground. "Just so they don't get nasty when they recover?"

"Yeah, good idea. Mask up first." Greg looked around for a moment, then pointed at one of the Reagans with a fringe of dark beard around the chin of his mask. "Take him, too. He'll be helpful." Greg assumed an Iraq vet would have experience disarming a civilian.

Henry and the young vet encountered little resistance while relieving the Liberation Army of their weapons, from which they ejected the magazines and threw them into the adjacent field. They returned the empty weapons to their owners with a shove.

After most of the Liberation Army trucks sped away, Greg gave a single long blast on his whistle to signify "all clear." "Ears off," he called. When the Reagans removed their hearing muffs, he said, "Just dump everything you're wearing here by the gate post. See Bill before you leave to get paid."

Bill went to where Gary was on his hands and knees vomiting; as the front man, he probably inhaled the brunt of the repellant. The commandant of the Liberation Army of Michigan struggled to get to his feet. "Sorry, Gary, you didn't leave me any choice. I guess we're kind of even. Down in Grand Rapids, I hired a bunch of actors to protest on Joliet Street. And you brought a bunch of clowns acting like soldiers here. But I brought real soldiers here. That's checkmate."

"Fuck you." Gary spat weakly at Bill, but his spittle landed on the butt of his own rifle instead. "Should have left my parents alone."

Bill grasped Gary's right hand, glad he had decided to wear surgical gloves, just the same as the Reagans. "Oh, now family matters to you?" Bill twisted Gary's hand back toward his wrist with a thumb in the middle of Gary's palm. "Who is it you work for? The Conservative Family Agenda? Family matters to them, right?" He applied more pressure on Gary's palm, forcing him back down to his knees on the ground. "You could have gone to any campground in the state, but you came here because of a sick child. Don't talk to me about your family values." Bill leaned closer and spoke directly into Gary's ear. "Oh, dear. Your troops are retreating." Gripping his scalp, Bill turned Gary's head so he could see the line of trucks abandoning the protest. "They didn't even wait to get their three hundred dollars."

Bill stood and pulled Gary to his feet by the collar. "Come on, time to go home to mommy. Let's hope you get paid after all the live streaming. Be sure to check the corners of the dark web. You'll be all kinds of memes tonight." Bill dragged the man over to his truck and opened the door to shove him inside. "Don't come back." He resisted the temptation to slam the truck door on one of Gary's limbs.

Bill walked back to the gate where Greg and Henry stood, both armed in multiple ways. Bill eased his 1911 Colt out of its holster and held it at his thigh in case Gary's pick-up lurched toward them.

"Glad I never pissed you off," Henry observed. "You're kind of touchy."

"No, I just get annoyed with people pretending to be military. Like that whole Stolen Valor thing."

As they watched, Gary backed his truck into a sharp turn and headed back out of the campground, Henry unloaded his rifle. "So what would you call those boys? Two Minutemen?" he asked. "Like the uniforms and the weapons, but not the discipline." He turned to face Greg. "By the way, I liked the noise to disrupt any command structure. But you're not concerned about assault charges for the grizzly gas?"

"I don't think Reagan's got anything to worry about; he's got a pretty strong alibi," Greg said.

"Besides which, no way to trace an aerosol or get a fingerprint off these." Bill held up a flimsy plastic exam glove. "Especially after I throw them in a burn barrel."

"How did you zero in on the leader?" Henry asked.

"Annette identified him from a news story. Idiot was recruiting online. She sent me his background. He flunked out of Junior ROTC, so he wasn't going to any service academy. But his Dad's connections got him a new job — field organizer for some political group."

Henry groaned as he leaned against the gate. "I hate all that shit. My Dad worked in the West Virginia coal mines a long time ago, and it was all political. There was a fight over union officers back in the Sixties, and this guy named Yablonski wanted the union to do more for miners with black lung. So he ran to be president of the union. You know what his opponent did? He hired a bunch of thugs that murdered Yablonski and his family in their home."

Bill looked at the Reagans dumping their gear into garbage bags. "I don't think this army is like a mobbed-up union. They're more like MLM sales things; recruit more people, and they promote you and give you more cleaning products." Then he looked toward the campground proper, where several men leaned against socially distanced trees, cradling rifles in their arms. From that distance, Jerry gave an informal salute.

"All things considered, I'll call this a win," Greg said.

Bill holstered his Colt. "Well, round one in our favor."

Henry stopped unloading the 30.06 in his hands. "How many go-rounds you expecting? More today?"

"If so, let's move your friends out of the open," Greg said. "Between us, we can likely arm most of them."

"No, not today. The Liberation Army will be halfway back to Grand Rapids before Gary catches up. Oh, excuse me." Bill took out his phone and pressed an autodial button. "Mission accomplished. Pay out and go." The phone went dead. He turned back to Henry and Jerry. "But please keep a low profile on social media for a few weeks. We haven't seen the last of little Gary."

April 25

The number of confirmed cases of the coronavirus (COVID-19) in Michigan has risen to 37,203 as of Saturday, including 3,274 deaths, state officials report.

Saturday's update includes 562 new cases and 189 additional deaths. Friday's numbers included 36,641 coronavirus cases and 3,085 deaths.

As of Saturday, April 25, the official recovery total is 8,342.

Michigan's Governor extended Michigan's stay-at-home order through May 15 while loosening some restrictions on the state's businesses.

Michigan residents are now required to wear masks in public places, such as grocery stores, under the governor's reversed stay-at-home order.

State officials say despite the increase in daily cases this week, the rate of growth is continuing to slow, while testing rates continue to rise. Officials on Wednesday noted a 15 percent decrease in virus hospitalizations over the last 10 days.

Michigan's chief medical officer said the state processed 7,400 tests on Thursday, a one-day record in the state.

— ClickonDetroit.com

April 25

When Doc Mac, Regina, and Mary returned from Hamlin Lake, Frank hugged his family and extended his hand toward the Major. Throughout the homecoming, Rick stood 10 feet away, wearing a mask. After his trip to Grand Rapids, he was back in quarantine. All he could do was watch the reunion from a socially responsible distance, at least a caribou and two ravens away.

Frank hugged Mary and asked how she liked staying at Jack's cabin for a couple of nights.

"The house is beautiful, it has everything we have at home. I've never seen such a large television. It's right on the lake, so we could sit on the deck and just watch the sunlight shimmering on the waves, making little water babies."

Frank smiled and brushed her hair from her face in the breeze off the lake. "And did Mommy like it there?"

"I hope so, because I'd like to go back again. Do you think Jack would let us stay there? If we take good care of Sand Lake?"

"We can ask him. He's a nice man, but that's a big favor. And he's already being very nice, just letting us stay here."

Mary nodded in understanding. "Daddy, do you know if they call it Hamlin Lake in honor of Lincoln's first Vice President?"

"Why do you think that?" he asked.

She went to sit on the bench of a picnic table, and everyone but Rick settled across from her. "In the cabin, we found an atlas of Michigan that showed the townships. Just north of the lake was Grant Township. And there's townships named for Meade, Sherman and Sheridan. Along with other townships called Freesoil and Victory. There's a town named Custer."

"We didn't have internet at the cabin, so she couldn't look it up," Regina said. She seemed rather proud of Mary's detective work. "I was planning to go over to the library tomorrow to download mass, and she can come with me." She also reached over to brush hair from the child's face.

"That's very good thinking. But how did you know about Hamlin?" Rick asked. "I never heard of him."

"Mom had me memorize the Presidents in order. So I went back and learned the Vice Presidents as well."

At his unwashed table, Rick smiled and nodded. At that age, he was most concerned with learning the line-up of the Detroit Tigers, guys like "Hot Sauce" Saucier and "Rosey" Rozema. Add characters like Denny McLain and Joe Niekro, and you could write one hell of a history on baseball in Detroit.

"So how did it go here yesterday?" Regina asked. "No troubles?"

Frank shifted so he could look at her and Doc Mac. "We got busy. We had the tribal drummers here in the campsites. There were three retired officers from the Forest Service. And ten or so guys dressed in camouflage wearing Ronald Reagan masks. There were maybe ten guys from the Liberation Army. But it ended pretty quickly. The officer that Bill put in charge seemed to know what he was doing."

"Bill? That man who brought us Easter dinner?" Regina asked.

"And my bunny." Mary added.

"Yes. One of the law officers came to the camper to be sure I was OK. He said the guy in charge, Greg, was Military Police."

Regina clasped her hands in prayer. "Thank you, Lord. I'm so relieved that is all done."

"I hope it is," Rick said. "When I talked to Bill on the phone last night, he seemed concerned that Gary was going to make another visit."

Mary spoke up. "And they are angry because we can be here but they can't? Because of the stay home order?"

Regina put her arm around the child's shoulders. "People get crazy ideas. We just have to focus on what we need to do. Right now, I need to take the frozen strawberries out of the freezer so we all can have pie tonight. Will you help me?"

The three men remained quiet while the mother and daughter walked to the Damon camper. Finally, Rick spoke up. "You haven't told her? She doesn't know why she had to hide in the cabin?"

"Regina was afraid Mary'd be scared," Frank said. "Pretty vile stuff online."

"Oh, I think that child knows exactly what's going on," Doc Mac said. "While we were there, she asked me why Regina was so afraid, and why you wanted them to stay in Jack's cabin. You can't fool that little girl."

"Am I the only one who doesn't know the names of all the Vice Presidents?" Rick asked.

April 26

Michigan's governor signed an executive order Sunday that imposes safety measures to protect consumers and employees from further exposure to COVID-19.

The new order encourages customers to wear face covering over the nose and mouth at food establishments. Grocery stores and pharmacies must also set aside at minimum two hours each week for the most vulnerable populations to shop.

Additionally, the order requires that if an employee at a store tests positive for COVID-19, other employees must be notified without infringing on the personal health information of the infected employee.

"While Michiganders fight this virus, we must continue to take aggressive action to reduce exposure and prevent a second spike in cases," the governor said. "This is not the time to slow our efforts; we must continue to be smart. By establishing these guidelines, we can protect Michigan families and our frontline workers. When we come together, we can slow the spread of this virus and save lives."

– WXYZ, Detroit.

April 26

The Cadillac office of the Huron-Manistee was quiet on Saturday afternoon. Apart from the future fleet sale, only three "privately owned vehicles," or POVs were in the parking lot when Bill rolled the Wagoneer to a stop on the North end. The other cars belonged to the watchstanders in the dispatch center. He assumed things were very quiet on a weekend in the midst of a pandemic.

He spent several hours hauling the records from his file cabinet down to the photo copier in the mailroom. While the copier flashed through the many pages, he created a duplicate set of file folders. He then began the tedious process of collating the stacks of paper with the dated files. He periodically stopped to ensure that no stray copies had ended up on the floor or in the recycling bin. Ring 3 of the circus required the same level of security as the Manhattan Project. With the addition of two more statements, these records would detonate in the Regional Office like Little Boy.

In the middle of the afternoon his personal cell phone whistled while he was back in his office on the North end of the building. "Do I need to take this call outside?" he asked as he punched up the speaker.

"Anybody around?" Annette asked.

"Just in Dispatch."

"OK. So far, you're cruising just below radar. Some chatter on the dark web, but nothing crazy. Don't stow your Kevlar just yet."

"It's so old now, you could cut it with a butter knife."

"Yet another reason I don't want your job. Added to the parking and, of course, working for the boss. How can you not have new Kevlar?"

"I don't think this job qualifies for combat gear. Not most days." He paused. "Annette, don't you have a family? Don't you have something better to be doing than watching my shadow on the internet?"

"So if not me, who?"

"You think I need a guardian angel?"

"Well, you tell me. You met Gary, right? He seem like a reasonable guy to you?"

"Not exactly. But you think he's a Reggie Strickland?"

"You talking sports again?"

"You never heard of Reggie?" Bill sounded astonished. "He was a middleweight out of Cincinnati who fought 363 bouts and lost a record 276 times."

"OK, you want to come back from man world now?"

"Sorry. Lot of testosterone in my former career."

"Sure. When I go on fire assignments, you can smell it more than the smoke."

Bill chuckled. "Just between us, I'm going to try to do something about that, too."

"You get close to retirement and develop a messianic complex?"

"Like I've never had one before now?"

"Hey, I should probably go spend a little time with my family, just like you said."

"Listen, I do appreciate that you're looking out for me online. I have no idea what's going to happen, so I'm glad for any warning I can get."

"I'll stay on top of it."

"Thank you kindly. You have a great weekend."

April 27

LANSING, MI -- Michiganders are now required to wear non-medical-grade face masks or coverings whenever they are in enclosed public spaces, under the state's newest stay-home order.

That mandate went into effect at 11:59 p.m. Sunday and applies only to people who are able to "medically tolerate" wearing a mask. There is no criminal penalty for not wearing a mask but, businesses can refuse service. Masks can be homemade, fashioned from scarves, handkerchiefs or other materials.

The governor's order further set that deadline for businesses to start providing workers performing in-person tasks with non-medical-grade masks.

The move comes about three weeks after state and federal health officials first recommended wearing non-medical-grade masks in public. Officials urge reserving N95 and surgical masks for medical professionals.

– Mlive.

April 29

Robert looked unhappy. When Jack and Bill entered, he did not greet them. Instead he merely pointed at the two chairs opposite his desk. He mutely motioned for Bill to swing the office door closed. The boss remained seated, apparently skimming through his e-mail messages and pausing at times to glower at his visitors. Finally, he stood and came around to sit on the desk with one leg\ dangling so he could easily kick their shins with his Italian dress shoes if the mood struck him. He continued to stare at them a full minute before he spoke.

"So, gentlemen, feeling pretty good about what you've done?" At least the boss wasn't trying to sugar-coat anything.

"Maybe," Jack said, after some hesitation. "Could you narrow it down a little?"

"Not sure where to begin because I've heard now from the White House, the Department, the Chief's Office, Office of General Counsel, the Regional Forester, Congressman Van Den Berg, the U.S. Attorney in Grand Rapids, and a group called the Conservative Family Agenda. Oh, and some guy named Gary leaves messages threatening to burn down the Pere Marquette State Forest."

"I'd turn the messages from Gary over to LEO Winchester," Jack suggested. "Can't ignore terroristic threats."

The boss glared at the District Ranger as if to rebuke him, but what Jack had said was the simple truth. He abruptly changed direction of the conversation and the object of his anger. "Why didn't you warn me that Renee was planning an ambush about the 2nd District race?"

"Boss, you didn't tell me about the rumors," Bill said. Technically, true, because the two men had never discussed the topic. Morally questionable, because Bill had baited the trap.

"Well, Van Den Berg complained to Judith, who went to the Chief. The Congressman also went to the House Minority Leader, who took it up with the White House. That led to a call from OGC."

"Ouch," Jack observed.

"Yeah, but worse than that," Robert said. "You both take the Hatch Act refresher each year? Now imagine it with direct threats."

"Ouch," they both said together.

"Now to my final point. I understand that on Friday the National Forest had a visit from the Liberation Army of Michigan. I was not informed of a planned protest."

Shifting in his chair, Bill spoke up. "Plausible deniability. We didn't want to involve you in case it went badly."

"Oh, I see. Did it go badly?"

Jack looked at Bill and shrugged. "I don't think so. I heard it went pretty well, all things considered."

"Really? And was the Liberation Army of Michigan given an opportunity to exercise their First Amendment rights on federal land?"

Bill's turn to shrug. "I heard them."

"Over the car alarms?"

"No, before that."

"And were the protesters tear-gassed?"

"Well, no. Not technically," Bill said.

"See, I think that's a yes-or-no question," the boss said.

"Robert, those campground hosts have been there for nearly a month," the District Ranger said. "There have been reports of black bears in the surrounding areas."

"That's right. Perhaps the protesters got sprayed with bear repellent," Bill said. "Might have been an accident."

"So when the Liberation Army of Michigan arrived at Sand Lake, why was Rory stationed out on Nurnberg Road to protect a 9-year-old?"

Bill and Jack managed not to look at each other. The story had unraveled at the very end.

Robert waited a moment for an answer. Sighing, he walked back around to his desk chair. He slumped back in the most relaxed position either Jack or Bill had seen him take. "Gentlemen, I don't know who this Conservative Family Agenda represents or how much money their PAC donates, but they managed to reach directly into the White House. Last night, I spoke with the Deputy Chief of Staff to the President. They just want a resignation, and I'll be allowed to run for Congress with the President's endorsement, at the request of an important donor. Congressman Van Den Berg has agreed to be ambassador to Japan."

"Wow. Congratulations," Jack said.

Bill paused, thinking through the political machinations. "Will it look strange if you resign abruptly? Won't it raise questions when you campaign?"

"I'm sorry if I wasn't clear. I will stay until I retire July 31st, just before the August primary. But they need a resignation now. So which of you will it be?" Robert stared at his wall of photographic glory. Bill realized that the open space at the top of the pyramid remained for the portrait of a future President Robert Fulbright.

Bill stood. "Well, boss, that will be me." He pulled an envelope from inside his binder. "Effective May 22." He dropped the resignation letter, executed a sharp right face and then opened the door before heading down the hallway to his office.

April 28

"Lunch?" Jack asked from the doorway of Bill's office.

"Twelve at Caberfae Trailhead?"

The ranger checked the time on his cellphone. "Where you been? It's already almost two in the afternoon."

"Sorry. Meant twelve-pack."

"Melissa says you're a terrible influence on me."

"Well, she's not wrong," Bill said. "I'm a terrible influence on me, too."

"Food, also?"

"If you insist. Just surprise me."

As soon as Jack disappeared from the doorframe, Elizabeth knocked. She came in without invitation, closed the door and sat in a chair along the wall.

"So, I gave you an incriminating letter about the boss, and now you're up and leaving?" She straightened herself in the chair and squared her shoulders. "Fuck off, you old bastard."

"I'm sorry. I knew I had to be ready if Robert sprung that on us. He was going to force one of us out, so it had to be me."

"I want my letter back," she said firmly. "Now."

Bill leaned forward, slightly violating her caribou space. "I am not done with Robert. Not by a long shot."

"Easy to shoot a slingshot from the other side of retirement."

"I'm planning to visit with the Regional Forester before I retire. In fact, you scheduled it for May 7th."

"Wait, that's when the boss and Jack are meeting with Judith. You have a meeting that same day?"

"Nope, same meeting. Jack kind of invited me along."

"You think Judith is going to listen to you during a review of Jack's mid-year performance?"

"I don't know. But you'll be safe." Bill smiled to reassure her. "Very safe."

April 28

As the wind rustled the towering red pines at the Caberfae Trailhead, Bill and Jack sat on the tailgate of the Wagoneer with a 12-pack of Two Hearted. Between them, they finished half a tub of the Colonel's best original recipe. Castigation is good for the appetite.

"You sure about this?" Jack asked.

Bill took a deep breath and let it out slowly. "Last day I was certain about anything was the day I married Camille. Don't think I've ever made another decision without doubt."

"You're done in just a few weeks. Why come with me next week?"

Bill took another beer from the box and opened it with his service knife. "Remember what we said. All in."

"That was for Mary."

"It's OK to do something for you, too. Unless you want to go to Yakutat."

Jack laughed, but not in a happy way. "You should have heard Melissa. She could be principal of the middle school next year, if things work out. I don't think that's going to happen very quickly in Yakutat."

"How's the orthodontia home course coming along?"

"OK, so I need to stay here. And maybe I need your help to make that happen."

"Nice ask."

"So what do you want for a retirement party?"

Bill took a long tug on his bottle. "Oh, I think that after next week that isn't going to happen. Just yesterday, Elizabeth's word calendar introduced 'persona non grata.' That'll be me."

"Great. Now I have to learn Latin?"

"No, just means I won't be welcome anywhere on the forest."

"I ever tell you I have a cabin over on Hamlin Lake?" Jack asked.

"Sounds nice."

"And a boat."

"Oh. Very nice."

"If the Governor gives the all-clear, maybe I'll have a little get-together on the Friday before Memorial Day. You think you could work up a discreet guest list?"

"Tell me why I always do the heavy lifting in this relationship?"

April 29

Rick sat cross-legged on a small bluff overlooking Sand Lake. Because of his trip to Grand Rapids five days earlier, he was relegated to the unwashed table and Coleman camper again for at least another five days. Maybe it was the transition from morphine to other medications that made him edgy. He had spent the day mowing and weed-whacking the entire campground. Rather than tired, he just felt grumpy. He wondered if there was another adjustment Doc Mac could make to the regimen. But Rick could not go ask at the Damon without intruding on the child's safe environment.

Pain is curious. People experience it differently. Rick had met patients suffering excruciating agony in waiting rooms who left relieved from just holding a paper prescription in their hand. At VA clinics, they often emerged from exam rooms enraged by the lack of treatment. How many times had he heard a clinician say, "Well, that's a natural effect of your injury." Translation: You were hurt, now get over it. After a particularly long and grueling spinal surgery, a Navy surgeon encouraged Rick to start training for an upcoming marathon.

He climbed into his Ford pickup truck and headed for the gate. Given the governor's orders, he knew there would be no bars or restaurants open to get a drink. So he headed east toward Garlett's Corner.

April 30

Lansing — Protesters, some carrying firearms, took their demonstration against the Michigan governor's stay-home order inside the Michigan Capitol on Thursday in a confrontational showdown with authorities. Dozens of protesters gathered outside the House chamber and demanded to be allowed in as Michigan State Police troopers stood in a line. The protesters chanted, "Let us in."

The state has long allowed guns inside the Capitol building — a policy that's previously drawn criticism from Democrats. A legislator from Livonia posted a photo of people in the Senate gallery Thursday with firearms. She said some of her colleagues "who own bulletproof vests are wearing them."

Outside the Capitol, 800 to 1,000 protesters participated in the American Patriot Rally throughout the day, according to the Michigan State Police. It was the second time in less than a month there's been a large demonstration against restrictions to combat COVID-19. But the event was much smaller than the one on April 15 that drew thousands of vehicles to Lansing.

"Just being here makes a real difference," said a protester from Grand Rapids, who carried an American flag and a sign that read, "Free MI."

Many protesters say they are frustrated by orders from the Governor that have forced residents to stay inside their homes and have shuttered businesses to prevent the spread of the virus. Most of the demonstrators' signs focused on that subject Thursday. But a few signs were more violent in tone. One attached to a truck outside the Capitol said, "Make treason punishable by hanging." Another person held a sign that said, "Tyrants get the rope."

— The Detroit News.

April 30

At dawn, Rick rested at the unwashed table. He chewed slices of summer sausage from his last visit to the Cherry Republic store in Traverse City. Nearby sat a bag of their Cherry Nut Mix gorp and a boxed 12-pack of Budweiser cans from Garlett's Corner. He studied a map of the campground, considering how he might post the open campsites to ensure safe social distancing. Although the individual sites weren't crowded together, campers have a tendency to fully occupy an area, with canvas chairs encircling the fire rings; sleeping tents; awnings over the picnic tables; their cars, trailers and bicycles.

After Doc Mac emerged from the Damon, he stretched and looked about as if getting his bearings. Suddenly he came straight at Rick. "What the hell is that?" he demanded, pointing at the box.

"The King of Beers?"

"We had an agreement." Doc's voice was closer to a snarl.

"We do." Rick ripped open a flap and removed one of the cans. He showed the unopened top to the major. "I haven't opened one."

"Why do you have it?"

"I got kind of edgy last night. No one to talk to. Nothing to do. Started to hurt more. So I went over and bought it," Rick explained. "When I put it in the truck, I wondered what I was going to do with it."

"Why not drink it?" the doctor asked.

"I realized I didn't want it. I can get to sleep without it."

"Even without the morphine?"

"OK, I'm not committing to that. But this new substitute is doing OK so far. What is it?"

"Let's keep that classified for now, like in a double-blind drug test. We're going to try a range of things. Might turn out that a placebo is all you really need."

"You want to put money on that?" Rick asked.

May 1

On the morning after hundreds of protesters gathered at the Michigan Capitol – with chants and signs — the President joined in the criticism of Michigan's Governor.

"The Governor of Michigan should give a little, and put out the fire," he tweeted at 8:42 a.m. on Friday. "These are very good people, but they are angry. They want their lives back again, safely! See them, talk to them, make a deal."

Michigan ranks third in the nation with 3,789 Covid-19 deaths and seventh in the U.S. with 41,379 confirmed cases of the virus.

– Mlive.

May 1

Over the years, Bill had amassed three file cabinets of correspondence, reports and miscellaneous paperwork, along with a bookcase and a two-door cabinet of books and documents. Somewhere in the stacks there could be the biological assessment for gathering a mating pair of every species and loading them onto a barge. To simplify the process of clearing out his office, he hijacked the big paper shredder from the mailroom and rolled it into his office. In keeping with official guidance on archiving files, he cast a critical eye over every page before shredding it.

History is written by the winner; Bill had lost.

After morning break, Elizabeth poked her head in to say hello. "Wow. A boomer and a hoarder."

"At least I didn't just douse it with lighter fluid and burn it all. Yet."

"Well, thanks for sparing me all the extra paperwork on an office fire."

"No, I'm saving the arson for the computer. If I buy it outright, can I take it for target practice?"

"Fine with me, if it's in cash." She shoved the shredder aside so she could enter and closed the door behind herself. "Look, I'm sorry about the other day. Even with everything that's going on, Randy would rather see me quit my job than keep working for the boss." She glanced back at the door. "He didn't say it so nicely. But if something comes of it all next week, maybe I can stay."

"I hope so."

"You need help? You've only got three weeks to get through all this crap."

"No. Not enough room in here for anyone else. Besides, I wouldn't want anyone to accidentally stumble across anything Top Secret."

Elizabeth laughed. "What, like the super-secret Smokey Bear handshake?"

"Well, you don't know it, do you?"

The office intercom came on, sharing a conversation at the front desk. "No, he's not gone yet. I thought I saw him earlier. 'Bill, you have a visitor up front. Bill, a visitor.' I think he's still allowed in the building …."

"Jeez, what kind of rumor did you start?" Bill asked Elizabeth.

"You mean how many rumors did I start? I'm kind of curious to learn what the district offices hear about you. You could be guilty of murder or treason by the time Oscoda knows." She seemed profoundly amused by her mischief.

"You never fail to surprise me. But let me go up front." They walked down the hall together, forgetting for a moment about caribou spacing.

"So you saw the president's tweet about more very good people this morning?" she asked.

"Oh, yeah. 'Make a deal.' Like what? You can open the gyms in exchange for another three thousand fresh corpses. Deal?" When they reached the reception area, Bill saw Ted waiting. "I'll talk to you later," he told Elizabeth as he went into the reception area. "Ted, how are you?"

"We're good. Can we go out front?" Ted asked.

"Sure." Bill turned to the front desk. "I'll be right back."

Outside the door, Ted started to extend his hand but pulled back abruptly. "Sorry. Can't take the risk with her condition."

"Of course. No problem. How is she?"

"Tolerating it all well. She says third time's a charm; I think it's hell."

Bill tried to avoid saying anything meaningless like *thoughts and prayers*. "You know if you need anything you just need to call."

"You've been great. So has Elizabeth. Don't get me wrong, she's got great people in her department. But they don't always keep her in the loop. They got used to working without her."

"It'll be OK when she comes back," Bill said.

"No, I hope she doesn't. She doesn't need the stress. Sure didn't need Robert to show up here." Ted reached under his jacket and took out a thick envelope that he handed to Bill. "She put it all down. Copies of reports. Everything. Please do her justice."

Ted turned abruptly and walked quickly back to his Chevy pickup. After he climbed inside and started the engine, he gave Bill a casual salute like those Hollywood pilots heading off to bomb Germany.

Of course it was now Bill preparing for one last mission.

May 2

The Governor took another step toward reactivating Michigan's economy by signing an order Friday for construction businesses, real estate activity and other outdoor jobs to resume May 7 as the coronavirus crisis continues into May.

The move came a day after hundreds of protesters gathered at the state Capitol, urging lawmakers not to extend a state of emergency.

Many were upset over the governor's stay-at-home order that has left people off work for weeks.

The legislature took no action with hopes the emergency declaration would expire at 11:59 p.m. Thursday, but the Governor issued executive orders to extend it through May 28 and she defended those orders in a Friday news conference.

"We're not in a political crisis, where we should just negotiate and find some common ground here," the Governor said. "We're in a public health crisis. We're in the midst of a global pandemic."

– Mlive.

May 3

Regina returned from the Wellston library in the afternoon, nearly bursting out of the Explorer in excitement. She called for Frank, who was sitting with Doc Mac outside, and brought the laptop into the camper. Mary came out from the big bedroom in the back of the camper.

"The news says that the governor is allowing construction, landscaping, golf, and boating to start up again. Doesn't that mean manufacturing will be next?" Regina asked Frank.

"I would think so, wouldn't you?" He wondered if and when the GM plants could re-open. There had been no e-mail warning yet from the company or the union.

She exhaled in relief, like she had been holding her breath for a month. "If you go back, we'll keep health coverage. And we'll have money coming in."

"Is that what you want?" Frank asked. "You'll be OK if I go back to the house in Grand Rapids?"

"Could you commute? From here?"

"Oh, honey, I think that would be about an hour and a half each way."

"If he goes back, I couldn't see Daddy, could I?" Mary asked. "He'll be with his co-workers all day." She hugged a Nancy Drew novel against her stomach.

"She's right, I guess. Even if I drove up, I'd have to stay outside. Same on the weekends."

Regina stood and headed for the camper door, gently touching Frank's hand as she passed. He smiled at Mary. "Why don't you go ahead and read. What's Nancy investigating this time?" He knew that brief touch was Regina's summons.

"She's on a cruise ship in the Great Lakes. Do they still have those?"

"I think so. Used to be only the ferries. But now there are cruise ships that sail all the way to Montreal. A woman at work did it for her honeymoon last year."

"Cool. That would be fun." She turned and went back to her room.

Something for Make-A-Wish, he thought, then instantly

regretted the mere idea. Surely this will all work out for her. He touched his forehead, chest and, shoulders as he spoke a silent prayer. Part contrition and fully half a plea. He stood and followed Regina outside. He saw her waiting abut 20 feet away from the camper. Just walking toward her, he knew from her stance that she was unhappy with him.

"I'm sorry, Regina," he began.

She raised her hands to stop him. "Don't. I don't want to hear it." She inhaled sharply, but he could see it did not tamp down her anger. "This was your idea, start to finish. I only agreed to keep her safe, but I never liked it. We're spending money like crazy, food, propane, gas here, but we're still paying the mortgage and utilities at the house. And unemployment barely covers the house payment. We're already dipping into savings. The news talks about Congress passing additional unemployment, but when will that be? No one will pay you to be a campground host; the pay is a place to park the camper. So you tell me how we can afford to stay here and you not go back to work?"

When he was a teenager, Frank spent summers helping on his grandfather's farm. The old man's business included slaughtering and butchering the steers he could not sell live, then offering the meat direct to the public. The process involved stunning the animal so it was senseless when the fatal shot came. Frank's job was to deliver the paralyzing blow to the animal's forehead with a 16-pound sledgehammer. For the first time, he knew exactly how that felt. Now was his turn to inhale deeply.

"I didn't know how bad it was getting," he said.

"I didn't want to burden you with it. I know you feel we're doing what we have to do for Mary. I do love you for that. But we can't keep going like this. Isn't there more work that Rick thinks the camper needs?"

"Nothing major. Some replacement parts." He now thought of the camper, his main inheritance from his father, as a huge burden.

"But see, all of that is coming out of our savings for the most part. I can show you the ledger."

"No, I believe you." Frank turned and walked down to the beach. He heard Regina following behind him.

"I am not your enemy," she said.

He stopped a few feet from the lake. The surface was smooth as a window pane, disturbed only by the ripples of fish rising to feed on the evening's insects. The warm air created a slight mist over the cooler water. "I will miss you," he said. "And I will miss Mary." He turned to face his wife. "And you'll need to ask Doc and Rick if they can stay and help you."

"Yes, I will ask for help when we need it." She stopped and looked up at him. "And that's bothering you."

"Of course," he said. He struggled a moment with what to say. "A man takes care of his family. He doesn't ask someone else to do it for him."

Regina wrapped her arms around him. "And you'll be taking care of us when you go back to work. We simply can't afford to go on this way. And when we get the call, you'll have more sick leave built up. It's OK to ask for help."

"I'll miss you both so much."

When he kissed her forehead, she turned her face up toward his. She whispered, "She can't see us here." So he kissed her more.

May 3

The President predicted on Sunday night that the death toll from the coronavirus pandemic ravaging the country might reach as high as 100,000 in the United States, far higher than he had forecast just weeks ago, even as he pressed states to begin reopening the shuttered economy.

The President, who last month forecast that 60,000 lives would be lost, acknowledged that the virus had proved more devastating than he had expected but said he believed parks and beaches should begin reopening and schools should resume classes in person by this fall.

"We're going to lose anywhere from 75, 80 to 100,000 people," he said in a virtual "town hall" meeting on Fox News. "That's a horrible thing. We shouldn't lose one person over this."

But he credited himself with preventing the toll from being worse. "If we didn't do it, the minimum we would have lost was a million two, a million four, a million five, that's the minimum. We would have lost probably higher, it's possible higher than 2.2."

– The New York Times.

May 4

A Family Dollar security guard who confronted a Michigan shopper for not wearing a mask inside the store was met with spitting, shouting and a fatal gunshot to the head, authorities said Monday.

Friday's senseless killing in downtown Flint has led to murder charges against the deranged customer, but police are still on the hunt for her adult son, who's accused of firing the fatal shot, as well as her husband.

The guard, 43, got into a verbal argument with a customer after asking her to cover her face to reduce the risk of coronavirus transmission inside the store, prosecutors said.

The customer responded by yelling and spitting at the victim, who then kicked the 45-year-old woman out of the store and instructed a cashier not to serve her, according to a press release.

Police said the suspect left the store, but her husband and son showed up moments later and confronted the security guard. It was the customer's son, 23, who then pulled out a gun and shot the security guard in the back of the head, authorities said.

The guard was taken to the hospital, but he was pronounced dead a short time later.

– The New York Daily News.

May 4

Bill was busy again shredding old files and records. He had placed the reference books acquired over 20 years on a table in the break room for employees to take. For years, he had carefully adhered to the federal rules for archiving government records. Everything that remained now was the personal copies that he maintained for a quick referral, like the many letters to a certain farmer. Much easier to open a file cabinet drawer than to submit a request to the National Archives and Records Administration.

He paused a few moments to prepare another Form 71, the official Request for Leave and Approved Absence from the Office of Personnel Management. This request covered his trip preparation, travel to Wisconsin, as well the day in Milwaukee and his return. He was not traveling on official business; the boss would not approve if he knew. No, better to have a little surprise in store for Robert.

A knock on the window startled him. "Good time?" Elizabeth asked. "Your daily to-do list."

"The dodo list?"

"Play nice. I'm just the messenger."

"How can I destroy evidence of years of wrong-doing if he keeps giving me actual work?" Bill asked aloud as he settled at his desk and shoved old files aside to find a notebook.

"Ready?" She lifted her clipboard. "Find out who else is on the RF's schedule the same day he and Jack are visiting. He said he wants to 'take the room temperature.' See if Rachel has time to talk about any outstanding Congressional issues, and give him a list of constituent concern you're dealing with, in case she brings that up."

"Maybe the Hatch Act?" he suggested innocently.

"Not touching that. And finally, are you doing an employee newsletter for May before you go? Please say yes, because otherwise I'll be doing one."

"Sure. I might have big news next week."

"You stay up at night plotting?" she asked.

"No, it's pretty spontaneous. I'm like Boris Badenov that way."

She rolled her eyes. "OK, Mooseketeer. I can probably find work to do. Sharpening pencils. Sorting paper clips. Something."

"Maybe give my leave request to the boss?" He removed it from the printer, signed it hastily and passed it to her. "Thank you kindly."

When she closed his office door, he reached for his personal cell phone and dialed. "How's your prep going?"

"Not good. Melissa says my best defenses are 'Do No Harm,' 'Caring for the Land and Serving People' or making Eagle Scout."

"Sounds like she does want to go to Alaska," Bill observed. "That or she's creating grounds for a divorce."

"Don't even joke like that. I've got friends my age who divorced. After alimony, they realize there's not a lot left over for that trophy wife."

"I hear a cooler of beer will get you a fishing buddy," Bill said.

"Yet another reason why I don't want to get a divorce."

"Don't worry. I'm locked and loaded."

"Yeah, Melissa says she's worried about the blowback from putting a former Marine in charge of my defense."

"OK, first you tell her there's no such thing as a former Marine. Second, let her know there's no better defense than a good offense."

"From *The Art of War*?"

"Maybe. I always thought it was George Washington."

Jack groaned into the phone. "I thought you were this great military tactician."

"Nope, just your *Cousin Vinny*."

May 4

A man asked to wear a mask at a Dollar Tree store in northern Oakland County allegedly wiped his nose on the shirt of a female clerk before leaving in a white van, police said.

The alleged incident took place about 1:30 p.m. Saturday, at a Dollar Tree on the 400 block of North Saginaw Street, south of Grange Hall Road.

Police said in a statement that the clerk advised the suspect that customers must wear a mask to shop the store.

Police say the man then approached the clerk, said "here, I will use this as a mask," and wiped his face and nose on her shirt.

The man then left in a large white van, police said.

– ClickonDetroit.com

May 5

Driving the Wagoneer, Bill left Harrietta early. He worked his
way through county roads until he came out on M-55, then turned
east. In Cadillac, he headed south on US 131 toward Grand
Rapids. He tuned to the talk radio station on AM to hear the news,
weather and rants. AM = Absolutely Mindless. After about 20
minutes of the political talking points, the range of the Traverse
City station began to fade. He dropped in an old cassette tape of
collaborative improvisation by Duke Ellington and John Coltrane.

He planned few stops on the trip. Gas refills were necessary. The
old Jeep had the gas mileage of a Sherman tank. Pit stops as
needed. In a cooler on the floor behind him was a couple of
Vernor's. On the front passenger's seat sat three MREs. Of course,
meals-ready-to-eat does not always mean edible.

Bill intended to keep his involvement in the RF meeting secret as
long as possible. Elizabeth had shared the boss' itinerary and
accommodations, so there was little chance of encountering Robert
along the way. While Robert and Jack had reservations at the
elegant Pfister Hotel in downtown Milwaukee, Bill was heading for
a no-name motel out by the airport. Surprise and superior force.

As he drove south, he tore open one of the MREs to see if there
might be cookies or another snack. Pistachios? Who thinks of pistachios as ready to eat? He wondered how a tank crew would dispose
of the shells from pistachio nuts. Load them into the 75mm gun?

Passing the Fifth/Third Ballpark on the northside of Grand
Rapids, he wondered what kind of a season the local minor league
baseball team would have with the pandemic. Before the accident,
he once brought his son to watch the West Michigan Whitecaps
defeat the Great Lakes Loons. The boy loved baseball games;
watching Major or Minor teams made no difference to him.

Bill then tuned into WOOD radio to catch the latest traffic. He
rarely traveled much farther than Newaygo at the South end of the
Manistee Forest. Congestion was not much of a problem the closer
you travelled north toward the 45th parallel.

South of the city on I-196, his phone rang in its cradle attached
to the air vent. He pressed to answer and punched up the speaker.
"Boomers United," he said.

"Oh crap. If you guys join forces, the world is screwed." Annette sounded genuinely distraught.

"Look at the bright side."

"I was."

"Real nice. Here I am trying to save a district ranger, a little girl and all unicorns everywhere, but you call to mock me."

"Not just you," she insisted. "You and everyone in your generation. We went from the greatest generation to the greediest. By the time I retire, they'll take 25 percent of my check to pay off all you boomers."

"I get the sense that you clearly need more work to keep you busy. Just so you're not searching the web so much. I'll chat with your supervisor about that."

"That's why I'm calling. Are you planning to see Ann on Thursday?"

Bill nearly choked. "Pardon?"

"You're not going to Milwaukee without stopping at the Regional Office, unless you're going for the License to Kill Mac and Cheese at the Safehouse."

"So you are a spy?" he asked. "How else do you know my plans?"

"Jack told Gwen, who told Elizabeth, who told me, naturally. You think we don't talk amongst ourselves?"

"Does the boss know?"

"Not from any of us. Are you kidding? Gwen subscribes to Soldier of Fortune, just to scan the classified ads for a solution to the boss."

"Careful. All those hitman ads are scams or FBI agents."

"Yeah, you tell Gwen or Billie that. They're hoping for a miracle."

He swerved to avoid hitting a car that merged into his lane without a blinker. "Sorry. I didn't know it was that bad."

"Ask any woman on the forest. They've all got a story to tell. I'm lucky that I started telecommuting back before he arrived. Take Angela, that new rec tech in Baldwin, to lunch sometime. One beer and she'll tell you a hell of a story about floating down the Pere Marquette with the boss."

"Thanks. But I don't take as many young female employees to lunch as I used to."

Annette laughed for nearly a minute. "Yeah. OK, given the topic, I get that. So do you need anything I can do for your Thursday meetings?"

"Ask Angela for a statement?"

"Seriously? Like Elizabeth?"

"Really? Do you know what I packed for the trip?"

"Sure. Two boxes of files; probably your blue suit, cordovan wingtips, gold tie with a herringbone pattern, the gray fedora; Dockers, an Orvis shirt and topsiders; and a few MREs."

"When I get back, I'm going to find those cameras, and then there will be trouble."

She laughed again. "Oh, come on, you only have the one suit. You only wear Dockers and Orvis. And you wouldn't go into a fast food joint if the fun meals had gold bullion."

"I stopped enjoying our chat five minutes ago."

"I've known you 15 years, Bill. You're not a creature of habit. You embody habit. I think it's that Marine thing."

"Tell me again why you called?"

"Torture. And to offer any help you need. You left me out of the fun in Grand Rapids, remember? I think you owe me."

"You know you don't work for me, right?" He paused to check the road signs. "Hey, I'm coming into the merge with I-94. Traffic is going to get crazy. If I need anything I'll call, but for now enjoy plausible deniability. We never had this talk."

He hit the red button on the phone. The sound system came off mute just as the cassette began with the Ellington and Coltrane epic opening of "In a Sentimental Mood." The music helped Bill maintain his calm as the tidal wave of traffic from Kalamazoo hit the highway. He could not decide if Kalamazoo or Detroit spawned the worst drivers in the state; it was a jump ball.

The phone rang again. The music went silent when Bill punched the green dot. "Not again, please."

"What did I do now?" Jack asked.

"Sorry. I thought you were someone else."

"OK, where are you?"

"Almost to Benton Harbor. What's up?"

"So when do you get into Milwaukee?"

Bill checked his wrist watch. "Three or four hours, depending upon traffic through Chicago. What's up?"

"Oh, not much, really. Judith has been summoned to a mandatory meeting in the Chief's office to discuss fire management and coronavirus."

"How far out did they reschedule your meeting for?"

There was a long pause on Jack's end of the phone. "Tomorrow. 10 a.m."

Bill took a deep breath. "Tomorrow? Wait, where are you?"

"Gladstone. The boss wanted to drive across the UP on U.S. 2. Somehow he's never been on the Hiawatha before. So we had to stop at the district offices in Saint Ignace and Rapid River. I'm hanging out in the car while he gets a tour of the new Forest Supervisor office here. I wasn't invited inside."

"What? You got left in the car? You're a district ranger, not a puppy."

"You know how Robert is."

"But you know the difference between a ranger and a puppy, right?" Bill asked. "Eventually a puppy will stop whining."

"Thanks. Smack me from the other side. I am house-broken."

"Hey, I'm sorry, but I've got to get some help I didn't think I'd need. Thought I had all day tomorrow to run down something important. I'll be there. *Semper Fi.*"

"Crap. Got to throw some Greek into the mix, huh?"

"Latin, Jack. *Semper Fidelis.* Always faithful. Reinhardt out."

Bill closed the line and immediately asked the phone to call Annette. "Welcome to my nightmare," he said when she answered.

"Just fifteen minutes ago, you didn't need any help. But Judith's schedule change caused a problem?"

"Seriously, are you CIA?"

"Well, I did apply out of college. Passed everything up to the ethics test."

"What? You're a good Catholic girl."

"Yeah, that whole not violating the Ten Commandments thing was an issue for them."

23

"Well, what I need is entirely ethical and moral. Can you follow up on a cold case with Ashland County Sheriff's department in Wisconsin? I'm waiting for a call back."

"Oh, is that all? You don't want the Holy Grail or the Shroud of Turin?"

"No, I've got those at home. You can get them on eBay now. Next rest stop I'll text you the date and case number."

"Is this what I volunteered for?" Annette asked.

"Not exactly," he said. "But you didn't mention any sidebars. Just to be clear, you cannot share anything with your friends. Promise?"

"The CIA wouldn't take me because I refused to violate my morals. You think I'm going to change now?"

May 6

The President said Wednesday he will continue trying to toss out all of the Affordable Care Act, even as some in his administration, including the Attorney General, have privately argued parts of the law should be preserved amid the coronavirus pandemic.

"We want to terminate health care under Obamacare," the President told reporters Wednesday, the last day for his administration to change its position in a Supreme Court case challenging the law.

More than 73,000 people in the United States have died from Covid-19, with more than 1.2 million reported cases, according to tracking by *The Washington Post*.

The President said the work of the White House coronavirus task force would continue "indefinitely," a day after the Vice President, who heads the panel, said it would probably wind down its work by the end of the month.

– The Washington Post

May 6

Yakutat.

Jack woke from a terrible dream. He had walked down the gangway of an Alaska Marine ferry onto the dock in Yakutat. On his back, he wore a Filson Ranger backpack. In one hand, he carried an oversized Cannondale duffel; the other held his prized Browning .308 Medallion Gold. His heart raced, but he wasn't screaming. Yet.

He thought about going for a quick run to start the day, but when he looked at the clock on the nightstand, it read 4:47. He sank back into the queen bed. The cool sheets were a comfort, but he just stared at the ceiling. Too late to sleep and too early to get out on the street. So much at risk today.

At 5:15, he rose and dressed for a run. Maybe a few blocks up Wisconsin Avenue and then back. Or down Wisconsin to Lake Michigan. He decided when he walked out of the lobby. To the West, people were already decamping from buses and taxis. The sidewalk looked clear toward the sunrise.

As he jogged toward the false dawn, he wondered how he had gotten into this situation. He didn't extend any invitations to Covid-19 refugees. Yet now they were on one of his district's small campgrounds. Why not an adjacent state campground? Or a National Park? Even another National Forest? The Upper Peninsula had two, the Hiawatha and the Ottawa, all to themselves. To paraphrase Bogey, of all the 193 million acres in all the 154 National Forests in the country, they had to drive into his campground. But Jack had no one to play *As Time Goes By*.

On the return to the Pfister, he slowed to a walk when he saw a woman sitting on a stoop, with a fully loaded garbage bag on either side. She barely responded when he walked past.

"Good morning," he said.

"Is it?"

"Clear skies so far." He stopped and tried to sound upbeat.

"If you say so. You have a few dollars so maybe I could get breakfast?"

He felt through the pockets of his running shorts. "I'm sorry. I didn't bring my wallet this morning. All I have is this key card from the hotel."

"You're OK. Be careful running on these streets. The taxis don't stop for anyone, even in the crosswalks."

Just a block later, he headed into an intersection when the illuminated white-lettered WALK sign appeared. Just as the woman had predicted, a yellow taxi zipped around the corner, heading at him at a surprising speed. The driver blared his horn and aimed an obscene gesture at Jack for crossing legally. This was not a good start to a day that could decide the future of a man who had wanted since childhood nothing other than to be a Forest Service District Ranger someday.

When he looked back, the woman was no longer sitting on the stoop. At least she was not there laughing at him.

Back in his room, he toweled off from his run. He intended to wait until closer to departure before showering. Now too sweaty for the dining room, he looked over the room service menu. On past visits, he had enjoyed the corned beef hash, with two eggs sunny-side up, hash browns and toast. Now he asked only for coffee and toast.

He turned on his laptop e-mail to read the daily list of retirement announcements. Old friends and mentors seemed to be leaving at a dizzying rate. He scrolled back looking yet again to see the announcement of Bill's departure. Still nothing.

At 7:30, his cellphone rang. A 414 area code. Would Bill be calling on a landline?

Remembering one of the last times he picked up a phone call cold, he put on his most business-like air. "Good morning, Jack Ferguson speaking."

"Hi, Jack. It's Tara, in the RF's office. Judith now has an earlier flight today. Can you start at 9 instead of 10."

"This morning?" he asked in surprise.

"Yes, Judith confirmed it with Robert personally."

What had Bill always told him about the Marines? "Last to know; first to go." He did not plan to say it aloud.

"I guess so," she said. "You can make it by then?"

"Sounds like there's not much choice."

Tara chuckled into the phone, then lowered her voice. "Sounds like the choice is Yakutat." She was not joking.

"OK. I'll be there." He hung up and immediately dialed another cell phone.

"Jack?"

"Sorry. Can you make 9 instead of 10?"

"Yeah. I've been ready to deploy since zero 630. I'll make it in plenty of time unless I hit traffic."

"Traffic in a pandemic?"

"Let's hope not."

Jack set his phone on the bathroom counter and stepped into the shower. He dressed in trousers, a button-down shirt and a necktie, for the first time since his last visit to the Regional Office. He left the hotel at ten minutes after 8, plenty of time to walk the less than three blocks to the Forest Service offices in the Gaslight Building. The Front Office had left his name at the check-in desk, so he was quickly on his way upstairs after signing the logbook.

May 6

Bill tapped his fingers on the steering wheel in frustration. He had left the hotel at 8 a.m. and turned north on I-794 within 10 minutes. How could he still be sitting in a single line of traffic to get around a road maintenance crew at 8:20? He punched the scan on the AM dial to see if anyone broadcast traffic reports. He would have done better looking for sports news. The two news stations he heard seemed to have moved onto their morning talk shows. At that moment, he did not need more talk in his life.

When he reached the city, he parked in a garage on the corner of North Jackson and East Mason. He loaded his file boxes onto a collapsible two-wheel dolly and slung a pack over his back. He hurried one block east to North Van Buren and then south to Wisconsin Avenue. The security guards examined his boxes and checked him with a magnetic wand. When he went to sign in, the receptionist challenged him.

"I'm sorry, but you're not on the list of visitors today."

Bill nodded. "Understood. Could you call Tara for me?" When the line connected, he said, "Hi Tara, Bill Reinhardt, PAO on the Huron-Manistee. I'm here for Jack Ferguson's meeting with Judith. Could I come up?"

"OK, let me talk with Becky," she said. Quietly she added, "But hurry."

Bill passed the phone back and headed for the elevator bank, with his load in tow. The worst possible outcome: being shot in the back by a rent-a-cop. When he punched the UP button, no one was threatening to kill him, so he went upstairs. When the doors opened, he weaved his way through the maze of cubicle walls. A few employees waved at him or stood to greet him. Given what Tara had said, he assumed he didn't have time to socialize.

When he reached the Regional Forester's suite of offices, Tara stood waiting for him. She was not smiling. At that moment, Judith's door opened and Jack emerged. Judith remained sitting behind her desk, with Robert in a seat facing her. Neither seemed to notice Bill.

"Sorry. Fucking construction. How did it go?"

"You watch movies. Try 'All is Lost.'"

Bill took a small notebook from his pocket and tore out a page.

29

"Call this number now. See if she can be here by 9:30, instead of 10:45. Beg as necessary." Bill stood and straightened his tie. "How do I look?"

"Really?" Jack asked.

"Never mind." Bill hauled his load past Tara's desk. "Tara, I'm going in now. You should try to stop me."

Perhaps Tara was an actress in a prior life, but she jumped to her feet and shouted, "Bill, you can't simply barge in there." She came around her desk and stood discreetly to one side of Bill's direct path into Judith's office. "Bill, stop." Her protests sounded rather convincing.

"Good morning, Judith," Bill said cheerfully. "Hello, Bob." He dragged his cargo to the conference table. "I see you're done with Jack early, so I was hoping I could take the balance of his time."

Judith sat back in her big leather chair; Robert appeared to bristle in his own seat. "I don't recall you were on the schedule," she said.

Bill nodded in agreement. "True. But my retirement came up suddenly, for reasons that we don't need to discuss. I'm hoping to have my exit interview."

She sat forward and rested her elbows on her big oak desk. "I don't normally conduct those. You can talk to Robert, or contact HR."

Bill checked his watch. Must slow this down. "You know, I have always hated being called a Human Resource. I would like to think I deserve just a little more consideration than trees or minerals. We call those Natural Resources. I like to think of myself as something more."

Robert stood and protested. "Bill, Judith has a flight to Washington shortly. We can have this conversation later."

Bill walked up to within a few feet of Robert and pointed a forefinger at his chest. "Sit down, Bob. I checked. Her flight is at 11:45." He pointed at an overnight bag sitting in the corner of her office. "Unless she needs to go home to get her toothbrush, she can give me ten minutes."

As many people do when confronted by an angry Marine, Robert sat back down.

Judith nodded. "All right. Ten minutes. Then I call security."

Bill checked his watch again. Timing would be close. He hoped he could engage Judith's curiosity to keep the conversation going as long as necessary. "Judith, every fall you ask for employees to provide input on the Forest Supervisor's performance. Unfortunately, I won't be here in September to send you my comments. So I thought I would just bring my input to you now. But just so you know, if you don't get a lot of response from the Huron-Manistee, it's because Bob likes to accuse employees of reporting unfavorable comments to you. But I don't have to worry about that anymore. Now do I, Bob?" He turned and hoisted the boxes off the cart and carefully dropped each with a thud onto the conference table room. "See, I'm a Marine, and we believe in being prepared. So here are my records of Bob's performance over the past two years. My notes, his e-mails, records of meetings, etcetera, etcetera, etcetera. I know it looks like a lot of documents, but you have a few months to wade through all this before it's time for performance evaluations." He waved his hand over the boxes, like a prize model on *The Price is Right*. He reached into a file box for one more folder, labelled April 2018. "Here, Judith, is evidence of Bob's ability as a supervisor." He placed in front of her one of the first e-mails he had received from Robert and quoted it. "'Bill, you must submit administratively acceptable evidence to support your request for bereavement leave. Robert.' Yes, Bob asked me to prove that my wife and son had died in a terrible car accident and I needed to bury them." Bill aimed a forefinger at Robert's head. "And you selected that man as a Forest Supervisor."

Robert turned in his chair. "Judith, this is all crap. He's just trying to defend Jack. It's too late for that."

Bill chucked as he glanced at his Timex. "But it's not too late for some things, is it, Bob? Some things can follow you for years and years."

"Bill, can you wrap this up soon?" Judith asked. "We'll look through your files, I promise."

"Thank you. Now there's a separate issue regarding how Bob treats women on the forest. I asked one of the admin folks to describe her experiences with Bob. Soon, my e-mail filled with comments from other employees." He opened a box and removed a thick brown envelope. "Here's a description from a recreation tech assigned to float down one of the rivers with Bob, during which he repeatedly invited her to go ashore for an intimate liaison." Bill held up another page. "Here's a receptionist who Bob cornered in a mailroom and invited to come to his hotel room. Now, maybe texting a rather explicit sexual request to a fire staffer was a mistake, but here's a copy, just the same."

Robert stood again. "This is outrageous! There's no proof of any of this." He turned on Bill. "I will sue you for slander."

"Good." Bill said. "You go for it, Bob." He held up the folder with the remaining statements. "Judith, I received all of these in just the past few days. But just prove one of these is wrong, Bob."

Judith sat back again. "OK, I think we can wrap this up."

At that moment, Judith's intercom buzzed. "Sorry for the inter-ruption, but there's a visitor here for Bill."

"Just one last thing before I go," Bill said. "Bob, do you remember back when you were a supervisory firefighter on the Chequamegon–Nicolet?"

"Of course, I had a great time there," Robert said.

Despite his fury at Robert's tone, Bill sounded sardonic. "That's nice. Because one of your crew doesn't recall such a great time there. At the time, she was a sophomore at University of Wisconsin, Stevens Point." Bill came to lean toward Robert. "Do you recall anyone like that, Bob. Her name was Ruth."

"We had so many interns; it's hard to remember them all."

"Oh, so you don't remember all the interns you raped?"

"That's enough." Robert stood and grabbed his briefcase. "Judith, he's just making stuff up now."

Bill went to Judith's desk. "Here's Ruth's statement. Medical record. Police report. Certificate of live birth. Adoption paperwork."

"I'm done listening to this nonsense," Robert said angrily. "I'm taking Jack back to Michigan so he can pack for Alaska."

Judith sat back, apparently to watch this play out before her. "Bill, anything else?"

Bill turned to face Robert directly. "Bob, Jack isn't going to be driving you anywhere. But I've arranged for someone who will drive you up to Ashland." He resisted the temptation to grip the man by his throat, even though Robert had lied repeatedly. "My visitor outside is a sheriff's deputy from Ashland County."

"I was there 30 years ago," Robert muttered.

"True, but see, Bob, in Wisconsin, the law on sexual assault is pretty clear. Rape resulting in pregnancy is First Degree Sexual Assault. There is no statute of limitations." Bill took a step closer toward Robert. "I suggest you shut up now. Judith and I could be called to testify about any excited utterance you make now. Come on, let's go meet the officer." He gripped Robert by the arm and pulled him out of Judith's office. Tara stood at her desk, watching in wide-eyed shock.

The Ashland County deputy wore an all-black uniform. Her badge was a polished silver six-pointed star. Monica stood a few feet behind the deputy, watching the events intently. As Robert and Bill approached, the deputy produced a set of handcuffs. "Robert Fulbright, I have a warrant for your arrest. Are you carrying any weapons? I will search you if I need to." She drew his arms back and placed the cuffs on his wrists behind his back. "You have the right to remain silent. Anything you say can and will be used against you. You have the right to an attorney. If you cannot afford an attorney, one will be provided for you. Do you understand these rights I just read to you?"

Robert made one more effort to face off with Bill, but the deputy pushed him forward by his cuffed hands. Bill turned back to Judith's office. From the doorway he said, "I apologize for this spectacle. With Bob back in Wisconsin, an arrest warrant could be served."

Judith stood and came around her desk to lean against the conference table where Bill's file boxes sat. "This had nothing to do with Jack, did it?"

"No, ma'am."

"You did all this for these women?" she asked, holding up the folder of statements that Annette had solicited from the women on the forest.

"Yes, but it started with a little girl. Well, and my wife," he said.

33

"Well, I don't think I need to fret over Robert's performance evaluation now."

"I'd like to clear up one detail about this business about Jack not doing his job. Did Bob tell you that Rory came to him for direction on Sand Lake because Jack wasn't available?"

She nodded.

"Yeah. See, the reason Rory couldn't find Jack that morning was because we were in Bob's office explaining the situation at Sand Lake and Jack's plan to deal with it. I suspect most of what Bob told you over the past month is pure bull." Bill turned to go, then stopped and came back to the doorway. "You should ask Monica to investigate the other districts and forests where Bob has worked. Or if you want, I'll have some spare time in a few weeks when I could do it myself. Share anything I learn with *The New York Times, Washington Post, Podunk Picayune.*"

"Are you trying to blackmail me?"

"Yes," Bill said, though it was a hollow threat. He pointed to the folder on her desk. "I'd like some assurance that those women won't be harassed for coming forward. Go through those statements. Maybe you could reach out to the women Bob harassed. You might keep the Forest Service from being the topic on the PBS NewsHour again."

"And?"

I'd like to see Elizabeth transferred into a different position; public affairs, fire staff where she's got quals already — just please let her do more than fetch dry cleaning."

Judith laughed at the thought of it. "You've heard of Merit Promotion, right? I can't just give people jobs."

"No, but she can transfer into any GS-9 admin position. Now, that's really just a cost savings. If Elizabeth files an EEOC complaint, you'll pay her more than the price of a lateral move in the same office. A *lot* more."

"Nothing else?"

"Well, Jack. If you ignore everything that Bob said, there's really no reason to send him to Siberia, is there?"

"Agreed. And nothing else? Do you want to change your retirement plans?"

"No. My father is 89, and my father-in-law is 92. They're both stubbornly trying to farm up in Gogebic County, the stone capital of Michigan. It's time I go help. Thank you for hearing me out."

"I understand." She put on a pair of reading glasses and opened the folder of statements from the women on the Huron-Manistee.

Bill then turned and went back to the outer office. Jack sat adjacent to Tara's desk. They were engaged in a lively discussion. Monica stood apart, waiting for Bill to emerge. "You could have told me. I'd have taken care of it, you know. I'm actually quite good at my job."

Bill leaned forward slightly so he could whisper. "I was hoping he would take a swing at me. But then you'd be arresting me instead."

Tara interrupted them. "Monica, Judith would like to speak with you."

Against all CDC guidance, Monica extended her hand and shook Bill's. "Nice work." She went into the Regional Forester's office and closed the door behind her.

"That was one of the most enlightening meetings I've had in years, at least since the time a past Chief called me an idiot," Judith said. She handed the folder of employee statements to Monica. "Here, please go through these and investigate any claims that may lead to charges."

"The deputy told me the state charges, and it sounds like there's good evidence. Robert is in a lot of trouble."

"So you think Bill's got all his facts straight?" Judith asked.

"I wouldn't expect any less from a Marine," Monica said.

Out in the foyer, Bill turned to Jack. "You want a ride back to Michigan? I think Bob's going to be busy for a while."

"Can we stop at the Pfister? I've got to grab my bags." Jack reached into his trouser pocket and fished out the keys to the government vehicle. "Would you give these to Robert? If he won't be needing the rig, we'll send someone to get it."

As they rode down in the elevator together, Bill gave a sigh of relief that he felt throughout his torso. "Strike the tent. The act in ring three has closed."

Jack asked, "So what did he do that got him arrested?"

"That's a long story. If we go up and around the lake rather than down through Chicago, I'll have plenty of time to tell you."

"OK, so long as you don't make me sit in the car every time we stop."

They went out the side exit of the Gaslight Building onto Van Buren Street. As they passed an alley entrance, Jack spotted the same woman from earlier that morning sitting on a back stoop in the shade. "You got any cash? I'll repay you."

Bill took his billfold from an inside jacket pocket. "I'm still burning through the cash I withdrew for the Resistance efforts. How much do you need?"

"Got a twenty?"

Bill handed over a hundred dollar bill. "Sorry, smallest I have at the moment."

"It'll do." Jack took the bill and went 20 feet into the alley. He gave the woman the money. "Sorry I didn't have anything for breakfast. How about lunch and dinner instead."

She accepted the money, looking at him with wide eyes.

"You probably saved my life. I think that taxi was aiming for me." He turned and walked back to where Bill stood on the sidewalk. "Thanks. Had to pay a debt."

"Wow. Your bookie is in deep cover."

May 6

Jack dropped his computer bag and canvas tote in the back seat. He draped his sports jacket over top of them. As he pulled his necktie loose, he climbed into the front seat of the Wagoneer. "I've got a couple of bottles of water and the bags of peanuts from the hotel room if you need any refreshments."

"You ever look at what they charge you for all that stuff? A bottle of water alone is probably five bucks."

"Really? I thought it was all free."

"You didn't take anything from the room's minibar, did you? That's where they really get you."

"Just a couple of Imperial Russian Stouts when we got here last night. Robert had an evening engagement, so I had a few beers in the room before I went to Blu for dinner and then the Belmont Tavern. Maybe a Heineken when I got back." He shifted in his seat so he could look directly at the driver. "And why am I reporting to you?" he asked rhetorically.

"Well, I hope Bob had a nice evening. May not be many more for a long time to come."

"Wait. I think you took a wrong turn." Jack reached to turn off the radio. "We're on I-41 instead of 43. 43 goes up to Sheboygan and Green Bay. I don't even know where 41 goes."

"We'll go through Fond du Lac and Oshkosh before we take 45 up to Watersmeet. I need to make a couple of stops in the morning. That OK?"

"You bet. I'm in no hurry to tell Melissa we have to pack in a hurry so we can catch the ferry in Bellingham."

"So you decided to go?" Bill asked.

"No choice now."

"Oh, I'd say give it a couple of days before you tell Melissa. Judith could change her mind. You just never know."

"In case she doesn't, I'm trying to look on the bright side. The hunting is great. I never got a moose while I was up there."

"Don't clear a space on the wall just yet," Bill said.

May 7

LANSING, Mich. – Michigan's Governor announced she has reopened manufacturing, including the Big Three automakers – Ford, General Motors and Fiat Chrysler – at the beginning of next week.

Manufacturing workers can return to the job Monday (May 11), the Governor said. This announcement comes after she loosened restrictions on landscapers, golf and motorized boating.

Manufacturing companies are required to take steps to protect workers from the spread of COVID-19, which includes daily entry screenings for everyone entering the facility, a questionnaire covering symptoms and exposure to people with possible COVID-19 and temperature checks as soon as no-touch thermometers can be obtained.

Companies must also create dedicated entry points at every facility and suspend entry of all non-essential in-person visits, including tours.

– ClickonDetroit.com

May 7

A new estimate of the U.S. infection fatality rate from the novel coronavirus puts it at 1.3%, making it deadlier than the seasonal flu, which in a typical season has a 0.1% infection fatality rate.

A professor in the department of pharmacy at the University of Washington in Seattle used publicly available data on infection numbers and deaths from the novel coronavirus through April 20.

– CNN.

May 7

"I'm viewing the third quarter as being a very important quarter because that's — as I said, that'll be a transition. I think you could almost say a 'transition into greatness,' because I think next year we're going to have a phenomenal year — a phenomenal year, economically."

> – The President of the United States,
> speaking at the White House.

May 7

Three men watched the 9-year-old as she walked along the shoreline of Sand Lake. Regina was at the library, downloading news and checking e-mail. Rick sat eating a frozen meal of Swedish meatballs while Doc Mac and Frank finished the leftover breakfast Regina had made of potato and egg scramble with onions and peppers. In another day, Rick would end his quarantine following his trip into Grand Rapids. Throughout his hibernation, his temperature had never gone above 98.1.

The morning calm was shattered by the blaring of a car horn as a Ford Explorer hurtled into the campground. Seeing her mother returning, Mary came running up from the water front, causing Frank to tense from fear that she would trip on a rock or an exposed tree root. The truck came so fast that when Regina stopped, it slid in the loose gravel. The transmission growled in protest when she shoved it into park.

"Frank, it's Monday!" Regina yelled through the open window. She jumped out and ran toward him. "The Governor said manufacturing can start back on May 11." She put her arms around his shoulders. "Isn't it great?"

Frank stood so he could hug her back. "Yes, it's just in time. Was there an e-mail?"

"Not yet. I can go back later today and first thing in the morning."

Mary joined the family embrace. "Can we go home now?"

"No, honey, not just yet," Regina said. "But your father can go back to work soon."

Frank rested his hand on the girl's shoulder. "We think it's best that you and your mother stay here a little while longer. Hopefully, Doc and Rick will be able to stay, too. And I'll come back every weekend." When he looked over toward the picnic tables, Rick and Doc Mac were nodding in agreement.

"And we'll be OK, right?" Regina asked. "We're still welcome, after all the trouble?"

"As long as you want to stay. When will you have to go back, Frank?" Rick asked.

"I don't rightly know. I imagine they'll bring us back in staggered groups. But supervisors will probably be first, so I'll go in at the start. The union said there will be training on Covid-19, like precautions and symptoms. The lines won't be running for at least a couple of weeks."

"I haven't heard anything from the hospital, but I will put in my retirement papers as soon as I do." He paused, considering all the possible complications. "I have to go to Grand Rapids and use the government computer to do it. Won't be gone more than a day. Glad you've got that doctor from Cadillac Mercy. Do you have her phone number?"

Regina nodded. "She gave me her personal cellphone number."

"She was nice," Mary said. "She said she went all the way to Baltimore, Maryland, for medical school." She turned toward Doc Mac. "Is there a good medical school there?"

"Did she say it was called John Hopkins?" Doc Mac asked.

"Yes, I think that was it."

"Oh, impressive."

Rick turned toward Doc Mac. "Where did you go?"

Seemingly irritated by the question, McKettrick said, "Indiana University. In Indianapolis."

"I nearly went to IU," Frank said. "But I didn't want to play ball for Bobby Knight. So it was MSU."

"Even Larry Bird went to Indiana State," the doctor observed.

"Well, I always liked the Spartans over the Hoosiers," Rick said.

Regina took Mary's hand, and they headed for the big camper. "Let's go see what we have for dinner." She wondered to herself why their conversations never once brought up the WNBA, even though it had been around more than 20 years. In her senior year at high school, her team had gone undefeated and was runner-up at state. Before she became pregnant, she consistently out-shot Frank from the three-point line. "How does spaghetti sound?"

"OK. Do you think Daddy will like it again?"

May 8

The President has been bullish about a coronavirus vaccine — so much so that experts have had to talk him off a more aggressive timeline for it.

But on Friday, the President seemed to shift his rhetoric on the topic, saying we don't even need one for the virus to go away. "I just rely on what doctors say," he said when pressed.

Except that's not what his coronavirus task force doctor says.

"I feel about vaccines like I feel about tests: This is going to go away without a vaccine," the President said. "It's going to go away, and we're not going to see it again, hopefully, after a period of time."

The President said that there could be "flare-ups," including in the fall, but that it would go away regardless. "There are some viruses or flus that came and they went for a vaccine, and they never found the vaccine," he said. "And they've disappeared. They never showed up again. They die, too, like everything else."

Pressed on the claim, he doubled down.

"They say it's going to go — that doesn't mean this year — doesn't mean it's going to be gone, frankly, by fall or after the fall," the President said. "But eventually it's going to go away. The question is will we need a vaccine. At some point it's going to probably go away by itself. If we had a vaccine that would be very helpful."

The director of the National Institute of Allergy and Infectious Diseases has said we need a vaccine. "There's truth to that. It's not going to be over to the point of our being able to not do any mitigation until we have a scientifically sound, safe and effective vaccine."

— *The Washington Post*

May 8

As Jack finished showering, his work cellphone rang on the desk. He recognized the 231 area code as northern Michigan. He decided to call back after he managed to towel off and pull on some clothing. A full two minutes elapsed before the same number rang again. He ignored it again, focusing on how to get a cup of coffee from the pint-sized pot in his room. On the third call, he surrendered to his fate.

"Good morning," he growled into the phone.

"Oh, woke you?" Elizabeth asked. "Sorry."

"Worse. Caught me between shower and coffee. I'm going to send an e-mail to your supervisor for your performance evaluation."

"Then I can save you the cost of an e-mail," she said. "This morning Judith sent out an e-mail stating that beginning May 24th, you, Jack Ferguson, will be Acting Forest Supervisor. And, therefore, my supervisor, at least for now."

"Oh. Really?" The surprised sounded in his voice. "What else did she say?"

"Apparently Robert will remain in Wisconsin on special assignment to the Regional Office." Elizabeth coughed discreetly. "Isn't that what they do with people who screw up?"

"Less said the better."

"It's OK, I gave Bill one of the statements he used. And just so you know, I don't pick up dry cleaning."

"Fine with me. I have exactly one jacket that is dry clean."

"And I prefer to be called Elizabeth. No Liz, Lizzy, or Beth. Remember that when you ask me to put in your travel claims."

"I've heard you were tough on Forest Supervisors. But the next claim will be easy. Just two nights of lodging. No mileage, parking, or anything."

"Hold your horses," she said with a chuckle. "I wasn't volunteering to do this trip. You're not my problem for two more weeks. So talk to Gwen when you get back. Be sure to ask nicely."

"Am I not going to enjoy this assignment?"

"Well, Bob was not big on returning phone calls or answering email. And, you won't have a public affairs officer. So how's the view from the frying pan?"

"I don't think I accepted this assignment, yet."

"OK, but Tara told me your only other choice is Yakutat."

The phone line went dead.

May 8

The old Wagoneer rolled up to the front of the Northern Waters Resort in Watersmeet at almost 10 a.m. After tossing his carryall into the backseat, Jack climbed into the front passenger seat with his waxed paper mug of coffee. "Late start this morning?" he asked.

"Sorry. I was just planning quick visits, but Dad gets wound up early if he's watching Fox and Friends before I get there. If I knew they came on at 6 a.m., I'd have been there at 5. The President was on this morning, so Dad was in a lather. You'd think a man in his eighties wouldn't get himself so worked up."

Jack looked around the Jeep's interior. "I would swear this Jeep isn't older than coffee. So why no cup holders?" He snugged the drink between his legs. "Why does your Dad watch if it makes him so angry?"

"Why does everyone poke at a loose tooth?"

"Good point. So you spent the morning at your Dad's place?"

"No, I also had to check on Camille's parents. I have to rethink moving back here. Or I'll have to puncture my eardrums when I do."

"All the parents pretty vehement?" When Jack checked his phone, he saw no bars of service. *Good*, he thought, *a little quiet time*.

"Yeah. Her parents were going off on MSNBC. I couldn't even figure out what topic bothered them."

"I think you're missing the simple solution here," Jack said.

"You can fix my families?"

"Tell your Dad to watch MSNBC and your in-laws to watch Fox. Change their cable packages if you need to."

Bill laughed and smiled at Jack. "See, this keen analysis is why you're going to be a great Acting Forest Supervisor."

"Who will need a great PAO."

Bill sipped on a Vernor's ginger ale. "I'll send you some names."

"No reason you couldn't hang around a little while."

"No reason I couldn't gargle with bleach to kill coronavirus, but I think I'll pass all the same."

"Yeah, but my offer pays every two weeks. Bleach just solves your parent problems." With his right hand, Jack fumbled with the power adjustments on the side of his seat.

"Again, you with the keen analysis, but no thanks."

May 8

In Manistique, Bill stopped at the Subway shop on U.S. 2 not far after the Manistique River bridge. Fully masked, they had to order their sandwiches to go. When they came out, Jack pulled off his blue cloth face covering. "You think we'll ever get on the other side of this thing?"

Bill removed his mask as he climbed into the Jeep. "I'll tell you the same thing I told Ruth. We haven't got a prayer. Like every invasive species or disease we're dealing with on the forest, we have people willing to spread it around because they just don't care. 'Gypsy moth or emerald ash borer on the firewood I'm taking to deer camp? Well, screw you.' 'Zebra mussels or Eurasian milfoil on my boat? I don't have time to hose that off.' People won't wear masks now, and in six months they won't get the vaccine. Why? Because they read online that a mask will activate the virus that's already in them, or a vaccine is just to achieve mind control. It's all a hoax; it will disappear in a miracle; and the world is flat."

Jack stared at Bill in astonishment. "So you've thought about this."

"Sorry. I really struggle with this whole intentional ignorance thing. But for my next career, I'm going to sell conspiracy t-shirts and hats online, like 'Covid-19 came from Area 51.'" Bill pulled out onto U.S. 2, heading east toward St. Ignace and the Mackinaw Bridge.

"Oh. I thought you were going to be a rock farmer." Jack sipped his new cup of coffee. "We're going to stop soon to eat these sandwiches, right? Otherwise, I'm chewing on your upholstery."

"Yeah, there's a great waterfront park up here a little way."

Just as promised, Bill turned just beyond the Big Boy restaurant into Lakeview Park. He parked so they could watch the frothy white waves of Lake Superior as they dined. Jack had ordered a foot-long barbecue rib sub with peppers, onions and the rest of the garden. Bill purchased a half-sized tuna with tomatoes and mayo.

"So, you really think the Liberation Army is going to come after Mary again?" Jack asked.

"Good news? No, I think that backfired on him. Can't say 'leave my family alone' while you're out threatening someone's child. You remember that old TV show with Chuck Connors? He was a cavalry officer stripped of his rank and branded a coward in the opening credits. Remember that?"

"Can I phone a friend on this question?" Jack asked. He brushed crumbs from the sandwich off his fleece vest onto the Jeep floor.

"You're going to vacuum that up next time we stop for gas. Anyhow. I think Gary got drummed out of his toy army over that little incident."

"Thank God." Jack heaved a big sigh of relief. "I was afraid we were going to be dealing with that until the pandemic ends."

"That's the good news. Annette tells me that Gary is looking for a little muscle to come after me. He's mad about upsetting his parents, and he's angry that I showed him up. You know, little Gary didn't get a young child killed, and the campgrounds are still closed. Something tells me Gary's got a Napoleonic complex. I've read that guys suffering small man complex are more likely to commit violence."

"Do Marines really talk like Sigmund Freud?" Jack asked.

"No, I think it's Adler."

"You're not especially tall. Are you prone to violence?"

"Did I grant you permission to speak?"

"No, and I didn't ask."

"We're three hundred miles from Manistee. Lot of places to hide a body in that distance."

Jack threw back his head as he laughed. "Oh, come on. I was an Eagle Scout. We're like Canadian Mounties. You kill me, and my fellow Eagle Scouts will hunt you down. Like the Mounties, Eagle Scouts always get their man."

Now came Bill's turn to chuckle. "I wouldn't use that as a recruiting slogan. How about 'always get their suspect'?"

"Are we just going to sit here and chat all day? I've got a forest to run."

"Yep, run it straight into the ground."

"And where else would a forest be?" Jack asked.

May 8

Regina was back at the library before noon; Mary could ride with her because they never left the truck while they were checking the news and e-mail. Frank was policing downed limbs from the individual campsites after the winter winds. He placed them in brush piles along the road where Rick would come along and gather them in to his pick-up truck later in the afternoon. At that moment, Rick collected a water sample from the main water well in anticipation of the Governor issuing an all-clear order for outdoor activities in the wake of the manufacturing return.

Doc McKettrick walked to where Frank was working. He tried to speak casually, despite his concerns. "Hey, Frank, how's the morning going?"

Frank stopped and rested his arm over the end of rake handle. "Do you ever think that maybe the apocalypse has arrived already?"

Major McKettrick stopped in his tracks. "No, I don't usually think about that stuff this early in the morning. I was thinking more along the lines of how are you and Regina doing with all the stress? I see how Rick and Mary are doing, but I never thought to ask about the two of you."

"It's not been easy, no. I worry about her a bit because she carries a lot inside. She worries about Mary, my job, the RV breaking down on the way to a hospital and the usual money thing. Just yesterday she admitted that she's rationing her insulin to make it last longer." Frank looked directly at the doctor. "Could you tell her how just plain stupid that is? She's smart enough to understand, but she's got this idea we can't spend any money. That's why I'm going back to work as soon as I can. I hope you and Rick won't mind helping them more once I'm gone."

Doc Mac walked over and sat at the picnic table that Rick and Frank had recently put back in the campsite. He motioned for Frank to join him. "OK, first things first. Does she have a renewal on her insulin prescription? If not, I can prescribe it and call it into the Meijer pharmacy. Does she need needles or test strips? I'm sure Jack would bring it out to us. But you're right. That's stupid. When she gets back, I'll tell her just exactly how dangerous that is."

"I hope she'll listen to you. I can't get through." Frank looked as discouraged as he sounded. "I try to tell her, but she doesn't want to spend our savings on herself. The unemployment money doesn't go far, and this big bonus they're talking about in Congress is probably months away."

Doc turned his head so it didn't appear he was staring at Frank too closely as he asked, "Do you need a little help to tide you over until you start working?"

Frank blinked and automatically shook his head. "No, we'll be … What kind of help are you talking about?"

Doctors learn how to talk about sensitive topics, a skill Doc Mac used now. "I'll be honest with you. Between my military retirement and my VA work, I do OK. My daughter wants nothing from me ever again. So I could give you, or loan you, what you need to keep Mary and Regina healthy, and help out until you're getting regular paychecks again. Otherwise, you'll worry yourself sick the whole time you're back home and working."

"I don't think I could," Frank said. "That stimulus money came just in time for Regina's sanity. So long as we don't have an emergency, I think we'll be fine."

"Understood. If you have an emergency, all you need to do is ask." McKettrick started to walk away, then turned back. "I'm admire what you and Regina are doing for Mary. Camping for more than a month like this? That's a sacrifice. But I see what a great kid she is. You're very lucky."

"Thank you. And thank you for your concern. I do appreciate the generous offer. I hope we won't need to take you up on it."

Doc Mac walked back to where the Damon and Coleman sat. Frank resumed raking the downed limbs into a pile at the entrance to each campsite.

May 8

"When I look at our country today, and see what we are
willing to do to protect and support one another, I say with
pride that we are still a nation those brave soldiers, sailors
and airmen would recognize and admire."

> – Queen Elizabeth of Great Britain
> on the 75th Anniversary of V-E Day,
> comparing the British sacrifices
> during the novel coronavirus pandemic
> to those of service men and women
> during World War II.

May 8

Two men on the run and accused of murdering a security guard in Michigan last week have been arrested, officials announced Friday.

The suspects were arrested after they allegedly shot and killed 43-year-old guard at a Flint, Michigan, Family Dollar store following a dispute over the store's policy requiring everyone to wear a face mask.

"Last Friday a simple request to wear a mask in order to protect others resulted in the brutal murder of a security guard," the Genesee County Prosecutor said in a statement Friday. "His family lost a dedicated husband and father, and we all lost a devoted member of our community."

– ABC News

May 11

Dozens of angry Michiganders, fueled by conspiracy theories and disinformation about the coronavirus, are promoting violence and mobilizing armed rallies against Michigan's Governor on Facebook, in violation of the social media company's policies.

Metro Times gained access to four private Facebook groups that can only be seen by approved members. The pages, which have a combined 400,000 members, are filled with paranoid, sexist, and grammar-challenged rants, with members encouraging violence and flouting the governor's social-distancing orders.

Assassinating the Governor is a common theme among members of the groups. Dozens of people have called for her to be hanged.

"We need a good old fashioned lynch mob to storm the Capitol, drag her tyrannical ass out onto the street and string her up as our forefathers would have," a man wrote in a group called "The People of Michigan vs. The Governor," which had nearly 9,000 members as of Monday morning.

Another person had the same idea: "Drag that tyrant governor out to the front lawn. Fit her for a noose."

"Either the President sends in the troops or there is going to be a midnight lynching in Lansing soon," someone chimed in.

Others suggested she be shot, beaten, or beheaded.

– Detroit Metro Times.

May 11

A noise woke Rick in the pre-dawn dark. He laid alone in the
Coleman, straining to hear it again. Voices whispered too low for
him to hear. A car door closed. He studied the luminescent hands
and numbers on this Timex Q diving watch to determine the time.
He didn't want to turn on any lights in case surprise would become
necessary. At 5:17, false dawn was just beginning. After another
door closed nearby, he dropped quietly from his bunk to the floor.
He felt along the edge of the lower mattress for his Savage 220, a
bolt-action .20 gauge shotgun.

Was the Liberation Army back for a night attack?

He worked his way forward into the front bedroom that housed
the queen-sized bed. Rick had insisted Doc McKettrick use that
bedroom when he stayed in the Coleman. That arrangement satis-
fied the chief petty officer's sense of privilege; on a Navy vessel, an
officer would sleep forward in "Officer Country." He went first to
the window in the exterior door on the starboard side of the
bedroom. That faced the gate and the road entering the campground. There were no strange vehicles on that side, and no one he
could see.

On the port side of the bedroom was an oblong window facing
the larger Damon camper, which was definitely the source of the
noise he had heard. As he kept vigil, Rick saw Frank emerge
carrying an oversized duffle bag. Doc Mac came out a moment
later, holding a full laundry basket. These items went into the back
of the Explorer. Regina brought out a large ice cooler, which was
placed in the back seat. The major waved to Frank and returned to
the camper, leaving Regina and Frank alone. They hugged, and he
kissed her forehead. Then he climbed into the Explorer and headed
toward the campground gate.

Rick knew for a week that was a possibility, but the word must
have come without warning. He and the doctor would stay at Sand
Lake to assist Regina in keeping Mary safe. Doc Mac had also
informed Rick that the kind doctor would pay for any repairs necessary to make the Damon roadworthy for the drive to the St. Jude's
hospital where Mary would eventually be treated. He was glad for
the extra work to keep him occupied. There was little left on his to-

do list for the campground. All the downed limbs from the winter were removed. The picnic tables and fire rings were in place. The only thing missing was actual campers.

As Rick watched, Doc Mac went back into the Damon, leaving the family to say their good-byes. The doctor had explained to Rick that once Frank returned to work he would need to stay away from Mary until he could quarantine for a two-week stretch, just as Rick and McKettrick had done after the Rory and Fritz visit.

When mother and daughter retreated from the Explorer, Frank climbed in and started the engine. Carrying a box from the camper's refrigerator, Rick went out and knocked on the window of the Ford's passenger door. Frank put the window down from his armrest. "Hey, I didn't see any lights on in the camper, so I wasn't going to bother you," Frank said, extending his hand to shake Rick's. "Thanks for all your help."

"It is my privilege. Can I ask you a favor though?" Rick hoisted the 12-pack of Budweiser through the truck window and put it on the Explorer's front seat. "Could you find a use for this? If I keep it, I'll just be tempted. Don't want to get the doc angry."

"Understood. I'll find some use."

Rick stepped away from the Explorer as Frank headed out to Grand Rapids.

May 11

Bill discovered his office lights already on when he arrived Monday morning. He found Elizabeth waiting inside in the midst of all piles of the future paper shredding. "Already?" he asked. "He isn't acting Forest Supervisor for another week yet."

"Close the door," she said. "We need to talk."

He shut the door behind him, then placed his fedora on the coat rack in the corner. "How can I be in trouble already? I've been out of the office for almost a week."

"Why don't you sit?"

When he did, she made a call on her cell. "He's here." She stood and opened the door, pulling on a mask as she held it open. Ruth came around the corner, followed by Wendy, the District Ranger from the Baldwin office. Technically, Visser was Wendy's problem, but the would-be cattle baron had been so persistent for so many years that Bill just asked to deal with it directly every time they received his request. Wendy was also masked, likely due to Ruth's condition.

Bill fished a back-up mask out of a desk drawer and donned it. "Look, I appreciate the thought, but you're a little early with the retirement party. I'm here two more weeks."

Ruth opened a leather binder across her lap. "Bill, this is a formal intervention at the request of the Regional Forester. Judith asked Monica to complete a threat assessment on the Liberation Army of Michigan, based on some information that Annette found online. This looks pretty serious. She asked me to fill in as acting forest supervisor until Jack is ready." She handed Bill a thick report bound in a wide black clip. "Judith is concerned that you won't take it seriously, so she wanted me to deliver it personally."

"Monica asked me to participate because I've had that MOSAIC training about identifying threats," Wendy said. "Turns out I made terrible choices in husbands."

Bill held the report in his hands to judge its heft. "Judith thought it would take all three of you to carry this in here?" He looked at the women intently. "And no donuts? Seriously?"

"You're lucky I don't have the strength to slap you across the face," Ruth said.

"I do," Elizabeth volunteered.

"Thank you. That won't be necessary," Bill said. "These guys are all mouth. On Facebook, they're talking about putting the governor to the guillotine. Does anyone think the Michigan State Police are going to stand around while some guys build a guillotine in front of the Governor's Mansion? First, where would they even get a hundred-pound blade like that?"

"Elizabeth and I may take turns slapping you," Wendy warned. "Please read what Monica sent. Let me have it for a minute." She held out her hand, then flipped through the pages of the report until she found a particular passage. She turned the page toward Bill. "Here, these guys have identified your house and posted photos. They have photos of both your Jeeps." She scrolled a few pages farther into the document. "Here's your father's house." Next page. "Here's Camille's parent's house."

"You're less popular than even the Governor right now," Elizabeth said.

Ruth leaned toward Bill. "Yes, most bullies are blowhards, but you can't just ignore this threat. Judith and Monica suggested that you spend a few weeks in Milwaukee."

He shook his head. "But if they can't find me, won't they just go to Watersmeet? No, I need to contain the problem down here."

"Damn Marine Corps training," Wendy said. "Why couldn't you have been Air Force? Coast Guard Reserve? National Weather Service?"

"Because I ..." he stopped, not wanting to tell the three women exactly why he had enlisted.

Ruth raised her hands. "Yes, I know. I heard it from my brother often enough, 'Once a Marine ...' So let's talk about alternatives. OGC suggested the online posts might justify a temporary restraining order."

Bill chuckled. "And the Office of General Counsel knows we need a specific identification of the person making the threat to get a TRO."

Ruth nodded in agreement. "Seemed a long shot. Annette asked about putting disinformation online about the Liberation Army members."

As if waving the suggestion off with his hands, Bill shook his head vehemently. "No, we can't risk having Annette engage these guys. They'll go after her family instead of me. No. Besides, they're already angry with me. Disinformation isn't going to help that."

"I'm running out of suggestions," Ruth said quietly. "But Ted volunteered to bunk with you for a couple of weeks."

"Thank you, Ruth," he said. "I'm sure you volunteered Ted to bunk with me. He knows he's needed more at home."

Ruth looked down at her hands in her lap.

"So you have a response in mind?" Wendy asked.

"You know what Warren Zevon said, 'Send lawyers, guns, and money.'" He stood and reached into the waistband at the back of his trousers. He laid a Springfield XD .45 caliber on his desktop, then placed his foot on the seat of his chair so he could draw a Smith & Wesson M&P .40 from an ankle holster. Small pistols with a lot of stopping power. He did not reveal that he carried a loaded back-up clip for each weapon.

"You can't have those in the office. Only LE can have weapons in the building." Elizabeth said, as she leaned forward for a better view.

He carefully stowed the pistols back into their respective holsters. "I have a concealed carry permit. I told Monica about these. I also informed the Cadillac PD; the Wexford and Manistee sheriffs; and the State Police of the threats." He looked at Ruth. "If you want me to lock them in the safe while I'm in the office, I will. But it will slow response time if the Liberation Army comes here."

"You're in the office ten more days?" she asked. She looked at Wendy. "What do you think?"

Wendy shook her head in doubt. "So let's step back from that question a moment." She reached forward and took the risk assessment from Bill's desk and flipped to the last few pages. "The RF asked us to come ensure Bill carefully considered the online threats against him. Which we did. But when we get to the end, there are no recommendations. So what is it exactly that Judith and Monica want him to do? Because if they don't have a plan, I'm OK with his."

"Do you need to come into the office at all?" Ruth asked. Bill worried that she might be tiring. "I know you have to be here physically on your last day to sign out, but what about the other days?"

He motioned with the sweep of an arm. "Here is where the shredding is."

Elizabeth raised her hand, even though it was unnecessary. "I can take care of that. If you sort it, I can get the shredding done. The front liners can shred old papers, and I can shred any sensitive materials." She smiled at Bill, "You know, all the nuclear secrets and the Secret Smokey handshake stuff."

"Bill?" Ruth asked. "Are you OK if you just finish the sorting and leave the shredding to us?"

"So you want me to stay out of the office as much as possible? But I can't take any more days of leave. They've already calculated my final annual and sick leave balances."

"He could work in the old admin building at Chittenden," Elizabeth suggested. "They're almost done with the renovation work."

"What do you think, Bill?"

He shrugged. "Sure. Just need to get Jack's permission. It's his district. He might be jealous he won't work there first."

May 12

OWOSSO, Mich. — Armed members of the Michigan Home Guard stood outside a barbershop, ready to blockade the door if police arrived. They were determined to help reopen the shop Monday, in defiance of state orders, and dozens joined them, wearing sweatshirts and cowboy hats and waving flags in support of the President.

They gathered not because they desperately needed haircuts but to rail against the Democratic Governor's approach to fighting the coronavirus outbreak in Michigan, one of the nation's worst hot spots. They were channeling the President's support of such protests, but some also were taking aim at the state's Republicans, who they say have not done enough to "liberate" the state from safety measures that have ground life to a halt.

The protest and others like it – including two last month that included demonstrators with swastikas, Confederate flags and some with long guns inside the Capitol — have alarmed lawmakers on both sides of the aisle. But after the President appeared to urge the militia members on, tweeting that they are "very good people" who "want their lives back again," they have forced Michigan's Republican lawmakers to strike a delicate balance, managing a deadly virus while also being careful not to contradict the President or alienate their conservative supporters.

Though the coronavirus has infected more than 48,000 people in Michigan and has killed 4,674 as of Tuesday — the fourth-highest total in the nation — many of the protesters live in areas that have barely been touched by the virus but have been struggling with economic collapse because of it. GOP state lawmakers, who hold narrow margins in both the state House and Senate, have tried distancing themselves from the most vocal protesters while being careful not to appear to hew too closely to the Governor's shutdown policies.

Generally, residents of Michigan agree with the Governor's approach, according to a Washington Post-Ipsos poll released Tuesday, in which 72 percent approve of her handling of the outbreak, and 25 percent disapprove.

— The Washington Post.

May 12

Doctor McKettrick found Rick inspecting the campsites, looking at both the height of the grass and what Jack called "hazard trees." Part of Rick's duties would be to take out any dangerous limbs that might fall on campers. One of the district recreation staff had stopped by the campground to explain how to identify the dangers. She told Rick and Frank that when she first arrived on the forest a limb fell on a tent during a storm, badly injuring one of the Boy Scouts inside.

"I saw you gave Frank a parting gift," Doc Mac said, walking a safe distance away from Rick.

"I don't have so much use for it now."

"I'm glad. You know, I never told you that I know exactly what it's like. After Connie died, I started quitting cigarettes and drinking at the same time. Took almost four years to get it done. Still days I came home from work thinking about putting on my favorite Keith Jarrett concert album on the stereo and sitting out back with a tequila sunrise and a Marlboro. I wish I didn't miss it so much."

Rick stopped and looked around him. "You know, I'm glad I'm here. I don't think I could go sober if I didn't have some work to keep me busy."

"Well, you might get even busier now. I'm thinking that pretty soon the hospitals will have to get back to treating other people. Think of all the patients who have been sitting at home while doctors and hospitals aren't seeing anyone in person." McKettrick perched on a picnic table in a nearby campsite.

Rick sat on the opposite side at the far end of the table. "So you think they'll be calling for Mary soon?"

Doc Mac nodded. "I hope so."

"How much time do you suppose we have? The Damon's going to need a little bit of work before a trip like that. Including some things that I can't do here. She's gonna need at least a day, maybe two, in the shop."

"So where will Mary and Regina be while their home is in the shop?" Doc rested his face in his hands.

"You suppose Jack would let them stay in his cabin for a couple of days?" Rick asked. "I hate to take advantage, but there aren't many places that are still safe from coronavirus."

"I guess we'll just have to ask."

May 13

An elderly barber shop owner who defied Michigan's governor's order to remain closed has had his business license suspended.

The state Licensing and Regulatory Affairs Department ordered the barbershop license for the barber shop on Main Street in Owosso be suspended. The 34-page document states that the public health, safety and welfare requires emergency action.

The barber's attorney says it's just not right.

"I guess the agency, and the AG's office and the governor don't believe in innocent until proven guilty anymore; you're guilty if charged," the attorney told WWJ. "I mean, our whole constitutional system and everything's getting turned on its head — all in the name of good intentions and trying to stop a virus that everyone knows can't be stopped in the sense that they're talking about."

– WWJ, Detroit.

May 13

Michigan health officials believe the stay-home model is working to reduce the spread of COVID-19 as new cases, deaths and the rate of positive tests continue to decline.

The infectious respiratory virus that has rocked the state and global economy in recent months appears to have peaked in Michigan during the first week of April.

Hospitalizations are down 64 percent from a month ago, the average number of cases a day has plummeted, and deaths are down 45 percent from last week's daily average.

"We are seeing cases decreasing over time, which is what we want to see," said an infectious disease specialist for the Detroit Medical Center.

Of the COVID-19 tests conducted Sunday, May 10, only 6.3 percent came back positive for the respiratory virus that has infected more than 48,000 Michiganders since mid-March. That marks the first time the percentage of positive tests dipped below 7 percent since March 11 when it was 0 percent.

– Mlive.

May 13

Sorting through old files and correspondence can be a very nostalgic task. Like the letter from the resident of Oscoda who was quite angry that the Forest Service would thin a stand of trees that he COULD SEE FROM HIS FRONT PORCH! A series of letters from a woman who recently moved to the Mio area challenged the need to create habitat for the Kirtland's warbler, an endangered species. The small songbird is like human snowbirds in the sense that it spends summers in Michigan, but overwinters in a warmer climate, primarily the Bahamas. Having done her research, the woman offered a simple solution for managing the birds; stop providing habitat among young jack pine trees where the warblers nest in Michigan so that the birds simply stay in the Bahamas year-round. Bill paused shuffling paper when he found a rather threatening letter from a gentleman in Freesoil addressed to him personally. After addressing Bill as an "idot," instead of idiot, the man claimed that Bill was himself to blame because the man had not taken a deer during the past three hunting seasons. If he was unsuccessful again, the hunter promised to track down Bill and hang the public affairs officer's carcass from a buck pole. The unhappy deer hunter was gracious enough to put his return address on the letter's envelope, so Henry had little trouble locating him and explaining the penalty for threatening a federal employee.

"Ah, good times," Bill mused aloud in an empty room.

In boxes filled from his file cabinets, he had old letters and notes collected over two decades. Records of public meetings; complaints; documentation of phone calls and other public interaction; plans and demands; environmental assessments and environmental impact statements; and the effluvium of lawsuits.

As he filled box after box for shredding, he considered whether it would be easier just to stack the boxes outside and douse them with an accelerant. Maybe he could use one of the drip torches that the fire crews use to spread flames across the boundary of a prescribed burn or ignite a back burn. He paused the sorting and opened a canvas tote bag. An inch deep into the paperwork related to retirement, he found the article that Ruth had given him back at Easter about dealing with misinformation in the post-truth era. Her husband Ted's direct response after reading the paper was "Back burn."

Bill came to the Forest Service too old to begin fighting forest fires. But he had grown up fly-fishing on the great rivers of the UP, streams where Hemingway had famously fished. So he thought about attracting a fish with a few fake casts, just to engage his target's interest. On his cell phone, he brought up recent calls and tapped a frequent number.

"You know I work, right? An actual government job that I'm not planning to leave in two weeks." From her tone, Bill could not quite determine if Annette was seriously annoyed by the intrusion or not. "I have a family. Even a husband. So keep those things in mind whenever you interrupt me."

"I think you're going to like this."

"If I had a million dollars for every time you said that."

"Come on, it will be fun. I want you to do some PR work for me. I need to be a total asshole. And I need it spread across Facebook, Twitter, all the chans, Instagram, Pinterest, TikTok, and anywhere else you can think of."

"So if you're finally going to be your real self, do you want to be on Tinder? Or Grindr?" She chuckled quietly.

"Oh, come on, you know I'd have to be on that site for old timers who share fiber recipes," Bill said.

"It disturbs me that you know about swingingoldies.sad. So you want me to turn you into a total jerk online. Is this some part of a grand plan?"

"Yes, because after you create me as a moron, I want you to show me bragging about beating the Liberation Army of Michigan. Lay it on thick, with a ladle. I want to make Gary so angry that he has to come find me."

"Did you recently have any sharp blows to your head?" Annette asked. "Any new medications that might explain this loss of reason?"

"Did you know Ted? Ruth's husband? He was legendary as an incident commander, the kind of IC they'd bring in when everything was going to hell. They used to say *Jesus could walk on water, but Ted could walk through fire.*"

"Are you sure about no recent head injuries?" she asked again. "You're kind of rambling here."

"OK, long story short. Through Ruth, Ted gave me a bit of advice about how to deal with all the online crap."

"So don't keep me waiting."

"Back burn."

"Well, Luke, the force is strange with you. Can you call me back when you're not seeing double?"

"A bunch of old vets scared the Liberation Army into running like a rafter of wild turkeys. Little Gary wants to sacrifice the weak, just not his own parents. All stuff like that. Put it all under my name. Include a picture of me if you have one. I want to be Gary's worst nightmare?"

"He suffers from leukophobia? Cause you're the whitest person I know."

"So you think I should skip the whitewalls next time I get a high-and-tight Marine haircut?"

Annette laughed until she choked. "And lose the cardigans and argyles, too. We're not living in Mister Reinhardt's neighborhood."

"That's way harsh."

"And stop with quoting movies and songs. You're too old for cool."

The line went dead. Annette thought she had finally crossed a line with Bill. On his end, he listened intently to the quiet. Another loud rapping came from the front entrance foyer. He drew the Springfield .45 from the belt holster and chambered a round. He knelt behind the table stacked with file boxes. He looked at the windows to see if anyone was getting into position to fire on the building. Unfortunately, there were plenty of conifers and structures on the grounds of the former tree nursery that might provide cover for a sniper or other unfriendlies.

The same knocking came from the front door. Slightly more insistent the second time. Bill moved his Smith and Wesson from the ankle holster to a hip pocket. He moved closer to the windows for a better view. Nothing out of the usual. He went out the side door and moved quietly toward the front corner of the building. A fire engine and three POVs sat in front of the adjacent garage. He knelt and peered around the corner of the main building toward the front entrance, still holding the Springfield in the ready position. Near his Wagoneer sat a Volvo. He stood and walked toward the front entrance. A woman knocked loudly on the exterior door, but she turned to go toward her car before she saw him. He tried to discretely put the pistol back into its holster. Doctor Pelletier looked much younger without the mask and face shield she wore at the hospital.

"They told me at your office that you are working out here now," Doctor Pelletier said. "I hope it's OK that I came."

Bill wondered about the value of working alone in the old tree nursery if the employees at the Cadillac office happily told strangers his location.

"Sure, it's fine. I owe you an apology for not coming in for those other tests." He motioned toward the grey steel doors. "Why don't we go inside? It's not really warming up yet with this breeze."

When he reached to open the door, she stepped back and removed from her pocket a blue surgical mask. "It's nothing personal," she said, pointing toward her face. "With my job, I can't take any chances."

"Understood. I'll go get mine from my work space."

When he returned from his make-shift office, she was sitting on the countertop of the reception desk. "I hope this is OK. You don't seem to have any chairs yet." Her wool coat was draped over the counter next to her.

"You're fine. I have to say, I think this is my first house call."

"Oh, dear," she said with a laugh. "I'm sorry, but I'm not really here about you. I came to ask about the little girl. How is she doing?"

"I really don't know. Jack and I have stayed away, hoping to keep the campers as isolated as possible. I understand that Frank, Mary's father, just left to go back to GM."

"If he starts working, that means he can't be around Mary. He'll have to quarantine for 14 days before every time he comes up for a visit."

"I had the impression from Jack that they were planning on that. Regina also asked if she and Mary could stay at his cabin while their camper went into the shop for a couple of days." Bill leaned against the wall at least two caribou away. "I think they have all the precautions covered."

She nodded, shifting uncomfortably on the counter. "I've been in contact with my friend at St. Jude's, but so far no real information."

"I think she's safe here. I can't imagine anyone getting close as long as Doc Mac and Rick are on duty."

"A couple weeks back I had a handful of guys in the ER complaining about being tear-gassed. You know anything about that?"

He chuckled quietly. "Depends. Is this an official inquiry of any sort?"

"No, they didn't want to put down anything official." She slid forward so she could stand and lean against the countertop. "And they all had health insurance from the same religious cost-sharing scheme."

Bill nodded and laughed. "Sometime I can tell you all about it. Maybe after the statute of limitations runs out."

"Deal. I never knew the Forest Service had clandestine operations." She put on her coat.

"Maybe someday I'll show you the super-secret Smokey handshake."

"You got Zoom? Maybe FaceTime or Skype?" She raised her eyebrows in anticipation. "We could start there."

"I happen to be a certified Lean Six Zoom Black Belt."

"Meaning you'll go home and spend the night figuring it out?" She pulled her coat closed. "Let me know when you've got it down." She started toward the door.

"Mademoiselle, I look forward to our next conversation."

"One thing about this video chat stuff." She stopped and faced him. "I'll expect you to wear pants."

May 14

Michigan's Governor says more protests at the state Capitol are making it increasingly likely that Michiganders may have to stay at home past May 28.

During an appearance on morning talk show "The View" on Wednesday, she was asked about the protests that have taken place at the Capitol.

"I do think the fact of the matter is, these protests in a perverse way make it likelier that we're going to have to stay in a stay-home posture. The whole point of (the protests) supposedly is that they don't want to be doing that and that's why I'm asking that everyone with a platform call on people to do the right thing," the Governor said.

– Mlive.

May 15

The number of confirmed cases of the coronavirus
(COVID-19) in Michigan has risen to 50,079 as of Friday,
including 4,825 deaths, state officials report.

– ClickonDetroit.com

May 15

Gwen felt frustrated. She wanted to give Jack a big send-off before he went on his detail as acting Forest Supervisor, but hardly anyone planned to work in the Manistee district office today. She also wanted to plan a welcome for the incoming acting district ranger, but that person was yet unnamed. Finally, she was offended that Robert was in legal custody rather than abducted by the nefarious assassins she had dreamed about for years. Often she had heard about bodies buried on the empty acres of the National Forests.

Shortly before 8 a.m., Rory and Fritz came past her office, the dog poking its snout in briefly in an ongoing quest for foot. "You seen Jack this morning?" Rory asked. "I wanted to ask him about the campers out at Sand Lake." He spit a small glob of masticated tobacco into a paper coffee cup.

"Something new?"

"The big Damon is gone, and the Coleman is empty. I wonder if they told Jack they were going away."

"I'm sure he'll be in soon. He's got a lot of paperwork to finish before he starts in Cadillac."

Rory dropped into the seat opposite Gwen's desk uninvited, much to her chagrin. The dog settled next to her. "So who's coming in while Jack's in Cadillac?" He spat a bit of tobacco cud into his mug, reminding her of her first husband's ever-present brown spittle.

"Haven't heard yet. I heard that ten people on the forest put in, and more from other forests. A lot of people want to work with me."

Rory chuckled, and the dog raised it head in concern. "Oh, yeah, tons of people can't wait to hear you whining."

Gwen sipped her coffee. "I do not whine. Elizabeth says that I 'kvetch.'"

"I heard the boss isn't coming back because he was arrested in the RF's office. You heard why?" he asked.

"Me? You're the one who's in law enforcement. Don't you guys have some kind of bat phones to discuss secret things?"

"I wish. Most days I can barely raise Dispatch on my truck radio. I hope I never have to rely on them for support. It's like half the forest is a dead zone."

"Good morning, Gwen," Jack called as he passed her office doorway. "Oh, hey, Rory. How's the morning?" He continued on to his office.

Gwen and Rory stood and followed him down the hallway. Fritz tagged along as well, likely associating the District Ranger with lemon loaf.

"You go first," she told Rory when they reached the doorway. "I've got a long shopping list of things for him."

Jack stopped calling into his voicemail and put down the receiver of his phone. "Tell me what you've got." The dog settled at his feet.

"Do you know what's happening out at Sand Lake?" Rory asked. "The big motorhome is gone, and the little one looks vacant. If it's unattended for 24 hours, that's a violation of 36 CFR 261.58(e). I can cite them now, or we can wait a few days and confiscate the trailer as abandoned property."

Jack always marveled at the ability of law enforcement officers to cite the exact number of each order within the Code of Federal Regulations. This was not an ability he envied; frankly, he thought it was a waste of otherwise useful brain cells. "Can we give it 24 hours? If we take possession, there are all kinds of hoops to jump through. What if they left a narcotic?" He did not say it aloud, but he wished Fritz would stop staring at Jack's leg like roast beef.

"OK, I'll keep an eye on it." Rory snapped a small clicker in his hand, and the dog lumbered to his feet to follow his master down the hallway.

After reflecting a minute, Jack stood and went into the hallway. "Hey, Rory, let's monitor the site for 48 hours, then let's talk about it some more." He went back into his office and closed the door. "This should be easier."

Gwen cocked her head to one side and gave him a quizzical look. "Which, getting ready to be Forest Supervisor or dealing with Rory?"

"Why does that dog always look hungry?" Jack asked. "I feel like Beef Wellington."

"That's good. Fritz might prefer steak tartare." Gwen settled at the round table in the office. "You have time for a list of questions?"

"Do I have a choice?"

"So do you think we're staffed up for the Governor opening up camping and boat ramps? Do you think we'll be overrun?"

"Of course. And I expect we'll have no warning before it happens. I'd like to stay closed for a week, just to shift the immediate rush onto DNR sites, but I suspect I won't get to make that choice. I'm already seeing a lot of dispersed camping outside the campgrounds. Can't keep people from their mushroom hunting."

"Next. Did you finish reviewing the Pandemic Preparedness Plan for fire incidents? The boss wanted all rangers and fire staff to review it? Although I guess you're the boss now."

"Twice. I reviewed it when the boss sent it out. And when NIFC issued this at the start of the month, I read it again." Jack reached for a binder on his desk. He removed an alert from the National Interagency Fire Agency and read from it aloud: "The earlier models did predict 'significant large fire potential' for northern California, much of Oregon, and eastern Washington by July — due to warmer and drier than average conditions going into summer. However, the latest models show a potentially alarming development since that report." He stopped reading and looked up at Gwen. "Now NIFC is saying it's going to be bigger and hotter than expected."

Gwen laughed. "You know, my husband wanted to go on a big road trip out west this year. Not sure I want to be living in a trailer and breathing all that smoke."

"I hope we don't have any idiots this year. Remember that fire in Arizona where some guy burned 50,000 acres to announce the wife was having a boy?"

"They call it a 'gender reveal' party. Shouldn't they wait? My daughter thinks the real gender reveal happens in freshman or sophomore year at college."

"How's she like Grand Valley State? She's doing med school and a law degree at the same time, right?"

"Yeah, but she'd like it a lot more if they were having all classes in-person. She hates having virtual classes on Zoom."

"I thought I would hate online meetings at first, but I like to listen to what people say when they forget to mute. Somebody's got to be collecting all these bloopers for a television special." He opened his canvas bag to get to his water bottle and took a drink.

"Like 'America's Favorite Zooplers?'"

He nearly snorted water through his nose as he laughed. "Yes. We should start a YouTube channel. We could be millionaires."

"And give up all this?" Gwen asked. She motioned around his office with her hand.

"I'd give this up in a minute," he said, earnestly. "In a minute, with 59 seconds to spare. There are probably 20 disciplinary actions on Robert's desk that he hasn't signed. Who knows what else he didn't deal with."

"I've got to go check the phones." Gwen stood and opened the office door. "Just remember to find us some money for new furniture at Chittenden."

May 15

"We think we're going to have a vaccine in the pretty near future, and if we do we're going to really be a big step ahead."

"And if we don't, we're going to be like so many other cases where you had a problem come in, it'll go away at some point, it'll go away," the President said. "It may flare up and it may not flare up, we'll have to see what happens, but if it does flare up we're going to put out the fire and we'll put it out quickly and efficiently. We've learned a lot. "

> – The President of the United States,
> speaking at the White House.

Lansing – A 32-year-old Detroit man is facing a felony charge after allegedly making "credible threats to kill" Michigan's Governor and Attorney General, the Wayne County Prosecutor's Office said.

The Prosecutor charged the suspect with false report of a threat of terrorism, a felony that carries a maximum penalty of 20 years in prison, according to a press release.

The suspect allegedly communicated through a social media messenger with an acquaintance, making threats to kill the office holders on April 14. Later that day, the Detroit Police Department arrested him at his home in Detroit, the release said.

"The alleged facts in this case lay out a very disturbing scenario," the prosecutor said. "We understand that these times can be stressful and upsetting for many people. But we will not and cannot tolerate threats like these against any public official who are carrying out their duties as efficiently as they can."

The Governor called on Republican lawmakers Monday to denounce death threats levied against her on social media. Recent protests against the Governor's stay-at-home order to combat COVID-19 have also seen signs with violent themes, like one on April 30 that said, "Tyrants get the rope."

On Tuesday the Senate Majority Leader, condemned those "who have populated a number of social media posts with crude, violent and threatening messages about our governor."

"These folks are thugs and their tactics are despicable," he said. "It is never OK to threaten the safety or life of another person, elected or otherwise, period."

A press secretary for the Attorney General, said earlier

this week that the Attorney General's Office takes "every threat seriously and will continue to monitor the situation with our partners in law enforcement."

– The Detroit News

May 16

Again, standing before a fridge and debating the merits of breakfast, Rick heard a car driving up the entrance road to the main gate at Sand Lake. He was the only person on the property, so he worried that the Liberation Army of Michigan had come on a surprise visit. Rick was confident that they couldn't recognize him from Joliet Street in Grand Rapids. He had carefully disposed of the demonic masks at the Citgo station off U.S. 131 in Cedar Springs.

He went down the hallway to the rear bedroom and took the Savage 220 shotgun from under the mattress on the lower bunk. As he moved forward in the camper, he crouched to peer out each window facing toward the closed gate. One vehicle, one driver, no passengers.

When Rick was confident there were no other vehicles coming into the campground, he stepped out of the camper. He carried the shotgun in his right hand, barrel down and his forefinger over the trigger guard. The car's driver door opened and a woman stepped out. She wore gloves and a wool coat against the morning chill. She tugged her facemask strings over her ears. He wondered why Doctor Pelletier had arrived when neither Mary or Regina were there.

"Good morning," he called. "I'm sorry, but I'm the only one here." He set the safety on the shotgun and stood it upright, the gunbutt resting on the toe of his boot. "Were they expecting you?"

"No, they weren't. That's the problem. My friend at St. Jude's says the hospital has called and e-mailed Regina, but they haven't had a reply. She's worried that Mary might lose her place."

"Oh, crap. I don't know where they are or how to reach them. Frank went home to Grand Rapids to go back to work. I took their camper to get some work done on it. Regina, Mary, and Doc Mac are staying at the ranger's cabin out on Hamlin Lake. They stayed there back when the Liberation Army came. Regina said she had no Wifi and Doc had no cell service."

Pelletier sat at the closest picnic table, braced her elbows on the tabletop and rested her forehead against her fingertips. After a few moments, she raised her face toward him. "You have any coffee? Maybe that's why I'm not thinking yet."

"Sure, Doc brought his fancy cup brewer. Let me get you something."

"Starbucks, by chance?" she asked.

"No, sorry. Doc's old Army. Strictly a Maxwell House man." He chuckled as he climbed the steps into the camper. After starting the coffee machine, "According to Doc, Teddy Roosevelt created the slogan 'Good to the last drop,' when he was staying at the Maxwell House Hotel in Nashville. And anything good enough for Roosevelt is good enough for Major McKettrick."

"Bleeds green?"

"And walks in cadence." Rick called from inside the camper.

She smiled, nodding to herself. Aloud, she said, "My father, too. A full-bird colonel. Any boy I wanted to date was afraid of him. All the boys he liked mostly wanted to date a colonel's daughter."

Rick came out of the trailer carrying a steaming mug. "So what did you do?" He sat nearly two caribou away at an adjacent table.

"Married badly. Three times." She held the mug cupped in her hands as if it radiated heat in the chilly morning air. "What about you?"

"My father worked on the line at Ford for 35 years. Put me through college so I could get a white-collar job there. Year I graduated, Ford cut like 30 percent of the white-collar jobs. So I went to see recruiters, and went Navy because they had the earliest opening at boot camp." He laughed. "I should have asked why that was."

He exhaled a long breath. She inhaled the fragrance of the coffee.

"So how do we get word to Regina and Mary?" she asked.

"Maybe through the Forest Service?"

"No, I stopped by their Cadillac office and that place in Wellston, but Bill's truck wasn't at either. Unless I just got there too early." She paused for a sip of coffee. "I called his cell, but it went to voicemail."

"So here's what we've got: Regina has no Wifi; Doc has no cell coverage; we don't know how to find Jack's cabin; we don't know where Jack lives or his phone number; Bill's not answering his cell; the Forest Services offices are closed. Am I missing anything?"

Pelletier sat upright and stared at Rick. "Thanks. You're just a

Little Miss Sunshine, aren't you? Anything else you'd like to contribute?"

"Another coffee?"

"Sure." She held out the ceramic mug with the VA logo. "Thanks."

Rick went inside and put a new cup into the brewing machine. Suddenly he was back on the camper's steps, without the fresh coffee. "Should we try law enforcement? The Forest Service guy with the dog was babysitting at Jack's cabin when the Liberation Army was here. And I think Jack may be friends with the sheriff."

"So, we can call 911?"

A minute later, Rick was back with her coffee. "It *is* life or death, right?"

Pelletier fished her cellphone out of her purse. "Here we go." She dialed three digits and then hit the green button. "And then you'll tell me about a Liberation Army?"

May 15

Lansing – A 32-year-old Detroit man is facing a felony charge after allegedly making "credible threats to kill" Michigan's Governor and Attorney General, the Wayne County Prosecutor's Office said.

The Prosecutor charged the suspect with false report of a threat of terrorism, a felony that carries a maximum penalty of 20 years in prison, according to a press release.

The suspect allegedly communicated through a social media messenger with an acquaintance, making threats to kill the office holders on April 14. Later that day, the Detroit Police Department arrested him at his home in Detroit, the release said.

"The alleged facts in this case lay out a very disturbing scenario," the prosecutor said. "We understand that these times can be stressful and upsetting for many people. But we will not and cannot tolerate threats like these against any public official who are carrying out their duties as efficiently as they can."

The Governor called on Republican lawmakers Monday to denounce death threats levied against her on social media. Recent protests against the Governor's stay-at-home order to combat COVID-19 have also seen signs with violent themes, like one on April 30 that said, "Tyrants get the rope."

On Tuesday the Senate Majority Leader, condemned those "who have populated a number of social media posts with crude, violent and threatening messages about our governor."

"These folks are thugs and their tactics are despicable," he said. "It is never OK to threaten the safety or life of another person, elected or otherwise, period."

A press secretary for the Attorney General, said earlier this week that the Attorney General's Office takes "every threat seriously and will continue to monitor the situation with our partners in law enforcement."

– The Detroit News

May 17

Across the state, many Michiganders are making it abundantly clear: They want to reopen the economy.

That was the message at a "Beach Bash" protest Saturday in Grand Haven, where residents from around the state gathered to express their frustrations about the Governor's stay-at-home order and called for it to be lifted.

The plea for reopening was also evident at a Branch County drive-in theater this weekend, where cars were lined up for about a quarter of a mile when the theater opened in defiance of the executive order.

A Holland salon owner became the latest of several Michigan barbers and stylists, who opened up shop despite the restrictions in place until May 28 on businesses deemed non-essential such as hair salons.

"It's about the principle of everything," said a salon owner. "We need to open our economy."

The Governor has defended her executive orders as necessary to battle the coronavirus pandemic.

– Mlive.

May 17

Doctor Pelletier felt she had created a panic, like shouting free popcorn in a crowded movie theater. A Manistee County dispatcher asked the Forest Service dispatch to send Rory Winchester to Jack Ferguson's cabin. The sheriff himself volunteered to go to Jack's house. A Wexford County deputy went to conduct a safety check at Bill's place. Even the State Troopers from the Cadillac post put out an APB for Bill's Wagoneer.

"Anything else we're missing?" she asked Rick. Her second coffee was starting to grow cold, but she hesitated to have a third.

"Something like a Goodyear blimp?"

"Should I drive out to Hamlin Lake? I think I'd recognize that big camper if I saw it again."

Rick took a deep breath and exhaled slowly. "See, there's a hitch. They don't have the Damon at the cabin. It's in a shop in Ludington, getting ready for a drive south."

"Oh, crap."

"Yep." He nodded, thinking about the parts on order and the work still to be done. "Even if they get the parts Monday, there's probably still two days of work in the shop before she can go."

She stood and pitched the dregs of the coffee into the brush. "We don't have that kind of time." She dialed Bill's phone number again, hoping he'd have a fix to this problem. When he answered, he sounded a little disoriented, as though he had been sleeping. She checked her watch; the sun was up, why wasn't he?

"What the hell time is it?" Bill asked gruffly.

"Half past six. You planning to get up today?"

He groaned into the phone. "Sundays I sleep until 7, thank you. Then usually go to St. Bernard's in Irons, but now they put everything online from Saint Andrew's because of the pandemic."

"Must be nice to lay about that way."

"I'm sorry. Did we have a Zoom date that I forgot?"

"A date? You wish." Her voice abruptly took a more urgent tone. "Look, we've got a real problem here. Can you get your friend Jack over here? You too?"

"Let's start with where. And then pick a time."

"Can we meet you at that tree place?" She paused a moment. "Bring anyone who can help in a crisis." She abruptly pressed the red button on her smartphone screen. "Can I have another coffee?" she asked Rick.

May 17

"So, if I understand you correctly, Mary should be in Memphis by Tuesday morning at the latest, is that right?" Jack asked.

Doctor Pelletier nodded. "The earlier, the better."

"But the Damon won't be available for that kind of trip until Tuesday at the earliest?"

"My best guess," Rick said.

"Alternatives?" Jack asked. He sipped from a McDonald's coffee because the drive-thru was the only place in Manistee open so early on a Sunday.

"I looked online. The drive is likely 13 hours," Bill said. He finished a coffee from Garlett's Corner.

"I think that's still the best option," Pelletier said. "Planes or trains both increase her possible exposure."

"Can we put her in a car for the trip safely?" Rick asked. "I know there'll be stops for gas, food, and restrooms. Is even that too risky?"

"Wouldn't be my first choice," the doctor said. "I'd like to put her in a bubble."

"What about your rig, Rick?" Jack asked. "Could you give up your camper if I can put you up in one of the apartments here? We just renovated a couple of the old cone sheds into summer lodging."

Rick shook his head. "Doc Mac would say it's unwashed. I just took the Damon to that repair shop in Ludington, so I may have been exposed. Wouldn't it be best to let it sit for a few days?"

Jack turned toward Pelletier. "Could we sterilize it?"

"Or rent something that's new?" Bill suggested. "My neighbor runs that RV lot over near Cadillac. Maybe we could rent one of campers that's been sitting empty."

"The CDC hasn't confirmed how long the virus lasts on a surface, so it would be better if we had a camper no one has been living in," the doctor said. "And I could ask someone from House-keeping at the hospital to give it a thorough wipe down."

The four looked at each other from their respective tables, ranging from washed where Pelletier sat alone to unwashed where Rick sat. Jack took a final sip of the cold coffee. "OK, so we have almost a plan. Bill, you'll go check to see what your neighbor has available for, I guess, two weeks?" He looked around for confirmation. "Doctor, you'll see about someone to clean it out? And I'll go out to Hamlin Lake and give them the good news. It's going to be bit of a scramble to get them on the road, but it's good news."

Doctor Pelletier objected, "No, this is great news. Really great."

May 18

Michigan's Governor will reopen parts of the state this week, including bars, restaurants and retail businesses, as coronavirus (COVID-19) numbers continue to drop, she announced at Monday's briefing.

The move will affect two of the eight regions identified in the governor's gradual reopening plan amid the coronavirus pandemic: one covers the Upper Peninsula and another includes 17 counties in the northern Lower Peninsula, including Traverse City.

Bars and restaurants will have to limit their capacity to 50 percent. Groups will be required to stay six feet apart, and servers will have to wear face coverings.

Office work also will be able resume if work cannot be done remotely.

"This is a big step, but we must all remember to continue doing our part to protect ourselves and our families from the spread of COVID-19," the Governor said in a statement.

There has been heavy opposition to the Governor's handling of the coronavirus pandemic in the Republican Legislature. State legislators are suing the Governor for extending her executive orders without their approval.

Michiganders have also taken to the Capitol Building for three major protests in the past month.

Despite the lawsuits and protests, the Governor has continued to take a cautious approach to reopening Michigan. While the Big Three automakers reopened Monday and other services, such as landscaping and construction, have been methodically resumed, she said her priority is safety.

"I know many people in our state are feeling frustrated," the Governor said. "Some are scared. Some are angry. That's understandable, but now is not a time for division, for hatred, certainly not a time for violence. Now is a time for us to pull together. Now is a time for unity."

– ClickonDetroit.com

May 18

At 0600, Bill left his house in Henrietta, towing a 2019 Wild-wood with his Wagoneer. Although the big camper was new, one of the Housekeeping staff from Mercy Hospital spent several hours Sunday evening disinfecting every conceivable surface. When the young woman finished, Bill tipped her generously; she had one of the most important tasks in Operation Relocate Mary.

The Wagoneer drove west on M-55, and Bill stopped again at Garlett's to top off the Jeep. He went into the deli and purchased a breakfast sandwich and a coffee. He continued west toward Lake Michigan, but took the left to go through Filer City and come out on U.S. 31 south of Manistee. In a few miles, he turned right onto West Forest Trail, which he followed to North Quarterline Trail. He went south, until a right on Nurnberg Road, where the pavement ended. Already the volume of weekend traffic heading into the Nordhouse Wilderness had created a washboard-like surface on the roadway. The camper bounced wildly and bucked against the back of the Wagoneer. Twice Bill came to a full stop to cease the herky-jerky motion of the Wildwood.

Jack's cabin was located on the southside of Janecyk Road. With luck, Jack had found a little parcel outside of Forest Service owner-ship with waterfront and a nice, cozy cabin. Bill maneuvered the long RV so that Doc Mac could get back to Nurnberg Road without a complicated operation. As he walked up the driveway, Bill found Jack already waiting in his pick-up. The ranger waved and climbed out of his big Ford. "Good morning for a drive," Jack said. "You going to be OK letting someone else drive your Wagoneer?"

"I'm trying not to think about it too much. When I do, I remember it's an excuse to drive the M38 more."

Extending his hand, Jack asked, "And that thing is street legal, right?"

"Of course. You should be more respectful of the Jeep that made the world safe for democracy."

At that moment, the front door of the cabin opened and Doctor McKettrick stepped outside. "Good morning, gentlemen. Mary and Regina are ready to come out. I'm sorry, but would you please walk a little farther away?"

The two Forest Service employees walked to the back end of Jack's truck. They watched as mother and child came straight from cabin to camper. Mary stopped on the step of the RV and gave a quick wave before she went inside. Regina made two more trips, carrying duffle bags. Finally Doc Mac closed the door and folded the steps against the body of the camper. He approached Jack and Bill, then gave each a white envelope. "Just a little something from Mary." He extended his hand toward Jack. "Thank you, you've done so much more than I would ever have thought possible." After shaking Jack's hand, he stood slightly more erect and raised his hand in salute. "Captain, thank you."

"Good luck, Major. We'll see you in a few days. Call if you have any problems."

McKettrick walked to the front of the Wagoneer and climbed inside. Soon the big V-8 rumbled to life. After a moment or two, the Jeep shifted into gear and rolled forward. Jack and Bill walked to the end of the driveway and watched the camper roll away. A young girl stood inside the big window at the rear of the trailer. She waved at them until the Jeep and Wildwood turned the corner. The two men waved back.

"You're worried about your Jeep, aren't you?"

"That and the camper," Bill said. "I have to pay extra if he brings it back scratched."

"Come on, I'll give you a ride to work." Jack chuckled. "Sounds like you may need the money."

May 22

Bill spent his last day before retirement back in the Cadillac office. He hung the parts of his sickly green uniform in the warehouse where someone else might be able to use them. He returned to Elizabeth his cell phone, laptop, keys, government charge card, government travel card, government identification card, and bronze badge with the etching of a conifer. When he did, she asked what kind of last bacchanalia he had planned.

"Oh, by the way, Judith called me," she said. "When there's a new PAO, there's going to be a temporary assignment as a public affairs trainee. She asked if I was interested."

"Congratulations."

"I'd ask for a reference, but I think I've already had it."

"Between me and Jack, I think you're good."

"So what's going to happen to Robert?" she asked.

"I think Bob's going to spend several years as the guest of the State of Wisconsin. Then hopefully, he'll spend a few years in some menial job paying back individual claims to the many women he hurt. At least that's my ambition for him."

"Anyone tell you that you're just mean?"

"All the time. Now I have to go submit my final timesheet."

"After that?"

"I need to go thank Ruth. You'll respond whenever she calls, right?"

"Of course. She put the stake in the vampire's heart."

"Exactly." He extended his hand. "Thank you."

Still masked, she stepped closer and gave him a hug. "Don't you want a party at all?"

"You mean a fully sanitized, socially distanced, and sterile soiree in an open-air stadium?"

"Not exactly what I was thinking, but these days ..." her voice trailed off.

"Look, if Jack doesn't work out, you call me. I've got pictures."

Back in his office on the North side of the building, Bill logged into his computer for a final time. He submitted a last time sheet. With all official documents saved in the appropriate databases, he deleted all the draft letters, news releases, and reports from his hard drive. He created an auto-forward e-mail message directing all public affairs inquiries about the forest to Rachel in the Regional Office. He recorded the same message on his desk phone. That should keep her busy for a while. Finally he opened a new e-mail message, addressed to all employees on the national forest: "As the great Groucho said, *'Hello, I must be going. I cannot stay. I came to say I must be going. I'm glad I came but just the same I must be going.'* And let me end on a personal note: Thank you for your relentless kindness." He punched SEND then looked out the window toward the towering oak tree in the cemetery. At least they had managed to get Mary safely to St. Jude's. No one could predict what would come for her. But at least he could claim a victory at the bitter end of his career.

Nothing left to do. He snugged his hat in place and went out the backdoor. The warm air outdoors surprised him. Summer had arrived swiftly with temperatures increasing by more than 40 degrees in the past two weeks. The weather had warmed enough that he liked to drive with the Wagoneer's windows open the past few days since Doctor McKettrick had returned from Tennessee.

"So what do you have planned?" a voice called. Jack came across the parking lot to meet him. "Elizabeth said something about a crazy Dionysian party. I don't understand what she's talking about."

"Well, the good news is that she's only got another seven months of that calendar."

"Oh, crap, we're going to need a Latin interpreter in our meetings now," the new acting forest supervisor said. "I owe you for this."

"But just think about how much it annoyed Bob every time Elizabeth said a word with more than four syllables."

Jack cocked his head as he looked at the new retiree. "Wow, that's devious. I salute you." He touched his fingertips to the right side of his forehead. "So what do you have planned for the holiday weekend."

"I don't know now that the Governor opened up everything across the Upper Lower. I think the RVs are already swarming north like locusts."

Jack reached into his pocket. He held out a key ring on a leather fob. "You know where our cabin is located. Take a few days. You'll have to restock the fridge."

Bill shook his head. "I couldn't. You might want to get away for the long weekend."

Jack shook his head as he jangled the key ring. "No, you should see the 'honey-do' list Melissa has at the house for me. I'll be busy right through Labor Day."

"OK, then. I appreciate it. Maybe you can stop by for a beer."

"We'll see. It's not exactly on my way to the hardware store. Oh, I don't have the boat out of storage yet. But you could bring a skiff."

"Canoe, OK?" Bill had yet to launch a wooden canoe that Brandon and his grandfather had finished while he and his mother had stayed on the farm in Watersmeet for the summer before the accident.

"Sure. You'll probably have free run of the lake. Most of our neighbors are snowbirds, so they probably won't risk traveling north with Covid-19 happening."

Bill accepted the keys and shook Jack's hand. "So, I'm thinking I owe you a lunch or at least a beer now."

"Let's see how this acting forest supervisor thing goes. You're responsible for it. You could owe me big time." Jack turned and headed into the building.

May 23

The President teed up fresh controversy on Saturday, by leaving the White House for his golf course in Virginia.

Early on a fine morning in Washington DC, the president was seen by reporters "in his typical golf wear of white polo shirt and white baseball cap ... before he departed the White House" for an undisclosed location. Secret Service agents accompanying the president were photographed wearing masks. The President was not seen to cover his face.

He later arrived at his golf club, where he was pictured playing a round.

As of Saturday morning, more than 1.6 million cases of Covid-19 had been confirmed in the United States, with the death toll approaching 100,000.

– The Guardian

May 24

Over the past two years, Bill had come to hate the long void of a holiday weekend. Friends made plans to travel or visited family. Campgrounds and popular recreation areas like the Nordhouse Dunes and the Pine River were packed with drunks. Usually he spent those days working. On Saturday, he stayed on the deck of Jack's cabin overlooking Hamlin Lake, reading a thick collection of Douglas Adams' satiric novels about a universe only slightly less crazy than the current one. On Sunday, he drove down and put his canoe in at 9 Mile Bridge on the Little Manistee River. He took out at the weir, where Angela, the summer rec tech from Baldwin met him. After they loaded his canoe on the roof rack of her old Volvo, she dropped him back at the Wagoneer. She invited him to the Club M 37. After lunch, when she left for Baldwin, he drove north on M-37 and walked alone down to the suspension bridge on the Manistee River Trail.

As dusk fell, Bill drove the Wagoneer into the steel Quonset hut behind his house. He had constructed a cable and pulley system so that he could easily hoist the canoe from the Jeep's roof rack. With everything secured, he headed for the kitchen door. A single exterior light illuminated his path. He never quite understood people who moved Up North then immediately surrounded their property with massive street lights. How could they ever enjoy a starry night?

After flipping on the kitchen light switch, Bill opened the refrigerator door and removed a tall bottle of Two-Hearted Ale. The red light on the house phone flashed. He pulled the cradle that held his cell phone from his belt. That phone also blinked to alert him of incoming voicemails and text messages. He put it on the countertop next to the land-line phone. Once you're retired, phone calls lose all urgency.

After opening the cold ale, he flipped on the light switch in the living room. He found a squad of the Liberation Army of Michigan waiting for him. Unlike cockroaches, they didn't run when exposed to light.

"You don't have any friends with you now, do you?" Gary asked. "No muscle to protect you."

"Funny that you brought so much. A young guy like you needs

99

all this help against an old retiree? As your boss would say, Sad."

Gary stood up to glare into Bill's face. He did not seem sure about how to play the heavy. Just a lightweight. He waved a Glock in the space between them.

Bill glanced about the room. There were seven. His best was four, way back in the day. "You sure you brought enough friends? Don't want to call for help?" Never show fear.

"Let's show the old man," Gary said, turning his head toward his squad.

A small red light flickered on the wall above Gary's head, then went out. Bill watched that space. After two seconds, the light returned and disappeared immediately. He counted one, two, and took a quick step to his left, just as the shot came through the window. As the falling crystal light fixture crashed onto Gary's head, Bill grabbed the Glock in Gary's hand. Twisting it upward, Bill fired a shot that sent the hot expended shell casing into Gary's face.

Wrenching the pistol from the falling man's hands, Bill opened fire. He aimed low to avoid any body armor. Three collapsed to the floor, screaming. The other three dodged behind the couch for cover. Dragging Gary as a shield, Bill backed into the kitchen. Once there, he shoved Gary back toward his mini-militia with enough force to send him sprawling across two of his own men wailing on the floor.

Battle assessment: Three intruders remained healthy, still heavily armed, and crouching behind the sofa as a shield. Four wounded on the ground, still possibly armed. Bill assumed he had at least four rounds left in the Glock. He dialed 911, then put the handset on the kitchen counter. From behind the refrigerator, he saw the supplies remaining from the Reagan Platoon on the table.

Running through the kitchen, he swept the pile onto the floor. He quickly put in earplugs, with hearing protectors over top. He added an N95 mask and googles. Then he began pulling lanyards on the personal protection devices, tossing five into the living room. 140 decibels times five should get their attention. Next he rolled a few of the remaining cans of bear repellant in behind the audibles. With a deep breath, he went to the doorway and fired rounds into the three aerosol cans. They exploded with considerable force, filling the room with a pepper spray designed for 500-pound grizzlies. Quickly the cloud became too thick to fire accurately

Bill escaped out the kitchen door into the yard. Once there, he heard the undulating wail of a loon. Thirty yards away, a set of headlights flashed and went off. Crouching low, Bill made a zig-zag run in that direction.

The shooter leaned against the fender of a big Ford pickup. The rifle rested on a tripod on the hood. Jack's Browning .308 pointed at the house; his eye remained at the scope.

"Nice shot," Bill said. "You were aiming for the light fixture, right?"

"I worried you wouldn't see the laser sight."

"I appreciate the warning." Bill lifted the binoculars from the hood of Jack's truck. "Anyone standing yet?"

Jack's eye remained at the scope. "Not that I can see. What's in that cloud?"

"Bear repellant."

"That'll keep them busy for a minute. I called 911, but not sure where my cell call pinged. Operator didn't know Harrietta."

"I called on the house phone, so they should have a GPS location. I hope they're coming. All I have are handguns." He set Gary's Glock on the truck's hood and added the two pistols he carried.

"My 30.06 is on the seat. You know how to use one?"

"I grew up in the UP. Had a Winchester before my first Huffy." Bill shoved the pistol into the back of his trousers as he retrieved the rifle. "Loaded?"

"Of course. Why bring an unloaded rifle to a gun fight?"

Bill looked at Jack, then laughed. "Look at us. Like Wyatt Earp and Doc Holliday."

"Better than Butch and Sundance."

"You mind if I plink a few rounds? Just to keep the boys on the ground?"

"Your house. Feel free. Good luck with your home insurance." Jack made a chuckling noise in the dark. "You know, you might go a couple of rounds just to keep them on their toes. Pass the time until the sheriff arrives. Don't want them to get any ideas about running off."

With little noise, Rick emerged from the dark. "No need to keep them pinned down in the house. They're not going far." He set a wheel wrench and a canvas bag on the hood of Jack's truck. "Very few people use locking lug bolts these days."

"I'd say let them go. In 200 yards, they'll be wading through Slagle Creek. In the dark, they'll find that bottom is pretty soft there."

Sirens wailed in the distance.

"Sounds like they're still out on the highway," Jack said. "You OK leaving everything to the police?"

"Of course," Bill said. "Unless the cops take Gary's side." He peered through the binoculars at the bay window in the living room. He saw no motion inside. "So how'd you know to come to my rescue?"

Jack laughed aloud. "Because Annette has been screaming all weekend, trying to alert you. Apparently you don't answer your phone, cell phone, texts, e-mails or telegraphs. The Wexford sheriff did a couple of safety checks out here, and I drove out to the cabin this morning."

"Jack had me come out here yesterday and today," Rick added.

"So where were you hiding out this morning?" Jack asked.

Bill thought this seemed a little invasive. "Canoeing a swift river, lunch with a charming young lady and inspecting an architectural beauty in the forest."

"OK, you don't have to tell me if you don't want to." Jack pointed toward the main road at the blue flashing lights flickering through the pines. "I think we should meet them without the rifles. Might go better for us."

Jack handed Bill a canvas carrying case for the 30.06. The Browning went into a hard case with a foam inset custom fit to the rifle. Jack laid these on the rear seat of his truck.

As three cruisers pulled up the driveway with their lights glimmering in the twilight, the men raised their hands and walked into the light cast by the headlights.

"I just saved your life," Jack said to Bill. "I expect something good. No citrus beers."

May 25

Doctor Pelletier's doorbell rang just after noon on Memorial Day. After several minutes, she opened the front door to find Bill Reinhardt standing on her porch. She kept the storm door shut tight and raised her voice to talk to him.

"They told me at the hospital that you were in quarantine," he said. "Thought I'd come see how you're doing."

"The hospital shouldn't be giving out my personal information," she said sharply.

"Everybody's just trying to be helpful these days. The Forest Service told you where to find me. They probably helped the Liberation Army of Michigan find me, too."

"I read about that in the *Cadillac News*. Probably lucky you weren't killed before the cops got there."

"Let's hope your job won't get you killed."

She smiled at him. "You have such a comforting way with words. What was it you did for the Forest Service?" She looked much younger without the mask.

"Mostly told people to keep their cows and their ORVs off federal land."

"How are you still alive?" she asked.

"So which would you prefer? Do you want me to stay out here and visit every day to run errands, or come live in your basement to keep you company until your quarantine finishes?"

"Hold up. You can't come in. I might expose you to the virus."

"So could the nozzle on the gas pump when I fill up. Or touching a door knob."

"No, wait a minute. Surely, you can't be serious. Asking to move in with me in the middle of a pandemic?"

He started to respond with *I am serious, and don't call me Shirley.* Then he remembered Annette had told him he was *too old to be cool.* "I know what it's like to be alone and looking into the great abyss of death," he said. "I brought a sleeping bag, two versions of Trivial Pursuit, a case of my ale and a collection of Michigan Rieslings for you. Other than that, we can order delivery." He didn't mention the two pistols and the full box of ammunition.

She stared at him a moment through the closed door. "You come in, you can't leave for two weeks."

"Understood. I said my goodbyes to a few folks, just in case. You're free to kick me out at any time. I've been wondering, do you have a first name other than Doctor?"

"That's a pretty brazen question before a first date." She unlatched the storm door. "Just like our FaceTime chats, I expect you to wear pants. Agreed?"

May 25

More than 98,000 people have died from coronavirus in the US

There are at least 1,657,441 cases of coronavirus in the United States, and at least 98,034 people have died, according to John Hopkins University tally of cases.

Johns Hopkins reported 14,195 new cases and 314 deaths on Monday.

– CNN.

ACKNOWLEDGMENTS

The author thanks W. Edward Wendover and Jim Thompson for their editorial guidance regarding Michigan.

The author is grateful to the journalists and media sources quoted in this novel that provide the historical context for the events depicted.

Made in the USA
Columbia, SC
08 December 2020